PRAISE FOR

"[A] polished medieval mystery..."

—*Publishers Weekly*

"This is a terrific book with wonderful characters, both good and evil."

—*Mysterious Women*

MORE PRAISE FOR
SHARON KAY PENMAN

"Penman's lively, articulate prose brings to life history as it could have happened—high praise for a historical mystery."

—*Houston Chronicle*

"A glowing, living tapestry. This is storytelling at its finest."

—*The Philadelphia Inquirer*

"The historical detail is luscious."

—*Library Journal*

"Penman is a superb storyteller."

—*The Miami Herald*

"[Penman] has made quite a niche for herself in the historical genre: novels based on historical fact, embroidered with lively imagination to breathe life into her characters and their times."

—Knoxville *News Sentinel*

"It is through the characters created from her imagination that Penman manages to create a believable twelfth-century environment."

—*Chicago Tribune*

DRAGON'S LAIR

A Medieval Mystery

SHARON KAY PENMAN

BALLANTINE BOOKS • NEW YORK

Sale of this book without a front cover may be unauthorized. If this book is coverless, it may have been reported to the publisher as "unsold or destroyed" and neither the author nor the publisher may have received payment for it.

Dragon's Lair is a work of fiction. Names, characters, places, and incidents are the products of the author's imagination or are used fictitiously. Any resemblance to actual events, locales, or persons, living or dead, is entirely coincidental.

2005 Fawcett Books Mass Market Edition

Copyright © 2003 by Sharon Kay Penman
Reading group guide copyright © 2004 by Random House, Inc.

All rights reserved.

Published in the United States by Fawcett Books, an imprint of The Random House Publishing Group, a division of Random House, Inc., New York.

FAWCETT is a registered trademark and the Fawcett colophon is a trademark of Random House, Inc.

This book published by arrangement with G. P. Putnam's Sons, a member of Penguin Group (USA), Inc.

ISBN 0-449-00728-6

Cover design: Allison Saltzman
Cover illustration: The Art Archive/Archeological Museum Cividale Friuli/Dagli Orti

Printed in the United States of America

www.ballantinebooks.com

OPM   9   8   7   6   5   4   3   2   1

To my father

PROLOGUE

July 1193
Nottingham Castle, England

The English king was dying. Despite the bone-biting chill of the dungeon, he was drenched in sweat and so gaunt and wasted that his brother barely recognized him. His skin was ashen, his eyes sunken, and his chest heaved with each rasping shallow breath. Even the vivid reddish-gold hair was dulled, so matted and dirty that vermin were burrowing into the scalp once graced by a crown. Would their lady mother still be so eager to cradle that lice-ridden head to her breast?

As if sensing he was no longer alone, Richard struggled to rise up on an elbow, rheumy, bloodshot eyes blinking into the shadows. The voice that once could shout down the wind, that was heard from one corner of Christendom to the other even when he whispered, now emerged as a feeble croak. "John . . . ?"

"Yes." Stepping into the meager light of the lone candle, John savored the moment to come. Had Fortune's Wheel ever spun so dizzily as this? The irony was exquisite, that the brother so scorned and belittled should be Richard's only chance of salvation. "What would you, brother? You wish for a doctor? A priest? A king's ransom?" The corner of John's mouth curved, ever so slightly. "You need only ask, Richard. But ask you must."

Richard stretched out a stranger's hand, one that trembled as if he had the palsy, palm upward in the universal

1

gesture of supplication. John reached for it reluctantly, for it would be like clasping hands with a corpse. Their fingers touched, then entwined. As John instinctively recoiled, Richard tightened his hold. There was surprising strength in this deathbed grip; to his alarm, John found he could not break free. Richard's fingers were digging into his flesh, leaving talon-like imprints upon his skin. So close were they that John could smell on Richard's breath the fetid stench of the grave, and his brother's eyes were as grey as their sire's, burning with fever and an inexplicable gleam of triumph.

"Rot in Hell, Little Brother," Richard said, slowly and distinctly. "Rot in Hell!"

John jerked upright in the bed, so violently that his bedmate was jarred abruptly from sleep. Ursula felt a surge of drowsy annoyance, for this was not the first time that John had awakened her with one of his troubled dreams. She was not so naïve as to complain, though, indulging herself only with a soft, put-upon sigh and a pout safely hidden in the dark.

As the German dungeon receded before the reality of his bedchamber, John began to swear, angrily and profanely. Why had that accursed dream come back? It made no sense, for Richard was not being held in irons; last report had him being well treated now that negotiations had begun for his release. Nor would he ever be Richard's deliverance, not in this life or the next. Each time he remembered Richard's taunt, his blood grew hot and his nerves hummed with hate. Upon being warned that his brother was scheming to claim his crown, Richard had merely laughed. "My brother John," he'd said, "is not the man to conquer a country if there is anyone to offer even feeble resistance."

John cursed again, feeling such rage that he could almost choke upon it. Richard's mockery trailed him like a ravenous wolf. It was always there, hungry yellow eyes aglow in the dark, awaiting its chance.

When he finally fell asleep again, his dreams were still unsettled and he tossed and turned so restlessly that Ursula heaved another martyred sigh, putting as much space between them as the bed would allow. John stopped squirming once he rolled over onto his back, but then he began to snore and Ursula conceded defeat.

Sliding out of bed, she padded across the chamber and drained the last of the wine from John's night flagon. A young squire slept soundly nearby, and she was tempted to fling the flagon into the floor rushes by his pallet, begrudging him the sleep that was denied her. She reconsidered, though, unwilling to risk waking John. She stubbed her toe getting back into bed and added yet another grievance to her ever-expanding hoard of wrongs.

Most men looked peaceful in their sleep and younger, too, unfettered by earthly cares. But not John. Studying him dispassionately, she decided he looked haunted, and older than his twenty and six years. She supposed most women would consider him handsome, even if he was the dark one in a fair family, for he had his mother's finely chiseled cheekbones and expressive mouth. His eyes were deep-set under black brows, fringed with surprisingly long lashes, and his hair was thick, as glossy as a raven's wing. If she'd been inclined to entwine a strand around her fingers—which she wasn't—she knew it would be clean and soft to the touch, for one of his quirks was an enjoyment of bathing. She had been taken aback at first, thinking it wasn't quite manly, but she'd soon come to appreciate the benefits: He did not stink like the other men who'd shared her bed and her favors.

John had once told her that he liked to watch people unaware. Regarding him now as he slept, Ursula under-

stood the appeal; there was a vulnerability about someone who did not know he was under observation. He'd
stopped snoring, though, and she settled down beside
him, closing her eyes and crossing her fingers. It was then
that the pounding started, as loud as summer thunder,
chasing away the mice scurrying about in the floor rushes
and any hopes of sleep.

John sat up in alarm. "Holy Mother, what now?" Ursula just groaned and put her pillow over her head. The
squire was sleepily stumbling toward the door. They
could hear the murmur of voices, and then the door was
shoved back and Durand de Curzon pushed the squire
aside, striding into the chamber.

John's protest died in his throat, for Durand's presence
validated the intrusion. The tall, swaggering knight was
one of the few men whom he trusted with some of his secrets. Durand was carrying a lantern and his face was
partially illuminated by its swaying pale light. He looked
as he always did: self-possessed, capable, and faintly sardonic. But John knew his demeanor would have been no
different if he'd come to deliver word of Armageddon.

"Are you going to tell me why you're in my chamber in
the middle of the night, Durand, or must I guess?"

Durand shrugged off the sarcasm. "A messenger has
ridden in, my lord, bearing a letter for you from the King
of the French."

John often received communications from the French
king. They were allies of expediency, united in their
shared loathing for his brother the Lionheart. It was from
Philippe that John had first learned of Richard's plight:
captured by his enemies on his way home from Crusade
and turned over to the dubious mercies of the Holy Roman Emperor. But he'd never gotten a message so urgent
that it could not wait till daylight.

"I'll see him," he said tersely.

The man was already being ushered into the chamber. His travel-stained clothes told a tale of their own, as did his bleary eyes and the involuntary grunt he gave as he sank to his knees before the bed. He held out a parchment threaded through with cord and sealed with wax, but John's gaze went first to his ring. It was a silver band gilded in gold leaf, set with a large amethyst cut into octagonal facets, corroboration that the courier did indeed come from Philippe, for royal signets could be forged but only John knew to look for the ring that had once encircled the French king's own finger.

"Give me your lantern, Durand," John said, reaching for the letter. As impatient as he was to read Philippe's message, he still took the time to examine the seal, making sure that it had not been tampered with. Durand observed this with a flicker of grim humor, so sure had he been that John would do exactly that. He studied John as a Church scholar studied Holy Scriptures, for a misstep might well mean his doom.

As John frowned over the letter, Durand sauntered over to the table, found flint and tinder and struck sparks until he was able to ignite the wick of a large wax candle. When John raised his head to demand more light, Durand was already there, holding out the candlestick. He took the opportunity to appraise John's bedmate at close range, his gaze moving appreciatively over the voluptuous curves so inadequately draped in a thin, linen sheet.

Ursula was well aware of his intimate scrutiny, but she made no attempt to cover herself, regarding him with an indifference that pricked his pride. Durand could not make up his mind about Ursula. Was it that she was too jaded to care about anything but her own comfort, disenchanted and distrustful? Or was it merely that she was dull-witted, a woman blessed with such a lush, desirable body that the Almighty had decided she had no need for brains, too?

Durand had flirted with her occasionally, if only to alleviate the boredom when they were trapped at the siege of Windsor Castle, but to no avail, and he'd soon decided that she was a selfish bitch and likely dumb as a post. Not that he would have lain with her even if she'd been panting for it. He'd long ago concluded that John's sense of possession was even stronger than his sense of entitlement. Still, the risk had its own appeal, separate and apart from Ursula's carnal charms. He'd learned at an early age that danger could be as seductive as any whore. Irked by Ursula's blank, impassive gaze, he stripped her with his eyes, slowly and deliberately. By God, she was ripe. Would it truly matter if her head was filled with sawdust? All cats were grey in the dark.

Belatedly becoming aware of John's utter silence, he glanced toward the younger man and all lustful thoughts were banished at the sight of John's ashen face. Durand held no high opinion of Queen Eleanor's youngest son. He thought John was too clever by half and as contrary and unpredictable as the winds in Wales. But he did not doubt John's courage; treason was not for the faint of heart. So he was startled now to see John so obviously shaken. What dire news was in the French king's letter?

"My lord? You look like a man who's just heard that there was hemlock in his wine. What is amiss?"

John continued to stare down at the letter. A muscle was twitching faintly in his cheek, and the hand resting on his knee had clenched into a fist. Just when Durand decided that he was not going to respond, he glanced up, eyes glittering and opaque. "Read it for yourself."

Many men would not have been able to meet that challenge, but Durand was literate in both French and Latin. As he approached the bed, John thrust the letter at him like a knife. He did not flinch, taking the parchment in one hand and holding the candlestick in the other, then stepping back so he could read it.

The French king's seal had been broken when John unthreaded the cord and unfolded the letter. There was no salutation, no signature, just seven words scrawled across the middle of the page, written in such haste that the ink had bled before it dried, blotted so carelessly that a smudged fingerprint could be seen.

"Look to yourself for the Devil is loosed."

1

July 1193
Westminster, England

Walking in the gardens of the royal palace on a sultry, overcast summer afternoon, Claudine de Loudun recognized for the first time that she feared the queen. This should not have been so surprising to her, for the queen in question was Eleanor, Dowager Queen of England, Duchess of Aquitaine, one-time Queen of France. Burning as brightly as a comet in her youth, Eleanor had shocked and fascinated and outraged, a beautiful, willful woman who'd wed two kings, taken the cross, given birth to ten children, and dared to lust after power as a man might. But she'd survived scandal, heartbreak, and insurrection, even sixteen years as her husband Henry's prisoner.

The older Eleanor was wiser and less reckless, a woman who'd learned to weigh both words and consequences. Her ambitions had always been dynastic, and in her twilight years she was expending all of her considerable intelligence, political guile, and tenacity in the service of her son Richard. She was respected now, even revered in some quarters, for her sound advice and pragmatic understanding of statecraft, and few appreciated the irony—that this woman who'd lived much of her life as a royal rebel should be acclaimed as a stabilizing influence upon the brash, impulsive Richard.

To outward appearances, it seemed as if the aged queen

had repudiated the carefree and careless girl she'd once been, but Claudine knew better. Eleanor's tactics had changed, not her nature. She was worldly, curious, utterly charming when she chose to be, prideful, stubborn, calculating, and still hungry for all that life had to offer. She had a remarkable memory untainted by age, and although she might forgive wrongs, she never forgot them. As Claudine was belatedly acknowledging, she could be a formidable enemy.

Claudine was not a fool, even if she had done more than her share of foolish things. It was not that she'd underestimated the queen, but rather that she'd overestimated her own ability to swim in such turbulent waters. It had seemed harmless enough in the beginning. What did it matter if she shared court gossip and rumors with the queen's youngest son? She had seen it as a game, not a betrayal, just as she'd seen herself as John's confederate, not his spy. How had it all gone so wrong? She still was not sure. But there was no denying that the stakes had suddenly become life or death. Richard languished in a German prison. John was being accused of treason. The queen was sick with fear for her eldest son and vowing vengeance upon those who would deny Richard his freedom. And Claudine was in the worst plight of all, pregnant and unwed, facing both the perils of the birthing chamber and the danger of disgrace and scandal.

She'd never worried about incurring Eleanor's animosity before, confident of her own power to beguile, putting too much trust in her blood ties to the queen, distant though they might be. But in this fragrant, trellised garden, she was suddenly and acutely aware of how vulnerable she truly was. It was such a demoralizing realization that she quickly reminded herself how understanding the queen had been about her pregnancy. She'd feared that Eleanor would turn her out, letting all know of her shame. Instead, the queen had offered to help. So why, then, did she feel such unease?

She glanced sideways at the other woman, and then away. She'd often thought the queen had cat eyes, greenish-gold and inscrutable, eyes that seemed able to see into the inner recesses of her soul, to strip away her secrets, one by one. Claudine bit her lip, keeping her own eyes downcast, for she had so many secrets.

Eleanor was aware of the young woman's edginess, and it afforded her some grim satisfaction. She bore Claudine no grudge for allowing herself to become entangled in John's web; she'd had too many betrayals in her life to be wounded by one so small. And so once she'd discovered Claudine's complicity in her son's scheming, she'd been content to keep that knowledge secret, reasoning that a known spy was a defanged snake. She'd even used the unwitting Claudine to pass on misinformation from time to time. But if she felt no desire for vengeance, neither did she have sympathy for Claudine's predicament. Every pleasure in this world came with a price, be it a dalliance in conspiracy or one in bed.

Glancing about to make sure none of her other attendants were within earshot, Eleanor asked the girl if she was still queasy. When Claudine swallowed and swore that she no longer felt poorly, Eleanor gave her a skeptical scrutiny. "Why, then, is your face the color of newly skimmed milk? There is no need to pretend with me, child. Only men could call a pregnancy 'easy,' but some are undoubtedly more troublesome than others. For me, it was my last. There were days when even water could unsettle my stomach. I've sailed in some fierce storms, but God's Truth, I was never so greensick as when I was carrying John."

Claudine's eyelashes flickered, no more than that. But she could not keep the blood from rising in her face and

throat. Watching as her pallor was submerged in a flood
of color, Eleanor smiled slyly. This was new, like an involuntary twitch or a hiccup, this sudden discomfort
whenever John's name was mentioned. Not for the first
time, Eleanor wondered who had truly fathered Claudine's child. Was it Justin de Quincy as she claimed? Or
was it John?

"I think it is time," she said, "for you to withdraw to
the nunnery at Godstow."

Claudine nodded reluctantly. This was the plan, with
cover stories fabricated for the court and her family back
in Aquitaine. She should have gone a fortnight ago, but
she'd found excuses to delay, dreading the loneliness and
seclusion and boredom of the coming months. "I suppose so," she admitted, sounding so forlorn that Eleanor
experienced an involuntary pang of empathy; she knew
better than most the onus of confinement. It was true
that this confinement was by choice and temporary, but
Eleanor could not help identifying with Claudine's aver-
sion to the religious life. There had been times in her past
when she'd feared being shut up in some remote, obscure
convent for the rest of her days, forgotten by all but her
gaolers and God.

"I will speak with Sir Nicholas this eve," she said
briskly, determined not to soften toward this foolhardy,
unhappy girl. "The arrangements have all been made. It
remains only for you to settle in at Godstow."

"Sir Nicholas de Mydden?" Claudine echoed in dismay. "But Justin was to escort me to the nunnery."

"Justin cannot—"

"Madame, he promised me!" Claudine was so flus-
tered that she did not even realize she'd interrupted the
queen. Lowering her voice hastily lest they attract attention, she said coaxingly, "Surely you understand why I
would prefer Justin's company, Your Grace. I know I can

trust him. And . . . and he wants to accompany me. This child is his, after all."

Eleanor looked into Claudine's flushed, distraught face, striving for patience. "Well, this is one promise Justin cannot keep. He is away from the court, and I know not when he will return. As for Nicholas, he is no gossipmonger." Unable to resist adding, "Those in my service know the value I place upon loyalty."

Claudine's lashes fluttered down again, veiling her eyes. After a moment, she said meekly, "Forgive my boldness, madame. It was not my intent to argue with you. If you have confidence in Sir Nicholas's discretion, then so do I. But could I not wait till week's end? Mayhap Justin will be back by then."

She took Eleanor's shrug for assent and fell in step beside the queen as they cut across the grassy mead. "I did not even know Justin was gone, for he did not bid me farewell."

She sounded both plaintive and aggrieved, and Eleanor found herself thinking that Justin might be fortunate that he was not considered a suitable husband for this pampered young kinswoman of hers. It would be no easy task, keeping Claudine de Loudun content.

"Madame . . . it is not my intent to pry," Claudine said, with such pious prevarication that Eleanor rolled her eyes skyward. "Whatever Justin's mission for you may be, it is not for me to question it. I would ask this, though. Can you at least tell me if he is in any danger?"

Eleanor paused, considering. Her first impulse was to give the girl the reassurance she sought. But the truth was that whenever her son John was involved, there was bound to be danger.

It was a sparse turnout for a hanging. Usually the citizens of Winchester thronged to the gallows out on Andover

Road, eager to watch as a felon paid the ultimate price for his earthly sins. Luke de Marston, the under-sheriff of Hampshire, could remember hangings that rivaled the St Giles Fair, with venders hawking meat pies and children getting underfoot and cutpurses on the prowl for unwary victims. But the doomed soul being dragged from the cart was too small a fish to attract a large crowd, a criminal by happenstance rather than choice.

The few men and women who'd bothered to show up were further disappointed by the demeanor of the culprit. They expected bravado and defiance from their villains, or at the very least, stoical self-control. But this prisoner was obviously terrified, whimpering and trembling so violently that he had to be assisted up the gallows steps. People were beginning to turn away in disgust even before the rope was tightened around his neck.

Luke's deputy shared their dissatisfaction, for he believed that a condemned man owed his audience a better show than this. "Pitiful," he said, shaking his head in disapproval. "Remember how the Fleming died, cursing God with his last breath?"

Luke remembered. Gilbert the Fleming had been one of Winchester's most notorious outlaws, as brutal as he was elusive, evading capture again and again until he'd been brought down by Luke and the queen's man, Justin de Quincy. His hanging had been a holiday.

"Luke."

The voice was familiar, but it should have been seventy-two miles away in London. Spinning around to face de Quincy, Luke scowled, for the younger man's sudden materialization was unsettling, coming as it did just as he'd been thinking of him. "Sometimes, de Quincy, I think you do it on purpose."

Justin was not put off by Luke's brusque welcome. While they'd started out as adversaries, they'd soon become allies, united in their common desire to ensnare Gilbert the Fleming. "Do what?"

"Appear like this in a puff of blue smoke and scare the daylights out of me. If I did not know better, I'd suspect you were a warlock instead of a harbinger of evil tidings."

Justin couldn't argue with that; he and Luke shared a past marked by murder, mayhem, and treason. "I'm here," he said, "to invite you to join a hunt."

Luke regarded him warily. "And just what are we hunting this time?"

"Our usual quarry," Justin admitted, "the one we track by following the scent of brimstone."

The port of Southampton lay just twelve miles to the south of Winchester, and it was still daylight when Luke and Justin reined in at the Bargate, a square stone tower that guarded the northern entrance into the city.

"Do you not think it is time," Luke declared abruptly, "that you were more forthcoming? Suppose you do find John here. What then? We cannot very well arrest him by ourselves, and I do not fancy arresting him at all, not when the man might well be king one day. This seems a long way to come merely to verify a rumor, de Quincy. I'd wager you have something else in mind, and naturally you are loath to share it with me. I've known Anchorite hermits that were more talkative than you. You need not confide every last detail of your battle plan, but I want more than you've so far given me."

Justin knew Luke would not be mollified with less than the truth, or at least a goodly portion of it. "I've not misled you," he insisted. "The queen wants me to confirm that John is in Southampton, making ready to sail for France. But you are right, and there is more to it than that. The queen has a spy in John's service. This may be the last chance he has to convey any messages to the queen, and since I am the only one who knows of his mission, I am also the only one who can seek him out ere they sail."

Luke was not about to ask for a name. He knew Justin would not tell him. Nor did he truly want to know; he'd learned long ago that Scriptures was right and "He that increaseth knowledge increaseth sorrow," at least when the knowledge was as dangerous as the identity of the queen's spy in her son's household. Instead, he concentrated upon the logistics of Justin's mission, suggesting that they search the docks first, find out which ships were preparing for the Channel crossing. That made sense to Justin and they split up soon after they'd passed through the Bargate, Luke heading for the castle quay and Justin continuing down English Street.

Turning onto the Fleshambles, where the city butchers had their shops, Justin was dismayed to see so many people still out and about. He reminded himself, though, that John was not a man to pass unnoticed. The streets were narrow, crowded with passersby, and Justin had to keep ducking his head to avoid sagging ale-poles and the overhang of buildings extending out into the roadway. When he saw a smithy close by the fishmongers' market, he hastily dismounted and soon struck a bargain with the blacksmith: a few coins in exchange for a stall for his stallion in the farrier's stable.

He decided to search the docks next and turned into the first alley that led toward the river. It was not much wider than the length of his sword, and he had to squeeze past a couple who'd ducked into the alley for a quick sexual encounter. The man was too preoccupied to notice Justin, grunting and thrusting with such force that the woman's body was being slammed against the wall; she made no protest, gazing over her partner's shoulder at

Justin with indifferent, empty eyes. She was so young, though—barely old enough to have started her flux—that Justin felt a flicker of pity as he detoured around them. Luke would have called him a softhearted dolt—and often did—but Justin had a foundling's instinctive sympathy for the downtrodden, God's poor, the lost, the doomed, and the abandoned. He saw no harm in offering up a brief prayer for the soul of this child-woman selling her body in a Southampton alley.

As he emerged from the alley, Justin came upon a lively waterfront scene. There were a few ships moored at the quays, but the larger vessels were anchored out in the harbor. Several small lighters were shuttling back and forth between these ships and the docks, where sailors and passengers mingled with vendors and merchants come to supervise the unloading of their cargo. Although Vespers had sounded more than an hour ago, the crew of a French cog was still hard at work, using a block and tackle to transfer wine tuns into a waiting lighter. The casks were heavy and unwieldy and one was balanced so precariously that Justin would normally have lingered to watch. But now he gave it only a glance, for his attention had been drawn to a cluster of well-dressed men gathered on the West Quay.

Stepping back into the mouth of the alley so he could observe without being seen, Justin had no difficulty in picking out the queen's son. The highborn were always magnets for every eye, even in these dubious circumstances, and John was surrounded by the curious, the hopeful, and the hungry. Peddlers cried out their wares, ships' masters jockeyed for position as they offered the hire of their vessels, and beggars huddled in the outermost ring of the circle, being kept at a distance by hard-faced men in chain mail. Justin found himself wondering what it would be like to live his life on center stage, like an actor in one of the Christmas plays. John would never be a supporting player; for him, it must be the lead role or nothing.

John started toward the alley and Justin withdrew farther into it. The first part of his mission had been easy enough to accomplish. But Durand de Curzon was as slippery as a conger eel and not even a forked stick would be enough to pin him down. Justin still remembered his shock upon his discovery that Durand was not John's "tame wolf," bur Eleanor's. He had never loathed anyone as much as he did Durand, and it vexed him no end to have to give the other man even a sliver of respect. He could not deny Durand's courage, though, for if John ever discovered his betrayal, death would come as a mercy.

Justin was so intent upon his surveillance that he was slow to heed the muffled sounds behind him. He did not swing around until he heard a choked-off scream. At the end of the alley, the young prostitute was struggling to get away from her customer. She kicked him in the shin and almost broke free, but he caught the skirt of her gown, and when she stumbled, he shoved her back against the wall. Justin took one step toward them before halting. His first instinct was to come to the girl's aid, but if he did, he risked alerting John to his presence. This was none of his concern, after all. Whores were used to being slapped around.

But then the man backhanded her across the face and grabbed her throat. Justin spared a second for a regretful glance over his shoulder before lunging forward. He had no interest in fighting fair, only in fighting fast, and made use of a maneuver he'd learned from a battle-scarred serjeant named Jonas, seizing a handful of the man's long, scraggly hair and bringing his fist down hard on the back of his neck. It proved as effective in Southampton alleys as it had in London's mean streets; the man staggered, then sank to his knees, mouth ajar, eyes dazed and unfocused. Snatching up a broken piece of wood, the girl swung it wildly at her assailant. When it missed, she threw it aside and began to scream curses and abuse at him, revealing an impressive command of profanity for one so young.

"Gutter rat! Misbegotten devil's spawn! Shit-eating sousepot, you tried to kill me!"

He gaped up at her, then lurched unsteadily to his feet. "Lying bitch!" Blinking blearily at Justin, he showed no resentment, instead appealed to him, man to man. "The little slut was going to rob me!"

"You're the liar, not me!" She, too, now addressed her complaints to Justin. "This besotted, poxy bastard did not want to pay me!"

"Filthy whore!"

"Rutting swine!"

By now they both were shouting loudly enough to awaken all but the dead, and a large, curious crowd had gathered at the entrance of the alley. Justin glared at the two of them. "Shall I send for a bailiff?" he asked coldly, and as he expected, that cooled their rancor considerably. The girl flung one last curse over her shoulder, then disappeared into the throng of spectators, while her accuser tried to recover some dignity by adjusting his disheveled garments before he, too, made a hasty retreat. Seeing that the show was over, their audience began to disperse, leaving Justin alone in the alley.

Justin was thoroughly disgusted with himself. When would he learn to heed his head, not his heart? He had no rational hope that John would not have been drawn by the uproar, and he turned slowly and reluctantly, already sure what he would see. As he feared, John and his men were blocking the alley.

John was the most unpredictable man that Justin had ever known, and he proved it now by reacting with amusement, not hostility. He looked utterly at ease, leaning against the wall, arms folded, eyes filled with laughter.

"God love you, de Quincy, but you are a source of constant wonderment," John said with a grin that told Justin he knew exactly what had transpired in this alley. "I can always rely upon you to be the veritable soul of chivalry. Is it just knighthood you aspire to, or have you a craving for sainthood, too?"

While Justin usually had no trouble laughing at himself, his sense of humor seemed to shut down whenever John was around. "I'm gratified that I was able to entertain you, my lord," he said dryly. "That makes my journey to Southampton worthwhile, then."

John's grin flashed again. "Come on," he said, "and I'll buy you a drink ere I sail. You can even wave farewell from the quay if you choose."

Justin submitted to this raillery with what grace he could muster, following John back toward the docks and into a riverside alehouse. It was poorly lit with reeking oil lamps, its floor deep in marsh rushes that looked as if they'd not been changed since the reign of the current king's father, its wooden benches splattered with dried mud and candle wax, not the sort of place where a man as highborn as John would usually be found. But Justin suspected that John often turned up in unlikely surroundings.

John was feeling generous and ordered ale for his men, too, even for several delighted customers. Claiming a corner table, he beckoned to Justin. "Sit," he commanded, "and drown your chagrin in ale. Once you've tasted their brew, you'll be willing to gulp down goat piss without flinching. So . . . you intend to tell my lady mother about this chat of ours? That her loyal spy let himself be undone by a Southampton street whore?"

"Yes," Justin said, so tersely that John had to hide his laughter in his ale cup.

"What was I thinking? Of course you will tell her. I daresay you'd go to daily confession if you could find a priest who'd stay awake during them."

Amused in spite of himself, Justin held up his hands in mock surrender. "I yield, my lord. God has indeed cursed me with a conscience."

John's mouth twitched. "I know you have questions, de Quincy. So ask away. I might even answer one or two."

"I have no questions, my lord. I am in Southampton to be able to reassure the queen that you got off safely for France. It was her hope that you'd convey her good wishes to the French king."

This was the way their conversations usually went, verbal jousting that reminded Justin of those boyhood winters when he'd strapped on bone skates and ventured out onto the newly frozen ice of Cheshire ponds. Thrust and parry. He waited now for John's counterstroke, but the other man was gazing over his shoulder toward the door.

"It is about time you got here," John said.

Justin caught a whiff of sandalwood perfume as a woman approached the table. She looked even more out of place in this seedy alehouse than John did, clad in a floor-length green mantle, her face framed in a white linen wimple, her fingers adorned with rings that testified to John's generosity. Justin recognized her at once as John's concubine from the siege of Windsor, and he started to rise.

Her manners had not improved any since then; Justin could have been invisible for all the notice she took of him. Gazing around her, she wrinkled her nose in disgust. "Must we wait for the tide in this hovel?" She added a perfunctory "my lord" in acknowledgment of the public setting, but it sounded neither deferential nor convincing. She had not impressed Justin as a particularly likable woman, but she was undeniably a desirable one, and he was wondering what she called John in the privacy of their bedchamber when a familiar voice sounded behind him.

"I did not think we'd ever get here, my lord. Mistress Ursula insisted upon stopping to view a street peddler's wares . . ." Durand's complaint trailed off in surprise as his eyes came to rest upon Justin. "Damn me if you're not the spitting image of a man I know back in London. Of course if you knew him, too, you'd take that as a mortal insult, for de Quincy is the most self-righteous, irksome—"

"It gladdens my heart to see you, too, Durand."

"What did I tell you lads about this unseemly squabbling?" John said, in a dead-on imitation of a father chastising his young sons. Pushing the bench back, he got to his feet and draped his arm around Ursula's shoulders. "You might as well finish my ale, Durand, if you can stomach drinking with de Quincy." His gaze flicked from Durand to Justin, his eyes guarded, utterly at variance with his affectation of good-humored nonchalance. "Tell my mother," he said, "that I'll be sure to pass on her regards to King Philippe."

Reaching for his money pouch, John spilled coins onto the table with the casual largesse that was expected of the nobility, even one in John's precarious straits. He sauntered out, then, with Ursula in tow. He did not look back.

Durand swung a leg over the bench, picking up John's ale cup as if he meant to drink it. As soon as John had exited the alehouse, he sat it down with a grimace. "I was wondering how you'd manage to find me," he said, with a studied drawl that grated upon Justin's nerves. "It never occurred to me that you'd simply ask John. Now why did I not think of that?"

"It worked, did it not?" Justin pointed out laconically. He'd be damned before he'd offer any explanations to Durand, and he met the other man's gaze evenly, refusing to take the bait.

Durand knew from past encounters that Justin's temper was easily kindled, and he was sorely tempted to keep on until he'd struck some sparks. But they dared not linger in the alehouse without arousing John's suspicions. Leaning forward, he said softly, "The French king warned John that Richard has come to terms with the Holy Roman Emperor and his release is nigh. This news alarmed John enough to send him racing for the coast and the first ship for France."

He laughed soundlessly. "Richard casts a long shadow, indeed, if the mere prospect of his return can scare men half out of their wits. It took John an outlandishly long time to remember that even if Brother Richard were released on the morrow, it would take him weeks to make his way back to England."

Justin understood why Richard could inspire such fear. There was no greater battle commander in Christendom, and all knew he was a soldier first and foremost, only secondly a king. "I grant you John is not acting like a man in the throes of panic. So if he knows the danger is not imminent, why is he still in Southampton, making ready to sail?"

"Once common sense took over, he realized that deals are made to be broken. There is only one offer on the table . . . so far. What if the emperor were promised even more money to keep Richard caged up in some godforsaken German castle?"

"He'd probably pounce upon that offer like a hungry weasel," Justin said slowly, and Durand grinned.

"Exactly. John well knows that the emperor has the scruples of a pirate and the honor of . . . Well, let's just say that the noble Heinrich makes John and Philippe look like Heaven's own angels. He'd sell Richard in a heartbeat if the price were right."

Justin nodded grimly, thinking that this would be a bitter message to bring to his queen. At least she would be forewarned that this storm was brewing on the horizon. Shoving his ale cup aside, he rose to his feet and was faintly amused when Durand immediately did the same; he'd never known another man so keen on securing each and every advantage, no matter how small or trivial. "Is that all?"

"Is it not enough?" Durand adjusted his scabbard, making sure that the weight of his sword was well balanced, then reached for his hat. It had a broad brim, turned up in the back, a style that Justin had not seen before, and was doubtlessly the newest fashion. It always surprised Justin that a man as ruthless and predatory as Durand de Curzon could also care about the petty concerns of royal courtiers. Someday he would have to resolve the mystery of this baneful, blood-hungry wolf, surely better suited to serving the Devil than their queen.

Almost as if reading his thoughts, Durand said, with a cold smile, "Well, as one queen's man to another, are you not going to wish me luck, de Quincy?"

He deserved it, Justin knew, and likely would need it, too. "Go with God," he said, with equal coldness. "And if we are both truly lucky, this will be the last time that we need lay eyes upon each other."

Durand's smile faded. "Ah," he said, "but John will be back. You can wager the kingdom on that."

2

July 1193
Windsor Castle, England

Justin de Quincy had not been back at Windsor since that spring's siege when he'd infiltrated the castle at the queen's behest, his mission to convince John to accept a truce. He'd ended up shackled in a dungeon hellhole, with Durand to thank for his awful accommodations, and although he'd eventually succeeded in his objective, his recollections of Windsor were not fond ones. Claudine did her best to replace them with more pleasant memories, sneaking him into her bedchamber as soon as the rest of the household was abed. But the night's daring, seductive rebel vanished with the coming of first light. Upon awakening, Claudine was beset by morning sickness, low spirits, and a heightened fear of being found out.

"I am so sorry," she whispered as Justin washed her face with a wet cloth. "A woman's lover ought not to have to hold a basin for her whilst she vomits—"

"Do not talk rubbish," he said and leaned over to kiss her on the forehead. "The pleasure was mutual, so it is only fair that the penance be mutual, too."

He spoke in jest, but that was how Claudine did view her pregnancy: as penance. He was stroking her hair, smoothing it away from her face, and she blinked back tears. "Do you think we will reach Oxford by nightfall, Justin?"

Oxford was not much more than thirty miles from Windsor, a distance Justin could easily have covered in one day. But they'd ridden only twenty-three miles yesterday and that had exhausted Claudine. "I think so," he said, hoping he did not sound as doubtful as he felt, for travel accommodations could not be left to chance, not when his traveling companion was gently born and pregnant.

Her thoughts had obviously been following the same route as his, for she said, with sudden determination, "We will just have to, won't we? But where will we stay in Oxford? It was safe enough to spend the night here at Windsor, but I do not want it known that I was so close to the nunnery at Godstow, for someone could connect gossip like that with my disappearance from court. So that eliminates both the castle and the king's house. Nor can I go to St Mary's Abbey, for I've met Abbot Hugh."

It occurred to Justin that his life had been much simpler prior to his involvement with Claudine. She was gazing up at him with a worried frown and he smiled reassuringly. "I promise, love, that you'll not have to sleep in the street."

Some fourteen hours later, though, he was not so sure about that. Due to Claudine's resolve and the lingering daylight of high summer, they had reached Oxford by dusk. The Wednesday market was just breaking up, and the streets were still crowded around the Carfax, the city's ancient crossroads. Leaving Claudine with their horses, Justin went in search of the closest inn. As Oxford was a prosperous town with more than five thousand citizens and a thriving university community, he was utterly taken aback to be told there were no inns. Making his way back to Claudine, he realized how easily he'd been spoiled by living in London, honeycombed with inns, cook shops, taverns, and alehouses, and he marveled anew at the vast changes his life had undergone since that December night when he'd finally learned the truth about his paternity.

Not the least of those changes was waiting for him in the churchyard of St Michael's. Claudine was attracting more than her share of attention, for she was fair to look upon, fashionably dressed, obviously a gentlewoman. She usually enjoyed creating such a stir, but now she seemed oblivious to the admiring glances being cast her way. Her face was pallid, her exhaustion evident in the drooping eyelids, down-turned mouth, and dejected slump of her shoulders. She managed a wan smile, though, as Justin drew near, even a small, irreverent joke. "Please do not tell me that there is no room at the inn."

"Worse than that, love. There is no inn at all, just lodgings for students from the university."

Claudine groaned. "Oh, no . . . now what? I seem to remember a nunnery here from a past visit . . ."

"I was told it burned in the great fire of three years ago. But I have found us a bed for the night, Claudine. A family on Catte Street has agreed to take us in—for a generous sum, of course."

Claudine opened her mouth to speak, then thought better of it. Justin could guess what she'd been about to say. The highborn did not take shelter at inns when they traveled. While monastery guest halls were always open to wayfarers and pilgrims, those of Claudine's class were accorded special status, often the honored guests of the abbot himself. If not an abbey or priory, there was usually a castle in the vicinity, and a welcome assured whether the castellan was known to them or not, for rank and blood were the keys to the kingdom. So Claudine was not troubled at the prospect of lodging under the roof of strangers—provided that they were of the gentry.

Justin came from a different world. Neither fish nor

fowl, he thought sometimes, for the mother he'd never known had been a vulnerable village girl and his high-flying hawk of a father would eventually become a prince of the Church. There was a certain security in knowing one's place in the natural order of things, none in balancing precariously upon the sword's edge. But Justin's dubious birthright did give him one advantage. He was bilingual, both literally and figuratively, in the Norman-French of the Conquest and the English of the conquered.

He proved that now by the ease with which he assuaged Claudine's qualms, volunteering that Benet Kepeharm, their host, was kin to John Kepeharm, Oxford's current alderman, and that he had gone ahead to prepare his household for their arrival. Reassured that she'd be dealing with people of property, Claudine let Justin assist her back into the saddle.

The Kepeharms' residence on Catte Street looked like all of its neighbors: timber-framed, slate-roofed, fronting on the street, and abutting the houses on either side. The interior chamber was where the family ate, worked, played, and slept, with a screened-off bed for Benet and his wife at one end, pallets for their children and maid servant at the other, and trestle table, benches, and coffers squeezed in between the sleeping spaces. Justin could see the pride that the Kepeharms had in their home; it glowed in their faces as they ushered their guests inside. But he knew, too, how shabby their prized possessions must look to Claudine, a child of privilege reared in palaces, and he felt again a sense of surprise that this woman could have become his bedmate.

Because it was a Wednesday fast day, they had a supper of baked lamprey eels, cabbage soup, and stewed pears, washed down with a red wine flavored with ginger and sweetened with honey. Benet and his wife insisted that their guests sleep in their own bed. Lacking a pillow, Claudine cradled her head in the crook of Justin's shoulder and apologized drowsily for her exhaustion, for they both knew this might be their last chance for lovemaking. Godstow's nunnery awaited them on the morrow.

This was only the fourth time that they'd passed the entire night together; their liaisons had usually been catch-as-catch-can. Listening to the soft, even sounds of Claudine's breathing, Justin recalled them, one by one. Their first night had been in a London inn. Their second night was when she'd arrived, drenched and shivering, at his cottage and blurted out that she was with child. And then these two nights on the road. Four nights and a handful of stolen afternoons, no more than that. He was almost asleep when the thought came to him, unwelcome and unbidden. Their night in that inn had been Claudine's doing. She'd admitted that she knew little of inns, so how had she known of this one? From John?

Justin did not want to go down that road again. It served for naught. He knew Claudine had been John's spy. He did not know if she'd been his concubine, too. In truth, he did not want to know. He looked down at the woman asleep beside him, letting his hand rest upon the rounded curve of her belly. God help him, he never wanted to know.

A sudden rainstorm had drenched London at midday, but the sun soon blazed through the clouds again and by dusk, the city was sweltering in humid July heat. Aldred was parched by the time he reached Gracechurch Street, his open, freckled face streaked with sweat, his cap of untidy yellow hair plastered damply against his scalp. He was already tasting one of Nell's ales, but he was a polite youth and he paused to exchange greetings with passersby. It was well known in the neighborhood that he worked for Jonas, the laconic, one-eyed serjeant who struck fear in the good and the godless alike. After joking briefly with Odo the barber, Aldred waved at the man standing across the street in the door of his smithy. "Gunter!" The blacksmith waved back, but by then Aldred had ducked into the alehouse.

He halted, blinking until his eyes had adjusted to the shadows. It was more crowded than he'd expected, for Vespers had not rung yet. Customers clustered around the rickety wooden tables, perched on stools and benches, sat on upturned empty barrels, voices pitched loudly to be heard above the din. Most were men, although there were a few local women happy to gossip and drink in a place where they could feel comfortable and safe. In the midst of this chaos was Nell, looking more harried than usual, pouring ale and scolding her helper, Ellis, for being a laggard and slapping away hands if they got too familiar as she squeezed past.

Aldred found a spot for himself and when Nell noticed him, he held up two fingers, hoping that she'd be tempted to take a break and have an ale with him. He'd always assumed that any woman managing an alehouse would have to be a hag, ugly as sin and as strapping and hulking as a Kentish quarryman. But Nell was a little bit of a lass, not even reaching his shoulder, with curly flaxen hair that was always escaping the constraints of her veil, a ripe, pouting mouth, and eyes as blue as a harvest sky. Aldred's shy courtship had not progressed very far; he suspected that Nell dismissed him as a green country lad, even though he'd lived in London for nigh on two years and proudly bore a scar on his throat from the blade of the notorious Gilbert the Fleming.

Eventually Nell made her way over, and Aldred's hopes rose at the sight of two tankards of ale. "Move your bum, Firmin," she directed and the man obediently slid down the bench, allowing her to sit next to Aldred.

"Lord have mercy, what a day . . ." She drank, sighed, and drank again. "I vow, Aldred, I've been on the run since daybreak, with nary a chance to catch my breath. First my Lucy was chasing about with that mad beast of Justin's and she tripped, scraping her knees and getting blood all over her skirt. Whilst I was getting her cleaned up, the sausages I was frying burnt to cinders. Then Hardwin finally showed up to whitewash the walls, after promising and putting me off for nigh on a month. So what happened next? Look for yourself," she said, pointing toward a patch of brightness, an island in a sea of smoke-smudged, murky grime.

"He mixed the lime and salt with water, painted that small section of the wall, and then told Ellis he was off to the cook shop for his supper. That was hours ago! I'll wager he's not coming back tonight, and all I've got to show for his day's work is one half-done wall, a lot of clutter, and that trough over there slopping over with whitewash! Ellis already put his foot in one of the buckets, damned near broke his leg. When I catch Hardwin, I'll make him rue the day he was ever born!"

Aldred did not doubt it; Nell's temper was legendary on Gracechurch Street. "You know how painters and carpenters and their ilk are," he said sympathetically. "If you are fool enough to give them their money ere the job is done, they're off in a puff of smoke—" Suddenly realizing that he'd just inadvertently insulted Nell, he said hastily, "Is Jonas here yet? He told me to meet him at Vespers. He and Justin have been chasing their tails all over London, trying to track down those rumors about some of the sheriff's men keeping a portion of the ransom for themselves."

In his eagerness to distract Nell from his gaffe, he was being very indiscreet. Normally Nell would have seized upon this intriguing bit of gossip, but she was only half-listening to Aldred, her eyes narrowing upon a corner table. "I cannot believe it," she muttered. "Now that knave is harrying poor Leofric!"

Following her gaze, Aldred did not see why she was so vexed. The object of her anger seemed to be a stranger of about thirty or so, well-dressed in a stalked cap and bright blue tunic, long legs stretched out in front of him, revealing leather ankle boots that Aldred would have loved to own. Several men were seated at the table and he glanced back at Nell. "Which one is Leofric?"

"The lad in the short tunic with the ripped sleeve," she said, gesturing toward a lanky redhead. "That lout has been hanging around all day, goading others into dicing or arm wrestling with him, for a wager, of course. When men balk, he shames them into it . . . and always wins. I am sure he is cheating somehow. I knew he was a wrong one the first I laid eyes on him. I warned him to let Leofric be, too!"

Aldred found himself begrudging Leofric the warmth in Nell's voice. "Is he mute that he cannot speak up for himself?" he asked, unable to keep an edge from his tone.

Fortunately for him, Nell didn't notice. "Leofric is a good lad, but he is slow-witted. When he first started coming in, some of the others made sport of him till I put a stop to it. He never causes trouble, just drinks his ale and smiles when spoken to. He helps out at the butcher's and has a few pence to spend, so I suppose that makes him fair game to that two-legged snake."

Embarrassed by his jealousy, Aldred sought to redeem himself in Nell's eyes by offering to arm wrestle the "snake" himself. "I do not like to boast, but I've won more than my share of bouts. I'll be right glad to teach him a lesson for you, Mistress Nell."

His effort was wasted, though, for Nell had turned aside to confer with Ellis. Setting down her ale, she rose reluctantly to her feet. "I'll be back," she said. "Ellis says one of the barrels has sprung a leak."

When she returned, there was a crowd around Leofric's table. Aldred was standing nearby, looking indignant, and immediately pushed his way toward her. "He prodded the lad into wrestling. But then he said they ought to make it 'interesting,' and he put a candle on the table so the loser would get burnt!"

Nell shoved and squirmed her way through the circle of spectators. Beads of sweat had broken out on Leofric's forehead, and his knuckles were bone-white in the other man's grip. But try as he might, his arm was slowly being forced toward that flickering candle. Wincing as the yellow flame licked at his skin, he looked up at Nell with such bewilderment that she felt a surge of outrage. Reaching for a tankard on the table, she knocked it over onto the candle, soaking the sleeves of both men with ale.

"How clumsy of me," she said, as evenly as her anger would allow. She looked toward Ellis, signaling for a refill as the best way of easing the tension. But the gambler gave her no chance.

"You stupid cow! This is Flemish wool!" Glaring at Nell, he brandished the wet blotch on his sleeve as if it were a wound. "If the fuller cannot get the stain out, you'll owe me for a new tunic." As she started to speak, he cut her off with an imperious gesture. "I want no apologies, woman, not from the likes of you. Just get me another drink and get it now."

Color flooded Nell's face. "You want an ale, do you?" She spun around and snatched a tankard from the closest table. "Here you are," she said, swiftly upending it over his head.

He sprang to his feet, sputtering oaths, and lunged for her. But she'd already darted out of reach, putting the table between them. "Lowborn bitch!" He started for her again, only to be brought up short when Aldred and Ellis blocked his way. His curses spilling over onto them, he raged for another moment or so before becoming aware of the utter silence. Glancing over his shoulder, he discovered that he was ringed in by a half dozen men.

"This is none of your concern!"

"Ah, but it is," one of his new adversaries explained. "We look after our own here."

His eyes slid from one face to another and then he began to back slowly away. The men followed.

It had been a long day, and both Jonas's and Justin's steps were flagging as they turned onto Gracechurch Street, trailed by Shadow, Justin's panting black dog. They'd covered at least ten miles since that morning, all of it on foot, for seasoned Londoners knew better than to brave the crowded city streets on horseback when they had many stops to make.

"I never thought I'd miss chasing after thieves and cutthroats," Jonas said tiredly. "But they're easier prey for certes. Hunt them down, catch them, hang them, and forget them."

"Well, at least we disproved the rumor." Justin smothered a yawn with his fist. "I can now assure the queen that the coffer from the nunnery at Clerkenwell arrived intact and the seal was not tampered with."

"This time," Jonas amended. "I daresay the money being collected in London is making it safely to the crypt at St Paul's. There are too many eyes watching for it here.

But there are a lot of lonely roads and moors and deep woods in the realm."

Justin nodded somberly. "Outlaws will be swarming like honeybees."

Jonas almost smiled. "So will sheriffs and bailiffs and aldermen and their sainted grandmothers, de Quincy."

Justin hoped Jonas was wrong. It was disheartening to believe that corruption was so contagious. And it would make his task all the more difficult, for he knew the queen would want every last half-penny accounted for. The ransom being demanded for King Richard was staggering, one hundred thousand silver marks, and no one was exempt. Churches, monasteries, towns, guilds, and subjects of the king were all expected to contribute a fourth of their year's income. Was Richard worth such a vast sum? That was a question Justin had never thought to ask. For him, it was enough that his queen thought so.

They had just reached the alehouse when the door flew open and a ghostly apparition stumbled out. He was coated in whitewash; it dripped from his hair and squished out of his boots, splattering the ground with his every stride. Justin and Jonas, with fine teamwork, veered off to either side, letting him splash between them. As they watched, he ran across the street and dived into the horse trough in front of the smithy.

The noise coming from the alehouse was loud and raucous. But a silence fell at the sight of the sheriff's serjeant and the queen's man. Jonas's gaze moved slowly over the crowd before settling on Aldred and Nell. Aldred flushed and tried to edge away. Nell stood her ground and shook her head when Jonas asked, "Is this something I need know about?"

"No," she said, and he nodded.

"Good," he said and entered the alehouse, carefully

stepping over a puddle of whitewash in the doorway. Justin followed him in toward a table that had suddenly become free; people tended to give Jonas space. Aldred soon sidled over and sat down. After a few moments, Nell joined them with a tray of ales. Pulling up a stool for herself, she smiled brightly.

"So . . . did you have any luck with your ransom hunt?"

"I see Aldred has been babbling again," Jonas said, sounding more resigned than irked.

Aldred squirmed and then seized his chance to deflect attention away from his latest lapse. "Look, Justin, your landlord is here."

Justin turned to see Gunter entering the alehouse. He didn't think of the blacksmith in those terms, but he supposed Aldred was right; he did rent Gunter's cottage. Half-rising, he beckoned to attract Gunter's eye, and Nell and Aldred moved over to make room for the farrier at their table. Gunter did not sit down, though.

"The queen sent a messenger to your cottage this afternoon, Justin. She wants to see you straightaway."

Justin was ushered at once into the queen's private chamber at Westminster, for her household knew that he was one of her agents, one of those mysterious men who came and went at odd hours on covert missions better left to the imagination. Eleanor was dictating a letter to St Martial's Abbey in Limoges. Justin heard enough to recognize it as a personal appeal to the abbot, requesting one hundred marks for Richard's ransom. He knew Limoges was in her overseas domains and he was interested, but not at all surprised, to learn that she was exacting payment from Aquitaine as well as England. He did not doubt that if she could, she'd have squeezed money from the Holy See.

Eleanor glanced up as Justin entered and knelt at her feet, then gestured to her scribe, who gathered up his writing utensils. She also dismissed her other attendants, an indication that she had a highly confidential matter to discuss. That was usually the case, for all the services Justin had performed for the queen were related, directly or indirectly, to thwarting John's schemes while still protecting him from his own folly.

Eleanor was in remarkable health for a woman of seventy-one years. The past seven months had taken their toll, though, as she'd first feared that her best-loved son was dead, only to learn that he was being held hostage in Germany by the Emperor Heinrich, an enemy who hated him as much as Philippe, the French king, did. Fatigue and dread and uncertainty had carved new furrows in her face, etched wrinkles around her eyes that none would ever call "laugh lines." This night she appeared exhausted, so pale and careworn that Justin felt a pang of alarm; he was not accustomed to seeing her look so vulnerable.

Eleanor signaled for him to rise, and when she spoke, her voice sounded as it always did, well modulated and deliberative, resonating with the authority she'd wielded for much of her lifetime. "I have a question to put to you, Justin. You grew up in the Marches, so I assume you are more familiar than most with the region and its labyrinthine politics."

Justin wasn't sure what *labyrinthine* meant, but he nodded, somewhat warily. "Yes, Madame. I know Shrewsbury well, Chester even better."

"You understand English and read Latin, so you seem to have an ear for languages. What about Welsh?"

"I am by no means fluent, my lady. But yes, I do have some grasp of it. I'd picked up a little as a lad, and whilst I was in Lord Fitz Alan's service, I learned more from another of his squires, who was half-Welsh."

"Make ready," she said, "to leave for Wales on the morrow. Money meant for Richard's ransom has gone missing." She turned and rifled through a pile of parchments on the table until she found the one she wanted. "This is a letter from the Welsh prince Davydd ab Owain. The ransom he'd collected for Richard was stolen by a Welsh rebel."

The name was vaguely familiar to Justin, and after a moment, the memory came into focus. Davydd ab Owain was a prince of North Wales, long allied with the English Crown. "What more can you tell me, Madame?"

"Unfortunately, not much. When I referred to 'money' earlier, I was using the term loosely. The Welsh princes do not mint their own money and so the bulk of the ransom was wool from the Cistercian abbeys, although there were some coins and silver plate and jewelry, mayhap furs, too. Davydd says he'd sent it under guard to Chester, but it was ambushed by an outlaw named . . ." She glanced briefly at the letter. ". . . Llewelyn ab Iorwerth. The guards were slain and the ransom stolen. Needless to say, I want it back. It will be a god-given miracle if we can raise all the money demanded by that hellspawn Heinrich. I am not about to let Welsh brigands ruin Richard's chances of release."

"You call this man an 'outlaw' and a 'rebel.' Which is he, Madame?"

"According to Davydd, both. He is kin to Davydd— the Welsh are all inbred—and he has been trying to stir up rebellion, without much success. But he makes do with robbery and thieving and extortion. Here, read the letter for yourself."

Justin moved toward the closest light, a sputtering cresset lamp. "Davydd is rather sparing with details. This letter tells us very little."

"You noticed that, too," she said dryly. "His overriding

concern seems to be escaping any blame for this disaster. Which is all I'd expect from the man."

"Have you met Davydd, Madame?"

The corner of Eleanor's mouth curved. "Met him? I'm related to him, Justin." She did smile then at his look of surprise. "Davydd ab Owain is my brother-by-marriage. He is wed to my husband's sister Emma."

Justin blinked. "I thought King Henry had two brothers. I remember nothing of a sister . . ."

"Emma is Harry's half-sister, one of Geoffrey of Anjou's bastards. Davydd pressed very hard for the marriage and because Harry needed Welsh support at the time, he agreed, albeit reluctantly. But he never thought very highly of Davydd. Nor did Emma. Or so I've been told," she added, an ironic aside so oblique that it took a moment for Justin to realize this was an indirect reference to her imprisonment; at the time of Davydd's marriage to the Lady Emma, Eleanor was far from court, being held prisoner in a remote castle of her husband's choosing.

Reading the letter a second time, Justin could not help thinking that this could well be the most challenging assignment that Eleanor had ever given him. "What would you have me do first, Madame?"

"The Earl of Chester will be your most useful ally. If you need men, he'll provide them. The bishop may be of some help, too, for he knows Davydd and Emma well. Go first to Chester, see the earl and the bishop. And then you'll have to seek out Davydd in Wales. He keeps his court at Rhuddlan Castle."

Justin was no longer listening. She'd lost him from the moment that she'd mentioned the Bishop of Chester. He stared at her, incredulous. Surely she could not have forgotten that Aubrey de Quincy was his father? Unless . . . unless this was a stratagem, a means of bringing them together?

"My lady queen, I . . ." He paused, not knowing what to say. But as his eyes locked with hers, he saw the truth. She had not forgotten. Nor was she seeking to arrange a reconciliation. She knew how loath he was to see his father. It did not matter. Nothing mattered but Richard and the recovery of his ransom.

3

The Bishop of Chester's palace was located southeast of the city, just beyond the ancient Roman walls, adjacent to the cathedral church of St John. Justin drew rein at the sight of the gatehouse, not moving until his stallion began to fidget. Several months ago, he'd had to enter a lazar hospital in search of a killer. With some of the same dread that he'd felt at facing the lepers, he urged his mount forward into the precincts of his father's domain.

He was dismounting at the stables when he heard his name called out. Handing the reins to a waiting groom, he turned to greet Martin, the bishop's steward. Martin's face was creased in a delighted smile, and Justin smiled back, thinking that at least there was one soul here who was pleased to see him.

"Justin, I cannot tell you how much the sight of you gladdens my eyes. When you rode away last December, it was as if you'd vanished from the earth. I have often wondered where you were, how you were faring."

Justin felt a dart of guilt that it had not occurred to him to let Martin know he'd landed on his feet. He owed Martin better than that, for his father's steward had always treated him with great kindness, almost as if he suspected the truth about Justin's identity.

"I ought to have written to you, Martin, and I am sorry I did not. I should have known that . . . the bishop would

41

not have told you that he'd encountered me in London after Whitsuntide. I hope we can find time to talk later, for I'd like nothing better than to buy you an ale. But right now I need to see the bishop."

Martin's face shadowed. His obvious dismay confirmed Justin's suspicions—that Martin knew he was the bishop's son. "You need not worry, Martin. I am not here to stir up trouble. The bishop will see me, for I am bearing a letter from the queen."

Aubrey de Quincy had taken Eleanor's letter to the open window, and as he read, the afternoon sun glistened upon the silvered strands at his temples. Justin hadn't realized he was going so grey, for it was usually disguised by the fairness of his hair. Justin's own coloring was dark, and try though he might, he could see nothing of himself in the man by the window. He supposed he must have gotten his black hair from his mother, though it was not likely that he'd ever know for sure. He had no memories of her, nothing but the gossip of an old woman who'd been the refectory cook in his father's parish. He'd never even been told her name.

Aubrey was taking a long time to read a brief letter, and Justin wondered if he felt the same unease, the same desire to be elsewhere, to be anywhere but the bishop's palace at Chester. The last time they'd spoken, it had ended badly, with his father angrily warning him to keep silent and him hitting back with the only weapon at hand, telling Aubrey that Queen Eleanor already knew the truth. Justin knew the queen's letter made use of the surname he had no legal right to claim, for she'd shown it to him before sealing it. He imagined the words *Justin de Quincy* must have leapt off the parchment at his father; had he taken it as a royal threat? A reminder that the queen knew the secret he'd sought to hide for so long?

When Aubrey at last looked up, it was with a smile that was as fleeting as it was forced. "Well, the queen must have great faith in you, Justin, to entrust a matter of such importance to you."

It had not sounded like a compliment—there was too much surprise in his father's tone for that—and Justin acknowledged it with a shrug. "It is not as if I am expected to find the missing ransom all by myself. I can rely upon the Earl of Chester for whatever help I need. And Davydd ab Owain, too. I daresay no one is more eager to retrieve the ransom than he is."

Aubrey nodded. "Yes . . . Davydd must be in a frenzy, and he has never been known for his serene, steadfast nature in the best of times."

This was an ideal opening and Justin was grateful for it; he much preferred to confine their conversation to the facts of the robbery, and he suspected that his father did, too. "The queen told me that you know both Davydd and his wife, the Lady Emma. What can you tell me about him?"

"Davydd's father was a remarkable man, a great prince. Davydd is neither."

It was a harsh assessment, but Justin knew that his father was not a man to make allowances for human frailty, not even his own. "What else?"

Aubrey gestured toward a carved wooden bench and they both sat, somewhat awkwardly. "I suppose you ought to know the manner of man you'll be dealing with. Davydd has ruled Gwynedd east of the River Conwy for the past twenty or so years. After his father's death, Davydd and his younger brother, Rhodri, banded together and ambushed their half-brother Hywel, the heir-apparent. Hywel was slain; a pity, for he was a fine poet. Davydd and Rhodri soon turned on each other and for a brief time, Davydd ruled all of Gwynedd. These days he divides his time between his castle at Rhuddlan and his manors in Shropshire."

Justin's eyebrows rose. "A Welsh prince dwelling in England?"

"I imagine his wife prefers Shropshire to Wales; how could she not? But Davydd also sets great store by his ties to the English Crown. He is King Richard's uncle, if only by marriage, and rarely misses an opportunity to boast of it."

"You do not like him much," Justin observed, and Aubrey's mouth quirked.

"Few do," he said dryly. "Davydd does not hold the hearts of his people in the palm of his hand. He is a man of mediocre abilities who has been blessed with good luck, high birth, and a very beautiful wife."

Justin was remembering what he'd been told, that Emma was the illegitimate daughter of Count Geoffrey of Anjou. Geoffrey had been dead for many years, so Emma must be well past her youth. "You mean she was once a beauty?"

"Was and is," Aubrey said, faintly amused by Justin's polite attempt to disguise his disbelief. "She is a year or two past her fourth decade, which doubtless sounds as old as Methusaleh to a lad of twenty. But trust me in this, Justin. Emma of Anjou is still a beautiful woman."

Justin was surprised, both that his father had remembered his age and that he spoke so warmly of the Lady Emma. "What can you tell me of her marriage?" he asked, suddenly very curious to see Davydd's wife for himself.

"They've been wed for nigh on twenty years, have a son and a daughter if my memory serves. I first met her some years ago in Shropshire, ere I was made an archdeacon. I found her to be a lady of grace and piety and dignity. I trust you will bear that in mind during this investigation of yours, Justin."

"I will do my best not to shame you," Justin said, saw the muscles clench along his father's jaw, and regretted his rash words. Rising, he bent dutifully over the bishop's ring. "I thank you for sharing your thoughts with me."

Aubrey rose, too. "I assume you will go now to see the Earl of Chester?" When Justin nodded, the bishop's eyes narrowed and his voice iced over. "You have been taking a great liberty in making use of the de Quincy name. That you do this with the queen's approval does not make it right. I shall expect you to conduct yourself with decorum and discretion whilst you are in Chester."

Justin was becoming accustomed by now to paternal threats, but if they did not intimidate, they still stung. "My lord bishop," he said, with such mocking deference that his father made an angry gesture of dismissal. They glared at each other, and had they but known it, in that moment they did indeed look alike.

The queen's letter gave Justin the same swift admittance to Chester Castle as it had to the bishop's palace. Ranulf de Blundeville greeted him in the great hall, but after reading Eleanor's message, he led Justin abovestairs to his solar. He did not offer Justin wine or ale, but Justin took no offense, sure that Chester's omission was not a deliberate rudeness. Those who knew the earl knew, too, that he was single-minded to a fault, a man who focused upon the most pressing problem to the exclusion of all else. While Justin had never formally met Chester before, he was well acquainted with the gossip that inevitably swirled around a man of such prominence. Chester prided himself upon being blunt-spoken and forthright, which occasionally caused the cynical to brand him as naïve or credulous. Justin knew better, for Eleanor had warned him not to undervalue the earl's discerning eye. If the queen respected Chester's mother wit, that was more than enough for the queen's man.

Putting aside Eleanor's letter, Chester studied Justin through hooded dark eyes. It was a challenging look, even antagonistic. Justin had expected as much. The Earl of Chester was a great lord, cousin to the king, wed to an even greater heiress, Constance of Brittany, widow of Richard's brother Geoffrey, mother of Arthur, Geoffrey's young heir. As stepfather of the Duke of Brittany, Chester was sure to exercise influence in the boy's domains, for Arthur would not reach his majority for many years. And there was always the chance that Chester might find himself the stepfather of a king. Richard had sired no sons from his Spanish queen, and he was not a man likely to die peacefully in bed. If he died without an heir of his body, some would argue that his brother Geoffrey's son, Arthur, had a better claim to the English throne than the youngest brother, John.

Whatever Arthur's prospects of outwitting or outrunning John in a race for the crown, there was no denying that Ranulf of Chester wielded vast and profound powers, and so Justin had assumed that he would be jealous of his authority, even with one of Queen Eleanor's agents. But however much he might have preferred to keep control of the investigation in his own hands, he would cooperate, for he was not a fool. If the ransom were not recovered, Chester and Davydd ab Owain would both be blamed by the irate queen and frantic mother.

Chester's first question showed that Eleanor's confidence in his intellect was not misplaced. "I would like," he said, "to know exactly what Davydd ab Owain told the Queen's Grace."

"We thought you would," Justin acknowledged, holding out a second parchment. "This is a copy of the letter that he wrote to Queen Eleanor, informing her that the ransom had been stolen on its way to Chester."

Justin waited while the earl read and was amused when Chester echoed his own words almost exactly, saying brusquely that Davydd had been miserly with the details of the ambush. "Fortunately, one of my knights was in Gwynedd, helping with the collection of the ransom, and he was able to give me a more thorough account of the crime."

This was the first piece of good news that Justin had gotten. "Was your man present at the ambush, my lord earl?"

"Luckily for him, no. There was but one survivor, and I'm told he was not expected to live. Thomas was at Rhuddlan Castle, though, and so he has some useful information for you. Davydd ab Owain has good reason to be closemouthed. Had I blundered as badly as he did, I'd be loath to share my shame with the world, too."

Justin was not surprised that Chester was eager to lay blame at Davydd's door. Marcher lords and their Welsh counterparts were natural rivals, for the borders were writ in sand, shifting or expanding as ambitious men jockeyed for advantage. "I would be most interested in hearing of these blunders, my lord. To judge by the prince's letter to my lady queen, all the guilt belongs to that Welsh bandit, who is apparently a kinsman of some sort."

"A kinsman of some sort?" Chester echoed, so sarcastically that Justin tensed. "You are not very well informed, are you, Master de Quincy? If you do not even know the players in this infernal game, how likely are you to come out as the winner? Llewelyn ab Iorwerth is no fourth cousin by blood or distant kin by marriage.

Nor can he be dismissed as a 'Welsh bandit.' He is Davydd's nephew and in the eyes of the Holy Church, he has a better claim to the crown than his usurping uncle, for he was begotten in lawful marriage and Davydd was born in sin."

Justin was angry at the injustice of Chester's rebuke; this was why he'd come to the earl in the first place, to learn about the "players in this infernal game." But earls were not men to be reprimanded, and he contented himself by saying coolly, "I thought that the Welsh allow a bastard to inherit as long as he is recognized by his father."

Chester's heavy black brows slanted down in a frown, for Justin's tone was not as dispassionate as his words. Justin held his gaze, and to his surprise, the earl was the one to look away first. "I am glad to see that you do have some knowledge of the Welsh and their ways," he said grudgingly, and Justin remembered that the earl had a reputation for more than pride and hot temper; it was said, too, that he was fair.

"I would like to meet with this knight of yours, my lord earl," Justin said, doing his best to sound like a suppliant, for his mission could be crippled if he made an enemy of Chester.

"I shall do better than that, Master de Quincy. It is my intent to send Sir Thomas de Caldecott with you into Wales."

Justin was less than thrilled by the earl's generosity, and there was a gleam in Chester's eyes that told him the earl well knew the presence of his knight would be a mixed blessing. It would be useful to have an ally who was so familiar with Wales and the Welsh. But this man would also be Chester's eyes and ears, and Justin was not yet sure if the queen's interests and the earl's interests were necessarily one and the same. Moreover, although he worked well enough with the serjeant Jonas and the under-sheriff Luke de Marston, he was more comfortable on his own. There was some truth in Luke's jest that he was a natural lone wolf, not happy hunting with the pack.

Justin now gave the only response he could, and thanked the Earl of Chester for his kind offer. "My pleasure," the other man said, with a brief smile. It was unexpectedly mischievous, and for the first time, he looked as young as he truly was, for Chester was only in his twenty-third year. "I've already sent for Thomas." Not at all uncomfortable with the prolonged silence that followed, the earl glanced again at the queen's letter and then back at Justin.

"De Quincy," he said, as if finally taking notice of Justin's surname. "Are you any kin to our bishop?"

It was the first time that Justin had been asked this question, although he'd often considered his answer. He did not want to lie, but neither did he want to admit the truth, for his candor could give rise to scandal and a public repudiation by his father. He compromised now by smiling and saying breezily, "I asked the good bishop that, too, but he says nay."

Chester nodded, asked Justin if he were kin to Saer de Quincy, who was wed to the daughter of the Earl of Leicester, and getting a denial, lost interest. Justin's words seemed to echo in his own ears, though, for there had been a bitter, bedrock honesty in his answer. The good bishop had indeed said nay.

"Two more ales, sweeting." Only then did Thomas de Caldecott interrupt his flirting with the serving maid to give Justin his attention. "Admit it, Justin. This is a better meeting place than the great hall under the eagle eye of my lord earl," he insisted, with an airy wave of the hand toward their smoky, noisy, and dim surroundings. "Of course here we have to buy our own ales, but the next round is on you, so who cares?"

"I may," Justin said, "if you keep swilling down these tankards faster than the girl can get them to us. I do not fancy having to drag you back to the castle like a sack of flour after you get stewed to the gills."

Thomas threw back his head and laughed loudly. "If you think you can drink me under the table, lad, you're in for a rude awakening. When it comes to carousing, I ought to be giving lessons. But then, you do not know me very well yet, so your ignorance can be excused."

"How kind of you." Justin lifted his own tankard in a playful salute. "To Sir Thomas de Caldecott, king of the carousers," he said, and Thomas laughed again, patting the serving maid on the rump as she sashayed by.

Justin slid his stool back so that he could lean against the wall and watched with wary amusement. Thomas was right. He did not know the other man well at all, and he was not sure what to make of the knight's easy affability. Justin had learned at an early age to keep his defenses up against a world that was indifferent at best and hostile at worst to a foundling without family, resources, or rank. He could not imagine lowering the drawbridges, opening the gates, and inviting people into the castle inner bailey as freely and confidently as Thomas was doing.

It had been a relief to find that the knight was not haughty and overweening as so many of his peers were. Unlike his lord, the Earl of Chester, Thomas seemed comfortable taking a secondary role in the ransom investigation. Justin had quickly realized that he'd found a valuable partner in Thomas. But he was bemused to be treated as an instant friend, for he was much slower to give his own trust. He was concluding that Thomas was that rarity, a man utterly at home in his own skin, with nothing to prove and nothing at risk, for failure would injure the earl, not his vassals and retainers.

The serving maids that Justin had known were far too jaded to blush, but Thomas managed it, whispering something that sent color flooding into the girl's face. As she withdrew in a gale of giggles, Thomas finally focused upon the matter at hand. "I suppose we ought to at least mention the robbery since we'll soon be on the road into Wales. The earl, God love him, will boot us out of bed at cockcrow. How good is your Welsh? Mine is more than good, if I may brag a bit. But the earl has a Welsh lad, Padrig, in his service, and I thought we'd take him along with us in case we run into anyone who cannot understand my elegant French accent. We'll need a goodly escort, too."

"Is North Wales that dangerous?" Justin asked, and Thomas grinned.

"I've heard that even the Welsh outlaws have their own bodyguards. But if we keep to the coast road, we ought to reach Rhuddlan without spilling any blood. I imagine Llewelyn is too busy counting his ill-gotten gains to be harassing innocent English travelers."

"Are you so sure that Llewelyn is the culprit?" Justin asked, intrigued by the other man's matter-of-fact manner. Thomas's indictment was more convincing than the Earl of Chester's fiery denunciation because of its very lack of passion or choler.

"If you're asking if Llewelyn is the one who stole the ransom, there is no doubt of that. But there is blame enough to go around and I'd not want to cheat Davydd of his fair share."

"The earl also talked of Davydd's 'blunders.' What were they?"

"Ah . . . where to begin? I suppose you want me to confine myself to those specific blunders relating to the ransom. A pity, for I have heard tales about Davydd's misspent youth that would have you rolling on the floor with laugher. Ah, well . . ."

Thomas heaved a comic sigh. "The trouble began with Davydd's bright idea to lure outlaws and bandits and Llewelyn away with a second convoy. He insisted upon sending a large escort with heavily loaded wagons by an inland road, whilst the real ransom was taken along the coast. But that was only part of his grand scheme. He loaded the ransom onto two ancient wains, piled hay on top, and to make it look even more convincing, he only dispatched four men with the hay-wains."

"That was lunacy," Justin blurted out. "How could he be sure they would not steal the ransom? The fewer the men, the greater the risk that they could reach an understanding amongst themselves."

"You'll get no argument from me, lad. But Davydd said he deliberately picked men without the ballocks or the brains to do more than follow orders. He chose a tough nut named Selwyn to give those orders. He'd been a member of the royal household for years, and Davydd swore he could be trusted. The others were downright pitiful: the lame, the halt, and the blind. A green lad of sixteen; he's the one left to die in the road. An aged grandfather, and a good-natured fool. Davydd thought that way no one would ever suspect these rickety hay-wains could be carrying anything but hay."

Justin shook his head slowly. "And did it never occur to Davydd that if his 'grand scheme' went wrong, these guards would have trouble fending off a dozen drunken monks?"

"Monks? You're too kind, Justin, my boy. That crew could have been overrun by nuns! But no, Davydd is not one for contingency planning. The Welsh rarely are."

"Llewelyn ab Iorwerth might disagree with you."

Thomas considered that and then conceded cheerfully, "I daresay he might. For certes, his plan went down as smoothly as the best-brewed ale. He pounced upon the hay-wains like a hawk upon a rabbit, took what he wanted, and left naught but bodies and the charred remains of the burned wains."

"He burned the wains? Why?"

Thomas gave Justin an approving smile. "A good question. He burned the hay-wains because he also burned the woolsacks."

Justin sat upright, nearly spilling his ale. "Christ Jesus, he burned the wool? Davydd said nary a word about that to the queen!"

"Naturally not, for he'd have to admit then that the bulk of the ransom was beyond recovery. Those hay-wains also held silver plate and jewelry and some fine pelts, but it was the Cistercian wool that was the real treasure. But woolsacks are heavier than lead, and Llewelyn apparently realized that he'd not be able to get the wool safely away in those decrepit carts without risking capture. So he took what he could carry off and burned the wool to deny it to Davydd and the English Crown."

Justin was still coming to terms with the realization that his mission had been doomed from the moment that those woolsacks went up in flames. "If he was clever enough to find out that the ransom was hidden in those hay-wains, I'd think he'd be clever enough to have some sturdy wagons on hand to haul the wool away."

"Ah, but it would have been no easy task to unload the sacks and reload them in the new wagons. The woolsacks are deliberately made so heavy for that very reason, to thwart theft. And even if he could have gotten them away, what then? They'd have to be smuggled into England and then sold to traders on the alert for that very stolen wool.

No, Llewelyn made a pragmatic decision to settle for what he could safely steal and took his vengeance upon Davydd with flint and tinder."

Justin saw the logic in Thomas's argument. He just did not want to admit that much of the ransom had gone up in a cloud of smoke, knowing what a blow that would be to his queen. The total ransom demanded was so huge that those sacks of fine Cistercian wool were needed, each and every one. He understood now why Chester was so critical of Davydd's part in this calamity. Thomas de Caldecott was right; there was more than enough blame to go around.

They headed into Wales on the morrow, keeping close to the Dee estuary. Although Wales was known as a mountain citadel, the coastal lands were flat. But the going was still not easy, for they had to contend with salt marshes and quicksand bogs while skirting the deep, tangled woodlands that lay just to the south. They stopped for the night at Basingwerk Abbey where Thomas was well known to the hospitaller, testifying to how frequently he'd made the journey between Chester and Rhuddlan Castle. He'd soon proved himself to be an agreeable traveling companion, one who took setbacks in stride and kept complaining to a minimum and knew what lay around every bend in the road. He was a talker, so he was good company, too, keeping up a steady stream of lively conversation as the miles plodded by.

By the time they'd reached Basingwerk Abbey, Justin had learned that his new ally was thirty and three, that his elder brother held a manor of the Earl of Chester at Caldecott in Cheshire, that he'd picked up some of his Welsh from his mother, who'd been raised in Pembrokeshire, and was taught the rest by a Welsh mistress. And by the time they were within sight of Rhuddlan Castle, Justin knew that Thomas took great pleasure in hawking, gambling, hunting, gossip, Gascon wines, and women, but he took little pleasure in sea voyages, tedious church sermons, sharing beds with strangers in flea-infested inns, salted herring during Lent, roan horses, cats, and his elder brother. He had Justin laughing more often than not, and since Justin was quiet by nature, they complemented each other quite well, the one offering entertainment, the other an audience.

Rhuddlan Castle was strategically situated at the lowest crossing point of the River Clwyd, the locale of several strongholds down through the years. The present fortress had long dominated the crossing, a bulwark of English power until captured by Davydd's formidable father a quarter-century ago. It looked impressive at first glance, with a rectangular keep situated upon a sixty-foot-high mound and a large bailey defended by steep palisades and a deep, wide ditch. But as they got closer, Justin saw that all of the castle's structures were wooden, not fortified in stone, as were the principal castles of the English Crown and baronage. Compared to the great citadels of Windsor and Chester, Rhuddlan no longer looked so invincible to Justin.

They were admitted without difficulty; Thomas was well known here, too. Dismounting in the bailey, they were welcomed by the Welsh prince's steward, and a man was sent to inform Davydd of their arrival. Justin watched him scramble up the perpendicular steps cut into the mound as he asked the steward about accommodating their escort; it was an unfamiliar experience, having men at his command, but he was learning to like it.

"Let's go into the hall," Thomas suggested, tugging at Justin's arm. "Princes like to make an entrance, so this could take a while." He switched from French to Welsh then, as he turned back to the steward, and Justin decided his boasting was justified; Thomas did indeed speak fluent Welsh. Thomas was joking with Garwyn, the steward, and Justin was pleased to find that he could follow the gist of their conversation.

As they approached the open door of the great hall, a man came striding out. He was of middle height, with flyaway reddish hair and beard, a sturdy frame, a square, sun-weathered face, and a fine Flemish sword at his hip. The beard identified him as a Marcher lord, for the Welsh were clean-shaven with mustaches. But Justin already knew that. He came to an abrupt halt.

Thomas was greeting the man with a smile and enough deference to indicate he was of greater rank than the knight. Justin already knew that, too. He was still standing as if rooted when Thomas turned to introduce him to Lord Fitz Alan, the sheriff of Shropshire, an influential Marcher baron . . . and the man who had taken Justin into his service as a squire, a personal favor for his friend, the Bishop of Chester.

4

August 1193
Rhuddlan Castle, North Wales

Recognition was mutual. Fitz Alan's look of surprise soon gave way to one of astonishment, for Justin was not quick enough to stop Thomas from introducing him with a flourish as "the queen's man." In other circumstances, the Marcher lord's befuddlement might have been comical, but Justin could find no humor in his present predicament. His feelings for his father were a confused welter of aggrieved, often contradictory, emotions. For all of his bravado, he did not truly want to alienate and embarrass his father with a public scandal. Now, finding himself face-to-face with the man he least wanted to see, one who was bound to realize the significance of his claim to the de Quincy name, he did not know how he could deflect Fitz Alan's curiosity or suspicions.

He was given a brief reprieve, then, when the prince's steward insisted upon ushering them out of the sun and into the great hall. Justin and Thomas and their men were soon herded inside, where they were offered mead or wine; hospitality was the Eleventh Commandment for the Welsh. Thomas was clearly at home here, exchanging jests and greetings with several of the Welshmen in the hall; almost as if reading Justin's mind, he said, "For the past year, I have acted as the earl's liaison with Lord Davydd, so I've been to Rhuddlan often enough to make a few friends and . . ." He grinned. ". . . tempt a lass or two."

Turning then to Garwyn, he slid smoothly into Welsh, telling the steward that once he was back in Chester, he'd arranged to have Masses said for poor Rhun's soul. Garwyn smiled, shook his head, and said something too quickly for Justin to follow. Thomas looked surprised, but then he smiled, too. "Rhun is the lad who was left for dead. We thought sure that he was not long for this world. But Garwyn just told me that not only is he still amongst the living, they think he is on the mend." He held up his hand before Justin could speak. "Alas, Rhun's good fortune is not ours. Garwyn says he has no memory whatsoever of the ambush."

Justin swore silently. "Is his memory gone for good?"

Thomas shrugged. "Who knows? Apparently loss of memory is not uncommon with head injuries like Rhun's."

Before Justin could respond, there was a stir at the end of the hall. Garwyn sprang to his feet, with Thomas right behind him. Justin rose, too, watching as Davydd ab Owain strode toward them. The Earl of Chester had described Davydd as "aged." Justin was surprised, therefore, to find that the Welsh prince was not that decrepit or doddering for a man who'd lived fifty-five winters.

Davydd's dark eyes were pouchy, his hairline was receding, and he'd long ago lost the lean, hungry look of his youth. But he was still a handsome man. His chestnut hair was only lightly salted with grey, his step had the swagger of one accustomed to wielding power, and he bore his years lightly. It was obvious, though, that the missing ransom was weighing heavily upon his mind; he looked starved for sleep and it was hard to imagine that tautly drawn mouth relaxing into a smile.

He held the queen's letter in one hand, crumpled in his

fist. Coming straight to Thomas, he said abruptly, "Is this the queen's man?"

Justin was glad it was a humid, summer's day. If it had been midwinter, the coldness of Davydd's welcome might have given him a bone-chill. "I do not understand why the queen has sent you to me, Master de Quincy. What I need are enough armed men to track Llewelyn ab Iorwerth to his lair and recover the stolen ransom. I do not see what you can do. What do you know about Llewelyn? About Wales? Do you even speak Welsh?"

Justin caught his breath, held it until he was sure his voice would reveal nothing of his inner fury. That brief moment gave him enough time, though, to devise a new stratagem, one born of Davydd's contempt. Rather than try to change the Welsh prince's low opinion of him, why not use it to his own advantage?

"I seek only to serve the Queen's Grace . . . and you, of course, my lord prince. I am deeply honored by her trust in me, and I am confident I can justify it. I grant you that I speak little Welsh, but I do not see why that would hinder my investigation. I have men with me to act as translators, after all." He'd been striving to sound ingratiating and indignant and just a bit pompous, and to judge by the disdainful expression on Davydd's face, he had succeeded.

"So be it," Davydd said coldly. "We will, of course, cooperate fully with your investigation." He was not particularly convincing, nor did Justin think he'd meant to be. Almost at once, he turned away, beckoning impatiently to Thomas de Caldecott.

"I will be relying upon you, Sir Thomas," he said, "to do what must be done. God alone knows what the queen was thinking to send me this green stripling. He is a nobody, not even a knight! I was a fool to put my hopes in a woman, ought to have known better. If I am to recover the ransom from that whoreson nephew of mine, I shall have to do it myself!"

This diatribe had been given in Welsh, and Justin sought to keep his expression bland, uncomprehending. He had not expected to reap benefits so soon from his professed ignorance of Welsh. He'd learned quite a lot in that angry outburst. That Davydd's dislike was not personal. That his pride was overblown and his temper easily inflamed. That he trusted Thomas, at least to some extent. And that his desire to retrieve the ransom was raw and real and desperate.

Thomas looked apologetically toward Justin. "My lord Davydd, I think you are too quick to dismiss Master de Quincy's capabilities. If Queen Eleanor has such faith in him, surely that says something about his—"

"It tells me only that the queen is in her dotage, entrusting a matter of such importance to a callow youngling like that!"

Justin wanted to hear the rest of Davydd's remarks, for he'd rarely have such an ideal opportunity to eavesdrop. But it was then that Lord Fitz Alan grasped his arm, pulling him aside. "We need to talk," he demanded, "now!"

Justin knew Fitz Alan well enough not to argue and followed the older man out into the bailey. Squinting in the sudden blaze of white sunlight, Fitz Alan at once took the offensive. "What sort of ruse is this, Justin? What is this nonsense about your being the queen's man? And why are you now calling yourself de Quincy? Does Aubrey know about this?"

Justin sighed, feeling rather ill-used by the fates at that moment. "It is no ruse, my lord. I *am* the queen's man. It was her suggestion that I call myself de Quincy. And of course the bishop knows."

Fitz Alan continued to scowl. "None of this makes any sense! It is not even a year since I dismissed you from my service, and you end up at the royal court?"

"As unlikely as it sounds, my lord, that is exactly what happened. I cannot satisfy your curiosity, for the queen demands discretion from those who serve her. I do not expect you to take my word for all this, though." Reaching for the scrip at his belt, Justin drew out a tightly rolled parchment sheet. "This is a letter from the queen, attesting to my authority to act upon her behalf. I am sure you recognize her seal."

Fitz Alan's eyes locked upon that wax emblem. Snatching the letter, he began to read, occasionally throwing Justin an incredulous glance. Justin waited, thanking God for Eleanor's foresight, for realizing that he might have need of such a warrant. The letter was deliberately effusive in its praises; after handing it to him, Eleanor had commented dryly that she hoped it would not go to his head. He saw now that her embellishments had done the trick. Fitz Alan was staring at him, mouth agape.

"For the life of me, I cannot imagine how you accomplished this act of sorcery," the Marcher lord blurted out, shaking his head in disbelief. "But it is indeed clear that you do Queen Eleanor's bidding. And . . . and your use of the de Quincy name, that is somehow meant to advance your investigation?"

Justin wasn't surprised that Fitz Alan sounded so tentative, for that was a frail reed. But it was the best he could come up with under the circumstances. He nodded, with what he hoped was an enigmatic smile. "The queen is relying greatly upon the bishop's assistance in this matter." Adding, "As is the Earl of Chester," figuring that name-dropping couldn't hurt his cause any.

It seemed to have worked, at least for now. Fitz Alan was utterly confounded by the series of surprises that had been sprung upon him this afternoon and would need time to sort them all out. Justin did not doubt that Fitz Alan's suspicions would surface again and hoped that he could warn his father before they did. Fitz Alan's entire demeanor had changed dramatically. Justin was no longer a former squire of dubious origins. He was a trusted agent of the Crown and, possibly, the Church, and the Marcher lord treated him accordingly, sounding almost friendly as they retraced their steps toward the great hall.

They were just about there when Fitz Alan paused to acknowledge a woman walking in their direction. She was strikingly attractive, with the dark hair and eyes so common to the Welsh. Later, Justin would realize that her allure came more from her exuberance and vivacity than from physical charms. Now he was aware only of the impact she made upon his senses. Fitz Alan introduced her as one of Lady Emma's handmaidens, and Justin was quick to kiss her hand, more than willing to linger there in the sun and flirt with this bewitching young Welshwoman. Her name was Angharad, her French was quite good, and when she smiled, he was bedazzled, until he realized that she was gazing over his shoulder, that beguiling, seductive smile meant for Thomas de Caldecott.

Justin's father had not been wrong. Emma of Anjou, then in her forty-second year, was still a lovely woman. Justin could only guess at the color of her hair, for it was covered by a white silk wimple and veil, but her skin was so fair that he'd wager it was flaxen, a shade of summer sunlight. Her eyes were blue sapphires, her cheekbones high and delicately drawn, her chin pointed, her mouth accented by two deep dimples. Hers was an ethereal, gossamer beauty, hers the elegance of queens, the purity of the Holy Madonna. Most men did not look upon her with lust. They gazed into the depths of those bottomless blue eyes and discovered chivalric impulses they did not even know they had, protective instincts that they thought had died in childhood.

Justin had been given a seat far down the table, as befitted his lowly status, whereas Davydd had seated Thomas de Caldecott upon the dais with Lord Fitz Alan. Justin did not mind the slight, for his seat afforded him an unobstructed view of the high table, enabling him to study the Welsh prince and his consort without attracting attention. He'd been told that Davydd and Emma had two children, but neither one was present at Rhuddlan, having been sent to live in noble households, as was customary for the offspring of the highborn. He conceded that Davydd and Emma made a handsome couple, although he saw little evidence of intimacy between them. They seemed very much the lord and lady of the manor, courteous to all, accessible to none. Justin had joined much of Christendom in taking an immediate and intense dislike to Davydd, yet he'd so far formed no impressions of Emma. She'd greeted him far more politely than her husband, but her formality was an effective shield, keeping her thoughts private and the world at arm's length.

The meal was more elaborate than the evening suppers Justin was accustomed to, for the Welsh served dinner at day's end rather than at noon, as they did across the border. He had his first swallow of mead, the honey and malt drink so favored by the Welsh, but he decided it must be an acquired taste. Once dinner was done, Davydd's bard was called upon to sing for the guests. Justin decided that he would not be missed, and slipped away with Padrig, the young Welshman on loan from the Earl of Chester.

The bailey of Rhuddlan Castle was crowded with wooden buildings: the great hall, kitchen and kiln, stables and barn, privy chambers, kennels, a chapel, and quarters for those not bedding down in the great hall. Justin had stopped a groom and was instructing Padrig to find out where the lad Rhun was lodged when he heard his name echoing on the evening air. Following the sound, he saw Thomas waving from the steps that led up the mound to the keep. Justin waved back and waited for Thomas to finish his descent into the bailey, noticing then that he was not alone. A woman stood on the steps behind him.

With Angharad on his arm, Thomas reached the ground and sauntered toward Justin. "We saw you make your escape and were not going to be left behind. Why should we be trapped listening to dirges and laments for the glory days of Wales whilst you fly away, free as a bird?"

"You're more than welcome to come along. I had it in mind to pay a visit to Rhun's sickbed."

They both seemed quite agreeable to that and fell in step beside Justin and Padrig. Directed by Angharad, they headed for a small building near the gatehouse. As they walked, Thomas entertained them with an accurate if unkind mimicry of Shropshire's roving sheriff. He had Fitz Alan's mannerisms down pat and soon had Justin and Angharad laughing as he parodied the Marcher lord's monopoly of much of the dinner conversation. He bragged that he could do a passable impression of the Welsh prince, too, but when he launched into it, Angharad feigned horror and slapped his wrist playfully, diverting the conversation onto safer ground.

Justin was amused by how deftly she managed it, not shaming Thomas while keeping him from uttering any mockery that might be carried back to Davydd's ears. It showed him that this young Welshwoman was as clever as she was comely, and that she'd obviously had some practice in reining in her lover's antics before they got out of hand. That they were lovers, Justin did not doubt; the intimacy he had not seen between Davydd and Emma shone in every glance passing between Thomas and Angharad, every lingering touch, every shared smile. Deciding he ought to help Angharad out, he distracted Thomas's attention from the Welsh prince by asking why Fitz Alan was at Rhuddlan, showing such interest in the robbery of the ransom.

"It surprised me to see him playing so active a part in the hunt for Llewelyn. He is a long way from Shropshire, after all."

"Aye, and when Will Gamberell and the Cheshire sheriff hear of it, they will be none too pleased," Thomas said, grinning. "Will's the city sheriff. As for the sheriff of the shire, he'll be sorely enraged, too, for not even a hungry dog with a bone is as loath to share as a sheriff."

"So why, then, did Fitz Alan ride all this way? What for?"

"What are you, man, blind? Did you not see the Lady Emma?"

"Thomas!" Angharad frowned, hastily looking around to make sure they'd not been overheard. "He is jesting," she assured Justin, "as always."

"I was not claiming that he is bedding her," Thomas protested. "The lady has better taste than that. No, I meant that he is a member of the brotherhood."

"I am probably going to regret asking," Justin said, "but which brotherhood?"

"I call them the Guild of Emma's Admirers. They esteem Lady Emma with the fervor men usually bestow on the Blessed Virgin Mary. Be warned, Justin, for it might happen to you, too. One day you're fine; the next you're sighing at the sound of her name and writing verses of bad poetry in her honor."

"Thanks, Thomas. I'll keep my guard up," Justin said lightly, wondering if his father had been a member of that brotherhood and wondering, too, if Thomas had always been so immune to the Lady Emma's charms.

Rhun was convalescing in the one-room cottage of Davydd's gardener and his wife, the castle laundress. He lay on a straw-filled pallet, a slight, pitiful figure under a worn woolen blanket. Justin knew the boy was sixteen, but he looked even younger, his face chalky in the meager illumination of a smoking rushlight. His head was bandaged in a wide strip of linen, smeared with ointment and soiled from handling. Lank brown hair stuck up around the bandage in spiked tufts, a splinted arm protruded from the blanket, and his chest rose and fell in the rapid rhythm of a troubled sleeper. Justin found himself thinking that the doctor who'd pronounced Rhun "on the mend" must have been besotted on mead at the time, for Rhun did not look to him like one on the road to recovery. In fact, he bore an eerie resemblance to a corpse, laid out before being sewn into a burial shroud.

His caretakers hovered on either side of the pallet, ill at ease and watchful, almost as if they feared being blamed for their patient's poorly condition. Padrig stood by, unneeded, as Thomas and Angharad took turns interrogating the couple, and Justin listened to the ebb and flow of Welsh, reassured that the translations being offered for his benefit jibed so well with his own understanding of what was being said. In this alien land of so many strangers, so many suspects, it was good to know that he could place some trust in Thomas and his Welsh mistress. As much as he wanted to question Rhun, he was hesitant to awaken the youth, for sleep was Rhun's only refuge. He was still deciding when the young Welshman's lashes began to flicker.

Rhun's eyes were dilated and dazed, and Justin realized he'd been given a potion for his pain. He seemed surprised to find so many people clustered around his bed. "You came back . . ." he murmured drowsily, smiling at Thomas, who seemed embarrassed at being caught out in a good deed and mumbled that he'd looked in on the lad earlier, wanting to see for himself how he was faring. When Thomas asked him again if he could remember anything about the ambush, his denial was clear, unambiguous, and convincing. No, he said softly, almost apologetically, he remembered nothing. And Justin saw that his one witness to the robbery was going to be of no help whatsoever.

The next morning, Justin and Thomas rode out to the scene of the ambush. Thomas had been there before, and so they did not need to put Davydd's grudging offer of help to the test by asking for a guide. The charred remains of the hay-wains had been dragged to the side of the road so travelers could pass by. Justin walked about in the ashes, finding a scrap from one of the woolsacks, kicking at a scorched wheel axle. He looked in vain for ruts in the road, but was not surprised by his failure to find any, given the amount of time that had gone by since the robbery; rain and trampling feet had obliterated whatever clues there might have been. The site told him little about the crime, nothing at all about the whereabouts of the ransom.

"It is an odd place for an ambush," he said to Thomas. "I assume they must have been waiting in that copse of alder trees over there. But we passed several spots that would have offered better cover. I suppose they felt they had nothing to fear, that those poor wretches would be able to offer little resistance. That is another thing I do not understand. Why be so brutal, kill them all?"

"I daresay to keep us from finding out who was behind it."

Justin was not completely convinced by Thomas's logic. Why should Llewelyn ab Iorwerth care if Davydd knew of his theft? He was doing his damnedest to overthrow Davydd, after all. But Llewelyn might care if the Crown knew he was the culprit. Why bring down upon himself the vengeful fury of the English queen if it were not necessary? The problem was that he knew almost nothing of this shadowy adversary. Was Llewelyn more than a mere outlaw? His ambitions were grand enough, for certes, but what of his abilities? Was he shrewd enough to look that far ahead, to consider his future relations with the English king? Most of the brigands Justin had encountered were rash, reckless men who acted on impulse, not considering the consequences until the morrow. The fact that Llewelyn had burned the woolsacks argued for a cool, calculating brain, one capable of sacrificing short-term profit for long-term gain. And yet there was something about this robbery that did not ring true to him, something shocking about this wanton destruction of property and men. He could not pinpoint his unease, knew only that as he looked around at this desolate, barren crime scene, he was not satisfied with the story Davydd would have him believe.

"Such a waste," he said somberly, raking the tip of his boot through the ashes, cinders, and soot that had once been wool worth its weight in gold. Wasted lives, wasted riches, wasted opportunities. How could he tell the queen that the bulk of the ransom was beyond recovery? Even if he somehow managed to retake a portion of the stolen goods, would that be enough for Eleanor?

Thomas had come over to stand beside him in the road. "What now?" he asked, and Justin shrugged. He would that he knew.

* * *

Upon their return to Rhuddlan Castle, Justin paid another visit to young Rhun, but it was more a courtesy call
than an interrogation. Even if the lad's memory did come
back, did it truly matter except to Rhun? What could he
know, after all?

Justin continued to use either Padrig or Thomas as his
interpreter, and by day's end he'd questioned all of the
men who'd been sent out to search once word reached
Rhuddlan of the ambush. He learned that Davydd was
not held in the highest regard by those who served him.
He learned that the Welsh reputation for being recalci-
trant and blunt-spoken was well earned. They viewed
him with suspicion and scorn, doubly damned as both a
foreigner and an Englishman. He did not learn anything
that even remotely resembled a clue, any information
that might help him to solve this frustrating crime or dispel his misgivings.

Dinner that evening was not a pleasant experience.
Once again Justin was banished to the far end of the
table, and once again he watched in brooding silence as
Davydd and Lord Fitz Alan dominated the conversation
and Lady Emma kept her eyes downcast and her opinions
to herself. The talk was mainly of Llewelyn, and the
prince and sheriff took turns damning him to the hotter
reaches of Hell. Justin was surprised to discover that
Llewelyn had been raised in Shropshire; his widowed
mother had wed a Marcher lord when he was ten. What
he learned next was even more surprising, that Llewelyn
had begun his rebellion against Davydd at the tender age
of fourteen. It was becoming quite clear to Justin that in
his letter to the queen, Davydd had greatly underplayed
the threat posed by Llewelyn. The truth was that the
Welsh prince was scared half out of his wits by his
nephew's rebellion.

Before retiring for the night, Justin went to the stables to check on his stallion, for Copper was his most prized possession, his heart's pride. Seeing no reason to hurry back to the hall, he found a brush and was currying the chestnut's burnished reddish-gold coat when Angharad appeared. She was looking for Thomas, she said; not finding him, she stayed to chat, overturning a bucket for a seat and arranging her skirts as gracefully as if she were sitting on a throne.

"You seemed downcast at dinner, Iestyn," she said forthrightly, flavoring her French with an appealing Welsh lilt and making use of the Welsh form of Justin's name. "Will the queen punish you if you fail in your mission?" When he shook his head, she smiled brightly. "I am glad you will not be blamed, for I do not think this will come to a good end."

"Nor do I, Angharad."

"Mind you, I cannot complain for myself. This robbery brought Thomas back much more quickly than I dared hope." This time her smile was impish. "So you might want to consider me a suspect, for I was one of the few to benefit from the ransom's loss."

Justin smiled, too. "Few, indeed . . . you and whoever took it."

"You do not think it was Llewelyn?"

"I do not know," he admitted. "Most likely it was. My trouble is that I've never been able to accept the easiest, most obvious answer. I want it all to make sense, to fit the puzzle pieces together. And in this case, there are several pieces missing."

"And they are . . . ?" she prompted.

He hesitated, but only for a moment. It often helped to muse aloud about the more baffling aspects of a case, and he saw no harm in testing speculations and suppositions upon an audience, especially an audience as attractive as

Angharad. "Well . . . I am bothered by the burning of the wool. Something does not feel right about that. It seems to be such an extreme measure to take."

"I know," she said. "I thought so, too. As for Lord Davydd . . . when he was told about the wool, I thought he was like to have an apoplectic fit, he was so distraught. I think it was only then that he realized the queen will blame him as much as Llewelyn for the loss."

"As well she should," Justin said ungenerously. "If he had not sent the ransom off in two hay-wains with no guards to speak of, the robbery would not have been possible. I could not imagine a man making a decision so foolish until . . ."

He let the sentence trail off, deciding it would be indiscreet, but Angharad shared his opinion of the Welsh prince. ". . . until you met Davydd," she said, and they grinned at each other.

"Actually," she confided, "he surprised me by how well he took the news at first. He has always been one for raving and ranting, cursing his lot and bewailing his ill fortune whenever he suffers a setback. But to give him his due, when they brought word of the robbery, he was quite calm and composed. It was only after he learned of Selwyn's death and the loss of the wool that he unraveled like a ball of yarn."

"I suppose it has been hard on the Lady Emma, putting up with his foul tempers."

"The Lady Emma," she said, "knows what a wife's duties are."

Justin was not sure what to make of that cryptic remark. Deciding to keep on fishing, he said innocently, "Then Davydd is indeed a fortunate man, having a wife who is as biddable as she is beautiful. I should be so lucky."

Angharad took the bait. The look she gave him was a

cool one. "It never ceases to amaze me," she said, "how easily you men are beguiled by a pretty face. There's not a one of you who wouldn't embrace mortal sin as long as it took a shapely female form."

Justin concealed a smile. "Especially if it took a shapely female form."

Angharad pretended to scowl. "I do believe you have been having fun at my expense, Master de Quincy."

"Yes, Mistress Angharad, I do believe so, too," Justin agreed gravely. But when their eyes met, they both began to laugh.

"There is no need to be underhanded," she chided. "If you have questions about the Lady Emma, ask me. How else can I know if I am willing to answer them or not?"

His first question was not one she was expecting. "You do not like her much, do you?"

"I do not like her at all."

"Why not, Angharad?"

"Well . . . I could tell you. But I do not think I will." Her dark eyes were teasing. "I think it best that you find out for yourself why I love that lady not." Rising, she smoothed her skirts without haste. Justin waited until she'd almost reached the door.

"Tell me this, then. I have been watching Fitz Alan, and I think your Thomas is right; he is smitten with Emma. Do you think she has been encouraging his attentions?"

"My Thomas. I like that," she murmured. "As you knew I would. Tall, dark, handsome, and devious . . . a dangerous mix. I think I shall have to keep a close watch on you, Iestyn." She started to saunter off, then glanced back over her shoulder. "Of course Emma encourages his attentions. She needs male admiration the way I need air to breathe. But to answer the question you were really asking . . . No, she is not an unfaithful wife."

"Are you so sure of that?"

"Yes," she said, "I am."

"Why is it," Justin asked, "that I do not think that you're praising her virtue?"

Angharad tilted her head, regarding him with a delphic smile. "I have a riddle for you," she said. "When is virtue not a virtue? If you can answer that, you'll know why I do not like the Lady Emma."

Justin could catch the scent of her perfume even after she'd gone; like her presence, it lingered. He stood there for a time, not moving until Copper nudged his shoulder. "Sorry, boy, I have no apples." Turning, he stroked the stallion's velvety muzzle. "Are you wondering what I was doing? Was I flirting, gossiping, or investigating?" Copper snorted softly, nudging him again, and Justin laughed. "Damned if I know!" And yet he sensed, for reasons he could not have articulated, that the Lady Emma was one of those missing puzzle pieces.

5

The lance came hurtling from the garden, thudding into the earth at Justin's feet. He recoiled so fast that he almost lost his balance. The lance was still quivering when several alarmed faces peered over the hedge, one of them belonging to Thomas de Caldecott.

"Justin, I am sorry! It was not my intent to skewer you, I swear. Tathan was showing me how to throw a lance and I overshot. Come on in so I can properly apologize."

Thomas was so insistent that Justin walked over. He at once regretted it, for the garden was filled with people, none of whom looked pleased to see him, with the exception of Thomas and Angharad. The Lady Emma was seated on a turf bench, attended by all three of her handmaidens, an older man Justin knew only as Oliver, several servants, and William Fitz Alan, who greeted Justin with a distinct lack of enthusiasm. Ignoring the tension, Thomas introduced Justin to Tathan, his obliging Welsh tutor, and explained that the Welsh in North Wales were known for their skill with the lance. "I've used it on horseback in tournaments, of course, but I've never thrown one . . . not until I nearly impaled you!"

"Your aim gets better with an ale or two . . . or six," Justin said, thinking of the drunken knife-throwing contest Thomas had gotten into during their evening at that Chester alehouse, and the knight gave a shout of laughter, thumping Justin playfully on the back. Feeling like an uninvited, unwelcome guest, Justin crossed the mead and wished the Lady Emma good morrow.

A trestle table had been set up on the grassy mead and draped in a white linen cloth; it held wine flagons, cups, and a platter of apples and wafers drizzled with honey. Several books were neatly stacked on the table, too, evidence that they had been having a reading. Justin knew these pastimes were popular with women of rank. Usually a chaplain would read aloud for the benefit of his audience, not all of whom would be literate. Since Emma's chaplain was nowhere in sight and she had a book open on her lap, Justin assumed that she'd been doing the honors. He was not surprised to learn that she could read. Her half-brother King Henry had been given a first-rate education and had harbored a scholar's love of books until the day he died; it was to be expected that he'd have seen to it that his little sister would be well-schooled.

Thomas made a show of introducing Justin to Emma's attendants; Justin was beginning to wonder if he did anything without a fanfare. Angharad was the only Welshwoman among them; under her mistress's eye, she pretended to be meeting Justin for the first time and then gave him a quick wink. The other two handmaidens, both from Emma's native Anjou, greeted Justin politely, but without any real interest.

Glancing up at the cloud-splattered sky, Emma closed her book and got to her feet. "We'd best be in; I'd rather not race the rain back to the keep." She had a very young-sounding voice, soft and breathy, like a little girl's. She'd spoken in French, as always. Justin had assumed that she'd have learned some Welsh during nigh on twenty years as Davydd's wife, but so far, he'd seen no indication of it. The servants at once began to collect the utensils, food, and tablecloth. Emma's ladies gathered up a bouquet of freshly picked flowers, hastened over to stop Emma's little lapdog from digging in a raised bed of daisies, and brought the errant pet back to its mistress. Justin found it interesting that Emma could command obedience faster with a smile than her volatile husband could do with a shout.

William Fitz Alan was hovering protectively by Emma's side, clearly intending to fend off any dangers she might face on the walk from the garden up to her chambers in the keep. But a cry from the gatehouse drew him reluctantly away from escort duty. A scout was coming in, and he and Thomas and Tathan made their apologies and hurried off. Justin was about to follow when Emma stopped him in his tracks with an unexpected request. Would he be so kind, she asked, to carry her birdcage back indoors?

Justin had not even noticed a wicker cage on a nearby turf seat. Since Emma had servants to do the heavy lifting and toting, he could not help wondering if this was a subtle insult, a reminder of his lowly rank in a prince's court. He had no choice but to obey, casting a curious look over his shoulder toward the gatehouse as he picked up the birdcage. There was a cluster of men around a lone rider, gesturing and talking loudly, but still too far away to be heard.

Justin soon decided he'd misjudged the Lady Emma, for she fell in step beside him as they crossed the bailey; so whatever she had in mind, it was not humiliation. She was carrying her lapdog, which looked to Justin like a feather duster with feet, but he knew such small creatures were de rigueur for ladies of rank. They walked in silence for some moments. Justin was amusing himself by imagining Nell's reaction to the Lady Emma's pampered pet when Emma brought him up short with the one thing he'd never have expected from her—an apology.

"I am sorry, Master de Quincy, that my lord husband has been so short-tempered with you. His nerves are not usually so raw. But this missing ransom is causing him great distress."

"That . . . that is kind of you, my lady," Justin stammered, caught utterly off balance. "But you owe me no apology. I understand quite well why Lord Davydd has been so . . . out of sorts." Because Davydd was a flaming arsehole. For a mad moment, those words hovered on Justin's tongue. He would never have said them aloud, of course, but for a heartbeat he allowed himself the pleasure of flirting with sedition.

"I am glad that you are so wise," Emma murmured, for the first time turning upon him the full power of those glowing blue eyes, and Justin coughed to camouflage an involuntary laugh. He'd been so stunned by her apology because eight months at the royal court had taught him that the highborn did not apologize, not ever, certainly not to the likes of him. And Emma had struck him as a woman very much aware of her prerogatives, privileges, and position. So her apology must conceal an ulterior motive. And now that she was casting sidelong glances through her lashes and complimenting him upon his "wisdom," he saw what it was.

She wanted something from him, wanted something badly enough to resort to her ultimate weapon—coquetry. Justin had been watching women charm men to get their way for much of his life, and he gave Emma high marks for her effort. She was not overtly flirtatious, but she still managed to create a sense of intimacy between them; he could understand how men like Fitz Alan were won over by a smile that promised nothing but hinted at much.

Emma's dog had begun to squirm, and in attempting to calm it, she dropped the book she'd tucked under her arm. Setting down the birdcage, Justin retrieved the volume for her, resisting the urge to do so with one of Thomas's flourishes. Emma thanked him with the gratitude usually reserved for life-saving heroics. The book flipped open as he handed it to her, and seeing his gaze drop to those fluttering pages, she said:

"These are lays written by my sister, Marie, very skillfully done, and very popular at the court. She prefers that her identity not be bruited about, though, for when not ministering to her muse, she serves the Almighty as abbess of St Mary and St Edward's Abbey in Shaftsbury. You may borrow the book if you like."

"Thank you, my lady. That is most kind of you." Justin wondered how many more times he'd call her "kind" before they reached the keep. He wondered, too, why she should have shared this family secret with him, a disclosure that her sister the abbess would not have appreciated. After a moment to reflect, though, he realized why, and commended her cleverness. What better way, after all, to establish a rapport than to reveal something confidential? The Lady Emma had a deft touch, he thought admiringly, flattering him with this display of trust at the same time that she reminded him of her patrician pedigree, which of course made her cordiality all the more flattering.

"How is your investigation progressing, Master de Quincy?"

So that was it. "Slowly, my lady."

"It grieves me to see my husband so heartsick. Is there no hope, then, for a quick resolution of this unfortunate matter?"

Justin met her gaze levelly. "No, my lady, I fear not."

"Do you think the ransom might not be recovered?"

He saw no reason not to be honest with her. "I regret to say, my lady, that may well be the outcome."

"May I ask you something in confidence, Master de Quincy?" Her eyes held his, just long enough. "Will you tell me the truth? If my husband fails to retrieve the ransom, will the queen be very wroth with him?"

"Yes, my lady," he said quietly, "she will." He waited, then, for her to argue for Llewelyn ab Iorwerth's guilt, as Davydd and Fitz Alan had been doing at every opportunity. She surprised him, though.

"I see," she murmured, and then, "That is as I feared." Her lashes veiled her eyes, and they walked the rest of the way without talking. Upon reaching the keep, she roused herself to thank him again, although with none of her earlier appreciation. Justin gave the standard reply, that it was his honor, and set the birdcage upon a table for her. The bird inside was small and drab, unfamiliar, not at all like the usual tame magpies or popinjays. Seeing his curiosity, Emma smiled.

"I brought him out for some fresh air, a glimpse of the world denied him. No bird in Christendom has a sweeter song than the nightingale. It sings at night, not during the day; is that not odd?" Still smiling, she looked from the caged bird to Justin. "There are no nightingales in Wales," she said. "Did you know that?"

Justin was starting down the steps into the bailey when he heard his name. Angharad was hurrying to catch up. "Lady Emma thinks she left her dog's ball in the garden, so I generously offered to search for it," she said, with a grin. "I have a strong suspicion that I will find it in the herb bed, under the Saint-John's-wort."

Justin grinned back. "But you will not be able to find it right away."

"No . . . probably not. Is it not pitiful, Iestyn, that I must resort to such trickery to steal a few moments with Thomas?" She did not sound put-upon, though, but quite pleased with herself. "So . . . you got to see my lady in action this afternoon. You must be made of sterner stuff than most of your brethren. I've seen men melt like candle wax when she flutters her lashes."

Justin couldn't help laughing. "Well, I'm a little singed around the edges, no more than that. She wanted to ask me about the investigation, and I confess that I could find no sinister intent in that."

"Sinister, no. Surprising, yes, for she rarely bothers with Davydd's doings. And did she try to convince you that Llewelyn ab Iorwerth is the Antichrist as Davydd claims?"

"No," Justin said, "she did not. I understand why Davydd would like to blame Llewelyn for this robbery, whether he is guilty or not. What better way to rid himself of a troublesome rival? But I did not expect him to demand that the Crown provide men-at-arms. I'd think that most Welsh princes would do all in their power to keep English soldiers out of Wales, not invite them in."

"There is no mystery to that. Davydd is losing this war with his nephew. He can send out patrols to hunt Llewelyn's men, but he'd have difficulty mustering up an army for a long campaign and that is what it would take. He ought to have quashed Llewelyn a few years back, when he was more of an irritant than a threat. Now . . . now it may be too late, for Llewelyn has been winning more than skirmishes. He has been winning the support of the people. Not that popular support counts for much on a battlefield. But it means that Llewelyn has eyes and ears everywhere, that he need not fear betrayal, that his men believe they will win."

Justin thought that was an astute appraisal of the military situation and assumed that she was giving voice to Thomas's opinions. But when he imagined his queen's caustic response to that, he smiled ruefully and offered up a mental apology to Eleanor and Angharad both. By then they'd reached the bailey and headed for the great hall by mutual consent.

Almost at once they ran into Thomas, who slid a proprietary arm around Angharad's waist and led Justin aside to tell him that Davydd was in a tearing rage for his men had gotten the worst of it in a skirmish with Llewelyn's men near Llanelwy. This setback was all the more disturbing to Davydd because the cathedral church of Llanelwy was only a few miles south of Rhuddlan, alarming evidence that Llewelyn was growing ever bolder.

"Where is de Caldecott?" Davydd raised his voice, and Thomas could no longer pretend he hadn't heard. With a resigned grimace, he moved toward the Welsh prince.

"I am here, my lord. How may I serve you?"

"I want you to leave for Chester straightaway, tell the earl that I need assistance in bringing this rebel hellspawn to a reckoning. I'll leave it to him to determine how many men to send, but tell him that the more he can spare, the faster we can recover the ransom for the English queen."

Thomas was silent for a moment. "I am sorry, my lord Davydd. The queen's letter to my lord earl made it clear that this is a Crown investigation. She did request the earl to provide men-at-arms if need be . . . if Master de Quincy asks for them. You're talking to the wrong man."

Davydd stared at him in disbelief, and then his rage erupted. "That is lunacy! You're telling me that the fate of Wales lies in the hands of a meager whelp like him?" He thrust an arm in Justin's direction as Justin struggled to maintain the pretense that he spoke no Welsh.

Thomas was not intimidated. "My lord prince, what

would you have me say? I serve the Earl of Chester and the earl serves Her Grace, the queen."

Davydd's fury and frustration spilled over then in a torrent of invective, teaching Justin some new and choice Welsh curses. As Davydd stalked toward him, the other men moved aside, leaving Justin exposed to the Welsh prince's wrath. "Do you understand what happened this day?" Davydd demanded, dredging up his French as if the very words tasted foul on his tongue. "I lost some good men this morn because of Llewelyn. But the next time blood is shed in my domains, it will be Llewelyn's own, that I vow upon the sanctity of my soul. Go back to Chester and tell the earl that I need as many men as he can spare."

"I am sorry for the deaths of your men, my lord." Justin paused to draw a deep breath, bracing himself for the storm about to break over his head. "But I cannot oblige you in this matter. The Queen's Grace was very clear in her intent. My one and only mission is to recover the ransom, not to assist you in suppressing a rebellion."

"You dare to refuse me?" Davydd sounded incredulous. "I *am* seeking to recover the ransom, you fool! Since Llewelyn was the one who stole it, it makes sense that when we find him, we find the ransom." He was speaking now through gritted teeth, spacing the words out slowly and deliberately so that even a dolt like Justin could comprehend. "As long as this renegade is free to raid and plunder my lands, we have not a hope in Hell of retrieving the ransom."

"I am not convinced of that, my lord. I've yet to be shown any hard evidence that Llewelyn ab Iorwerth is to blame for the robbery. I know you are convinced that he is guilty. As are you, my lord," he said politely, glancing toward the glowering William Fitz Alan. "And I am not arguing for the man's innocence. I am saying simply that his guilt has not been proven, not yet, not to me. And until it is, I am not willing to ask the Earl of Chester for military aid."

"For the love of Christ!" Fitz Alan could hold his tongue no longer. "If Llewelyn was not the one who sprang that ambush, who did?"

"I cannot answer that, my lord, for the same reason that I cannot agree to Lord Davydd's demand. My investigation is not done, and until it is, I am not willing to pass any judgments."

Davydd's face was seared with heat. "I cannot believe that I am forced to argue what is obvious to all but the deranged, to all but you, de Quincy! You want proof? Will a dying declaration satisfy your delicate scruples? One of the men still lived when my scouts came upon the burning wagons. With his dying breath, Selwyn accused Llewelyn of ambushing them."

Justin did not believe him, not for a moment. This "dying declaration" was much too convenient, as suspect as any confession coerced in the depths of a castle dungeon. "Why did you not tell me this before, my lord?" he said, striving not to sound as skeptical as he felt.

"I am telling you now," Davydd snapped. "Do you want to question the man who heard Selwyn's deathbed denunciation?"

Davydd flung down the challenge as if it were a gauntlet and was infuriated when Justin picked it up. "As a matter of fact, I would, my lord."

Davydd started to speak, coughed, cleared his throat, and then spat into the floor rushes, looking as if he wished he'd aimed at Justin's face. "I will see to it, then," he said, managing to make it sound more like a threat than a promise.

* * *

By day's end, Justin had begun to feel like a leper. Word had gone out about his confrontation with the Welsh prince, and people were shunning him as if he might infect them with Davydd's ill will. Even Thomas and Angharad were keeping a discreet distance and despite his best efforts, their retreat hurt. Wherever he went, Justin found himself the cynosure of all eyes, attracting either scowls or pitying side-glances. When he'd had enough, he took himself off to the only place in the castle that offered even a modicum of privacy.

Caring for his stallion gave him some peace of mind, but all too soon there was nothing more to be done. The stables were empty, the grooms over in the great hall having their dinner. Justin had no appetite, although he wondered if he was truly not hungry or just reluctant to face a hall filled with disapproval and hostility. Sitting down in the straw, he leaned back against the wall, watching moodily as Copper munched a mouthful of hay.

His anger had burned long enough to lose its heat, but it still simmered in his bone, muscle, and marrow, smoldering in the back of his brain. He'd doomed himself to failure, for he'd turned Davydd's distrust into outright enmity. Why had he been so rash? Yet what else could he have done? He would be damned ere he'd ask Chester to send Englishmen to fight Davydd's war for him. By now he'd not have believed Davydd if he said the sun rose in the east and sank in the west, and the Welsh prince's witness was not worth a shovelful of horse dung. But where did he go from here?

"Master de Quincy."

Justin had not heard the footsteps muffled in the straw, and he started, getting hastily to his feet. Instinctively his hand dropped to the hilt of his sword; his dealings with John and Durand had taught him to be wary even when there seemed no reason for wariness. The man standing there looked benign enough: not yet old but no longer young, with a scholar's slump to his shoulders and a hesitant smile. He looked vaguely familiar, too, and after a moment, Justin placed him: Davydd's scribe.

"May I speak with you?" When Justin nodded, the man advanced into the wavering pool of light spilling from a lone rushlight. "My name is Sion ap Brochfael. I am Lord Davydd's clerk."

"I know."

Sion came closer, his eyes probing the shadows. "We are alone?"

"Just you and me and the horses." Justin smiled, without much humor. "So you do not want to be seen with me, either?"

"No, I would rather not." Sion's nervousness was obvious; he kept shifting from foot to foot, clenching and unclenching his fists. "I might as well just say this straight out. I was in the hall this afternoon when you and Lord Davydd had your disagreement. Is what you said there true, that you are not yet convinced of Llewelyn ab Iorwerth's guilt?"

Justin was tempted to respond with sarcasm, to say that No, he'd made a mortal enemy of the Welsh prince just for the fun of it. But he said only, "Yes, it was true. Why?"

"I do not think Llewelyn did it, either. And I know a man who might be able to help you prove who did."

"Go on," Justin said. "Tell me more."

"It may amount to nothing. But Davydd dismissed one of his men soon after the robbery. The man—Guto—was sorely vexed and got roaring drunk. I happened upon him, pounding on the door of the buttery, vowing that he would have some of Davydd's best wine. Since I knew Davydd would punish him harshly for such a theft, I coaxed him away with the offer of more mead. As I said, he was in his cups and rambling, as besotted men are prone to do. Much of what he said was nonsense. He cursed Davydd roundly and swore he'd be sorry, and eventually became mawkish and maudlin, overcome with pity for himself. But one of his threats stayed with me. He said that Davydd would regret letting him go, that he knew Davydd's secret, he knew the truth about what really happened in that ambush. When I asked him what he meant, he became sly and furtive, and he'd say only that I ought to 'ask Selwyn.' Since Selwyn had been slain during the robbery, I did not know what to make of that. But later I remembered that Guto and Selwyn had been friendly, and I . . . well, I wondered."

So did Justin. Selwyn's name was being bandied about very freely this day. First Davydd and his tale of Selwyn's dying accusation. And now Sion with his story of vengeful drunks and secrets. Sion might be right, and it might well come to naught. But what other leads did he have to follow?

"Can you tell me where to find this Guto?"

"I regret not. But I can take you to someone who is likely to know. Guto's cousin Pedran is a lay brother at Aberconwy, the Cistercian abbey to the west of here. It is not that far; we could easily make it in half a day."

Justin's eyes narrowed. Was he being set up? Sion seemed almost too helpful. But try as he might, he could not see what Sion hoped to gain by luring him into a trap. He was no tempting target for robbery. All he owned of value was Copper, and there were easier ways to steal a horse. Nor was it easy to envision Sion—this earnest, greying, mild-mannered clerk—allied with an outlaw band. For certes, the man himself posed no threat; he wielded a pen, not a sword.

"You would accompany me, then?"

Sion nodded, oblivious to the sudden edge that suspicion had given to Justin's voice. "We would have to slip away separately, let none see us together. There is a ford just south of the castle; we could meet on the other side of the river."

"And why would you want to do that?"

The other man looked surprised. "How else could we do it? I must come with you, for you do not know the way to Aberconwy, and you'll need me to translate for you once we're there. Neither Guto nor Pedran speak your foreign tongue."

"No . . . I meant why would you be willing to take such a risk? We both know what Davydd would likely do to you if he found out. Why endanger yourself . . . for what?"

Sion smiled thinly. "You've had a chance to observe my lord Davydd. Think you that he is a joy to serve? Nothing would give me greater pleasure than to be free of his demands and petty cruelties. This ransom matters greatly to your queen. So it seems to me that she would amply reward anyone who helped you recover it . . . would she not?"

"Yes," Justin conceded, "I daresay she would."

"So what say you, Master de Quincy? Shall we ride out on the morrow to find Guto?" When Justin did not respond at once, Sion looked searchingly into his face. "You still have misgivings? This will not work without mutual trust. You must trust me to take you safely to the abbey and I in turn must trust you to keep your word and make sure that I am rewarded for my help. Think about it if you wish, and let me know once you've made up your mind. I must insist upon one thing, though—that we go alone. I am willing to trust you. That does not hold true for Thomas de Caldecott."

That presented no problems for Justin, for he had no intention of involving Thomas, not wanting to put the other man at risk. Nor did he think Thomas would be keen to join this wild-goose chase. The knight seemed quite sure that Llewelyn ab Iorwerth was the culprit they sought.

"Very well," he said. "What do I have to lose?"

6

As Justin and Sion rode west, the land began to look like
the Wales of legend: mountain peaks silhouetted against
the sky, woods deep and dark and primeval, so impene-
trable that trees had never felt the bite of an axe and only
meager shafts of sun could filter through the wild, un-
tamed tangle of undergrowth, brush, and bracken. The
road hugged the coast and clouds hovered low on the
horizon, as grey and foreboding as the choppy, wind-
swept sea. Welsh weather was notoriously erratic, hostile
to invaders and inhabitants alike, and by the time they
reached the estuary of the River Conwy, rain was falling,
a chill drizzle that threatened to become a downpour at
any moment. Sion hailed the boatman and they were
soon being ferried across the river. To their right, the castle of Deganwy stood sentinel over the bay, and ahead of
them lay their destination, the Cistercian abbey at Aberconwy.

Justin was restless, edgy, and bored. He'd been stranded
in the outer parlour for at least two hours by his reckoning. Sion had vanished within moments of their arrival,
hurrying off to fetch Pedran, the lay brother, promising
to bring him back to the parlour straightaway. But as
time dragged by, Justin's patience began to fray. What if
Pedran did not know the whereabouts of his cousin?

What if Guto could not be tracked down? And even if they did find him, what if he knew nothing about the ambush? If his loose talk had been no more than the maunderings of a man deep in his cups?

Rising again from his seat on an uncomfortable wooden bench, Justin paced the cramped confines of the parlour. He ought to have accepted the hospitaller's offer of milk and cheese. But he'd expected to be riding off in search of Guto once he'd interviewed Pedran. He was not truly troubled yet by Sion's failure to return with Guto's cousin. He knew the Cistercian lay brothers did the heavy labor at the abbey, and Pedran was not likely to be permitted to abandon his chores to chat with a stranger, however much he might like such a brief respite. He could even be off on one of the abbey granges, although if so, Justin could not understand why Sion would not have returned with that information. Had he been foolhardy to trust Sion? The reasons that had seemed so convincing behind the sheltering walls of Rhuddlan Castle were more dubious now that he found himself deep in Wales, with no resources to draw upon but his sword, his wits, and a stranger named Sion.

When he felt unable to pass another hour in his spartan seclusion, he shoved the parlour's far door open. As he'd guessed, it led out into the cloisters. He stood for some moments in the walkway, breathing in the damp salt air, listening in vain for the ordinary, familiar, comforting sounds of daily life. The abbey was shrouded in silence, for the church bells had not rung since None several hours ago. Monks glided by, their sandals making no noise on the wet paving stones. Dressed in the unbleached wool habits that had caused people to name them the White Monks, eyes downcast, hands tucked into their sleeves, they seemed almost like ghosts to

Justin, pale shadows of mortal men no longer burdened with temporal concerns.

He attracted a few oblique glances, and tried to remember if lay people were allowed in the abbey cloisters or not. The Cistercians were the most austere of all the holy orders, and they might well frown upon too much contact with intruders from the world they'd renounced. He greeted these mute, wraithlike men of God with a polite "Good Morrow," but received only grave nods in return, for the White Monks were sworn to silence for much of their day. Justin admired them for their piety, their discipline, their willingness to give over every waking hour to God, for he knew he would have found it well nigh impossible to follow in their footsteps. But his esteem notwithstanding, he was feeling more and more like a trespasser in their midst, and headed for the one place where laymen were welcome, God's House.

Even there, the monks were segregated from their lay brothers, who heard Mass in the nave. At this time of day, between None and Vespers, the church was empty, still. Justin paused to bless himself at the holy water stoup, then slipped into a chapel in the south transept, where he knelt and offered up prayers for Claudine and their unborn child.

Soon after, he heard the door creak open, heard footsteps pause before the holy water stoup as he had done. When they began to echo in the nave, he stepped from the chapel to see who this newcomer was. He'd been half-expecting one of the monks, but the man he was now facing was no monk. Nor was he clad in the brown habit of a lay brother.

"Are you Justin de Quincy?"

The words were French, and excellent French at that, but the cadence was Welsh. Justin was suddenly alert, his eyes taking in every aspect of this stranger's appearance. "I am. But do not try to tell me you are Pedran, not with that sword at your hip. And I suspect you are not Guto, either."

"No, I am not Guto. But I think you'll want to talk with me, nonetheless. I am Llewelyn ab Iorwerth."

Justin expelled his breath slowly. "Well, well," he said softly. "I was trying to flush out a rabbit, and instead, I've flushed out the fox."

The Welshman's mouth quirked at one corner, as if he were suppressing a smile. "In light of what you've been hearing about me from my loving uncle Davydd, I should probably consider 'fox' a compliment. I daresay you could have come up with much worse."

"I daresay," Justin agreed. They were both standing in the center aisle of the nave by now, and a wall torch gave off enough light for them to do a mutual inspection. They were about the same height, for Llewelyn was taller than the average Welshman. Both had dark coloring, although Justin's eyes were grey and Llewelyn's were brown. Justin judged them to be about the same age, too. It was like looking into a pond and seeing a wavering reflection that was almost, but not quite, a mirror image of himself.

Llewelyn saw the resemblance, too. "Sion said you were fair-minded—for an Englishman." Again there was the hint of a smile. "But he did not tell me that you look like kin. A pity my father is dead, for it would have been interesting to ask him if he'd broken any English hearts."

Justin stiffened. But he remembered, then, that the Welsh did not view illegitimacy like the rest of Christendom. Here a man could be bastard-born and a prince, for the Welsh balked at punishing children for the sins of their fathers. "Alas, my mother's heart was not one of them. I say 'alas' because I can well imagine the look on

Davydd's face when I returned to Rhuddlan with the happy news that I'd found my long-lost brother, Llewelyn."

This time there was no mistaking Llewelyn's amusement. "Ah, but that would make Davydd your uncle, too," he pointed out and laughed outright at Justin's expression of mock horror.

Justin found himself wondering if the Welshman had been testing him with that dubious jest about broken English hearts, wanting to see how quick he was to take offense. "Be sure to tell Sion that he lies very convincingly. That was an inspired move on your part, whether you deliberately placed him in Davydd's household or won him over. I cannot imagine a more useful spy than Davydd's scribe."

"What of Davydd's confessor?"

"Jesu!" Justin was genuinely shocked before he realized that Llewelyn was joking. It was a shame that he could not introduce this Welsh rebel to his lady queen; he suspected they'd get along famously. "Just out of curiosity, how can you and Sion be so sure that I will not reveal his true identity to Davydd?"

"Because you've had a week to enjoy the pleasure of Davydd's company," Llewelyn said, very dryly. "Sion felt the risk was worth taking. He believes that you truly want to find out what happened. Is he right, English?"

Justin nodded. "I want the truth, yes. I also want the ransom. And if I must choose between the two, I'll take the ransom. I was sent by the queen on a mission of recovery, not retribution."

"So . . . you're saying that if I were to know the whereabouts of said ransom, you'd be willing to settle for its return, no questions asked?"

"Yes."

"That is an interesting offer. But it is not one I can accept. You see, Davydd's claims to the contrary, I do not have it."

"I do not think you do, either," Justin admitted. "But it was an offer I had to make, just in case I was wrong. I spoke true when I said that the queen's only concern is getting back what was stolen . . . or what is left of it."

" 'What is left of it'?" Llewelyn echoed, sounding surprised. "Are you saying you believe that the wool was really burned?"

Justin felt a sudden surge of hope. "You do not think it was?"

"By the rood, no! Even if Davydd were the world's greatest fool, and he well may be, he still would not have burned the wool. Have you ever seen any man throw money into a fire?"

There were two intriguing suppositions in Llewelyn's retort, but Justin chose to focus first on the one that would matter the most to his queen. "How can you be so sure of that? I visited the scene, saw for myself that wool was burned."

"So did I," Llewelyn said laconically, and Justin blinked in astonishment.

"You dared visit the ambush site? I'm surprised you did not stop by the castle afterward for an ale!"

"I prefer mead." Llewelyn moved closer, and when Justin tensed, he said, "Look, we've been circling each other like wary cats. We can keep on dancing about if you wish, but I'd rather not." As he was speaking, he was removing his rain-dampened mantle. Slowly and deliberately, he then unbuckled his scabbard, placed it on the floor at his feet. Justin had left his own mantle in the outer parlor, but after the hesitation of a heartbeat, no more than that, he took off his sword, too, laying it down next to Llewelyn's weapon.

Llewelyn looked pleased. "Good," he said. "Now we can talk." There were no seats but he found two prayer cushions, sat down cross-legged on one and invited Justin to do the same. "Have you found out about the hay-wain horses yet?"

"What . . . the horses stolen in the robbery? What is there to find out?"

"One of them turned up a few days after the ambush, still wearing a halter. And a second one was seen in the hills, running loose."

Justin frowned. "I was told none of this. How do you know about it? How can you be sure these were the same horses?"

"I have friends in surprising places. Sion talked privately to the grooms at Rhuddlan, and their descriptions of the horses matched perfectly."

"That makes no sense. No one would steal horses and then turn them loose like that . . ."

"No," Llewelyn agreed, "they would not. Any thief worth his salt would want the horses, too, if only to sell them. You can always find a buyer who'll ask no questions if the price is cheap enough."

Llewelyn did not bother to state the obvious, that his men would never have let the horses go, either. Justin tucked this new information away for further reflection and leaned forward. "So what evidence do you have that the wool was not burned?"

"The wagon tracks were still visible when I inspected the scene. We'd actually had several dry days in a row, which qualifies as a drought in Wales. The wheel ruts were shallow, nowhere near as deep as they ought to have been if they'd been loaded with woolsacks."

"So you think they removed the wool ere they fired the hay-wains? Mayhap burned part of a woolsack or even some wool to convince us that it had all gone up in smoke? I want to believe that, I really do. But if so, what happened to the wool? What did they do with it?"

"I have not worked that part out yet," Llewelyn conceded. "We could find no other wagon tracks in the vicinity. I have no doubts, though, that the wool is still intact, hidden away somewhere till it is safe to transport it."

He saw that Justin was not yet convinced, and leaned forward intently. "My people have a saying, '*Gorau amheuthun, chwant bwyd*.' 'Hunger is the best sauce.' We know that particular sauce well in Wales, for mine is a poor country. I will not believe that any Welshman would have set fire to a year's worth of wool, not unless one of God's own angels whispers it is so in my ear, and even then, I'd have doubts. No, this was a clever trick, no more than that. It is still out there, waiting to be found."

Justin decided it was time to tackle the second of Llewelyn's suppositions. "And you think the mastermind behind this scheme is . . . ?"

"A 'mastermind,' no, I'd not call him that. But he is guilty. I'd wager you know whose name I am going to say, too . . . my uncle Davydd."

Justin did not trouble to conceal his skepticism. "Is this some sort of a family game? Davydd is one for playing it, too. We both know he has reasons to blame you that have naught to do with the missing ransom. But it seems to me that your charges are equally suspect. Why keep on fighting this war if you can get the English Crown to fight it for you?"

"First of all," Llewelyn said, "I am winning this war. And even if I were not, I'd not be mad enough to seek English aid. I'm not going to invite a man to dinner unless I am sure he'll go home afterward. No offense, but you English are too hungry for lands that are not yours."

"It has been my experience that it is the highborn who

are hungry for lands not theirs . . . no offense, of course."

Llewelyn's dark eyes narrowed slightly, and then he began to laugh again. "I'd wager you are giving my uncle fits!"

Justin grinned. "Well, I do my best. I've been honest with you about my doubts. But I've an open mind. If you can make a persuasive case against him, let's hear it."

Llewelyn was quick to take the challenge. "To begin with, that scheme of his was too absurd for even my uncle to concoct. Lure me away with a false patrol and then send the ransom off in two unguarded hay-wains? Talk about begging to be robbed! Even his use of hay was suspect, for no one sells his hay at market; the need for it is too great. As soon as I heard about it, I knew Davydd was up to no good. I think he arranged to 'steal' the ransom, doubtless leaving it in Selwyn's capable hands to make the necessary plans. Selwyn was with Davydd long enough to know where all the bodies were buried, and my uncle has never been a man for details."

"Yes, but Selwyn was slain."

"Davydd's plans never end well." Llewelyn's smile came and went, almost too quick to catch. "Obviously, something went wrong. I cannot believe that my uncle would have wanted Selwyn dead; he was too useful."

Justin considered for a moment and then shook his head. "No, it still does not make sense to me. I grant you that your theory explains some of the holes in Davydd's story. But there is just one problem with it. I have been watching Davydd closely for the past week and I am sure that he does not know where the ransom is."

When Llewelyn would have argued, Justin held up his hand. "Wait, I heard you out. You're going to have to trust me on this. Unless your uncle's true vocation was to be a player, he could not be so convincing. He is well and truly fearful. Unless . . ." A memory had just surfaced. "A reliable witness told me that Davydd was unusually calm when told of the robbery. She says he did not panic until he found out that the wool had been burned and Selwyn slain. Suppose . . . suppose he did set up the robbery as you claim. What if Selwyn's hirelings decided they'd rather have the whole than a share?"

"Possible," Llewelyn acknowledged. "Men capable of murder and robbery would not have any qualms about betrayal. Still, though . . . there is one weakness in that argument. Whoever carried out the robbery made no mistakes. It was well planned, well executed. I very much doubt that anyone hired by Selwyn could have done it. He'd have been looking for men who were stupid and strong, men who could be relied upon to take orders without getting any notions of their own."

"'Men without ballocks or brains,'" Justin said thoughtfully, remembering what Thomas de Caldecott had told him in that Chester alehouse. "Those are Davydd's own words about the men he sent out on the hay-wains. I see your point. Selwyn would be too shrewd to use men likely to turn on him."

"It is not enough that he sent those men to their deaths. No, he must slander their memories, too." Sion had come in so silently from the sacristy that neither Llewelyn nor Justin had heard him, and they both leapt to their feet at the sudden sound of his voice.

"You did not know those men, Master de Quincy," Sion said quietly. "I did. They did not lack for 'ballocks or brains.' Alun's only failing was his age; he'd lived more than sixty winters and had wobbly, aching bones. Madog . . . well, Madog may have been slow-witted, but he was a strong, strapping lad with a good heart. And Rhun may be just a stripling, but he is clever and capable, never has to be told twice to do a task. They deserve better than to be dismissed out of hand as simpletons. All the talk has been of recovering the ransom. But no one—not even you, my lord Llewelyn—has spoken of the need to give them justice. Someone ought to pay for their deaths."

"Iestyn was not voicing his own opinion, Sion. That scornful phrase 'ballocks or brains' came from Davydd's own mouth." Llewelyn had spoken in Welsh, but he now switched back to French for Justin's sake. "You are right, though. This attack upon three innocent men deserves our attention, our outrage."

" 'Three men'?" Sion queried. "What of the fourth—Selwyn?"

Llewelyn shrugged. "If we are right in our suspicions, Selwyn was no innocent."

Sion's eyes flicked from one to the other. "You think Selwyn was involved in the robbery? For what it's worth, he never struck me as a man overburdened with scruples. But I very much doubt that he would have dared such an audacious undertaking on his own. It is more likely that he was obeying orders."

Llewelyn nodded. "Ah, but whose?"

Justin saw where the Welshman was going with that. "You are suggesting that Selwyn was the one who betrayed Davydd, only to be betrayed himself?"

Llewelyn nodded again and elaborated for Sion's sake. "We are proceeding on the supposition that Davydd planned to steal the ransom and blame it on me. But Iestyn is convinced that Davydd does not know where the ransom is, so we are assuming that there is another player in the game. We've dismissed the idea of Selwyn's hirelings turning on him, so if not them, who then?"

Sion was frowning pensively. "Selwyn never lacked for

ballocks. Mayhap he was the one who decided to turn on Davydd?"

Llewelyn and Justin exchanged glances and saw that here, too, they were of one mind. "We have the same problem with that," Justin explained to Sion. "Selwyn would not have hired men likely to show too much enterprise, whether they were robbing for Davydd or robbing for him. But we think it possible that Selwyn was induced or bribed to change sides, only to discover that his new allies were even less trustworthy than Davydd. You knew the man, Sion. How loyal was he to Davydd?"

Sion was not one to make quick judgments, and he took his time in responding. "Selwyn was loyal only to Selwyn. But he was shrewd and would not have been easily duped. If he decided to throw his lot in with these 'new allies,' he must have been convinced they could outwit Davydd or protect him from Davydd's wrath. In other words, people who either had power of their own or were slick enough to convince Selwyn they did."

"So . . ." Llewelyn concluded, "Iestyn need only find out the identity of these unknown evildoers, and we can recover the ransom."

"'*We* can recover the ransom'?" Justin echoed, with enough emphasis on the pronoun to set a grin tugging at the corner of Llewelyn's mouth.

"Yes, 'we,'" he said blandly. "We have a common interest here, after all. You want the ransom and I'd rather not let Davydd get away with blaming me for the theft, not when it would bring down the wrath of the English Crown on my head."

Later, it would surprise Justin to realize how easily they had begun to exchange the barbed banter that was the coin of the realm in male friendships. Now, he shot back with a sardonic "What are you saying, Llewelyn? That we are allies all of a sudden?"

"You could do worse, my lad," the Welshman gibed. "To be more accurate, though, I'd say we are friendly adversaries."

"If word of this gets back to Davydd or the Earl of Chester," Justin said, "we'll be seen as partners in crime!" He was fast learning that Wales was a mystery maze that few could penetrate, an enigmatic land in which naught was as it first appeared. But nothing seemed more unlikely to him than that he should find himself in this peaceful Cistercian church, sharing a laugh with Llewelyn ab Iorwerth.

Justin spent the night at the abbey guest house, while Sion rode off with Llewelyn, promising to return on the morrow. It had been agreed upon that he would escort Justin back to Rhuddlan Castle, although he was not going to accompany him all the way; he planned to stay away another few days, having gotten leave from Davydd to visit his brother. He did not want anyone to connect Justin's disappearance with his absence, he'd explained, and Justin could only marvel at the shadow world of spies like Sion and Durand, where even the most minor detail could mean discovery and discovery could mean death.

Sion turned up at the abbey guest house the next morning, and to Justin's surprise, Llewelyn was with him. When Justin asked about his safety, he smiled and shrugged, saying the White Monks of Aberconwy knew how to tell genuine coin from a counterfeit, and Justin remembered Angharad's comment about the support Llewelyn enjoyed amongst the Welsh. "Poor Davydd," he said wryly, and the Welshman laughed. But as they rode away from the abbey, it would be Llewelyn's last words that Justin would remember, not his laughter.

Llewelyn and a handful of his men were standing by the abbey gatehouse as Justin and Sion waved in farewell. "English!" he called out suddenly. "You are going into the dragon's lair. Bear that in mind, and watch your back!"

7

"Iestyn!"

Dismounting in the castle bailey, Justin turned toward the sound of a familiar voice. He was getting used to responding to the Welsh version of his name. Angharad was hastening toward him, looking so distraught that he quickly handed the reins to a waiting groom and strode toward her.

"Iestyn, thank God you are back! Where have you been for the past two days? Do you know what a hornet's nest you stirred up?"

"Angharad, I left a message for Thomas. Are you saying he did not get it?"

"No, he got it, but he found no comfort in it. You told us nothing, after all, just that you were going off on your own. Thomas was vexed at first that you'd not confided in him, but when you did not return last night, he began to fear the worst. He was so disquieted that he insisted upon returning to Chester and letting the earl know that you'd gone missing."

"God's Blood!" This was a complication Justin did not need. He was sorry he'd worried Thomas, even sorrier that he'd have no answers for the knight. He could hardly tell Thomas that he'd been meeting on the sly with their chief suspect. "Is Davydd wroth with me, too?"

"Actually," she said, slipping her arm through his as

they headed toward the hall, "I think he is hoping that you fell off a cliff or were eaten by a wolf."

"Well, the day is not a total loss, then. At least I get to disappoint Davydd."

And disappoint Davydd, he did. "You're back, are you?" the Welsh prince said sourly. "You'd damned well better have a good explanation for all the trouble you've caused. De Caldecott insisted that I send men out to search for you. Why he should care is beyond my comprehension, but he made an utter nuisance of himself until I agreed. So suppose you tell us why you took off like that and just where you've been for the past two days."

"I cannot do that, my lord, not yet. As I told you before, I can share my findings with no one until I've completed my investigation."

"Surely you can confide privately in my lord husband?" Emma's contribution to the conversation came as a surprise to Justin and Davydd both. She'd approached them soundlessly and was now regarding Justin so coolly that she seemed a totally different woman from the one who'd sought him out in the castle gardens. "These are Lord Davydd's domains, after all," she continued. "So he of all men ought to be kept informed of whatever you discover."

Looking startled but gratified by this wifely support, Davydd glared at Justin. "Indeed! I'll tell you straight out, de Quincy, that I find your secrecy offensive."

"As well you should, my lord husband." Emma was addressing Davydd, but those beautiful blue eyes were taking Justin's measure and finding him wanting. "What you do not seem to realize, Master de Quincy, is that by balking at sharing information with Lord Davydd, you raise suspicions in other men's minds. People might well think that you do not trust him or even that you suspect him of complicity in this wretched business."

"Me?" Davydd protested, swinging around to stare at his wife. "How could I possibly be involved?"

"I can only promise you, my lord Davydd, that once I learn what happened to the ransom, you will be the first one to know." Justin saw that he had satisfied neither Davydd nor Emma, and as he looked about the great hall, he was acutely aware of his isolation, an unwanted alien in a land not his, not knowing enough to solve the mystery of the missing ransom, knowing just enough to put himself in peril.

Justin had been stung by Sion's accusation that no one seemed to care about getting justice for the murdered men. There was too much truth in it for comfort when he thought of those involved in what Emma had called "this wretched business." His lady queen. The Earl of Chester. His father. William Fitz Alan. Thomas de Caldecott. Prince Davydd. Lady Emma. Llewelyn ab Iorwerth. And if he were to be honest, himself. For them all, the greatest concern, mayhap even the only concern, was the recovery of the ransom. Who amongst them had given much thought to Selwyn, Alun, Rhun, and Madog? And of the lot of them, his failure was the worst. A queen, an earl, a bishop, a baron, a knight, a prince, the sister of a king. Llewelyn was highborn, too, the grandson of one of the greatest Welsh princes. But what was his excuse?

Justin had brooded upon this during the ride back to Rhuddlan, and eventually an idea had come to him, an ember sifted from the ashes. "Clever and capable," Sion had called Rhun, and Justin had no reason to doubt him. As the only surviving witness, Rhun could confirm Davydd's claim that Llewelyn was the culprit—or refute it. A quick-witted lad would realize the danger he was in. Was that memory loss of his genuine? Or a way to stay alive?

Justin decided it was worth trying to question Rhun again. But he did not know if his Welsh would be up to the task. Padrig had gone back to Chester with Thomas de Caldecott. He could wait till Sion returned to Rhuddlan. If he did, though, whatever he might learn would be passed on to Llewelyn, and Justin was not sure how much he trusted this newfound ally of his. There was only one person at Rhuddlan Castle whom he had no reason to doubt, and he did not know if he ought to involve Angharad in this or not. Was it fair to ask her to keep secrets from her lover? More important, could he be putting her at risk?

Deciding he could not chance it, he slipped away while the rest of Davydd's household was dining in the great hall. But when he entered Rhun's lodging, he found that fate had taken a hand. As he'd hoped, the gardener and his wife had gone to eat. Rhun was lying listlessly upon his straw pallet, sipping mead from a cracked cup, and Angharad was sitting beside him, changing his head bandage with quick, deft fingers. Looking over her shoulder, she smiled at the sight of Justin's surprised expression.

"What . . . you thought I was merely the Lady Emma's handmaiden?" she teased. "I happen to be a woman of many talents. In my free time, I serve as Rhuddlan's angel of mercy."

Justin knew that women were often skilled in the healing arts, for doctors were readily available only to the highborn and the wealthy. He did not suppose that Davydd's private physician gave high priority to treating a lad like Rhun, so Angharad's kindness was a godsend to the boy. That she should be here now was clearly God's Will, and Justin no longer resisted it.

"Rhun, I need to talk to you," he said, speaking slowly and deliberately and in Welsh. Out of the corner of his eye, he saw Angharad's head swivel toward him. "I can speak better Welsh than I've led people to believe. I am trusting you to keep my secret, and I promise to keep any secrets of yours. Upon the surety of my soul, I promise that."

Rhun's eyes were as green as any cat's, and as difficult to read. "What secrets do I have?"

Justin knelt by the boy's pallet. "I do not believe Llewelyn ab Iorwerth was the one who stole the ransom. I think you can prove that, and that puts you in danger, for Lord Davydd wants Llewelyn to be guilty."

"Why would I be in danger? I cannot remember what happened."

"That is your good fortune. But I do not know how long it will last. If there are men who do not want you to talk about the ambush, they may well worry that your memory could come back."

He saw a flicker in Rhun's eyes, no more than that, but it was enough to confirm his suspicions. Angharad had seen it, too, for she leaned forward then and placed her hand upon Rhun's.

"Is Iestyn right, Rhun? Can you remember more than you've let on? If so, he is right, too, about your danger. Whoever ambushed you has no scruples about killing. They've proved that in a very bloody way already."

Rhun said nothing, his eyes downcast. Justin was close enough to see the Adam's apple move in the boy's throat as he swallowed. "With your help, Rhun, we can find out who did this and see that they are punished. I will not lie to you. Yes, there is risk in speaking out. But there is greater risk in keeping silent."

Rhun gnawed his lower lip. He was too young to grow a proper mustache, and those patchy, sparse whiskers gave him the vulnerable look of a child playing at being a grown-up. "Lady Angharad, you trust this Englishman?"

She did not hesitate. "Yes, Rhun, I do." Seeing him look toward the mead cup, she reached for it, held it to his mouth while he drank.

When he spoke, there was a tremor in his voice, the husky hint of tears. But his gaze did not waver from Justin's. "I lied," he said, "because I was scared. I do remember. And if Lady Angharad thinks I ought to tell you, I will."

The sun was hot on his face, and a vagrant breeze ruffled the hair on Rhun's forehead. It was that rare summer's day in Wales, warm and dry and altogether delightful. Rhun hated to waste it like this, jouncing around in the back of a swaying hay-wain. His physical discomfort he could have borne; he was used to it. But his unease of mind was different. No matter how often he tried to convince himself that there was nothing to fear, his disquiet lingered. He was acutely aware of the fact that he was sitting on a fortune, a nesting bird prey for any passing hawks.

When he could endure the bone-bruising jolting no longer, Rhun slipped from the wagon, preferring sore feet to a sore bum. The horses were plodding along so slowly that he had no trouble keeping pace. "Can you pitch my wineskin to me, Uncle?" Alun eased up on the reins and obligingly reached for the wineskin. Rhun jogged over to catch it, pretending it was a pig's bladder camp-ball. Alun was not really his uncle, but the other man was so much older than Rhun that he used it as a courtesy. He found it hard to imagine living as long as Alun had, more than sixty winters. From the vantage point of Rhun's sixteen years, that was as old as God.

There was no warning. As the hay-wains came around a curve in the road, the brigands were waiting for them. Even before he saw that the men were masked, Rhun's heart began to thump wildly in his chest. Selwyn was driving the first hay-wain, and he jerked on the reins as the outlaw leader ordered them to halt. Alun did the same. He looked more resigned than fearful and shot Rhun a reassuring glance. Rhun wished he could be so calm, too, but he did not have Alun's decades of experience to draw upon.

The outlaw chief held the reins in one hand, a drawn sword in the other. The lower half of his face was covered by a knotted cloth, and a wide-brimmed hat shadowed his eyes. "Get down off the wagons," he commanded, and then glanced over his shoulder at his men, saying something in a language that was utterly foreign to Rhun. Selwyn and Madog did as they were told, and Alun had begun to climb stiffly down to the ground when the outlaw suddenly thrust his blade into Madog's chest. Looking surprised, Madog sank to his knees, then began to cough blood.

After that, everything seemed to happen in slow motion to Rhun. Two of the outlaws cried out in that guttural tongue, sounding alarmed. Alun shouted, "Run, lad!" to Rhun, and then he, too, was struck down by the outlaw's bloodied sword. The leader snapped a command to his men, but only one responded, kicking his horse forward as Rhun spun around and sprinted for the woods. Rhun did not get far. The outlaw caught him in a few strides, and leaned precariously from the saddle to swing a club at the boy's head. Rhun tried to duck, but he still took a glancing blow that sent him sprawling.

Rhun rolled down an incline, thudding into a tree. For several moments, he was stunned, digging his fingers into the earth to keep from spinning off into space. Blood was streaming down his face and a red haze danced before his eyes. When he tried to move, bile rose in his throat and he vomited weakly into the grass. After that, he lay still, praying to Almighty God that they'd think he was dead.

He could hear more shouting in that unknown language, and then Selwyn's voice, sounding eerily calm. There was more talking that echoed in Rhun's ears like the buzzing of a beehive, incomprehensible and oddly muffled, as if coming from a great distance. Suddenly he heard Selwyn's voice again, clear and piercing and panicky. "What are you doing? Wait—no, wait!" There was a scream then, which ended in a sickening gurgle. Rhun shut his eyes tightly, trembling so violently that his teeth had begun to chatter.

The outlaws were yelling again. Rhun could make out one word—Joder—repeated several times. Slitting his eyes, he risked a glance toward the hay-wains, and his heart seemed to stop when he saw the outlaw chieftain looking in his direction. He said something to one of the men, pointing at the boy. Rhun's throat constricted, for he knew he was watching his death trudge toward him. The outlaw's mask had slipped down, revealing a reddish-blond beard, a face fair-skinned and youthful. He held a cudgel at his side, almost as if he were trying to hide it. Coming to a halt, he loomed over Rhun, and the boy looked up helplessly, pleading with his eyes. The other outlaw shouted, sounding angry, and he hesitated, then raised the club.

Rhun gasped, flinching away from the weapon. He heard a whistling sound as it cut through the air, and then a thud, loud enough to rock his world. It took him a moment or so to realize that there had been no pain, that the club had struck the ground by his head. The outlaw dipped the club in the blood that had pooled at the base of the tree, then turned back to face the others, holding it aloft for them to see. The chieftain strode toward them, and Rhun held his breath, staring up blindly at the summer sky. But the man seemed satisfied, for he came no closer. Rhun bit his lip until he tasted blood in his mouth, not daring to move, barely daring to breathe. Soon after, he mercifully lost consciousness.

It was quiet after Rhun was done. Angharad took Rhun's hand again, squeezed gently. Justin exhaled his breath, very slowly, having gotten more than he'd bargained for. "Do you think you'll soon be able to travel, Rhun?" he asked at last.

The boy hesitated. "I suppose so. Why?"

"If I can find you work, would you be willing to leave Rhuddlan Castle?"

Rhun's eyes widened. "Am I in as much danger as that?"

"I do not know," Justin said honestly, "but I think we'll both sleep better if you're sleeping elsewhere," and after a moment, Rhun nodded.

"Woe unto the mouse that has only one hole. I'd be much beholden to you, Master de Quincy, if you could find me another hole."

"I will," Justin said. "I promise you that I will. Rhun . . . this language they spoke, you could understand none of it, not even an occasional word?"

"No, just that word I told you: *Joder*. I think it may have been a name."

"What about their leader? He spoke Welsh, but was he Welsh?"

Rhun thought about it. "No . . . his Welsh was very good. Much better than yours," he added, with a small smile. "But he was not Welsh. I am sure of that."

"Is there anything else you can tell me about these men? Anything at all?"

"No . . ." But Rhun did not sound certain, and after a pause, he said slowly, "It seemed to me that . . . that the foreigners were not that comfortable on horseback, not like the man in command. The one who ran me down . . . he ought to have splattered my brains out, but he swung his club too short. Does this help?"

"Yes," Justin said, after a long pause. "I think it might."

Dusk had fallen by the time Justin and Angharad began to walk across the bailey toward the keep. "So," she said, "are you keeping any more secrets from me, Iestyn?"

"One or two," he allowed. "I want to thank you for your help. Angharad. Not just for translating when I had need of it, but for persuading Rhun to talk to me."

"Do not make me regret it," she said softly. "Are you not going to ask for my silence?"

"Do I need to?"

"No. The only way I can protect Rhun is by keeping quiet. But you need to do more for him. Can you, Iestyn? Can you keep Rhun safe?"

"Yes," he said, "I think so." Who could better protect Rhun than the man who had the most to gain from Rhun's story?

"And can you stop Davydd from blaming Llewelyn ab Iorwerth for this crime?"

"That I do not know," he admitted. "There are answers I still need. But because of Rhun, at least I know now where to search for them."

"And where is that?"

"Chester," he said, with more confidence than he actually felt. "I think I'll find my answers in Chester."

8

August 1193
Chester, England

On the following morning, Justin rode away from Rhuddlan Castle, and two days later, he was within sight of the walls of Chester. It had been an uneventful trip and a safe one, for William Fitz Alan had decided to depart with him, and he had a sizable escort. While Justin was glad that he need not worry about outlaws, he was soon weary of fending off the Shropshire sheriff's heavy-handed queries, and his spirits rose as the estuary's blue waters darkened with the mud, silt, and mire of the River Dee.

Entering the city from the south, they continued up Bridge Street until they reached the cross, where their paths diverged, to Justin's relief. Fitz Alan and his men headed on toward the abbey precincts of St Werburgh, and Justin turned off to find a cook shop. After eating, he rode back out of the city, because the Bishop of Chester's palace was located just beyond the town walls. He'd originally intended to seek out the Earl of Chester first, but with Fitz Alan on the loose in the city, he owed his father some advance warning.

Justin had been half-hoping that his father would be away; much of a bishop's time was taken up with official visitations to the monasteries within his diocese. Not only would that have avoided a meeting with Fitz Alan, it would have postponed his own reckoning with the bishop. Luck was not with him, however. As soon as he was announced, Aubrey came hastening into the great hall to greet him.

"Justin, you are well?"

Justin blinked in surprise. "Yes, I am fine. Why would I not be?"

Aubrey's brows drew together in a familiar frown. "Why, indeed? Mayhap because the Earl of Chester told me that you'd vanished without a trace. He said the knight he'd sent with you returned yesterday, claiming that you'd gone missing like the ransom."

"I was trying to find out what really happened to the ransom. What did you think, that I was off carousing or drinking myself sodden in some Welsh alehouse? They do not have alehouses in Wales," Justin said sharply and Aubrey's scowl deepened.

"No, you young fool, I thought you might be lying dead in a ditch with a Welsh lance in your chest!"

Justin opened his mouth to retort, then stopped, not knowing what to say, and the bishop remembered that their quarrel was taking place in a public setting, his own great hall. "Come with me," he said and strode off without waiting to see if Justin was following or not.

He led Justin upstairs to the greater privacy of his solar, neither one speaking until they could close the door upon the rest of the world. Gesturing for Justin to sit, Aubrey began to pace. Justin sat down on a bench, taking longer than necessary to readjust his scabbard. He still did not know what to say, and as the silence lengthened, he wondered if Aubrey did not, either.

"You said you were trying to find out what *really* happened to the ransom." The bishop halted his pacing and turned abruptly toward Justin, as if finally realizing the import of those words. "The earl led me to believe that you already know what happened, that it was stolen by Davydd's nephew, Llewelyn ab Iorwerth."

"So everyone wants to believe. The only problem is that it is not true."

"No?" Aubrey sounded surprised, but not skeptical, and Justin realized that his father had no cock in this fight, no preconceived notions about Llewelyn's guilt or innocence. "You seem very sure of that, Justin. What do you know that the earl does not?"

"Quite a lot, actually," Justin admitted, making up his mind then and there to confide in his father, at least as much as he was able. If his idea was a daft one, Aubrey would tell him so. That he did not doubt. "I must ask you to keep whatever I say in confidence. Is that acceptable to you?"

Aubrey was beginning to look curious, even intrigued. "Of course." Settling himself in his high-backed chair, he said, "What makes you think that Llewelyn is not guilty?"

"Because I've learned who the robbers were and they were not Welsh. Nor were they English or Norman-French. I was told that they spoke a foreign tongue. I know it was not Irish or Breton, for they are somewhat akin to Welsh. One of the men may have been named 'Joder,' and that sounds to me like it might be German or Flemish."

Aubrey nodded thoughtfully. "I agree. I suppose you'd rather I not ask how you came into this bit of interesting information. Are you sure that you can trust your source?"

"Yes."

Aubrey smiled faintly. "If words were coins, you'd be the despair of beggars everywhere. Assuming, then, that your source is correct, what next? How would you even begin to hunt for these men?"

"Well, I have a little more to go on. I was told that these outlaws did not seem to be experienced horsemen," Justin said and saw by his father's expression that Aubrey was not following his line of reasoning. Hoping he was not about to make an utter fool of himself, he continued cautiously, "I thought about that, and it occurred to me that men who are not used to riding horses and who speak a foreign tongue might well be sailors."

" 'Sailors,' " Aubrey echoed, sounding startled. After a moment, he smiled. "That is very clever of you, Justin. I doubt that I would have thought of it. So . . . that is why you are here. Chester is the closest port to the Welsh border."

"That was my thinking," Justin acknowledged. "I know it is a road that may not take me anywhere. But I thought it was worth exploring."

"Does the Earl of Chester know about this?" When Justin shook his head, Aubrey said, "Well, you need to tell him straightaway, lad! Surely you do not think that the earl is somehow involved in this wretched business?"

"Passing strange, for that is exactly what the Lady Emma called it, too. And no, I do not suspect the earl. But I do not want to risk exposing my source until I am sure he is out of harm's way."

"That is commendable, of course. Do not confuse your priorities, though. Nothing must matter more than recovering the ransom for the queen." The bishop was beginning to sound like a tutor instructing a well-meaning but slow pupil. As Justin was accustomed to being lectured by Aubrey—most of their past conversations had been sermons of some sort—he took no offense. Aubrey continued on in this admonitory vein for several moments and then grinned unexpectedly. "Was I not right," he demanded, "about the Lady Emma?"

Justin grinned, too. "Indeed you were." It was a

strange sensation to be sharing a companionable moment like this with his father; he could not remember it ever happening before. Nor was it ever likely to happen again. "There is something I must tell you. When I arrived at Rhuddlan Castle, I encountered someone I had not expected to find there, and he took me by surprise." Justin exhaled his breath slowly. "It was Lord Fitz Alan."

"What?" Aubrey was on his feet, staring down at Justin in dismayed horror that was not long in giving way to outrage. "And you told him I was your father? Jesu, what a fool I was to trust you!"

"No, I did not!" Justin rose so swiftly that his scabbard banged against the edge of the bench, hard enough to leave a bruise upon his thigh. "But he heard me introduced as Justin de Quincy and naturally that aroused his curiosity."

"I cannot imagine why!" the bishop snapped. "So what did you tell him, then? What could you possibly have said?"

"Other than the truth, you mean? I told him that you and the queen were involved in the recovery of the ransom, and I implied that this was why I'd taken your name."

"For the love of God, could you not have done better than that? How long do you think it will take Fitz Alan to come to me with questions I cannot answer?"

Justin gave a half-shrug. "It could not be helped."

"Oh, but it could. If you had not chosen to claim a name that is not yours and will never be yours, none of this would have happened!"

Justin flinched. "You are right. But it can also be said that none of this would have happened if you'd not broken your vows and seduced my mother!"

"Your mother was—" Aubrey cut off the rest of that sentence so abruptly that he all but choked on his own words, and Justin went cold, for his father had always refused to tell him anything at all about the woman who'd died giving him birth.

"My mother was . . . *what*?" he challenged. "Go on, say it!" But the moment was already gone. Aubrey's jaw was clenched, his the unfriendly, guarded eyes of a stranger. He shook his head and gestured toward the door. Justin had seen him dismiss servants and underlings like that over the years, waving people away when he no longer had need of them. It was easy enough to obey, far easier than it would have been to resist, to stay and demand answers he was not likely to get, answers he might even be better off not knowing.

As he entered the great hall of Chester Castle, Justin bumped into Thomas de Caldecott, quite literally. Thomas swung around with a reprimand that never left his lips. "De Quincy! Christ Jesus, man, where have you been? I told the earl that you might well be dead!"

"Well, I am not," Justin said tersely, not wanting to deal with Thomas's interrogation, not now. His brusqueness did nothing to mollify the other man, who glowered at him with the indignation of the unfairly wronged.

"Forgive me for being fool enough to worry about you!"

The heat had yet to fade from Justin's face, for he'd come to the earl directly after leaving his father. He sensed dimly that he ought to have given himself some time between confrontations, but for now, his anger ruled both his brain and his tongue, his nerves too raw to tolerate even the lightest touch. "I left you word that I was checking out something on my own. What more could I have said?"

"You could have told me what you were doing, where you were going, and who you were meeting!"

"No," Justin said, "I could not," and the look in Thomas's eyes belied his mien of easy affability.

"So you do not trust me? What have I done to deserve your suspicions? No . . . do not answer, for I do not really care. You can rest assured that I'll not fret about your safety in the future. From now on, you're on your own!" Spinning on his heel, Thomas stalked off, shoving aside a man who'd inadvertently stepped into his path. Justin almost called him back—almost. But it was easier once again to take the path of least resistance, to let him go.

The Earl of Chester was shorter than average and Justin topped him by at least a foot. But he showed none of the self-consciousness Justin had often encountered in other men of small stature, striding alongside his taller companion with utter indifference to the disparity in their heights. They were out in the castle tiltyard, watching as the youths in the earl's household practiced their fighting skills, riding at the quintain and feinting clumsily with swords they could barely lift. Justin had undergone such training, too, when he'd first entered Lord Fitz Alan's service. But these boys were of higher rank than Justin could ever have aspired to, for there was great prestige in learning life lessons from an earl.

"Does Thomas know yet that you are still amongst the living?"

"He does, my lord."

"So . . . where were you?"

"I cannot tell you that, my lord . . . not yet. I have suspicions and suspects, but no hard proof. I'd rather wait until I have conclusive evidence to present to you."

"You can do better than that," Chester scoffed. "You think if you give me a name, I'll pounce upon the poor wretch and haul him off to the gallows? What is the real reason you are so loath to confide in me, de Quincy?"

"I fear endangering those who are helping me, my lord earl."

Chester subjected Justin to a hard-eyed scrutiny before nodding grudgingly. "That I can accept . . . for now. I ask for no names. But I do want to know where you think this investigation is heading." When Justin hesitated, he said impatiently, "It is common sense, man, no more than that. What happens to your secrets if you come to grief back in Wales? I'll tell you what happens. They die with you."

Now it was Justin's turn to give ground. "You are right, my lord," he conceded. "I will tell you this much, then. Llewelyn ab Iorwerth is not the one who took the ransom. His uncle seeks to blame him falsely and may even have gone further than that. As for the actual outlaws, I think they were hirelings, men who may not have known what they were stealing. And they were not Welsh."

Chester's reactions were subtle: a tightening of the corners of his mouth, an upraised brow. He was silent for some moments and then swore softly, "Hellfire and damnation. It would have been so much easier if Llewelyn had been guilty. I am going to pay you the great compliment of assuming you know what you're doing. Just in case you do run into a stray arrow or get your throat cut in your sleep, are you saying I ought to look in Davydd's direction first?" When Justin nodded, the earl seemed more cheerful. "That I will do right gladly. In the meantime, I suppose you want me to keep this to myself?"

"I would be beholden to you, my lord, if you did."

"What of Thomas? Surely he ought to know . . ." The earl was quick enough to catch the faintest glimmer of doubt in Justin's eyes. "What? You do not trust him?"

Until that moment, Justin would have said he did. But hearing the question put so baldly was a revelation. He looked across the tiltyard, where Thomas de Caldecott was showing one of the young squires how to execute a shifting cut, changing his sword's direction in mid-attack. Thomas appeared to be ignoring their presence entirely, but Justin had seen him shoot a covert glance their way from time to time. "Thomas has given me no reason not to trust him, my lord," he said slowly, choosing his words with care.

"Men like you need no reasons, de Quincy. You breathe in suspicions like other men breathe in air."

The words themselves were sharp enough to wound, but oddly, the tone was neutral, as if the earl were making an observation, not an accusation. " 'Men like me,' " Justin echoed. "And what men are they, my lord?"

The answer surprised him. "Men who serve only the Crown. Spies, agents, scouts, call them what you will. I admit I was puzzled when the queen put you in charge. You seemed an unlikely choice for such a mission, lacking in years, experience, or authority. But I'm beginning to understand. Something smelled foul about this to the queen, so she sent one of her own, one of those men from the shadows, the sort who've learned to leave no footprints and cast no reflection in mirrors."

"You make it sound," Justin protested, "as if I am in league with the Devil!"

Chester's lips twitched in a sardonic smile. "No," he said, "only the queen."

There weren't that many hours of daylight remaining, but Justin did not want to waste them, and from the castle, he went directly to the waterfront. He'd known from the first what a difficult task he faced; trying to find three nameless, faceless sailors was akin to the hunt for the proverbial needle in a haystack. Even if he was right in his suspicions, the sailors could have returned to their ship and sailed for their homeport by now. Or they could have fled with their newfound wealth, and their ship could have sailed without them. He'd chosen to gamble that they would not have gone back to their old lives and that their flight would have left a hole for him to discover. But so far, he'd had no luck at all. By nightfall, he'd hunted down several ships' masters, and all he had to show for his efforts was a blister on his heel, a throat sore from asking questions that got no satisfactory answers, and a powerful desire to drown his disappointment in drink.

He was looking for a sailors' hangout and found one in a waterfront tavern. It was cleaner than most of its kind, twice as large as Nell's alehouse back in London. Half a dozen men were sprawled on benches, dicing and drinking and laughing at a curley-haired youth who was doing his best to charm the serving maid. She might have been pretty in other surroundings, another life. But in this dockside tavern, she merely looked bored and somewhat sullen, and Justin shared the majority view, that the lad was wasting both his time and his money.

Over a cup of red wine heavily spiced to hide the sour taste, Justin brooded upon the day's events. He tried not to think about that ugly scene with his father. Instead he sought to focus his thought on Thomas de Caldecott. Why was he of a sudden harboring doubts about the knight? Was it because Thomas had overreacted to his disappearance?

Why had the other man been so alarmed that he'd gone off on his own? Was it genuine concern for his safety? Or something more sinister? If Thomas had been the one to disappear, would he have been as worried? He thought not, not unless Thomas had vanished without a word. The message he'd left ought to have been enough to allay his misgivings, at least for a few days. Nor had Thomas seemed all that relieved to see him surface, alive and well.

But would he not have been affronted if Thomas chose to withhold information about the robbery? He damned well would, so how could he blame Thomas for bristling at his secretiveness?

But he could not explain to Thomas that he was being so close-mouthed out of fear for Rhun's safety, for that very revelation might put the boy at risk, even if Thomas was utterly without ulterior motives. This entire puzzle was beginning to resemble a game his dog Shadow liked to play, spinning around in circles trying to catch his own tail.

He was somewhat disquieted, too, by the Earl of Chester's jaundiced view of his employment skills. All that had been lacking in the earl's description was the scent of sulfur. It was flattering to think that the queen had indeed chosen him because she'd sensed that there was more to this robbery than met the eye. But he did not want to see himself as a creature of the shadows, a being never quite belonging anywhere. That was Durand de Curzon.

A bellowed curse drew his attention toward the dice game. The loser had sprung to his feet and was loudly accusing the winner of using weighted dice. The accused was blinking up at him in befuddlement. As young as he was, he might have been a student if he hadn't been so proper in appearance, for there was nothing about him of the hell-raiser or mischief-maker. Insisting that he'd not been cheating, he held out the dice, offering to let anyone examine them for himself. He seemed confused and scared, and when Justin studied his accuser, it was easy to see why. Not only was the burly loser taller and heavier than the winner, he bore the battle scars of a man who'd had more than his share of tavern and back-alley brawls, a man who'd fight for the fun of it, aroused by the smell of fear.

Justin took a better grip upon his drink. The other tavern customers were doing the same, bracing themselves in case stools and cups and bodies began flying through the air. But even those who were anticipating some entertainment were taken aback by the brutality of the attack. Lunging forward, the instigator grabbed his opponent by the front of his tunic and smashed his head down upon the table. Before his victim could recover, the bigger man had flung him to the floor and kicked him in the ribs. Too dazed to defend himself, the youth scrabbled instinctively to get away. But before he could crawl under the table, his assailant seized him by his hair and dragged him out into the middle of the floor.

By now the tavern was in an uproar. Drunken fistfights could offer good sport, but no one wanted to watch a helpless man being beaten to death. The serving maid spun around, yelling to the youth who'd been flirting with her, "Fetch Ben!" Other voices were being raised now, too, protests coming from most of the witnesses. But only two offered more than verbal objections, Justin and a sailor with hair and beard as long and bright as a Viking's.

The sailor was closer than Justin and got there first, seeking to wrap his arms around the attacker and immobilize him in a bear hug. He was a big man and clearly he'd had success in the past with this maneuver. But his opponent broke the hold with alarming ease and kneed him in the groin. The sailor gasped and dropped like a felled oak. By then Justin was there, burying his fist in the aggressor's stomach. He'd put the full weight of his body behind that punch, but the other man only grunted. In the moment that Justin was slightly off balance, his foe shoved him backward, with enough force to send him reeling into a table. The man turned back to his victim then, kicking him in the head.

So intent was he upon his prey that he paid no heed to the entrance of another man. This one was taller than most, but lanky and rail-thin, with such long arms and legs that he looked a little like a scarecrow. There was nothing at all intimidating about his appearance, nor did he seem unduly alarmed by the bloody scene meeting his eyes. But when the drunkard drew back his foot to kick the body on the floor again, the newcomer moved with the speed of a snake, catching hold of that foot and jerking with enough force to send him sprawling. Even that fall did not seem to have slowed the man down much. His eyes, small and close-set, gleamed with the bloodshot fury of a cornered boar, and with a rumbling, wordless roar, he launched himself at this new enemy.

He barely got off the floor, though, before he was down again. The other man whipped out a lethal-looking cudgel and brought it down upon his skull with an audible thud. Two more blows followed in close order, delivered with the impersonal, practiced skill of a master carpenter. The second blow had rendered the man unconscious.

Poking him with the tip of his boot, the victor said, "God's Cock, Berta, what the hell happened? I leave the place for an hour and come back to a butcher's paradise. We'll never get rid of all this blood, not unless we paint the walls red." Prodding the downed man again with his toe, he said, "Anyone know who this offal is?"

Berta edged around a pool of blood, her nose wrinkling in disgust when she saw that some of it had splattered her skirt. "I think he may be off that French cog out in the harbor. It is a good thing that Algar found you, Ben, else we'd have had a killing here for certes."

"That whoreson sheriff is looking for any excuse to close us down, too," Ben agreed. Glancing around at the tavern customers, he picked out two, told them to drag "this lump of lard" down to the docks and leave him there. His gaze raked the room, taking in the sailor still on his knees and Justin, who was untangling himself from an overturned table.

"Holy Mother Mary, it looks like we have two heroes amongst us, lads. Berta, free drinks for the Good Samaritans." Striding over to examine the youth on the floor, he winced at the sight of the damage done by the sailor's heavy clogs. Drafting another volunteer, he ordered the man to fetch Osborn the Leech and leaned over, saying, "Someone give me a hand. We'll put this one in the back room till Osborn gets here."

By now Justin was back on his feet and had determined that he'd suffered no injury except a few bruises and a spilled drink. "I'll help," he said, starting toward Ben.

The other man was bending over the inert body of the dice game winner. "You take his legs," he directed Justin, "and I'll get his shoulders—" But as he looked Justin full in the face, he stopped, almost dropping the injured man back into the floor rushes. "Christ on the Cross! Justin?"

Justin studied him in surprise. He looked to be about Justin's own age, with jet-black hair, a pirate's scruffy beard, and the bluest eyes to be found this side of Sweden. It took a moment for Justin to realize that this thin, angular face was one from his past. "Bennet?"

9

"By Corpus, it is you, Justin!"

As soon as Bennet grinned, Justin was sure, too, for Bennet had always had a smile that lit up an ordinary face and made it unforgettable. This man beaming at him was indeed the friend of his boyhood, the only person he'd ever truly trusted, his brother in all but blood.

They'd always had an uncanny ability to read each other's thoughts, and Bennet proved now that he'd not lost the knack, turning around and saying to the tavern at large, "Justin and I were thicker than thieves growing up. God's Truth, we were like brothers. At least until he was sent off to serve a high-and-mighty lord down in Shropshire!"

Seated at a table in the back of the tavern, they regarded each other with amazement, pleasure, and belated wariness. "How long has it been?" Bennet marveled. "Five years? Six?"

"Actually, closer to seven, for I was fourteen when the bishop placed me in Lord Fitz Alan's household."

"I hope you noticed that I let your 'lord' remain nameless," Bennet said and grinned. "I could not think of a quicker way to clear out this den of thieves than to announce that this blood brother of mine works for the sheriff of Shropshire!"

Justin started to correct Bennet's mistake, but the words never left his lips. What could he say? The truth was too fantastic for Bennet to accept. How could he expect Bennet to believe that he was now the queen's man?

"I wondered so often how you were doing, Bennet. But I did not even know where you were, and I could hardly . . ."

He let the words fade away, but Bennet finished the sentence for him. "Write to me. Not bloody likely. And do not remind me that you'd offered to teach me to read, if you please! We both know I was never much of a student."

Not a student at all, Justin thought, for he knew that neither Bennet nor his sister had so much as a day's schooling. They had been children forgotten by family, townsmen, the Church, even by God, it sometimes seemed. Born to a woman who'd disappeared soon after Bennet's birth and a belligerent, blustering fishmonger who'd drunk away what little he'd earned, they had grown up as wild as stable cats. But from the time he was eight until his fifteenth year, Justin had been closer to Bennet than he ever had to another living being.

"That is not true," he objected. "You were always a quick study for the things that interested you."

"Aye, when it came to trouble, I went right to the head of the class," Bennet agreed cheerfully. "We thought about you, too, Moll and me. We figured that you were doing good. You were always as clever as a peddler's ape. But what about me, Justy? Admit it, you likely expected to hear that I'd ended up dancing on the gallows!"

"No," Justin said with a grin, "not as slick as you were. You were ever one for ducking around corners and squeezing under fences when it counted. I will admit, though, that I did not expect to find you as the owner of a Chester tavern. How did you manage that, Bennet?"

"What . . . you think this sty is mine?" Bennet shook

his head, laughing. "That would be the day! I tend to it, keep these fools from breaking heads when they're soused, and make sure that they remember to pay for their drinks. But it belongs to Piers Fitz Turold."

"I . . . see." Justin was not happy to hear that, for Piers Fitz Turold had long been a figure of speculation and suspicion in Chester. Supposedly, he was a vintner, but the general belief was that he made much of his money in other, less legal ways, including smuggling and prostitution. "So you work for Fitz Turold, Bennet? For how long?"

"For a while now. I look after his warehouse by the docks, too. In fact, I sleep there most nights for Chester breeds bolder thieves than anywhere else in the realm. I also do other tasks for him when the need arises."

Justin knew better than to ask what those tasks might be. He was sorry to learn that Bennet had gotten ensnared in Fitz Turold's web, but not surprised. What choices did Bennet have in the world he'd been born into? As a lad, there had been times when he'd had to steal to eat, and by the time their friendship was ruptured by Justin's departure for Shropshire, he suspected that Bennet was practicing the skills of a cutpurse.

"Ben . . . I thought you might want another flagon." Berta leaned over the table, offering them both a close-up view of her ample cleavage. She let her gaze linger upon Justin, moistening her lips with the tip of her tongue. Since she had not given him so much as a glance before, Justin assumed that his worth had gone up because of his friendship with Bennet.

As she sauntered away, they both watched her swaying walk before Justin said, "So you are Ben now? Should I cast Bennet aside?"

"No need. Moll still makes use of it. Also, to hear you call me Bennet brings back a lot of memories."

Justin had been almost afraid to ask about Bennet's sister, for if any girl seemed predestined for a bad end, for certes it was Molly. "Molly . . . she is well?"

"Well enough. She'll not believe you turned up like this, not unless she sees you with her own eyes. So can you stay for a while? She ought to be back by week's end."

"She lives in Chester, then? Has she taken herself a husband? Most likely she has . . . any children?"

"Yes, no, and no." Bennet reached for the flagon, poured for them both. "I might as well tell you straight out. Molly is with Piers now."

Justin sat his cup down so abruptly that wine splattered upon the table, set the candle flame to sizzling. "Jesu! And you let her, Bennet?"

"And when's a mere man ever been able to keep Moll from doing what she pleased?" Bennet looked more closely into Justin's face and realization dawned. "I did not mean that, Justin! Molly is not one of Piers's whores. They have an understanding, an arrangement. Piers lets her live rent-free in one of his cottages and goes to see her when it strikes his fancy. It seems to suit them both," he said, with a half-shrug that was very familiar to Justin, the gesture he'd always make when happenings were beyond his control.

"Molly could have done so much better." But even as he said the words, Justin knew they weren't true. Molly's choices had been even more limited than her brother's. "She deserves better," he amended. "There is no future for her with Piers, not unless his wife has gone to God since I left Chester."

"Nay, she is alive and thriving, the last I heard. But I doubt that Moll would have Piers even if she could. Have you forgotten how often she made mock of marriage and wedded wives?"

"I remember," Justin admitted. "She'd say that a woman without a man was like a cat without a collar." Their eyes met and they both laughed, theirs the laughter of nostalgia, remembrance with a bittersweet tang. "I might as well confess," Justin said. "I was besotted with your sister."

"You and half the men in Chester, my lad."

"Are you mocking my broken heart? It was the great regret of my life that Molly saw me only as her little brother's friend, this green stripling of fourteen. Of course I *was* a green stripling of fourteen, but even so . . ." Enough years had passed so that Justin could smile at the memory of his first infatuation. "You said she's gone from Chester?"

"Piers had to visit his salt house in Wich Malbank. He has a finger in every pie, does that one. He took Molly along because . . . well, what else is a man to do in a salt wich?" Picking up his wine cup, Bennet held it aloft in a playful salute. "To days gone by and—holy shit!"

"I'll drink to that if you insist," Justin grinned, "but surely we can do better?" Bennet was no longer paying him any mind, though, staring over his shoulder toward the door. Turning in his seat, Justin saw an officer of the law blocking the doorway. There was nothing in the man's appearance that proclaimed his rank. It was the air of authority that he exuded. Justin had seen Jonas swagger into a London alehouse and have it fall silent just as this Chester tavern had stilled.

"Watch yourself," Bennet muttered. "That is Will Gamberell, the city sheriff. He'd like nothing better than to blame Piers for an affray in one of his taverns." Raising his voice, he said, "What brings you here, Master Gamberell? Berta, fetch wine for the sheriff and his men."

"As if I'd drink the swill you sell here," the sheriff said

with a sneer. "I hear you had yourself some sport tonight. We found a man half-dead down on the docks, and he says you beat him to a bloody pulp. Dare you deny it?"

"Good of you not to pass judgment till you heard my side of it," Bennet said, but he sounded more sullen than sarcastic and there was a note in his voice that Justin had heard before—the embittered understanding of a man who knew the law was never going to protect the likes of him. "You'd do better to ask your 'bloody pulp' what he'd done to warrant a beating. I am not saying I gave him one, mind you. But he damned near killed a man, would have for certes if he'd not been stopped."

"So you were just doing your duty as a law-abiding citizen of Chester?" the sheriff drawled, and his men laughed.

"You need not take my word for it. His victim is in the back room, being patched up by Osborn the Leech. Ask him yourself what happened."

"You may be sure I will. But right now I am asking you."

"Ben?" Almost as if it had been staged, the doctor chose that moment to appear in the doorway of the storeroom. "The poor sod is asking for you. He lost some teeth so he sounds like he's got a mouth full of mush, but I think he wants to thank you. I told him that if not for you, we'd have been measuring him for a burial shroud."

Justin turned toward Bennet, expecting to share relief that this was so easily cleared up. But Bennet looked grim, and one glance at the sheriff's face told him why. Gamberell was grinning like a man who'd just discovered a forgotten hoard of coins in his money pouch. "Well now," he said happily, "I do believe my life just got easier."

The doctor realized that he'd done Bennet no favor and said quickly, "But I may have misunderstood what happened. Look in on the lad, Ben, and whilst you do, you can reassure me that someone is going to pay for my services."

Bennet rose slowly, and while he said nothing, his body language dared the sheriff to stop him. "With your permission, Master Gamberell."

"Why not?" The sheriff waved him on with a magnanimous gesture, before adding, "I happen to know the only way out of that room is through this door and the only way out of this tavern is through me."

By now it was deathly quiet. The sailor who'd intervened in the beating had stood up as the sheriff began to speak, but he'd soon sank back in his seat again. Having gotten the lay of the land, he was studiously staring down into the floor rushes. None of the other customers were meeting the sheriff's gaze, either, doing their best to appear as inconspicuous as possible. Justin had gotten the lay of the land, too, by now. The sheriff did not care why Bennet had struck that drunken lout. What mattered to him was that one of Piers Fitz Turold's underlings had made a misstep, and who knew where that might lead?

Justin shoved his seat back, deliberately drawing the sheriff's attention, and got to his feet without haste, making it clear his intentions were peaceful. "I think I can help, Master Gamberell. I can tell you exactly what happened."

The sheriff's expression was skeptical. While Justin was wearing a sword and spoke the Norman-French of the educated, he'd been sharing a drink with Bennet, and the sheriff was a firm believer that a man could be judged by the company he kept. "Who in the blazes are you?"

"I am the man who hit that misbegotten knave you found on the docks."

If possible, the tavern became even more silent. "I have witnesses who say otherwise," the sheriff said curtly.

Justin doubted that, but he said calmly, "They are wrong. Bennet and I are both tall, with dark hair. They must have mistaken him for me."

The sheriff's eyes were blue-ice. "I'd not be in such a hurry to claim credit for this if I were you. Even if you were defending yourself, you can still be charged with attempted murder and mayhem. It will be up to a court to decide who is telling the truth."

"I understand that." Justin picked up his wine cup, drank the last of it slowly. He was hoping that the gesture would appear coolly confident, but he also needed the liquid, for his mouth had gone dry. "I ask only that we stop first at the castle so I might tell my lord earl what happened and why I am being detained."

Justin had discovered with William Fitz Alan that the Earl of Chester's name carried considerable weight. It had an even more telling effect upon the sheriff. "Why would the earl care?" he asked, but he sounded wary.

"You know, of course, about the ransom that was stolen in Wales." Reaching into his scrip, Justin drew out the queen's letter and handed it to Gamberell. He thought he probably could have bluffed the sheriff with the earl's name alone, but he wanted to end this before Bennet reemerged from the storeroom.

The sheriff read rapidly and when he glanced up at Justin, his face was guarded, revealing nothing of what he was thinking. Returning the letter, he reached over and emptied Bennet's cup into the floor rushes. "We are done here," he said, turning on his heel as his startled men hastened to follow.

The hush continued even after the sheriff had gone. Justin retook his seat, and Berta scurried over to refill his cup. She asked no questions, nor did she meet his eyes, and he realized that to a tavern serving wench, power was dangerous, be it in the hands of the city sheriff or a mysterious stranger.

When Bennet returned to the common room, his expression was one that Justin had seen before, chin jutting out, wide, mobile mouth set in granite, eyes heavy-lidded and opaque. So he'd looked when facing down his drunken father, bracing for the beating that was sure to come. "Osborn misunderstood what that poor lad said. It was not me who—" He halted in midsentence, looking around in astonishment. "Where the Devil is the sheriff?"

"He left."

"I can see that, Justin. But why? Is he coming back?"

"I do not think so."

Bennet's eyes narrowed on Justin's face. Sitting down again, he waved his hand to indicate the others were to resume their own conversations, and then said in a low voice, "What did you do, Justy? And do not tell me you bribed the bastard. The man is honest!"

There was such genuine indignation in his voice that Justin burst out laughing. "You remember that time we were caught stealing apples in the abbey orchard?"

"I remember. I thought sure we were in for it, but you got the gardener to let us go by making free with the bishop's name."

"Well, let's just say I did some name-dropping tonight, too."

Bennet did not look satisfied, but he said only, "I did not realize that Fitz Alan cast a shadow clear into Cheshire." Raising his cup, he clinked it against Justin's. "Here's to friends and secrets and sheriffs and better days." He drank, watching Justin over the rim of his wine cup. "It is good to know that some things never change. You always were as closemouthed as a clam."

"That is because you talked enough for the both of us. You never let me get a word in edgewise."

After that, the past seven years melted away. Bennet sent out to the cook shop for supper and they swapped memories and insults as they drained several more flagons dry, taking perverse pleasure in recalling a boyhood that had not been easy for either of them. When curfew rang, Bennet closed the tavern and they continued to drink, reminding each other of half-forgotten escapades: playing camp-ball and hunt the fox, sneaking into the abbey fish stews to swim, getting greensick on their first flagon of ale, fighting and forgiving, going to St John's Fair and the hanging of a notorious outlaw, growing up in a world that put little value upon a fishmonger's brat and a foundling born of sin. And for one night, Justin was able to forget about ransoms and captive kings and double-dealing Welsh princes and the dangers that awaited him upon his return to the dragon's lair.

10

Justin's first thought was that someone had hit him on the head. He was becoming all too familiar with that experience, for it had happened twice in the past year, first by Gilbert the Fleming and then Durand de Curzon. When he moved, he felt as if his brains were going to spill right out of his skull. Slitting his eyes, he found himself staring up at wooden rafter beams. The air was musty and damp, smelled of straw and sawdust and other odors better left unidentified. Where in holy Hell was he?

He forced himself to sit up, at once regretted it, for his stomach was in no better shape than his head. The last time he'd gotten this drunk, it had been after he'd discovered that Claudine was John's spy. Wisps of memory were beginning to etch themselves upon the night's blank slate. Being at the tavern with Bennet. The floor littered with empty flagons. Staggering through the deserted streets, ducking into an alley to evade the Watch, muffling their laughter with their mantles. A misplaced key, hunting for a spare behind a cistern. More laughter. Even snatches of a bawdy alehouse song.

Lord God have mercy. *We sang?* Justin shuddered at the memory and sought to extricate himself from his tangled blankets. He'd slept on top of a large wooden crate; no wonder his spine felt as if a horse had walked on his back. At least he knew now where he was, in Piers Fitz

Turold's waterfront warehouse. Across the room Bennet lay sprawled upon a straw pallet. He twitched at the sound of Justin's boots hitting the ground but continued to snore softly until Justin wobbled over and shook his shoulder.

"Wha . . . ? Go 'way . . ."

"I will if you tell me where I can go to piss."

One bloodshot blue eye opened. "Hey, Justin . . ." The rest of his words were swallowed up in a yawn, and Justin had to shake him again. "I use the privy out on the docks . . ."

The glare of sun off the river was blinding, and when nearby Holy Trinity Church began to toll, Justin felt as if the bells were echoing inside his head. But by the time he got back to the warehouse, he thought he was likely to live and was furious with himself for wasting so much of this day. The sun was so high in the sky that it must be nigh onto noon.

Bennet was still sleeping, and Justin roused him only by threatening to pour water on his head. Blinking owlishly, he peered out of a cocoon of blankets, sounding puzzled and peevish. "Why are you up? Is the place on fire?"

"I have things I must do today. So do you, Bennet."

"Yes, go back to sleep." Bennet tried to burrow under the blankets again, but Justin persisted and he reluctantly poked his head out. "Do what you must, then. We can meet back at the tavern tonight. I ought to be able to drag myself out of bed by then . . ."

Some things never changed. Even as a lad, Bennet had been one for sleeping the day away if he could. Justin retrieved his sword, thankful that it had survived their drunken carousing with nary a scratch, and braced himself before opening the door and stepping back out into that painful dazzle of pure white sunlight.

He returned to the castle before resuming his search for the missing sailors, checking upon Copper and checking in with the Earl of Chester in case there had been new developments that he needed to know. He did not run into Thomas de Caldecott and was grateful for that. The last thing his throbbing head could take would be another shouting match. After stopping at an apothecary's shop where he bought wood betony for his headache and a saffron potion for his hangover, he headed for the quays.

Chester was a river port, and the larger ships were anchored downstream. Smaller boats were tied up at piers, and the tide was running high enough to lap at the western town walls. Justin's expectations were low after the previous day's failures, but he was to get a pleasant surprise. The second ship's master he spoke to, captain of a sturdy merchant hulk christened the *Gulden Vlies,* told him that he was indeed lacking three members of his crew, hitherto reliable lads who'd deserted without any warning whatsoever.

This entire voyage had been accursed, he complained bitterly. First he lost three good men, and since then it had been one misfortune after another, leaks to be caulked, a mainmast to be repaired, shrouds to be replaced; he'd be lucky if they sailed by Michaelmas, he predicted dourly. Once he saw that Justin was not a candidate for his crew, he had no further interest in prolonging the conversation, but Justin was able to extract the names of the missing men: Geertje, Karl, and Joder.

Failing to get anything else from the ship's master, Justin spent the rest of the day tracking down crew members from the *Gulden Vlies.* This was a process as frustrating as it was laborious. The ship was moored in the estuary, and the few sailors he found ashore either spoke only Flemish or claimed to know nothing about the disappearance of their shipmates. He was concluding that he'd have to find a way to get out to the hulk when a small, wizened man with skin like leather sidled up to him. He had such a strong Flemish accent that his French was not easy to understand, but Justin's hopes soared when he grasped that this was the cook of the *Gulden Vlies*. He could not help, but he knew one who could, he said, looking pointedly at the money pouch attached to Justin's belt.

With Baltazar, the cook, scurrying to keep pace, Justin began another search, this time for the ship's helmsman, who was a kinsman of the missing Karl. They finally found him in a cramped, dingy alehouse so poorly lit that it was like going into a tunnel. Rutger looked to be between thirty and forty. He had a deeply tanned face framed by lanky fair hair, close-set blue eyes, and the truculence of a man who'd been drinking for most of the day. With Baltazar acting as his translator, Justin attempted to find out what Rutger knew of his cousin's disappearance. But Rutger did not want to talk to Justin about anything at all, especially Karl, and cursed him out in slurred, thick Flemish when he persevered.

Justin at last conceded defeat, at least for now, and retreated out to the street, where he paid Baltazar the agreed-upon sum and arranged to try again when Rutger had sobered up. From the way Baltazar smirked, Justin suspected that Rutger had been drunk for most of their time in port, but he had no other leads. Unless he could persuade Rutger to tell him what he knew, he'd reached a dead end. Refusing to consider what he'd do if Rutger knew nothing useful, he headed back toward Bennet's tavern.

He'd begun feeling better as the day wore on. His head's pounding had subsided to a dull ache, and by mid-afternoon, he'd recovered enough of his appetite to buy a roasted capon leg from a street vendor. It was cold and greasy, but he expected no better fare from a peddler, and he was hungry enough to go back for a second helping, giving the bones to a skinny stray dog. His mood had improved, too, as his body recovered. It was too early to despair. He'd accomplished quite a lot this day. He'd confirmed his suspicions about the sailor-outlaws. They all had names now, had become flesh-and-blood men, no longer figments of his imagination. He would keep after Rutger until the helmsman agreed to talk. If need be, he'd buy the Fleming enough ale to swim in.

The sun had set, briefly turning the brown waters of the Dee to a muddy gold. Dusk was smothering the last of the light, and fewer people were out on the streets. As he neared the tavern, Justin became aware of a prickling at the back of his neck. Twice before that afternoon he'd experienced the same feeling, a sense that he was being watched. He had no evidence of that, had seen no one who'd looked either familiar or suspicious. But his unease lingered, for he'd learned to trust his instincts.

When he reached the tavern, he paused in the doorway to study the street but saw only passersby hurrying home through the deepening twilight, a beggar being berated by a stout man in a green felt cap, a thin, pale whore haggling with a prospective customer over her price. He was still not satisfied, and he vowed not to repeat last night's mistake. It was sobering to realize how vulnerable he would have been to attack as he and Bennet had blithely weaved their way homeward.

The tavern was already crowded, a mix of sailors and regular customers from the neighborhood, and several trestle tables had been set up to accommodate them. Justin had no trouble finding a seat, though. Berta at once hurried over to escort him to a corner table, shooing away the men already there. When they protested, she insisted, "Ben said he is to get whatever he wants," and that seemed to end the argument. Ben had been called away, she explained to Justin, but he'd soon be back. "He said you ought to wait for him. And I'm not to charge you for drinks."

There was something to be said, Justin decided, for having a friend who ran a tavern. Berta soon brought over a flagon and a cup and even offered to send someone out to the cook shop for food. Feeling like royalty, Justin declined and watched a rowdy dice game, taking an occasional swallow of Bennet's truly awful red wine, and pondering ways to win Rutger's trust. His fatigue soon caught up with him, and leaning forward, he rested his head on his arms and fell asleep.

He dozed off and on; he'd never been a heavy sleeper even in surroundings more conducive to sleep than a tavern's common room. He catnapped for a time, and when he opened his eyes again, he discovered that he was no longer alone. A woman had slid onto the bench next to him, so close that their bodies touched at hip and leg. Smothering a yawn, he said drowsily, "Sorry, sweetheart, I'm not looking for company," while prudently patting his money pouch to make sure it was still there. It was, and he was slipping back into sleep when the woman poked him in the ribs.

"If men are not the most fickle creatures on God's green earth! Here I thought I was the first great lust of your life, and now you do not even recognize me?"

Justin's head jerked up so fast that he almost gave himself whiplash. While Bennet had left boyhood behind and sprouted up nigh on a foot in their years apart, time had not wrought such dramatic changes in his sister. Molly had been seventeen when he'd last seen her, and this woman laughing at him was not so different from the girl he remembered.

She had vivid green eyes and Bennet's raven hair, and like his, her face was angular, with wide cheekbones that gave her a vaguely exotic appearance, a generous mouth, well-defined jawline, and skin that could not have been more unlike the pale complexion so idealized in songs and minstrel tales. Molly's skin was a warm shade that looked sun-kissed even in the dead of winter, and in summer it seemed to shine with a golden glow, no small defect in a society that so prized fairness, but one that never troubled her unduly. It had certainly not troubled the men of Chester, for she'd been bewitching them without even trying since her fourteenth year. As for Justin, he'd grown into manhood unheeding of the Church's warnings that "all wickedness was but little to the wickedness of a woman," that women were the Devil's pawns, daughters of Eve. To Justin, Eve was Bennet's wild child sister, and he'd have willingly forfeited Eden for a taste of her forbidden fruit.

"Hey, Molly," he said softly, greeting her as he always had, as if almost seven years had not gone by since their last meeting.

"Hey, Justin," she echoed, and they smiled at each other, savoring one of those rare moments of perfect happiness, in which nothing was asked or expected and it was enough. Then she said, "Well, do I not get a hug? I'll wager Bennet got one!"

They embraced like the old friends they were, like the brother and sister they were not, and for a brief time, they held each other without speaking. When they moved apart, they kept their hands clasped, and when they did speak, it was in unison, Justin saying he thought she was in Wich Malbank and Molly exclaiming that she had not believed Bennet at first, not until she made him swear upon her St James's scallop shell. They paused and then again spoke as one, Justin expressing amazement that she still had that pilgrim badge and Molly explaining that she'd returned early from Wich Malbank, getting into the city that afternoon.

"Let's start anew," she declared, "one at a time. Of course I still have my scallop shell. My father swore he'd gotten it from a man who'd made the pilgrimage all the way to Compostela." A pause. "Of course we both know what a liar my father was. But the odds are that he had to speak the truth at least once in his life, and I like to think this was that time."

Justin had learned from Bennet that their father had died five years ago. Now he hesitated, conflicted between good manners and honesty. Courtesy demanded that he offer his condolences, but he knew what a miserable excuse for a father the fishmonger had been, beating his children when he was drunk, beating them even worse when he was sober, making them his scapegoats for a life that had been joyless and harsh. He temporized by saying, "It could not have been easy for you and Bennet when your father died."

"And whose life is ever easy, my lad? Even Piers, who has money enough to buy all the indulgences he'd need to get through Heaven's Gate . . . even he finds much to mutter about these days, sure the fates are conspiring against him."

That answer told Justin much more than the words themselves. Molly did not want to talk about the hard times after her father's death. Neither had Bennet. But he also thought she'd deliberately thrust Piers's name into the conversation, a test to see how he'd handle her liaison with the notorious vintner. "Did Piers come back to Chester with you?" he asked, in what he hoped was a neutral tone of voice.

"No, he had to stay on at Wich Malbank for another week. But I could abide the place no longer and insisted that Piers send me home." Molly made a face. "Have you ever visited a salt house, Justin? It offers excitement beyond bearing. Fancy, all day you get to watch as the brine is boiled away and the salt collected!"

Justin's response was lost in the uproar that followed, for Bennet had just returned, laden with so much food that he'd gotten a street urchin to help him tote it from the cook shop to the tavern. He had wheat bread fresh from the baker's oven, he announced proudly, for that was the fare of the well-off and the wellborn, and Justin knew there had been many times when Bennet and Molly had not even had the money to buy rye torts, which were hard enough to hammer nails. He had an entire roasted chicken, Bennet continued, and little pies stuffed with beef marrow, and a dozen wafers flavored with honey and ginger. He must have spent a considerable sum on this meal, and Justin's first impulse was to offer to share the expense. But he caught himself in time, realizing that this lavish expenditure was something Bennet needed to do for his boyhood friend who served a lord, even if he could not afford it.

Bennet's first words confirmed his conjecture. "Guess who I saw out and about this afternoon? Lord High and Mighty himself, swaggering down Northgate with more lackeys than a dog has fleas. He thinks highly of himself, does that one. Not even the earl puts on such a show." Neither Justin nor Molly said anything, but Bennet must have realized that his comments could be misconstrued, for he said hastily, "Not that I meant you were one of his lackeys, Justy! It is obvious that you stand high in Fitz Alan's favor, and glad I am for it."

Justin was discomfited, well aware of how different their pasts and their prospects were. Taking refuge in humor, he said wryly, "I stand high in his favor? Hellfire, Bennet, for my first two years with him, he called me Jordan."

As he'd hoped, that got a laugh and they tucked into their meal with no further awkwardness. Molly ate as heartily as the men, but there was so much food that even three hungry young people in good health could not finish it all. Calling Berta over, Bennet instructed her to distribute the remains of their meal to God's Poor, sounding for all the world like the Earl of Chester dispensing alms to the needy. Again, Justin almost reminded him that there were enough leftovers for several suppers; again, he refrained.

The rest of the evening was spent in reminiscing, laughing over experiences that had not always seemed so amusing at the time. They remembered how Justin had taken it upon himself to defend Molly's honor when a stripling had called her a slut; since he was only twelve and his opponent seventeen, that had not ended well. Justin took their teasing in stride, and grinned when Molly confessed she'd tried to avenge them by casting a spell that turned the lout into a frog. "It did not work, alas," she confided. "But he did break out in right ugly warts!"

They recalled the time a young farrier had dared Molly to ride his gelding. She'd never even sat upon a horse's back, but she'd still scrambled up into the saddle and when she kicked it in the ribs, it bolted. "You scared us out of our wits," Bennet said, scowling at his sister as if her misdeed were still fresh and not ten years stale. "We thought sure you were going to kill yourself on that nag!"

"I remember poor Wat running down the street after you," Justin chimed in, "yelling for help in catching the horse, and someone shouting for the sheriff, thinking you were stealing it!" He also remembered that when Molly finally fell off, she'd lain there in the dust, laughing like a lunatic, saying it had been as close as she'd ever get to flying.

They shared with Molly the stories they'd been swapping the night before, and she in turn reminded them of ones they'd forgotten: the time they'd been chased up onto the Rood Cross by the miller's savage dog; the time they'd sneaked into the cemetery on All Hallow's Eve; the time they'd seen a wolf in the marshes; the time they'd won a goose at the Midsummer Fair races. But they did not talk about the times they'd gone to bed hungry or the times Justin had gotten thrashed for taking food for them from the bishop's kitchen and not once did they speak of their late, unlamented father.

Occasionally their remembrances were interrupted by a minor disturbance in the tavern, but Bennet was able to restore order without difficulty. He was drinking as much as he had been on the preceding night, and since he'd shown none of Justin's morning-after malaise, Justin thought he must regularly swill more wine than an abbey of Benedictine monks. Mindful of his disquiet earlier that day, Justin confined himself to several cups of wine, and Molly had taken her usual quota, one cup, for she'd always insisted that she could get giddy on a thimbleful and a drunken woman was like a plucked chicken, just waiting to be tossed in the pot.

When curfew rang, Bennet began to herd his customers out, a prolonged process since most of them pleaded for one more drink to tide them over till the morrow. Justin offered to see Molly safely home. When he told Bennet that he was not up to another night of serious carousing, Bennet derided him for being a "pitiful milksop" and then hurried over to the door to remind Justin that he knew where the spare key was if he decided to go back to the warehouse instead of the tavern.

Chester's streets were quiet, for most people were home and abed by then. Molly was tall for a woman and had a brisk, confident stride, easily keeping pace with Justin as they strode down the center of the street, avoiding any dark alleys that could give cover to men intent upon robbery or worse. They did not have far to go, for Molly's cottage was within shouting distance of St Mary's nunnery, and they could already see the convent walls.

"I live on Nun's Lane," Molly informed Justin gleefully, "although I daresay the nuns think I ought to be dwelling on Wanton Way! Ah, the looks I get from the good sisters when one of them ventures beyond the gate. Can you imagine, Justin, choosing to shut yourself away from the world like that? Even if that were the only way to save my eternal soul, I think I'd still balk."

"I know one who would agree wholeheartedly with that, lass," Justin said, thinking of Claudine, thinking, too, of the queen.

Molly's cottage had a thatched roof, for Chester did not have London's strict fire hazard prohibitions. Once they were inside, Molly told Justin where there was flint and tinder, and he kindled a fire in the hearth. By then she'd lit an oil lamp, and he looked about with unabashed curiosity. There was a bed in the corner, covered with a woven blanket, one high-backed wooden chair that was doubtlessly for Piers, two coffers, a wall pole for clothes, a trestle table and several stools. The room was immaculate, without a trace of dust anywhere, and the floor rushes were fresh, mingled with sweet-smelling herbs. But there was something oddly impersonal about this cottage. No one could walk in and know at once that this was Molly's home, for there was nothing of her in it, no small touches of comfort or decoration. It was almost as if she was not really living here, merely tarrying for a brief time. It was, he realized, very like the neat, sparsely furnished cottage that he rented from Gunter the smith in London.

Molly had left the door ajar, and a cat now strolled in. It was a large, grey male, sleek and well fed but bearing the scars of past combats, cocky as only a feline king of the streets could be. Most people did not view cats as pets, keeping them only to catch mice and rats, but this cat was obviously more than a mouser. It was purring and rubbing against Molly's legs with utter confidence that its overtures would be welcome, and when she stooped and picked it up, the cat draped itself across her shoulder like a pelt. "A slow night, Alexander?" she asked. "Usually you do not wander home till cockcrow."

"Alexander?" Justin said and grinned. "Whoever names a cat Alexander?"

"I do." Molly had crossed to the table and was pouring from a wineskin into a tin cup. Holding it out, she said, "You do not mind sharing with me?"

"I would be honored, my lady," he said, with his best court manners, and she smiled.

"You've grown into an interesting man, Justin, and, I suspect, far more interesting than I even know. You have not told us much about your new life, after all. Who knows what dark secrets you may be keeping from us?"

"Ask of me what you will," he offered. Their fingers touched as he took the wine cup, and even that brief touch was enough to sear his skin. He took a deep breath, but it was hard to listen to his brain when his body was sending such urgent messages.

"And would you answer my questions honestly?"

He considered and then smiled. "Mayhap not." Taking a swallow, he handed the cup back to her, watching as she drank slowly.

"My, my," she said softly, "a man who is honest about his dishonesty. Be still, my heart."

"Molly . . ."

"Do you really want to walk all the way back to the warehouse, Justin?" Her eyes were luminous, reflecting the firelight and his own desire. "You can always stay here. Of course I have only the one bed, but you said you'd not mind sharing, did you not?"

"Molly, there is not a man alive who'd say nay to you. I was daft about you for years, and not very good at hiding it. So, yes, I want to share your bed, God, yes. But I do not want to bring any trouble into your life."

"Piers?" She'd begun unfastening her veil, let it flutter to the floor at their feet. Her hair was coiled at the nape of her neck; she deftly removed the pins and then tossed her head so that it swirled about her face, cascading down her back. It was as dark as he remembered, a midnight river a man might drown in. "You need not worry about Piers," she murmured. "He does not own my body. He merely rents it on occasion."

Justin leaned over and pressed his mouth to the palm of Molly's hand. She smiled without opening her eyes and made a sound low in her throat much like her cat's purring. Turning his head, Justin realized it was the cat. It had jumped on the bed with them and was kneading the blanket with its paws, clearly staking out its territory. "I have a rival," he said, brushing his lips against her eyelids and then the corner of her mouth and getting an unblinking yellow stare from the tomcat. "I do not think your cat likes me."

"Probably not," she agreed, yawning. "He does not have much use for men." Shifting onto her side, she placed her hand on his chest. "From the way your heart is beating, I'd say I was worth waiting for."

"You seriously need to ask? If it had gotten any hotter in here, the bed would have gone up in flames."

She laughed softly, and Justin drew her closer. She nestled against his body, her breath warm on his skin. "Good night, lover."

"Good night, Molly." He stroked her hair gently, ignoring Alexander's baleful gaze, and drifted off to sleep before he could do any brooding about Bennet, Piers, or Claudine. When he awoke, several hours must have passed, for the hearth fire had burned down to embers. Molly slept peacefully beside him. She'd kicked the blanket off, her long hair trailing over the side of the bed. The cat was nowhere to be seen. Justin lay still, all his senses on the alert, for his awakening had not been natural. It came again, a muffled sound, but loud enough to have penetrated his dream. He started to sit up, listening intently, and Molly stirred.

"You want seconds already, lover? A girl does need some sleep, you know."

"Molly, listen. It sounds like people are shouting."

She cocked her head to the side, and then swung her legs over the side of the bed. "I hear it too," she said, padding across the room to the window. As soon as she opened the shutters, the noise came clearly to them both. She leaned out recklessly, heedless of her nudity, and then whirled back toward Justin. "Jesus God, fire!"

People were stumbling out of their houses into the street, some of them dressing as they ran. A few carried buckets. All looked alarmed, for the fear of fire was a primal one for city dwellers. None needed to ask for directions; they had only to follow the spiraling smoke.

As soon as she realized the fire was burning on the waterfront, Molly broke into a run, with Justin right at her heels. When she lost a shoe, she kicked the other one off rather than stop to retrieve it. To their right was the tavern, shuttered and silent. By now she was panting, but she did not slow down, for ahead of them the sky was an unearthly shade of orange.

"No, Jesu, no!" Molly's scream was swallowed up by the roar of the fire. Cinders and ashes were raining down upon the street, and the scene was bathed in eerie light, as if night had become day. People were milling about, shouting and gesturing, but not much was being done to fight the fire. One look and Justin understood why. The warehouse was already engulfed in flames.

"Bennet!" Molly lunged forward, only to be stopped by a burly man with a smoke-blackened face. She fought him until Justin caught her, grabbing her wrists and dragging her back.

"Molly, it is too late!"

"No!" She sobbed and scratched his hands, coughing as the wind blew smoke into their faces. It was so hot that breathing had become painful. More embers were being sucked up into the sky, and heads followed their drifting path, watching in horror as they were wafted toward other homes. Molly still resisted as Justin sought to get her farther away from the flames. There was a rumble and the roof collapsed in a shower of sparks and cinders.

"No!" Molly gave an anguished cry, but she no longer struggled against Justin's restraining hold. "Bennet!"

11

August 1193
Chester, England

The wind had carried embers onto the roof of a dockside alehouse, and people hastily formed a bucket brigade, taking water directly from the river. The warehouse had been set apart from the other buildings, deliberately buffered by open space. Piers's neighbors had thought it a shameful waste of good land and speculated that he wanted privacy for his illegal dealings. They benefited now from the isolation of the warehouse, and although people across the street were dragging what belongings they could from their houses, it was soon apparent that Chester would be spared a conflagration.

The city sheriff, Will Gamberell, arrived on the scene and took charge, sending his men into the throng of spectators to find witnesses. By now the crowd was a large one, and it was obvious from their murmurings that many of them had known Bennet. Several women began to weep, and Justin assumed they were his friend's bedmates. He had never felt like this—utterly numb, aware of no pain or grief, only an overwhelming sense of unreality. He watched the sheriff, the wailing women, Bennet's blazing tomb, and it was as if he were unable to accept the evidence of his own eyes and ears. He kept waiting to wake up.

Molly was sitting on an overturned wheelbarrow, her eyes never moving from the hellfire the warehouse had become. She did not speak, and when Justin sought to coax her into leaving, she did not seem to hear him. Her flame-lit face was expressionless, empty of emotion. Although he had his hand on her shoulder, it seemed to Justin that she had gone away, gone where none could follow.

After a while, the sheriff walked over. His eyes flicked to Justin, speculative and suspicious, before shifting to Molly. "This is likely a waste of breath, but if you know anything about this, now is the time to tell me. Who hated your brother enough to want him dead?" She did not react, and he said impatiently, "Do you understand what I just said? This fire did not happen by mischance, a candle knocked over. It was deliberately set."

Justin drew a breath sharp as a blade. "You are sure of that?"

"The first men to discover the fire said it was burning at both doors, front and rear, and it looked like kindling had been used to get it going. There was a trail of straw across the yard, that wheelbarrow had been left behind, and the air reeked of tallow. Now mayhap this was meant as a warning for Piers Fitz Turold. But it may well be that your brother was the quarry in this hunt. It was no secret that he slept there at night."

Molly gazed at him impassively, saying nothing, and the sheriff turned away with a muttered oath, sounding more vexed than surprised by her lack of cooperation. A stir at the end of the street heralded the arrival of the Earl of Chester and Lord Fitz Alan and their men. Chester nodded in acknowledgment to Justin as their eyes met, and he then beckoned to the sheriff. After a brief interrogation, he withdrew, apparently satisfied that the city was not in danger. Thomas de Caldecott was one of his escorts. He, too, noticed Justin, stopped abruptly, and then mustered a polite wave before hastening after his lord.

Fitz Alan lingered at the scene, letting loose a barrage of brusque questions that soon had the Chester sheriff bristling. To the east, the dawning sun struggled to break through the clouds of grey smoke. Once the alehouse fire was safely doused, a number of its rescuers pushed their way inside to celebrate their success. The crowd was dwindling rapidly.

Justin slid his arm around Molly's waist and got her onto her feet. "Come on, Molly-cat," he said gently. "Let's go home."

She looked at him blankly. "No one has called me that for so long . . ." Tears welled in her eyes, began to spill down her cheeks, and Justin drew her close. The shoulder of his tunic was soon wet and he could feel her body trembling, but she made no sound, and he'd never seen anything as heartrending as this mute, dazed grieving, silent and wholly without hope.

People soon started turning up at Molly's cottage: neighbors carrying kettles of soup, fresh-baked bread, and clay pitchers of ale, Bennet's friends and alehouse customers, a few tearful young women with heavily powdered faces and swollen eyes. The parish priest stopped by, too. He was very young and clearly had little experience yet in consoling the bereaved, his fumbling for words of comfort painful to watch.

To them all, Molly offered courtesy, but little else. She spoke rarely, nodded occasionally, but all the while her eyes were turning inward, her dark, dilated pupils reflecting no light at all, hers the unfocused, vacant stare of the newly blinded. Justin stayed by her side, ignoring the curious glances of the mourners, holding Molly's hand tightly, as if the clasp of flesh and blood and bone could somehow serve as a lifeline for them both.

People did not tarry, soon found excuses to slip away,

and at last they had all gone but Berta, the alehouse serving maid. As Berta puttered about the cottage, wiping away tears with her sleeve, Molly looked up at Justin, and for the first time in hours, he felt that she actually saw him. "When they find his body," she whispered, "will you . . . ?"

"I'll take care of it, all of it," he said huskily and refused to let himself think about what he'd just promised to do.

"I want . . ."

"What, Molly? Tell me."

Tears were brimming in her eyes again. "I want," she said in a small voice, "to get drunk, so drunk that I never have to sober up . . ."

So did Justin. He craved oblivion at that moment as he'd never craved anything in his life. He knew Molly had never fancied the taste of ale, but it was all they had and he was pouring out a cupful for her as Berta finally ceased her aimless meandering and went over to answer another knock at the door. A moment later, she let out such a bloodcurdling scream that Justin spilled half of the ale into the floor rushes.

"Christ Jesus!" He spun around to see Berta backing away from the door, her eyes wide, blessing herself with a shaking hand. And then there was another cry, this time from Molly, and he could only stare in disbelief at the man filling the doorway.

Bennet had never looked worse, his skin so sickly white he seemed bloodless, his eyes reddened and puffy, his hair as tangled as uncombed wool. "Molly," he said and held out his arms as she flew across the cottage into his embrace. They hugged each other so tightly that neither seemed to be breathing, as Berta continued to retreat and Justin stood, frozen, not yet able to credit this incredible mercy by their God. Opening his eyes, Bennet saw Justin for the first time and gave a sigh of relief before smiling down tenderly into his sister's tear-streaked face.

"It is really me," he said. "I am not a ghost, Molly—" His head jerked sideways then, as Molly slapped him across the mouth.

"Where were you? Damn you for doing this to me, Bennet, damn you!" She did not wait for him to react, buried her face in his shoulder again, and they stood motionless for a time, clinging together like shipwreck victims who'd at last reached shore. And as his own eyes blurred with tears, it occurred to Justin that Molly and Bennet had a bond that went deeper than blood. They were survivors, having weathered childhood storms together that would have destroyed either one of them alone.

Berta had gone to spread the word that Bennet had not died in the fire. Molly, Justin, and Bennet shared what was left of the ale and gathered around the trestle table as Bennet explained that he'd never gone back to the warehouse, deciding instead to spend the night with a friend. "I was already flying high, and we drained a few more flagons dry after I got there. The next thing I remember, it was daylight and I felt so vile I did not get out of bed till noon. I was heading for the warehouse when I ran into Alys, the barber's wife, and she well nigh swooned away at the sight of me. After she stopped stuttering and made some sense, I . . . well, I did not believe her, not until I saw the smoking ruins for myself . . ."

He fell silent, and Justin understood why. It must have been like gazing down into his open grave. "Thank the Lord that you took it into your head to go looking for a lass!"

"Yes," Molly said, but with none of Justin's enthusiasm. "This 'friend' of yours . . . by any chance could it have been Monday?"

Bennet looked sheepish. "Well, yes . . ." he admitted, adding for Justin's benefit, "Moll does not like Monday very much—"

"I like her not at all," Molly said and scowled at her brother. "I thought you said it was done between the two of you. God's Truth, Justin, this woman has feathers where her brains ought to be. She is greedy, sly, flighty—"

"So she must be blazing-hot in bed," Justin blurted out, for he was still so euphoric over Bennet's miraculous resurrection that he had a drunkard's control of his tongue. Molly glared at him, but Bennet burst out laughing and Justin soon joined in, theirs the shaken, giddy laughter of men reprieved on the steps of the gallows. Molly glowered at them both, and then she began to laugh, too, for they'd all seen enough of life to understand how rare it was to cuckold death.

Bennet ran his hands through his tousled hair, for a moment resting his palms against his eyes, like a man with a pounding headache, or one trying to blot a harrowing vision from his brain. "When I saw the warehouse this afternoon—what was left of it—I truly feared that you might have died for me, Justin. I know I have enemies, but who hates me enough to want to see me fried?" He could not repress a shudder. "God, what a way to die . . ."

He smiled at them then, as if fearing he'd revealed too much. "One suspect comes to mind—that lump of lard from the French cog. He seemed the sort to nurse a grudge."

"Can we dismiss any jealous husbands out of hand?" Molly gibed, and Bennet made her grin by crossing his eyes as if they were still bairns.

"Of course," Bennet said, sounding more cheerful, "it may well be that I got a message meant for Piers. Wait till he hears about this . . . Jesu! It could have been worse, though. The fire could have happened last week when he had far more to lose."

Justin had no interest in what Piers may have been smuggling, for he had much more on his mind than the law-breaking of a Chester vintner. "There is another possibility," he said slowly. "The fire might have been set for me."

That got their immediate attention. They both turned to stare at him, Molly looking dubious and Bennet downright skeptical. "I doubt that, Justy," he said, with a smile that was somewhat patronizing. "Who's more likely to have enemies with murder on their mind? Piers and me? Or someone who passes his days in the company of lords and ladies and bishops?"

"There are things you do not know, Bennet, that I have not told you. I am not in Chester to do Fitz Alan's bidding. I am hunting for a large sum of money, money that has already cost the lives of three men, mayhap more." Justin glanced from one to the other. "If this is my fault, Bennet, I'll never forgive myself. I truly did not think I was putting you in jeopardy—"

"You do not know that you have," Molly said briskly. "We know you, Justin. Give you some time to brood and you'll be blaming yourself for King Richard's capture and the flooding in Shrewsbury last spring. Ere you start with the mea culpas, tell us why you think someone wanted you dead, and badly enough to risk setting the entire town ablaze."

"You know about the ransom being demanded for the king's safe return," Justin said, and they nodded in unison.

"Who does not, with the Crown bleeding the realm white for the ransom." Bennet did not sound as if he considered the ransom money well spent. "What does that have to do with you, Justin?"

"A goodly portion of the ransom went missing in

Wales. I am one of the men trying to find it. I was in North Wales ere I came to Chester, at the court of the Welsh prince Davydd. He is blaming his nephew in the hopes that the Crown will send knights and men-at-arms to put down a rising against him. But it is a lie. The ransom was stolen by three Flemish sailors and the outlaw who hired them. And I am the only one who knows what truly happened. Now ask me again, Bennet, if you think I have a secret worth killing for."

"You've convinced me," Bennet said dryly. "Money is always worth killing for. But why does Fitz Alan not know this, too? Why are you keeping it from him?"

"Because I am no longer in Fitz Alan's service. Whilst I am trying to recover the missing ransom, I answer to the Earl of Chester."

There was a long silence. "God's Blood," Bennet said softly, "what have you gotten yourself into, Justin?"

Justin shrugged, looking over at Molly. She'd so far been silent, her face not easy to read. As their eyes met, she shrugged, too. "I did say you were a man with secrets, did I not?" she murmured. "So you tracked these Flemish sailors to Chester. Did you find them here?"

Justin shook his head. "They never came back to their ship. There is a man who may have some of the answers I seek, but he has balked at talking with me. He is suspicious and who can blame him? Even worse for me, he speaks only Flemish."

"Is that your problem? I can solve that for you just like this," Molly said, snapping her fingers. "A friend of mine speaks Flemish and she is also very good, indeed, at getting men to do her bidding."

"Barbele?" Bennet asked, and when she nodded, he grinned at Justin. "Moll is right. Barbele could lure the Devil out of Hell and yes, I speak from very pleasant experience."

"How good is her Flemish?" Justin asked, and Molly grinned, too.

"It is her mother tongue," she said triumphantly. "Her grandfather was one of the Flemings that the first King Henry settled in South Wales. Barbele still has kin down in Pembrokeshire, but she grew up here in Chester. So . . . shall we ask her to bedazzle this stubborn sailor of yours?"

"I'd be much beholden to you, Molly," he said, and she winked as Bennet pushed away from the table and got to his feet.

"I'd best find a man to ride to Wich Malbank and spoil Piers's week. I am also going to put the word about that Piers will pay to find out who burned his warehouse, and pay well. With luck, we might learn who was the true target last night. No offense, Justin, but I hope it is you and not me!"

"You took the words right out of my mouth," Justin said and they both laughed.

Molly was not amused. "If you two do not mind, I'd rather not jest about which one of you was supposed to be turned into kindling last night!"

"You are not usually so squeamish, Moll," Bennet teased, leaning over to give her a hug. "I'd say we were both lucky beyond belief, Justin. Where were you, anyway? Why did you not go back to the warehouse?"

Justin hesitated, not wanting to lie to Bennet but not wanting to tell him the truth, either. Bennet had always been quick; he glanced from Justin to Molly and then to the rumpled, unmade bed. "Well," he drawled, "you did not waste any time, did you, old friend?"

Justin could not blame Bennet, for he was sure that if he'd had a sister, he would be protective of her, too. That did make it difficult, though, to offer a defense. Fortunately for him, Molly was more than up to the task.

"What, you think he seduced me? Do not be stupid, Bennet. I may not have many choices in this life, but I damned well pick my own bedmates!"

Justin had once been told by a Norwegian trader that when they'd still worshipped the old gods, men believed that one who was slain in battle would be welcomed into Valhala or Paradise by beautiful, flaxen-haired maidens, the daughters of Odin. It was a pagan superstition, of course, but he could see how it might appeal to men facing death, and it had lingered in his memory. When he first saw Molly's friend, Barbele, he remembered, for she was almost as tall as he was, big-boned, with a plenitude of womanly curves, a mass of hair the color of honey, a lusty laugh, and a surprisingly carefree disposition for a woman who made her living in one of the most precarious of professions.

"Is that all you need done?" she asked blithely, waving her hand as if it were already accomplished. Justin described Rutger to her and told her where she could find him, at the alehouse where Baltazar had said he'd been passing all his days in port. She was so confident of her powers to charm that she waved aside Justin's offer of partial payment, saying she was content to wait until she'd gotten him the information he needed, adding playfully that she was not usually so trusting of men, but if Molly trusted him enough to take him into her bed, that was good enough for her.

They left her standing in the doorway of the bawdy house and continued down Cuppinges Lane. This was one of the more sinful streets of the city, and it amused Justin that it was in such close proximity to St Mary's nunnery. If the good sisters thought Molly was an unseemly neighbor, he wondered how they dealt with the bawdy house whores. "So how did she know we'd lain together?" he asked. "You introduced me only as a child-hood friend."

"Women always know." Slipping her arm through his, she turned to wave a final farewell to Barbele. "Let's stop at the cook shop, Justin, ere we go home. I do not think either one of us has eaten since yesterday eve, and I am for certes not in the mood to cook. Ah, wait, I forgot—we have the food that the neighbors brought. Unless we have to give it back now that Bennet is not dead!" She giggled at that, sounding like the Molly of memory, and he felt a vast, sweeping relief that she'd been spared more grief.

"I am still not sure I ought to go back to the cottage with you," he began, and she reached up to lay her fingers against his lips.

"Hush, now, we've already settled that. I truly would feel safer with you than if I slept alone tonight. And Bennet said he was going to put men to guarding all of Piers's properties till he gets back from Wich Malbank, and that includes the cottage. I doubt that there is a need for all that, but Bennet does love to spend Piers's money. For that matter, so do I!"

Justin knew he was making a mistake, but he could not help himself. "Have you given any thought, Molly, to what you'd do if you did not have Piers to keep you in such comfort? There must be other means to earn a liveli-hood—"

"Name three," she challenged. "Unless you want me to earn my bread on my back the way Barbele does, I'd say I'm doing right well for myself these days."

Justin was not ready to concede defeat. "But surely Bennet makes enough for the both of you with all he does for Piers?"

"I make more," she said matter-of-factly. "Ah, Justin, you are talking of plans and prospects as if such things were ever within my grasp. If I've learned nothing else in this life, it is that to plan for the morrow is folly, especially for the likes of Bennet and me. Now you . . . it may be different for you. It does sound as if you've risen in the world since we last met, lover. For example, you said that you 'answer to the Earl of Chester,' but I got the sense that this was temporary. Who do you answer to the rest of the time?"

"You would not believe me, lass, if I told you."

She gave him a pensive, speculative look that promised further interrogation. But before she could persevere, Justin heard his name called out behind him. "De Quincy!" He swung around, pulling Molly with him, to see Thomas de Caldecott striding toward them.

Thomas was smiling. "This is better luck than I expected, for I've been searching the town for you. The earl wants to know when we'll be returning to Wales." His eyes had already moved from Justin to Molly, subjecting her to an appraisal that was so openly admiring it evaded giving offense. "Are you not going to introduce me to your lovely lady, Justin? I understand now why we've seen so little of you at the castle!"

"Mistress Molly, may I present Sir Thomas de Caldecott?" Justin said, hoping he did not sound as trapped as he felt, and Thomas at once shifted into his courtier mode, kissing Molly's hand with a gallant flourish. Justin took some solace from Molly's composure. Unlike so many of the women he'd seen exposed to Thomas's practiced charm, she did not appear to be in immediate danger of succumbing to the knight's seductive smile and beguiling blue eyes.

Thomas turned his attention back to Justin then, saying candidly, "Look, about our earlier dispute, I want to offer my apologies. I ought not to have flared up like that. But you made me look foolish in the earl's eyes, and

I have my fair share of vanity. I hope you are not one for holding grudges?"

"No, Thomas, I am not."

"Glad I am to hear it. Well, I'll not intrude further upon your time with the fair Molly. What should I tell the earl about your plans?"

"Tell him," Justin said, "that I expect to be done in Chester by week's end," and Thomas bent over Molly's hand again. But as he started to turn away, Justin suddenly remembered something that the knight had shared during their ride into Wales.

"Thomas!" The other man glanced over his shoulder, a quizzical smile upon his face that disappeared with Justin's next words. "I was curious about something. I envy you your gift for languages. I was wondering if you'd ever learned any Flemish?"

Thomas's smile came back. "No, I cannot say that I have," he said, sounding faintly puzzled by the question. "Well . . . a pleasure, Mistress Molly. Justin, I'll see you at the castle, and I'll tell the earl that we'll be departing soon."

They stood watching as Thomas sauntered off. As soon as he was out of earshot, Molly said, "That one fancies himself too much for my taste. Why did you ask if he spoke Flemish?"

"I know little about the outlaw leader, only that he spoke both Welsh and Flemish. Thomas is quite fluent in Welsh, and I remembered his telling me that his mother was raised in Pembrokeshire."

"Ah, I see. But by asking him straight out, did you not risk putting him on the alert?"

"I hope so," he said, and she frowned.

"What are you doing, setting a trap with you as the bait?"

"I'd not go that far. I have no proof that Thomas is involved in any of this, just random suspicions. I might well be wronging him," Justin admitted. "Only time will tell."

"And so you think to get your proof by letting him know you are putting all the pieces together. That is well and good if he is innocent. But if he is indeed guilty, you could end up with your throat cut!"

"Have you so little confidence in my skill with a sword?" he joked, but Molly found no humor in his predicament.

"Sometimes I think men do not have the sense God gave to sheep," she said, with an aggrieved toss of her head. "We'll let that be for now, though. I'd much rather talk about what he called you . . . de Quincy."

Justin had known it was foolish to hope she'd missed that; Molly missed very little. "What? I think you misheard."

"The Devil I did. I have to admit that I was taken aback, too. I thought that was a secret buried too deep to be dug up."

Justin stared at her in astonishment. "You knew?"

"Well, not for certes," she said, sounding rather pleased with herself. "I had my suspicions, though."

Justin was incredulous. "Why?"

"Because he was good to you, Justin. Did you never wonder why?"

"I knew why. I was an orphan with none to look after me, and he took me in as an act of Christian charity."

"He was a priest, not a saint," she scoffed. "Not to let you starve to death—that is both commendable and believable. But he went beyond that, Justin. He brought you with him from Shrewsbury when he was made Chester's archdeacon. He did more than make sure you were fed and clothed. He saw to it that you were educated, that you had the schooling few foundlings ever get. For a time,

I thought that you might be the bastard get of a kinsman of his. The only other explanation I could think of was that he was one of those with a liking for boys, and—"

"Jesus God, Molly!"

Justin sounded so repulsed that she suppressed a smile. "I did not believe it! Word gets around when a man has a vice like that, and I never heard even a whisper that the bishop was depraved in that manner. Moreover, I could tell that you were not being maltreated, for you'd not have been able to hide that from us. But I knew there was more to this than your 'Christian charity.' And then, when the bishop placed you in Lord Fitz Alan's household like that, I realized there was only one possible answer. You were his son."

"But you never said, you never even hinted—"

"Why would I? It was plain that you had no suspicions of your own, so what would it have served to share mine? I did not think it even mattered that much, for I was sure it would never come out. That is why I am so astounded by this. I would have wagered any sum that he'd never tell you, much less acknowledge you!"

"He did not," Justin said bleakly. "I found out on my own and when I confronted him, he finally admitted it. And he has never acknowledged me, Molly, nor will he."

"But you use his name," she protested. "Are you saying you just . . . took it?" When he nodded, she whistled softly. "My heavens! That was very brave of you, Justin, or very foolhardy, mayhap both."

He could hardly explain that England's queen had given him the courage to claim the de Quincy name. "Does Bennet know . . . ?" Relieved when she shook her head, he said, "I'd rather you said nothing of this to him, Molly. I know it is unfair to ask you to keep secrets from him, but—"

She interrupted with laughter. "We keep secrets from

each other all the time, Justin. How else do we get along so well? You need not worry. I'll keep quiet for your sake . . . and for the bishop's."

That was the last thing Justin had expected her to say. "For his sake?"

He sounded so confounded that she gave him a surprised look. "Yes, for his sake, too. He tried to do right by you, lover, as much as he was able. There are far worse fathers in this world than one who cannot acknowledge you as his," she said quietly, and Justin could not argue with that.

Molly's revelation had brought them both to a halt. Now she tugged at his arm, saying, "Come, let's go home." They walked without speaking for several moments. From time to time, Molly glanced over at him, her eyes narrowed in thought. "So once Barbele gets you the information you need, you'll go back to Wales, to the court of this Welsh prince?" When he nodded, she said, "And you'll go with this Thomas de Caldecott, even knowing that he might have an excellent reason to wish you dead." It was not a question, for she already knew the answer, and they continued on toward her cottage in silence.

12

August 1193
Chester, England

As Justin and Molly entered the tavern, Bennet looked up in surprise. "Rather early in the day for the two of you, is it not? Now these poor sots . . ." With a genial wave of his hand toward the handful of regular customers. "If I did not chase them out at night, they'd never see the light of day, happily living out their lives here. But I've never seen you come by at this hour, Moll. Justin leading you astray?"

Justin hoped he was joking. Sometimes it was hard to tell with Bennet. "Barbele sent me word this morn that we should meet her here at midday. With luck, this may mean she has news for us about Rutger."

Bennet made no further comment, but once they were seated, he joined them with a flagon and several cups. "The sheriff paid me a call this morn," he said. "He was trying manfully to bear up under his disappointment, but I fear my resurrection is a hard morsel for him to swallow. I suspect he did not believe me even after I'd sworn upon our sainted father's soul that I knew nothing about the fire."

Molly's mouth thinned and she muttered "hellspawn" under her breath, but Justin was not sure if it was meant for her "sainted father" or the Chester sheriff or perhaps both. Before she could clarify, she saw someone passing by the open door of the tavern and jumped to her feet.

169

"Beatrix, wait! I need a word with you." Flinging an "I'll be back" over her shoulder, she hastened out into the street.

This was the first time that the men had been alone since Bennet had learned why Justin had not been in the warehouse that night, and the silence that followed was not a comfortable one. Justin raised his cup, set the wine down untasted, and finally said, although he knew how hollow the words would sound, "Bennet, I'd cut off my arm ere I'd ever hurt Molly . . ."

Bennet gave a noncommittal grunt. "Well, that was not the body part I had in mind for you to forfeit." But then he smiled. "Ah, Hell and damnation, Justin, I cannot pretend it did not take me aback. Once I thought about it, though, I decided that Moll could have done much worse . . . and has," he added, and Justin knew the same man was in both their minds: the notorious vintner, Piers Fitz Turold. "Just remember that if any hearts get broken, it damned well better be yours!"

They clinked their cups together, mutually relieved to have this moment over and done with, and after that, they kept their conversation on familiar ground, trading amiable insults until Molly returned. She'd no sooner reclaimed her seat than the door opened again, this time admitting Barbele, trailed by an obviously nervous Rutger. He looked as if he might bolt at any time, but Barbele was having none of that. Ignoring his skittishness, she linked her arm in his and steered him across the room toward their table.

"I have fetched for you this sweet man," she announced, "so he may tell you what he knows." Settling onto the bench, she drew Rutger down beside her and promptly took control of the conversation. "Rutger is sore afraid for his cousin Karl. But he does not want to get Karl into trouble with the law."

"Tell him," Justin said, "that I have no interest in punishing Karl or the others. I want only to find the stolen money and the man who convinced them to take part in the robbery. From what I know, I do not think Karl realized what he was getting himself into."

Barbele at once unleashed a torrent of words upon Rutger, gesturing with animation. England had been a bilingual land for more than a hundred years. Molly and Bennet spoke both English and French, and Justin could make himself understood in three languages, while able to read Latin, too. But Flemish was an utter mystery to him, and for all of Barbele's goodwill, he wished he did not have to rely so completely upon this bossy, blonde stranger.

"Rutger says he does not know very much, but he will tell you what he can. He says their family would be shamed if this becomes known. He is coming to think, though, that not ever knowing Karl's fate might be worse. He wants you to understand that Karl is not a bad man, merely a young and foolish one. He is sure that Karl and Geertje were talked into it by that malcontent Joder. Joder was ever one for dreaming big dreams, and Karl . . . he has a wife and baby to provide for back in Ypres." So thoroughly had Barbele thrown herself into her role that she now twitched her shoulders in unconscious imitation of Rutger's mournful shrug.

After another rapid exchange between the two, Barbele resumed Rutger's story. "Karl told him that Joder knew a lord who wanted them to do a robbery. They'd be stealing from foreigners and it was supposed to be right easy. No one need get hurt and they'd make much money, more than Karl could ever earn at sea."

"Did Karl ever mention a name? Did he say where they met this . . . this lord?"

Again, Barbele conferred with Rutger. "No, he never said any names. He thought the man was a lord because he wore a sword and was comfortable giving orders, like a ship's master. He does not know how Joder and the lord knew each other. They met with the lord at the alehouse, the one where you first saw him. He has been going back there every day, hoping he might hear something, hoping Karl might walk in of a sudden . . ."

Barbele stopped, and Justin saw that tears had begun to well in Rutger's eyes. "He says he does not want you to think badly of him, but he did not know what else to do. He'd tried to make Karl see this was madness, he says he truly did."

"Is there anything else he can remember Karl saying about the man who hired them? Anything at all?"

"Karl said he spoke Flemish right well, but he was not Flemish. He was friendly, joking with them as if they were lords like him. Karl liked him, trusted what he told them."

Rutger turned aside as if to clear his throat. He spat into the floor rushes, then kept his head down for several moments as he struggled with his emotions. He had been speaking slowly, tentatively, with long pauses. But now the words came out in a rush, spilling from his mouth as if they'd burn his tongue if he did not get them said. Barbele reached over, patted his hand, and then looked at Justin.

"Rutger says his cousin and Geertje planned to come back after they'd done this thing and gotten their money. Karl was sure he could get their ship's master to take them on again. They even damaged the mainmast so the ship could not sail without them. But that was weeks ago. What has happened to them? Why have they not come back?"

When darkness fell, Molly lit several oil lamps, but shadows still lurked in the corners of the cottage. The remains of their supper were growing cold, a far cry from the days when there had never been enough food for left-overs. Molly watched as Justin stared down at his trencher, cutting another piece of cod and then forgetting again to eat it.

"Enough," she finally said, rising and grasping his hand. "If you are going to brood, better you do it in some comfort." He offered no resistance and they were soon settled on the bed. "Turn over," she ordered, and when he rolled onto his stomach, she began to knead some of the tension from his neck and shoulders. "You might as well talk about it. You cannot get that missing ransom out of your head, can you?"

"No," he conceded. "I keep going in circles, Molly, never getting anywhere."

"You do have a favorite suspect, though."

"Yes . . ." he agreed slowly, "I suppose I do. The wind does seem to be blowing in Thomas de Caldecott's direction these days." Propping himself up on his elbow, he said, "This is what I know about the man who stole the ransom. First of all, he had to be in Wales at the time of the robbery. He had to know Wales, and he had to be familiar with Davydd's court, to be trusted enough to learn somehow about Davydd's plan."

"What plan?"

"I suspect that Davydd arranged the robbery in order to blame his nephew for it," he said, and Molly burst out laughing.

"I love to hear about the crimes of the wellborn. They are so much more interesting than the sort of common misdeeds we get to commit here in Chester. Go on, though. What else do you know about this unknown suspect, whom we can call Thomas for convenience's sake?"

Justin grinned and tweaked her nose. "I know he speaks fluent Welsh and Flemish, that he handles a sword all too well, and a man must be taught that skill, Molly; no one is born knowing it. I know he is bold, clever, and without mercy. I know he is either of the gentry or able to convince people he is. According to Rutger, he can be very good company. And he must have been in Chester the night of the warehouse fire."

"So how many of those shoes fit our Thomas's feet?"

"He can wear every shoe but two, and they might also fit. I do not know if he is ruthless enough to kill in cold blood, and I do not know if he speaks Flemish. But his mother grew up in Pembrokeshire."

"You know what we say in Chester, Justin: that if a creature looks like a dog and walks like a dog and barks like a dog, most likely it is a dog."

"You'd need more proof if the dog were facing the gallows. There is another twist to this puzzle, too, for I cannot be certain if 'our Thomas' has allies or not. He may have been in league with Selwyn, Davydd's man. It is possible that Selwyn was the one who told him about the intended robbery . . ."

He fell silent until Molly poked him, saying, "You do not sound convinced of that. Who else could have told him if not Selwyn?"

"From what I've learned about Selwyn, he was too wary to betray Davydd like that on his own; he'd have needed to be talked into it. But there is a Welsh lass at Rhuddlan who is hopelessly besotted with Thomas. It may be that she overheard something and passed it on to him. I would hope not," he admitted, for he did not want to suspect Angharad, and not just because he liked her. God help Rhun if she were not as innocent as she seemed to be.

"Do you have any other suspects besides Thomas?" she asked, and he smiled ruefully.

"I did for a time. As odd as it sounds, I did entertain

the thought that William Fitz Alan might somehow be involved in all this."

Molly's green eyes flashed. "Let it be so, Lord, for that would be a such a boon for Bennet!" Seeing his surprise, she smiled, somewhat sadly. "I know it was not easy for you, being sent off to Shropshire like that, having to leave the only world you knew, the only friends you had. But it was harder for Bennet, for he was the one left behind. I think he has borne a grudge against Fitz Alan ever since. As for me, I find it unlikely that Fitz Alan is guilty. This mysterious outlaw is said to be affable and charming, no? Well, when was the last time you heard those words applied to Fitz Alan?"

"That did occur to me, too. For the life of me, I cannot imagine Fitz Alan skulking around waterfront alehouses, treating Flemish sailors as if they were his peers. Moreover, I cannot find a satisfactory motive for the man, Molly. I could see Thomas doing it for the money, but not Fitz Alan. He already has what most men can only dream of—he is highborn, a baron with multiple manors, sheriff of a prosperous shire, in favor with the Crown. I do not think he would ever jeopardize all of that for material gain."

"So what are the motives for murder and mayhem and robbery? What will men kill for?" She gave him no chance to reply, ticking her answers off on her fingers. "Greed, lust, hatred, love, fear, vengeance. What did I forget? If I had to guess which one of *these* shoes might fit Fitz Alan's big feet, I think I'd go with . . . lust."

Justin raised an eyebrow. "Have you seen the Lady Emma, then?"

Molly nodded. "Every year she graces the midsummer fair with her presence."

"Women do not fancy the lady much, do they?"

"I do not imagine that the poor worker bees have much

fondness for the queen bee, either. Of course the drones adore her . . . until after they mate with her and die."

"Whoa!" Laughing, Justin leaned over and hugged her. "Ah, Mistress Molly, I've missed that sharp tongue of yours. And for what it is worth, I am not one of Lady Emma's drones. Now tell me why you dislike her."

"She has a cold heart, overweening pride, and no pity for the less fortunate. She saunters about the city as if she were the Queen of England, with her nose so high in the air she is in danger of drowning every time it rains. But I doubt that she'd ever take Fitz Alan as her lover, and I doubt that he'd take such a risk for her unless she did."

Justin found it very interesting that Molly and Angharad both seemed to share the same opinion of Davydd's consort. "A friend posed a riddle to me about the Lady Emma: 'When is virtue not a virtue?' I think you may have answered it for me, lass."

"Exactly," she said triumphantly. "She deserves no credit for keeping her marriage vows if she remains faithful only because she can find no lovers worthy of her! This friend of yours . . . is she one of Emma's handmaidens?"

"Yes . . . but how did you know the friend was female?"

"Because that was a woman's riddle. Unless the woman is blood-kin, men are more interested in her lack of virtue." They smiled and leaned toward each other, their lips almost touching when there was a sudden pounding at the door.

"It's me," a familiar voice announced. "And I'm giving you fair warning, as I do not want to see anything that will rob me of sleep at night!"

Justin swung off the bed, crossed the chamber to unlatch the door for Bennet. From the corner of his eye, he saw Molly straightening out the blanket, smoothing away the indentations of their bodies, no more eager than he was to flaunt their new intimacy in front of her brother. Not for the first time, he found himself hoping that he had not made a great mistake by bedding Molly. He of all men ought to have remembered the dangers of unintended consequences, and if he did not, he knew Claudine, cloistered and pregnant, would have been more than willing to remind him.

Sliding the bolt back, he let Bennet in, saying, "We've just gotten done with supper. There is fish left if you're hungry." Molly had moved to the table and was already spooning some of the food onto a trencher for her brother. They joined him around the table while he ate, breaking off chunks of bread to soak up the garlic sauce. Only after he finished the last mouthful of cod did he relax against the cushion in Piers's high-backed chair.

"We've all heard that old saying, that dogs do not eat other dogs. Thankfully, it does not hold true for thieves and cutthroats."

Molly's head came up quickly. "You've found out who fired the warehouse?"

Bennet's smile somehow managed to be both grim and complacent. "Chester has more than its share of lawless men. But if you had to pick the greediest and the most foolhardy, Moll, who would it be?"

She gave that a moment's thought, then her mouth dropped open. "No! Not the miller brothers?"

Justin glanced from one to the other. "Millers who are thieves, too? I know people take that as gospel. But most millers have so many opportunities to cheat their customers that they have no need to resort to outright law-breaking."

Bennet was grinning. "Nay, they are not truly millers. Hubert and Kenelm are petty thieves who've always yearned to be infamous evildoers. They are big and strong enough to be hired when someone needs brawn or brute force, but no one would use them for anything that requires brains. They'd steal mother's milk from a new-born babe, though, and that is God's Truth. One day a while back, I'd caught them trying to rob a cupshotten friend of mine and threw them out of the tavern. Soon after, a couple of customers started complaining about getting cheated at the Dee Mill, and one of them asked the tavern and the world at large if there was any thief worse than a miller. I was still thinking about those two louts and blurted out their names. We all laughed, but it stuck and ever since, they've been known as the miller brothers."

"And you are sure the miller brothers are the ones who set the fire? Do you know who hired them?"

"No names," Bennet admitted, "but they were hired by another 'lord,' and I think we can safely assume he is the same one who was lurking around waterfront alehouses with those missing Flemish sailors. So it looks like you win the wager, Justin. The miller brothers were working for your enemy, not mine."

"How did you find out about them, Bennet?"

"The usual way a crime is solved around here—they were sold out by their own. Their cousin Edred came running to me as soon as he heard about the reward being offered. According to him, they were paid to burn the warehouse down and told to do it in the middle of the night, which proves the intent was murder. They got some of the money then, the rest to come afterward. But when Hubert went to the agreed-upon meeting place, the 'lord' never came. I suppose he was only willing to pay if there'd been a pile of charred bones."

Molly flinched. "Bennet, stop it," she said, and he gave her an apologetic smile before turning back to Justin.

"Anyway, the miller brothers were hung out to dry in a

very cold wind. It seems they were not the total idiots we thought they were. Even they realized that it was not a good idea to make an enemy of Piers Fitz Turold, and they were planning to depart Chester as soon as they were paid. So . . . they panicked when they did not get paid and tried to borrow money from Cousin Edred. The rest you know."

"What happens to the miller brothers now?"

"I expect that we've seen the last of them, even if they have to beg their bread by the side of the road. They know they have far more to fear from Piers than from the law."

Justin was toying with one of the table knives, running his thumb along the dulled edge. It was not as blunt as he thought, though, and a thin, crimson thread became visible on his skin. This was not the first time that someone had sought to kill him. Gilbert the Fleming had come very close in Gunter's stable. Durand de Curzon had dumped him in a Windsor dungeon, in danger of being hanged as a spy, and to this day, he was not sure how he'd managed to win John over. But nothing had ever filled him with so much fury—or so much regret—as the attempt to murder him in the fire at Piers Fitz Turold's warehouse.

Becoming aware of the silence, he glanced up, found that his friends were watching him intently. Before he could speak, though, Molly reached across the table and covered his hand with hers. "Lord help us, Bennet, he has that remorseful penitent's look on his face."

Bennet cocked his head to the side. "By God, lass, you're right. Have some mercy, Justin. This was not your fault. We know that and you know that, so talking about it again will be even more tiresome than your confessions usually are."

Justin did his best to match their banter, insisting that

his parish priest always called his confessions "thought-provoking and compelling," but his words rang false even in his own ears. What if he'd been followed to Molly's cottage?

He looked so troubled that Molly did her best to distract him as soon as Bennet had risen and was no longer looking at them, bringing his hand up to her mouth and licking the scratch on his thumb as delicately as a cat. He smiled at her, but his eyes remained somber, and she sighed, let his hand slide out of hers.

"I thought that I was being followed," he said. "I never saw anyone, but there were a few times when I could feel the hair rise on the back of my neck."

"Well, you *were* being followed," Bennet commented. "We know that for certes now. How else could this murderous lord of yours find out that you were sleeping at the warehouse?"

They looked at each other and the same thought hit them at the same time. There was only one night when Justin could have been followed to the warehouse, the night they'd gotten so drunk together.

Bennet sucked in his breath. "Hell's bells, Justin, we were in no shape to fend off a one-legged beggar that night. Why did he not take advantage of an opportunity like that?"

Justin was quiet for a few moments, dredging up hazy, wine-drenched memories. "Mayhap he meant to, Bennet. Mayhap we're still alive only because he was scared off . . ."

Bennet's expression was perplexed. "Scared off? By what . . . ?" And then he understood Justin's meaning and his eyes widened. "Jesu, the Watch!"

"What are you talking about?" Molly demanded. "Tell me!"

Neither one wanted to answer her. It was Justin who said at last, "We almost ran into the Watch that night, ducked into an alley just in time. I cannot help wondering what might have happened if they'd not been patrolling."

Molly stared at them and then shivered, instinctively blessing herself. "I think we know what would have happened," she said, sounding both angry and frightened. "You both would likely have died . . . at the hands of the same man who'll be riding at your side, Justin, as you go back into Wales."

The sky had taken on the pale, milky pearl color of an August dawn when Justin arrived at Molly's cottage. She opened the door at once, already dressed, looking tired and wan.

"We will be departing within the hour," Justin said. "So I came to bid you farewell."

She nodded briefly, then handed him a small sack. "I packed some food for you, just bread and cheese . . ."

"Thank you," he said politely, and a silence fell, not broken until he took her in his arms. "I am not going to die in Wales, Molly. I mean to sleep with one eye open, I promise you."

"From your lips to God's Ear," she said, sounding more resigned than reassured. "I will walk with you back to the castle, for Bennet is going to meet us there."

"Bennet is actually going to be awake at this ungodly hour? The only time he's seen a sunrise is when he was up all night."

"Well, he said he'd be there." As Justin helped her with her mantle, Molly glanced around at the cottage to make sure all was in order. "He has a favor to ask of you. A friend of Berta's would like to ride with you. He has some Welsh blood and has kin living not far from Rhuddlan. Bennet thought it would be safer for him to travel in your company."

Justin wondered just how safe his company was going to be, but he agreed to take Berta's friend along, and they stepped out into cool, morning air that reminded one and all that summer was on the wane. They walked in silence for the most part as the city slowly came to life. By the time they reached the castle walls, Chester was bracing for another day.

Bennet was indeed there, yawning and blinking like a bat unused to bright light. "If you do get yourself killed in Wales," he complained, "at least have the decency to spare us a daybreak funeral. Did Molly tell you about Rolf? He is around here someplace, or he was . . ." Giving another huge yawn, he glanced about the street and then beckoned to a man leaning against a tree in St Mary's churchyard.

The man introduced to Justin as Rolf was not one to warrant a second glance. He was dressed in a dun tunic and mantle, a drab shade that matched his unkempt, long hair and shaggy beard. The only notable thing about his appearance was the oddity of his eye color; one was blue and one was brown. A taciturn sort, he thanked Justin in as few words as possible, although he did rouse himself to bid Molly a good morrow. When Justin invited them to come into the bailey, his friends refused, Bennet joking that he never liked to get too close to castle dungeons. And so Justin's last glimpse of them was out in the city street, standing side by side, ghosts from his past gazing after him with the same expression on both their faces, one of unease and foreboding.

13

August 1193
Rhuddlan Castle, Wales

"Rhun? Wake up, lad."

The boy blinked sleepily and, upon recognizing Justin, sat up quickly. "You're back! Thank God!"

Justin put his finger to his lips, jerking his head toward the sleeping forms of the gardener and his wife. "How do you feel? Are you fit enough to travel?"

Rhun nodded, pitching his voice as low as Justin's. "I'd crawl over hot coals to get out of here. But where am I to go?"

"You know Sion, the prince's scribe? Tomorrow he is going to take you to his brother's home and you will stay there until it is safe for you to return. But you'll have to leave here on your own, Rhun. Whilst it is still dark, you must slip out the postern gate and then hide yourself until Sion comes for you. Can you do that, lad?"

Rhun hesitated. "Can you not take me? I trust you."

"Sion is not in danger of being followed. He can ride out tomorrow and no one will think it suspicious, for he has no known connection with you. You can trust him, too, Rhun. He is in Lord Davydd's service but . . . but he does not serve the prince."

Rhun mulled this over. "If you think it best . . ." he said doubtfully. "You truly believe my life is in so much danger? I've already told you what I know."

"Yes, but you are the only witness, Rhun. Your testi-

mony could convict a man, whereas mine could not."
Justin was loath to frighten the boy any more than he already had, but he could see no other way. "I have food in
this sack for you tomorrow, whilst you are waiting for
Sion. Tonight I will sleep here. That will make it easier
for me to awaken you in time."

Rhun had already demonstrated that he had an agile
brain, and Justin did not really expect the boy to believe
that lame excuse for his presence. Justin heard the sharp
intake of his breath. He said nothing, though, merely
handed Justin one of his blankets. Justin slid his sword
out of its scabbard, laid it on the ground within easy
reach. They both settled down, then, for what was to be
an unquiet night. Justin's sleep was shallow, its surface
broken every time he heard an odd noise, an imagined
footstep. He dozed and awoke and dozed again, listening
all the while for a killer's tread outside the cottage door.

When there was still an hour of darkness, Justin roused
Rhun and, muffled in mantles, they stealthily made their
way across the bailey. Once they reached the small
postern gate, they stayed close to the wall in case any of
the sleeping sentries were actually awake and alert. In
whispers, Justin reminded Rhun where he was to wait for
Sion and the boy nodded politely, as if he'd not already
been told that before. His green eyes showed some of his
fear, but now that he was poised for flight, his natural
youthful impatience had taken over and he was eager to
go, eager to take action of some sort. Justin understood;
he was still young enough himself to consider waiting to
be a penance. When he lifted the latch, the postern door
opened noiselessly; Sion had sneaked out during the
night to oil the hinges.

Rhun smiled briefly, and then, with the suddenness of a
baby bird leaving the nest, he was gone, and there was
nothing more for Justin to do but slide the bolt back into

place and entreat the Almighty to look kindly upon the Welsh youth. The wind had picked up, and he quickened his pace. As he neared the stables, he decided to check on his stallion before going on to the great hall, so he detoured in that direction. Turning the corner of the smithy, he collided with Berta's friend, Rolf.

Recoiling, Justin exclaimed, "Good God, man, you gave me a scare! Why are you lurking about at this hour?"

The other man regarded him impassively. "I went out to take a piss."

Justin had his doubts about that. If a privy was not available, most men merely staggered outside to answer nature's call; why would Rolf go so far? He was not sure, though, if his suspicions were justified, for he found himself reluctant to give Rolf the benefit of any doubt. There was something about this man that unsettled him and had from their first meeting in front of Chester Castle.

"I expect that you'll be leaving today for your family's home," he said, and Rolf shrugged in what may have passed for assent.

Justin was not reassured, and he continued to think about Rolf as he resumed his walk toward the stables. It was unusual for him to take such an immediate, instinctive dislike to someone. It had happened with Durand de Curzon. And for whatever reason, it was happening with Berta's dour friend, Rolf. Each time he glanced over his shoulder, he saw Rolf still standing by the smithy, watching him, and that only reinforced his misgivings.

The tension blanketed the great hall like wood smoke. From his lowly seat far down the table, Justin watched the drama being played out upon the dais. Davydd was as jumpy as a treed cat. He'd accosted Justin earlier in the day, demanding to know what he'd accomplished in

Chester. And they'd had another confrontation when he learned that Rhun had disappeared, accusing Justin of complicity in his flight. Thomas de Caldecott had also challenged Justin about Rhun, with little of his usual amiability. Angharad was visibly subdued, and from the sidelong glances she kept casting in Thomas's direction, Justin concluded that they must have quarreled. And the Lady Emma was again assuming her role of ice queen, aloof and inscrutable.

Justin had passed most of the day thwarting their interrogations. He had a plan in mind, one that he hoped would flush out another fox, a Cheshire knight rather than a Welsh prince. But for now, he was content to wait, to let the storm clouds gather, and to watch his back.

He adhered to his plan the next day, too. He made several trips out to the stables, as if he were intending to ride out, for he was sure Thomas would attempt to follow him if he did, and this was an easy way to keep the knight off balance. He spent a lot of time hanging around the great hall, occasionally making cryptic remarks that implied much but actually said little. He did his best to be as conspicuous as possible whenever Davydd or Thomas were in the vicinity. And to his surprise, he discovered that he was actually enjoying this prolonged game of cat and mouse. Men who murdered ought to suffer for their sins, ought to fear exposure and capture, ought to experience a small measure of the dread their victims had endured in their last moments. It was a strange sensation for Justin, this realization that he, who'd had so little power in his life, now had enough to alarm a prince, to threaten a killer.

Coming back from one of his excursions to the stables, he entered the great hall and stopped abruptly, for Rolf was slouched in a window seat. Justin strode over, intent upon getting rid of this man he did not trust. As he drew closer, he saw that Rolf was sharpening a blade on a small whetstone. Most men carried a saex or eating knife, which could be used for protection, too, in a pinch. But the weapon Rolf was honing was a dagger and a lethal-looking one at that: double-bladed, with a wooden hilt covered with leather and bound in thin cord for a better grip. Rolf's appearance and clothing were nondescript, and his horse was equally unremarkable, a rangy bay gelding. His dagger, however, was one that a lord would not have scorned: expensive, finely crafted, and deadly.

"That is a handsome dagger," Justin said, noting, too, that Rolf was sharpening it on a personal whetstone, one threaded onto a thong that could be looped at his belt or worn around his neck. Most men were not that meticulous about keeping their blades so keen. Rolf acknowledged the compliment with a grunt, and Justin came closer to get a better look at the weapon. "May I ask where you got it, Rolf?"

Rolf glanced up, then back to his task. "It was a family heirloom," he said laconically, and once again Justin felt a prickle of unease.

"I thought you were leaving yesterday for your kin's house. Why are you still here?"

At last he had Rolf's full attention, although he could not tell what the other man was thinking. "I've been getting along right well with one of the kitchen wenches. She's been balking at firking so far, but I figure I need only another day or so to get her on her back. I thought it would do no harm to tarry here for a while longer." Those oddly colored eyes met Justin's evenly, almost challengingly. "I did not think you'd begrudge me a meal or two at Lord Davydd's expense."

*   *   *

After his unsatisfactory exchange with Rolf, Justin had loitered in the hall for a while, but he was fast growing bored with so much free time. Finally he returned to the bailey and climbed up onto the castle battlements. It offered a sweeping view of the River Clwyd, the salt marshes, distant mountains, and a slate-grey sea. Clouds had been obscuring the horizon since a muted, hazy dawn, but it was easy for Justin to imagine that on a clear day, he could have seen to the back of beyond. He watched a hawk soaring on the wind, a fox darting across an open patch of ground, an oxen cart slowly lurching along the road to the castle. Below in the bailey, a horse was being led toward the smithy, a woman was carrying eggs from the hen roost, several children were playing hoodman-blind, and, in the shadows cast by the stables, Thomas de Caldecott and another man were arguing.

Justin moved swiftly along the walkway, getting as close as he dared. He could not hear what they were saying, for even in their anger, they remembered to keep their voices low, but there was no mistaking their agitation. It was interesting to see Thomas off guard, dropping his public persona to reveal a tightly controlled temper. But Justin was far more interested in the identity of Thomas's adversary. It took him a moment to recognize Oliver. He was a member of the Lady Emma's household, a soft-spoken Norman well past his youth. Misled by his quiet demeanor and grey hairs, Justin had not paid him much mind . . . until now. Clearly Oliver deserved more scrutiny than he'd so far gotten.

Justin waited until Thomas and Oliver ended their mysterious quarrel and then descended to the bailey. He was passing the gardens when he glanced over the wall and saw Angharad sitting on one of the turf benches.

Swerving at once in her direction, he wasted no time in joining her on the bench.

"You are the very one I needed to find, Angharad. What can you tell me about Oliver?"

"Oliver? He has been with Emma since the snakes were chased out of Ireland. I think he was with her even before her first marriage to that Norman lord, most certainly since she married Davydd. He is not well liked, for he has some of his lady's haughtiness, and like her, too, he has no sense of humor whatsoever. Why do you want to know?"

"Just curious. I saw him squabbling with Thomas earlier, and was wondering what that was about. Is there bad blood between them?"

"No . . . I doubt that they've even spoken a dozen words. Thomas enjoys lively company and Oliver is about as lively as a corpse." Angharad mustered up a ghostly smile. "Iestyn . . . I was looking for you, too."

Justin had been so intent upon learning more about Oliver that he'd not given Angharad more than cursory attention. Only now did he notice her pallor, her swollen eyes, the forlorn slump of her shoulders. "Well, you've found me, lass," he said, reaching over to squeeze her hand. "What do you want to talk about?"

"Thomas." Her brown eyes met his in mute entreaty, glistening with unshed tears. "You have become friends. Has he told you what is wrong? He has been so strange since he got back from Chester, so unlike himself. He loves me, Iestyn, I know he does. But now he looks at me as if I were no longer there. Something is on his mind, something dark and brooding. I've tried to talk to him about it, to no avail."

Her words tumbled out in a great gush, giving Justin no chance to respond. "You two are friends," she repeated plaintively. "Can you tell me anything that will enable me to help Thomas? Anything at all? Did something happen in Chester? Did he . . . did he meet another woman?"

Justin was at a loss for words. Feeling as guilty as if he were somehow Thomas's accomplice, he said, "No, lass, no. I did not see Thomas all that much whilst we were in Chester. But I am sure there is no other woman."

"I did not think so, either . . . not truly. It is just vexing to see him so troubled and not know how to help . . ."

Justin understood exactly how she felt. He'd been hoping fervently that Angharad was not involved in Thomas's villainy. He'd not given much thought to the conesquences if she were innocent, not until now, sitting with her in the castle garden and listening to the echoes of her broken heart.

Justin rose early the next morning and put the next part of his plan into motion. Heading for the stables, he chose a time when the grooms were over in the hall breaking their night fast. After saddling Copper, he moved down the row. A grey stallion stuck its muzzle over the stall door, nickering loudly. Justin paused to admire Thomas de Caldecott's palfrey, for it was a handsome animal. Thomas's saddle was suspended on a hook by the stall. Drawing his knife, Justin cut partially through one of the saddle girths, and belatedly realized the significance of Thomas's lack of a squire.

Few knights were not attended by men—usually but not always young—who took care of their horses, equipment, and weapons. Prior to discovering the truth about his paternity, Justin had served as a squire to one of Lord Fitz Alan's household knights. He'd thought it odd that Thomas traveled without a squire, but now it made sense. A squire always underfoot would have been a hindrance to a man who needed utter freedom to come and go as he pleased, no questions asked. With a final pat for Thomas's stallion, he led Copper out of his stall, and was soon riding across the castle drawbridge.

After reaching the ambush site, he took cover and waited to make sure he'd not been followed. While he was reasonably sure that his sabotage had given him enough time to outdistance any pursuers, he could take nothing for granted, not when the stakes were so high. Once he was convinced that he had no unwelcome shadow, he spent the next few hours in search of a possible hiding place for the missing wool. He found two caves and each time his hopes soared, to no avail. He had not really expected to find the wool so easily, but was still disappointed when he did not. When there was an hour or so of daylight remaining, he turned Copper back toward Rhuddlan.

Dinner that evening was an ordeal to be endured. Davydd was in an even fouler mood than usual, although Justin actually found himself feeling a twinge of pity for the Welsh prince. Like the hapless miller brothers, Davydd would soon be hung out to dry in a cold wind, and the royal wrath would be fearsome to behold. Emma was no happier than her husband; preoccupied and tense, she looked as if she yearned to be anywhere but the great hall of Rhuddlan Castle. Thomas ate in morose silence, his gaze anchored upon Justin's end of the table. And Angharad did not eat at all, watching Thomas with such naked misery that Justin had to glance away.

The meal was done and servants were clearing away the dishes, starting to dismantle the trestle tables. Justin was leaning against a wall, waiting for Thomas to approach him. It did not take long. Striding toward him, the knight said brusquely, "We need to talk." He pointed toward the comparative privacy of a window seat, and Justin followed him obligingly. Once they were seated, Thomas wasted no time. Glancing about, he signaled toward a passing servant, laying claim to two wine cups on the youth's tray. Thrusting one of them at Justin, he said accusingly, "You lied to me."

"When?"

"When you told me in Chester that you were not a man to bear grudges."

Justin raised the cup, but only wet his lips, remembering that drunken walk from the tavern to the warehouse, possibly the luckiest night of his life. Before he could respond, the hall erupted into pandemonium, into sudden screams and what sounded like snarls, the thud of overturned chairs, curses, and total chaos. Justin and Thomas shot from the window seat like arrows from a crossbow. They made little progress, though, for they were struggling against an incoming tide, as people surged away from the source of the turmoil.

By now the snarls and growls were loud enough to be heard above the yelling, and it was becoming obvious to all what the trouble was: several of Davydd's enormous wolfhounds were embroiled in a noisy, savage fight over a large beef bone. Davydd was demanding that the dogs be separated, but after one youth was badly bitten when he rashly waded into that maelstrom of flesh, fur, and flashing teeth, no one else was eager to volunteer, and that included Justin and Thomas. By common consent, they retreated back to the window seat, where they watched as Davydd fumed and threatened and the big dogs were finally dragged apart.

"I once won the huge sum of five marks on a Chester dog fight," Thomas observed, sounding almost friendly. "That is one of my fondest boyhood memories, as I used the money for my first bawdy house visit . . . at the ripe young age of thirteen." Reaching for his wine cup, he clinked it against Justin's. "What were we talking about? Ah, yes, the grudge you bear me. Do not bother denying it, de Quincy, although I truly do not understand why you seem to mistrust me. I told you at the outset that I wanted us to work as allies, and that still holds true. But you guard your secrets as if I am the enemy. Take today, for instance. You rode off at dawn with nary a word, and I felt like a right proper fool when Davydd wanted to know where you'd gone and I had to admit I did not know."

Justin was impressed by how well Thomas had struck all the right notes: bafflement, righteous indignation, a willingness to let bygones be bygones, overlaid with a dose of hearty, man-to-man candor and charm. It was chilling to realize that evil could be so attractive. "You want to know where I went today, Thomas? I am quite willing to tell you. I was out looking for the missing wool."

"But the wool was burned," Thomas reminded him, with such convincing perplexity that Justin resisted an urge to applaud. To give the Devil his due, Thomas could lie better than any man he'd ever met, and that included such gifted liars as the queen's youngest son and his henchman from Hell, Durand de Curzon.

"No," he said, "it was not. It was a trick, like those you see performed at fairs with walnut shells and peas. Sleight of hand, Thomas, no more than that."

"I hope you are right," Thomas said, after a long pause. "If you are, at least we have a chance to recover it, then." But this time his delivery was no longer pitch perfect and Justin raised his wine cup to his mouth to hide a smile. "Have you proof of this, Justin? Or is this merely a good guess?"

"You'd be surprised how much proof I've managed to unearth, Thomas."

Thomas had already drained his cup and beckoned to the nearest wine bearer. Justin took advantage of that chance and poured most of his wine into the floor rushes. When Thomas turned back to him, he was gratified to see that the knight's smile had begun to fray around the edges.

"What sort of proof?"

"Let me tell you a story, Thomas, a right interesting one, if I say so myself. It begins in a Chester alehouse with three Flemish sailors named Joder, Geertje, and Karl," Justin said and Thomas inhaled wine, began to cough. When he got his breath back, he shot Justin a look that was stripped of all pretense, his eyes cold and flat and deadly.

"I think you've had too much wine," he said, "for you're beginning to babble, de Quincy. You are making no sense."

"That is passing strange, for you are the one man who ought to understand exactly what I am talking about."

"Well, I do not." Thomas got slowly to his feet, stood for a moment staring down at Justin with an odd expression, one that put him in mind of the unblinking stare of a peregrine falcon, pitiless and predatory and impersonal. When he moved away, Justin let him get several feet before firing the last arrow in his quiver.

"Maes!" he called out, and saw Thomas stiffen, a reaction as involuntary as it was damning. The other man swung around and as their eyes met, Justin smiled, with no humor whatsoever. "This is something else I learned in Chester," he said. "An obliging wanton with a gift for languages told me that Maes is Flemish for Thomas."

The knight said nothing, nothing verbal. He simply turned and walked away. But he stayed in the hall for the rest of the evening, and whenever Justin glanced up, he found Thomas watching him. Justin would have insisted that he was unaffected by that malevolent gaze, and he'd have been lying. The knight was sitting in another window seat, paying little heed to Angharad, who'd joined him uninvited and was talking with a forced, frantic animation that was painful for Justin to see. Thomas was drinking heavily, but showed no ill effects from the wine, and Justin remembered his jovial boast, that he could drink anyone under the table. It was barely a month since they'd had that alehouse conversation, but it already seemed a lifetime ago to Justin.

He bedded down again in the great hall, taking care to spread his blankets in the midst of Davydd's sleeping soldiers. He did not think that Thomas would risk waking any of the other men, but sleep still eluded him for much of the night. Every noise seemed magnified, the snoring of his neighbors, the thudding of his own heart, the haunting cry of an owl on the scent of prey. He hastily blessed himself at that, for all knew the owl was a harbinger of death. Sometime before dawn, he finally slept.

He was awakened with a jolt, jerking upright with a ragged gasp. All around him, men were stirring, cursing, yawning. Justin sat up, staring like the others, at the youth in the doorway. He was young and scared, but he looked excited, too, to be the bearer of such news.

"They found a body in the chapel," he cried. "There has been murder done!"

14

Justin's first fear was an illogical dread that Rhun was the victim. His second fear was for Angharad. He was unprepared, therefore, when he burst into the chapel and found himself looking down at the body of Thomas de Caldecott. The knight lay on his back, arms outstretched in a pose oddly suggestive of the Crucifixion. His gaze was blind, the pupils so dilated that his eyes looked black, the corneas clouded and opaque. There was no blood that Justin could see, but the cause of death appeared obvious at first glance: there was a dagger hilt protruding from his chest.

Since entering the queen's service, Justin had learned much about dead bodies, too much for his liking. Kneeling beside Thomas, he touched the man's face with the back of his hand. The skin was cool. It was also dark, the shade of raw liver. Justin's eyebrows shot upward. Mastering his distaste, he carefully lifted Thomas's head, just enough to see that the skin on the back of his neck was blanched of all color. The body was already stiffening, rigid and ungainly. Justin closed those flattened, staring eyes before making the sign of the cross over the corpse.

He already knew the body had been moved. One glance around the chapel told him that wherever Thomas had died, it was not in God's House. He was studying the dagger hilt, leather bound in cord, when Davydd noticed his presence. "You!" Striding forward, he thrust his finger in Justin's face. "This is your fault. His blood is on your hands!"

Justin was incredulous. "What . . . you think I killed him?"

Davydd's eyes narrowed, and for a chilling moment, Justin thought he was seriously considering such an accusation, wondering if he could get away with it. "No," he said, with pronounced reluctance. "I am saying that Thomas would not have died if you'd heeded me from the first."

By now Justin was on his feet. "I do not understand what you are talking about."

"That is the trouble, you've understood nothing! I told you that Llewelyn ab Iorwerth was the one who stole the ransom. If you'd done as I wanted and asked the Earl of Chester for his help, Llewelyn would be imprisoned or dead weeks ago. For certes, he would not have been able to murder Thomas!"

Justin could conceal neither his disbelief nor his scorn. "You expect us to believe that Llewelyn was skulking around your own stronghold in the dead of night?" Adding a prudent but unconvincing "my lord prince" as a sop to Davydd's vanity.

"He did not do the deed himself," Davydd said impatiently. "One of his henchmen did . . . and I know which one. A sullen cutthroat named Rhys ap Cadell." Pointing toward Thomas's body. "That is his dagger. Look how distinctive it is. I'd know it anywhere."

Justin did not bother to argue further; what would be the point? He waited until the priest approached Davydd, in great distress because the church had been contaminated by bloodshed and must be reconsecrated before Mass could be said there again. As soon as Davydd was occupied with his chaplain, Justin slipped out and went to look for the place where Thomas had really died.

The last time he'd seen Thomas, he'd been standing in the doorway of the great hall. Based upon what he'd observed about the body, the knight had been dead for nigh on eight hours. So he must have died soon after leaving the hall. Where would he have gone?

Glancing around the bailey, Justin saw several dogs hovering by the side of the smithy. He walked over, following a hunch more than logic. The dogs were nosing about the ground, licking the grass. As intently as Justin searched, he could find no traces of blood. He did notice an indentation in the earth, too oddly shaped to be a footprint. After a moment to reflect, he dropped to one knee, leaving an imprint similar to the first one. Whatever had happened to Thomas last night, it had happened here.

A small crowd had gathered by the chapel. In the brief time that Justin had been out in the bailey, another half dozen people joined their ranks. Their circle broke to admit a newcomer. At the sight of Angharad, Justin lunged to his feet. "Angharad, wait!"

He was too late. She was already in motion, running toward the chapel. She darted through the doorway, and then Justin heard her scream.

Angharad was huddled on the floor next to Thomas's body, sobbing so uncontrollably that she finally attracted Davydd's attention. Swinging around, he snapped, "Someone see to that woman!"

When one of his men moved toward her, Justin stepped in front of him. "Let her be," he said. "She needs to grieve."

The man backed away, raising his hands to show he was merely following his prince's bidding. Davydd scowled at Justin, welcoming an excuse to lose his temper. "Who are you to interfere with my orders?"

"Let me tend to her, then," Justin said tautly. Reaching down, he was attempting to get Angharad onto her feet when the door was pushed open and the Lady Emma entered the chapel.

"Davydd? What in the world has happened? The servants are babbling about a murder, but I . . ." Her words trailed off at the sight of the body. Justin was close enough to hear her gasp. The color drained from her face so suddenly that he instinctively took a quick step toward her. But her eyes were already rolling back in her head, and before he could reach her, she crumpled to the floor next to the corpse of Thomas de Caldecott.

Emma was the center of attention, being cosseted and attended to by her husband, his physician, his chaplain, and all of her handmaidens. It was left to Justin to do what he could for the anguished Angharad. Eventually he managed to get her away from her lover's body and back to Emma's chamber in the castle keep, where he pried the doctor from Emma's side long enough to give Angharad a mild sleeping draught. Then he went in search of Rolf.

He found the other man in the stables, making ready to saddle his horse. Rolf was positioning a sweat cloth on the gelding's back and continued with his task even as Justin approached. "I ought to be able to get to Basingwerk Abbey by dusk," he said, reaching for the saddle at his feet. "What . . . no cheering? I thought you'd be gladdened to see the last of me."

"You're right. I do want to see the last of you. But there is something else I want to see first—that dagger of yours."

Rolf paused, briefly, before adjusting the saddle girths. "And if I do not want to show it to you?"

"Then we have a problem."

Rolf paused again, giving Justin an inscrutable glance over his shoulder. "Well, if it means that much to you . . ." Opening his mantle, he turned so that Justin could see the leather sheath and dagger hilt. "I usually do not draw it unless I plan to use it," he said, "but I suppose I can make an exception for you."

Sliding the dagger from its sheath, he offered it, hilt first, to Justin, and then fastened the crupper to the saddle cantle. "Did you truly think I'd be stupid enough to knife a man and then leave it in his body? Especially a costly dagger like this one?"

Justin handed the dagger back without comment and watched as Rolf tied his saddlebag to the crupper. "So Thomas de Caldecott dies and you ride off."

"What other reason do I have to stay? The pleasure of your company?" Rolf smiled coldly. "Of course you might well have another mortal enemy lurking in the shadows, mayhap two or three. Somehow, I doubt you lack for enemies. But now that de Caldecott is on his way to Hell, you're on your own."

"If you were here to watch my back, why did you not tell me?"

"I'm sure you'd have been overjoyed to have me as an ally," Rolf jeered. "Anyway, I was not watching you. I was here to watch de Caldecott, and he made it insultingly easy. Lords like him always do."

Justin could not muster up even a whit of gratitude. Furious with himself for not guessing the truth sooner, he shook his head in disgust. "I ought to have known that this was Bennet or Molly's doing." Leaving unsaid the one reason why he hadn't reached that conclusion: because Rolf was too unsavory to connect to his friends. "How much did your help cost them?" he demanded, determined that they'd not deplete their meager savings on his behalf.

"Nothing." Justin looked so skeptical that Rolf added grudgingly, "I owed Molly a debt. Now I do not."

It was obvious to Justin that Rolf was not going to give him any answers, and he was not sure they were answers he would want. "There is no reason, then, to delay your departure, is there?"

"You're welcome," Rolf said sardonically. Picking up the reins, he began leading his horse toward the stable door. He'd been saving his best shot for last and delivered it now. "One more thing. It might interest you to know that de Caldecott tried to kill you last night."

"How?"

"Poison."

"No," Justin said. "He had no opportunity to poison me. We shared a drink, but we took them from a lad toting a platter of wine and mead cups—" He stopped, for Rolf was smiling, a thin, knowing smile that was full of mockery.

"Yes, de Caldecott had a friendly chat with that very lad earlier in the evening. From what I could overhear, he spun a story about his English friend—that would be you—not liking mead. After getting a coin, the boy was happy to saunter over once the two of you were sitting in the window seat, enabling de Caldecott to pick out two cups, apparently at random. Do I need to tell you that those two cups were ones he provided, supposedly filled with your favorite wine?"

He looked so smug that Justin fought back an urge to hit him. "I did not drink his wine," he said. "I poured most of it into the floor rushes."

Rolf smirked. "By then it was as pure as mother's milk."

Justin stared at him. "You got the dogs to fighting."

Rolf nodded complacently. "Whilst the beasts were fighting over that bone, I replaced your cup with one of my own. Simple, fast, effective. A pity I could not just have switched the cups; that would have been a joke worthy of the Devil himself. But de Caldecott had taken care to make sure there'd be no confusion. You may not remember, but your cup was wooden, his made of horn."

Justin did remember. "I find it hard to believe he'd be that desperate," he said, trying to convince himself more than Rolf. "If I died of a sudden, there would have been questions and suspicions for certes."

Rolf smirked again. "And that Welsh prince would have moved heaven and earth to bring your killer to justice . . . right? I'd wager you'd have been buried and forgotten in the time it took to dig your grave. I expect that de Caldecott was shrewd enough to pick the right poison, too. The man did seem to have a knack for killing. He'd not have wanted you to collapse at his feet, foaming at the mouth. Even Davydd would have been hard-pressed to ignore that. So that lets out some of the more popular poisons like hemlock, monkshood, henbane, or mandragora. De Caldecott would want something that would act fast, but not too fast."

"You are remarkably well informed about poisons," Justin said slowly. "I cannot help wondering how you came by all this knowledge."

"Are you not curious about de Caldecott's poison of choice? I figured he could have used saffron or cock's spur. I'd wager he went with nightshade, though. Not only would it take several hours to sicken you, you'd not have a prayer in Hell of recovery. With nightshade, death is certain . . . and none too pleasant."

He looked as if he expected Justin to ask for the gruesome details of a nightshade poisoning. Justin did not want to know. What if Rolf had not intervened? Would a sip or two of de Caldecott's poisoned wine have been enough to kill? He would not have drunk any more than that, but would even a mouthful have been too much? Rolf could probably tell him, but that, too, he preferred not to know.

"I owe you," he said tersely, aware of how ungracious that sounded. It was the best, though, that he could do. "How did you get rid of the wine? Are you sure that there was no way de Caldecott could have taken it by mistake?"

It was the first time that he'd seen Rolf look amused. "Did I poison him? If I did, I'd hardly admit it to you, would I? I took the wine out to the bailey with the idea of testing it on one of the dogs. Mead would have been sweet enough to tempt them. But they just sniffed at the wine, so I have no proof that it was poisoned. Nor does it matter now. De Caldecott is beyond the reach of earthly justice."

Justin had a fondness for dogs and he was looking at Rolf with such antipathy that the other man noticed. "What . . . ?" Getting no answer, he swung up into the saddle. "You do know that de Caldecott was not stabbed to death?"

"Yes," Justin said grimly. "I know."

15

August 1193
Rhuddlan Castle, Wales

The day after Thomas de Caldecott's death, it rained. The sky darkened and a stinging salt wind blew off the ocean, ripping leaves from trees in a barren, bleak foretaste of winter. Justin had spent the morning doing what little he could to console Angharad. Her grief alarmed him; it was so intense, so overwhelming. It troubled him that the object of her love had been so unworthy of it, but he thought it would not help her to know that. Nor was she likely to believe him. Without more proof, Justin doubted that anyone would.

He was dripping wet and disheartened by the time he returned to the great hall. He was drying off by the open hearth when the door opened and the Lady Emma entered. Davydd at once hastened down the steps of the dais and hurried to her, helping her with her mantle and escorting her toward the hearth with what Justin felt was exaggerated gallantry. She let Davydd settle her in a chair comfortably close to the flames, and Justin's ears pricked up. He did not expect to overhear anything of significance. Accustomed to living their lives on center stage, the Welsh prince and his consort were unlikely to be careless enough to choose a public forum for private discussion. But he was curious to watch them interact, for their marriage remained a mystery to him.

This was Emma's first appearance since she'd fainted

in the chapel, and Davydd was fussing over her so osten-
tatiously that he put Justin in mind of a brood hen with a
prize chick. She was well, Emma insisted, although she
proclaimed her health in such a languid, breathy voice
that Justin could not blame Davydd for harboring
doubts. It was to be expected that she'd still be disquieted
by the experience, Davydd declared. Women of gentle
birth were not meant by the Almighty to look upon
scenes of bloodshed and gore.

Justin fought back laughter. He wondered if Davydd
really believed that or if he was merely affecting a chivalric pose. The women in Justin's life bore little resemblance to the docile and frail females exalted as models of
ideal womanhood. Queen Eleanor had accompanied her
first husband on crusade and instigated a rebellion
against her second. Claudine had amused herself by spying for the queen's youngest son. Nell had been widowed
before she was twenty and was raising a daughter on her
own whilst managing a kinsman's alehouse. Molly had
been defying the odds and convention from birth. And he
suspected that the Lady Emma was steel sheathed in silk,
too. He found it intriguing that Davydd appeared so protective of the silk, so oblivious of the steel.

Accepting a wine cup, Emma took a small sip. "Have
you made arrangements for Thomas's funeral?"

Davydd nodded. "I sent a messenger to Bishop Reiner
at Llanelwy."

"Few men are fortunate enough to have their funeral
Mass said in a cathedral church," Emma said. "But might
not his family prefer that he be buried in England?"

Davydd shrugged. "It cannot be helped. By the time
the storm passes and the roads dry out, Thomas's body
would be too rank for transporting. Forgive me for being
brutally blunt, my dear, but by then the stench would be
too foul to endure."

Emma gave him an impatient, sidelong glance. "I know that, Davydd. Surely you have not forgotten the story of the burial of my brother Henry's great-grandfather, William, conqueror of the English?"

Davydd assured her that he remembered, while the eavesdropping Justin prodded his memory. It took only a moment, for the account of William the Bastard's death and burial was too grisly to be forgotten. There'd been a delay in burying him, and when it was discovered that the stone coffin was too small for a man of William's bulk, an ill-advised attempt had been made to force the body into it, causing the decomposing corpse to break open, emitting such a noxious odor that the mourners had fled the church in horror.

This was the sort of gruesome story to lodge in the morbid imagination of young male students, and Justin was not surprised he recalled it so quickly. What did surprise him was that Emma would have chosen to mention it, for it hardly seemed like a suitable topic for a woman of such delicate sensibilities that the mere sight of a dead body would cause her to swoon. He decided that she could not resist any opportunity to brag about her family's lofty bloodlines, but as he continued to listen, he realized that Emma had something else in mind.

"Surely that sad occurrence argues for a quick burial, Emma. Llanelwy is but a few miles away and even if the rain continues, we can take the body there without great difficulty. De Caldecott's family will just have to accept the fact that we did the best we could under the circumstances."

"Well . . . there may be a way to satisfy his family without taking any risks. Bury his body at the cathedral of St Asaph in Llanelwy and deliver his heart to the earl at Chester so it may be buried at Caldecott."

"An excellent suggestion, my dear." Davydd sounded

pleased, but Justin frowned, wondering why Thomas de Caldecott's burial would matter so much to Emma. She gave him the answer, though, with her next words.

"When you send men to the earl, I would like my man, Oliver, to accompany them. The last time I was in Chester, I ordered sarcenet silk, damask, and white kidskin gloves from France, and the mercer told me they ought to arrive by summer's end. Oliver is going to fetch them for me."

Justin's head came up sharply. Oliver looked to be in his sixth decade and had a limp that indicated he had a touch of the joint evil. This was not a man to send on a two-day ride for an ordinary errand.

Justin's arrival in Chester was not auspicious. The storm that had drenched Rhuddlan earlier in the week had moved east and was now buffeting the city with high winds and driving rain. Oliver balked at lodging with the others at the castle, insisting he preferred the guest hall at St Werburgh's, which meant that it would be more difficult for Justin to keep him under watch. And most troubling of all, Justin learned that the earl was gone from Chester, called away by the sudden illness of his youngest sister, Hawise. Justin had not realized how much he was counting upon Chester's aid until it was no longer available.

As soon as he could get away, he slipped out of the castle and went to make sure that Oliver had settled down for the evening at the abbey. He was convinced that Emma had sent her man to Chester to meet someone, which meant that he dared not let Oliver out of his sight for long. Since Oliver knew him and would be on the alert if he was up to no good, that was going to make surveillance no easy task.

* * *

Bennet instructed Berta to bring them cups and a flagon, then steered Justin toward a corner table. "So," he said, as soon as they were seated, "Rolf told us that your best suspect got himself killed. Where does that leave you?"

"Mired in the mud," Justin conceded, before giving his friend a quick, probing look. "I suppose I ought to thank you and Molly for Rolf . . . I think."

Bennet grinned. "Scary, isn't he?"

Justin heartily agreed. "Dare I ask how the man earns his livelihood?"

"I never asked, never wanted to know. He works occasionally for Piers, doing God knows what, and he disappears from Chester for weeks at a time, always comes back with plenty of money to spend on drink and whores and wagers."

"What did he tell you about de Caldecott's death?"

"That he'd been found dead in the castle chapel with a knife in his chest. Why . . . is there more to this tale than he let on?"

"No . . . apart from the fact that he was not killed in the chapel and he did not die from a dagger thrust." Justin took a swallow of wine, and then grimaced, both at the taste and his dubious prospects. "I think he was probably poisoned. I could find no other wounds on the body and I find it hard to believe that his heart just stopped beating of its own accord."

"What about the dagger? How can you be sure it did not kill him?"

"Because," Justin said, "there was no blood, no blood at all. The only way a man can be stabbed and not bleed is if he's already dead."

"This is beginning to sound very peculiar, even for Wales. Why stab a dead man?"

"For the same reason that his body was moved into the

chapel: so Davydd could blame his nephew, Llewelyn, for the killing."

Bennet shook his head, marveling at the duplicity of the highborn. "Moll told me about his grand scheme to steal the ransom and accuse the nephew. Has he gotten around to blaming Llewelyn for Chester's great fire and our last drought?"

"Not yet, but I'd not put it past him. As far as I can tell, Bennet, this is what happened. De Caldecott was poisoned in the great hall, a poison that did not take effect right away. He was crossing the bailey when it hit. I found the place where he collapsed. I think he became very ill very fast and died ere he could call out for help. Sometime later his body was discovered by someone, most likely a guard, who sought Davydd out straightaway."

"And Davydd saw another chance to put the blame on his favorite scapegoat," Bennet suggested dryly, and Justin nodded.

"He had the body moved into the closest building—the chapel—because the death scene would have given the lie to his claim that Thomas was stabbed. From the way the castle dogs were hovering around, I think Thomas vomited all over the ground ere he lost consciousness. Davydd's men did their best to tidy it up, but the dogs still caught the smell."

"So a dagger was found, and some poor sod was given the unholy task of stabbing a corpse. Think what an interesting confession he'll have to tell his priest! If you are right, Justin, it sounds very haphazard, like they were cobbling the pieces together as they went along."

Justin nodded again. "It was hastily done and poorly done. Thomas died face down; I could tell by the color of his skin. But he was stabbed in the chest. I suppose

Davydd assumed that none would dare to question his findings, and aside from me, he was right. I am sure the doctor saw the truth as soon as he examined the body. Was he likely to call his prince a liar, though? The same holds true for Davydd's men."

Bennet understood perfectly; he had far more experience than Justin in the inequities of power. "I need to ask you something, Justin. Have you gone to see Molly yet?"

"No, I came here straightaway. Why . . . nothing is wrong?"

"It depends upon who you ask. Piers is back in Chester. So I'd suggest you stay away from Moll's cottage. I'll arrange for you to meet her here."

Justin thought about that for a few moments. "Molly told me," he said, "that Piers is not jealous."

"As far as we know, he is not. But I think Molly does not fully comprehend how fiercely he guards his territory."

Justin did not like the sound of that, and he took advantage of this opportunity to discuss Molly's dangerous lover with her brother. Leaning forward, he said quietly, "There must be something we can do, Bennet, to untangle her from that man's web."

Bennet looked at him with the sorrowful sarcasm of one counseling a well-meaning but not overly bright friend. "You're right, Justy. Mayhap we ought to sit down and make the perils known to her. Why did I not think of that myself?"

Justin acknowledged the mockery with an abashed smile. He would have persevered, though, if a boy hadn't arrived then with the food Bennet had ordered from the cook shop. The food was not very good—a chicken pie that was greasy and too long out of the oven—but Justin had not eaten for hours, and he and Bennet finished it in record time. Only then did they return to the subject of murder.

"You've told me how Thomas de Caldecott died, and we both can guess why. But we have not talked yet about the most important question of all . . . who?"

"I would that I knew, Bennet," Justin said with a sigh. "Davydd has the best motive by far. If he found out that Thomas was the one responsible for the robbery, he'd have feared that his own duplicity might be exposed if de Caldecott was caught. Not to mention he'd have a very valid reason for wanting revenge, which the Welsh take quite seriously. But for the life of me, I cannot understand why he'd go about it like this. Davydd is one of the most vexing men I've ever met. He is not a total dolt, though, and only God's greatest fool would have poisoned de Caldecott and then made such a clumsy attempt to blame Llewelyn."

"So we acquit your Welsh prince on the grounds that he is stupid, but not quite stupid enough," Bennet said, sounding faintly amused. "Not exactly a ringing testimonial to his innocence, is it? But if Davydd is out, who is left?"

"His wife."

Bennet's eyes gleamed. "The lovely Lady Emma? This is getting interesting. Why do you suspect her?"

"Process of elimination," Justin said glumly. "I have three reasons to look more closely at Emma. First of all, I saw her trusted man, Oliver, quarreling with Thomas the day ere he died. Next, Emma fainted at the sight of his body, and it was no ladylike pretense. Lastly, she sent Oliver to Chester on an errand that posed a genuine hardship to a man of Oliver's years and health."

Bennet held his peace, but Justin saw his expression and sighed again. "I know what a thin gruel I've cooked up. There could be any number of innocent explanations for my suspicions. Moreover, I have no motive for her. Assuming she did ally herself with Thomas to steal the ransom, why? For the money? Not likely. To cause Davydd pain and trouble? I can safely say she loves him not. But his downfall would be hers, too, and what of their son? Unless . . . unless she hopes that Davydd would be deposed and her son put in his stead, with her as regent, of course. That seems a great risk to take, though, for she could not be sure it would happen that way. If Davydd were to lose his throne, her son would still have to fend off Llewelyn ab Iorwerth, and you can take it from me, Bennet, that one will not be easy to defeat."

"Motives are elusive, no easy quarry," Bennet said thoughtfully. "If it were up to me, I'd stay on the lady's trail. Who knows where that might lead?"

He was a loyal friend, refusing to voice the fear that had been shadowing Justin since his first glimpse of Thomas de Caldecott's body. What if Thomas had been working alone? If the only partner he'd had was the unfortunate Selwyn? That was a possibility Justin was not ready to acknowledge, for it would mean that the secret of the wool's whereabouts had died with Thomas and he would not be able to recover the ransom. He would fail his queen.

Justin ducked back into an alley, swearing under his breath. For three days and nights he and Bennet had been shadowing Oliver each time he ventured from the abbey precincts. By now they knew what to expect. Oliver's destination would be the docks. He'd go into wharfside alehouses and taverns, having a drink in each one before moving on to the next.

Justin had been quick to read sinister significance into

his actions, convinced that a meeting had been set up, mayhap weeks ago, and Oliver was taking Thomas's place, waiting to be contacted. They decided that Oliver was visiting more than one alehouse in a clumsy attempt to confuse anyone who might be following him, although they were not sure if Oliver was aware of their surveillance or was just being cautious. They'd taken care to keep their distance, benefiting from the continuing wet weather as men muffled up in hooded cloaks or mantles were not readily identifiable, and sending Bennet in to spy on Oliver in close quarters. Justin refused to entertain the thought that Oliver's evening excursions could be prompted by nothing more than an innocent fondness for English ale or bad wine, and if Bennet harbored any doubts, he'd so far kept them to himself.

On this damp September evening, Oliver had followed his usual routine. He'd already visited two alehouses, where he'd sat alone at a corner table; no one had approached him, Bennet reported, and after ordering one drink, he'd moved on. He was now entering the third alehouse, pausing suddenly to look over his shoulder. Justin and Bennet hastily faded back into the shadows. After a prudent interval, Bennet made ready to follow. Pulling his hood forward to hide most of his face, he reminded Justin of a turtle withdrawing into its shell. "The last time," he grumbled, "he did not even stay long enough for me to finish my ale." As he started across the street toward the alehouse, Justin stepped back into the alley, settling in for another irksome wait.

This wait was over almost before it began, for Bennet soon re-emerged and hurried back to the alley. "He has company," he said, sounding out of breath. "He is sitting at a table with two other men."

"Why did you leave, then? I need you to see what happens next, Bennet!"

"I had no choice, Justin. I recognized one of the men—none other than our city sheriff, Will Gamberell!"

"Christ Jesus," Justin whispered. Could the sheriff be Oliver's contact? Or was this just a wretched coincidence? "You say there was a second man with Oliver. Can you describe him?"

"Not well," Bennet said dubiously. "As soon as I saw Gamberell, my one concern was getting out of there ere he noticed me. The other man . . . he was steering the serving wench over to their table, so I did not get a good look at his face. I could not even tell what color his hair was, for he had a hood on, a fancy one, too, not attached to his mantle, with a little cape over his shoulders. I suppose that is not much help?"

"No," Justin said ungraciously, but soon repented of his rudeness; he could scarcely blame Bennet for wanting to avoid an encounter with a sheriff who loved him not. "I'll have to go in," he said reluctantly, for he could not risk losing this chance to see Oliver's mystery partner, even if it meant revealing himself to be a spy.

That did not strike Bennet as a particularly good idea, but he had no other suggestions to offer, and he waved Justin on with forced cheer, wishing him luck and asking if he could bring back an ale. That got him a quick smile, and then Justin was gone, and Bennet leaned against the wall of the closest building, marveling at the madness of this entire enterprise of theirs; what did it matter to him, after all, if King Richard never set foot again on English soil?

The interior of the alehouse was better lit than Justin had expected; each table held a large tallow candle or an oil lamp. It was more crowded, too, with more than a dozen men and several women sheltering from the rain at the end of a dreary, autumn day. Justin noticed the sheriff at once; there was a conspicuous space around the table where he was seated with several of his deputies or serjeants, a boundary line drawn between the law and the less lawful. But there was no sign of Oliver or his hooded companion, and Justin drew an alarmed breath. Where in blazes were they?

"Is there a rear door?" he demanded of the serving maid, and she looked at him incuriously, then nodded and pointed. In three strides, he crossed the chamber, barely missing a collision with a tipsy sailor who rebuked him in a foreign language that sounded vaguely Germanic. Jerking open the door, he found himself looking out into a small, dark, and very empty alley. There was no point in pursuit. His quarry was long gone.

He'd attracted the attention of the other alehouse customers, including the sheriff. "If it is not the queen's man," he said, sounding none-too-happy about it. "For someone looking for a ransom in Wales, you seem to spend an inordinate amount of time in Chester, de Quincy."

Having nothing left to lose, Justin bore down on the other man's table. "The men you were drinking with, you know where they've gone?"

Gamberell looked faintly surprised. "That old man and the coxcomb? No, why should I? I never laid eyes on either of them till tonight."

"I see. You always drink with men you do not know?"

"He does if they're buying," one of the serjeants volunteered with a cackle, which caught in his throat when the sheriff shot a withering glance his way.

"Whilst he was waiting for the old man, the younger one offered to buy me an ale," Gamberell said shortly. "What of it? How does this concern you?"

"I need to find them straightaway. What can you tell me about the younger man, the 'coxcomb'? Did he give you a name? Say anything that might enable me to seek him out? What did he look like?"

The sheriff glared at Justin, irritation giving way to outright antagonism. "I know nothing about the man. Nor would I tell you if I did. In Chester, we judge a man by the company he keeps, and the company you've been keeping reeks to high heavens!"

On the next day, the waterlogged residents of Chester got a rain reprieve, their first glimpse of the sun in more than a week. When Molly opened the door of the alehouse, she let in a blaze of light that did little to dispel the gloom that held the common room in thrall. Bennet and Justin acknowledged her entrance with such a lack of enthusiasm that she knew their news had to be bad. Hurrying over to their table, she pulled up a stool.

"Well? What happened last night? Did Oliver's phantom friend fail to turn up again?"

"He put in an appearance," Bennet said glumly, "but disappeared in a puff of smoke ere we could get a good look at him."

Molly was surprised, for she knew how good her brother was at tracking without leaving telltale footprints. "He was lucky to lose you," she said. "But surely there will be other opportunities?"

Justin shook his head. "Oliver stopped by the castle this morn and asked when I'd be returning to Rhuddlan. He was done in Chester, he said, and hoped we could travel together for safety's sake. So smug he was, I wanted to hit him."

He told Molly, then, of the sheriff's unexpected involvement, and she fell silent for some moments, pondering this new development. "If we assume Gamberell was telling the truth," she said thoughtfully, "then we are left with an interesting question. Why did our phantom buy the sheriff a drink?"

"We've been thinking about that, too," Justin said.

"We came up with three possibilities. One: Oliver some-how got a message to him that he was being followed and they made use of the sheriff as a distraction. Two: pure coincidence. Or three: that he was amusing himself by seeing how close he could come to the flame without get-ting burned."

"Three," Molly said promptly. "That seems the most likely . . . and the most troubling. Some men lust after danger the way others do after whores. If the phantom is one of them, Justin, you'd best beware, for men like that are unpredictable and reckless."

Justin shrugged, irked by her continued use of the term "phantom," for that only stressed how easily Oliver's confederate had outwitted them last night. Bennet was not eager to dwell upon their failure, either, and diverted Molly's attention by revealing Justin's more immediate problem, that the Earl of Chester was still gone from the city.

"Justin needs to send a letter to London, and he fears that if he waits until Chester gets back, weeks could go by. He is not likely to return until his sister recovers or, Jesu forfend, dies. Since this letter is overflowing with scandalous accusations against the Welsh prince and his consort, he needs to make sure it does not fall into the wrong hands. I offered to take it for him, but he says he cannot trust me not to sell it to the highest bidder."

Justin was not surprised when Molly rolled her eyes, for she held no high opinion of male humor. What she did not know, of course, was that he'd joked to keep from telling Bennet that his London letter was meant for the English queen. He remembered a common folk wis-dom—that it took only one drop too many to cause a bucket to overflow—and he did not doubt that his revela-tion about Queen Eleanor would be that drop.

He was lost in thought, regretting the need to lie to his

friends, and did not hear Molly's comment. It was not until Bennet gave him a playful poke that he focused again upon the alehouse and their conversation. "What . . . ?"

"Molly has solved your problem, Justin. It is so obvious, too, that we ought to have thought of it ourselves. You do not need to wait for the earl to return. You need only ask the bishop to send a courier with your letter."

Justin's eyes cut accusingly toward Molly. She met his gaze blandly. "Is there any reason why you'd not want to ask the bishop, Justin?"

"Yes," he said tersely. "We had a . . . a misunderstanding the last time we spoke."

Molly riposted with a wicked smile. "Well, this will give you a chance to make peace."

Justin was on the defensive even before he'd set foot in the precincts of the bishop's palace, already anticipating his father's rebuff, and that gave his voice a conspicuous edge as he requested an audience with the bishop. When he was told that the bishop was entertaining guests, he was too tense to wait and insisted that he'd need but a few moments of the bishop's time. He was still arguing when the bishop's steward happened by. One glance at Justin's face and Martin took over, smoothing ruffled feathers on the bishop's staff and offering to let Aubrey know of Justin's arrival.

Justin agreed to remain in the entrance hall. The last time he and his father had met, it was in the bishop's own chambers above the great hall. He watched Martin disappear into the corner stairwell, but he was too ill at ease to sit down. Noises from the great hall indicated that dinner would soon be served, and the entrance hall was crowded with petitioners, waiting with far more patience than Justin in the faint hope that the bishop might see them.

Only Aubrey's private chapel offered solitude and silence, but it was in that same chapel that Justin had confronted his father on a frigid December eve, and he had no wish to revisit either that scene or that night.

He was still pacing restlessly when the bishop came bursting out of the stairwell. Justin turned in surprise, for he'd never seen his father move so precipitately. As far back as he could remember, Aubrey had been regardful of his dignity, striving to maintain an air of deliberation and formality whenever he appeared in public. Now he was panting, flushed, and agitated, even somewhat disheveled.

"What are you doing here?" he demanded. "I have highborn guests. You must leave straightaway!"

Justin flushed, too. "I am here on the queen's behalf," he said, in a low voice that was not as steady as he would have liked. "I need a letter delivered to London, and that is my only reason for—"

Aubrey gave no indication that he'd even heard. "You cannot stay," he insisted, "for they'll soon be coming into the hall. Be gone whilst there is still time!"

Justin's anger was fueled by hurt. He was used to being treated as an insignificant stranger by his father whenever there were other eyes to see them, but never had Aubrey rejected him so vehemently, as if the very sight of him was shameful. "This is an urgent matter and I am going nowhere until you hear me out!"

Aubrey glanced toward the great hall and then grabbed Justin by the arm, jerking him toward the chapel. Shoving Justin through the doorway, he hissed, "Stay there until I come back, and do not let yourself be seen!"

Justin stumbled, regaining his balance as Aubrey slammed the door shut. His face burning, he stared in disbelief at that closed door. His first impulse was to stalk out, to put as many miles between himself and Aubrey as he could. But common sense told him that if he bolted, he'd have endured this humiliation for nothing. Slipping his hand into his tunic, he drew out the letters, handling them as gingerly as if they were hot to the touch. One for the queen and one to the abbess at Godstow, with a sealed enclosure for Claudine.

The chapel was deep in shadows, lit by a single rush-light in a wall sconce. Sunlight filtered through a stained glass window in colors like jewels: ruby, emerald, sapphire. The walls were painted with scenes from Scriptures and the gospels: the Annunciation, the Passion of Christ, the torments of Hell. It was too dim to distinguish them, but Justin had seen them so often that they were imprinted upon his brain. He'd passed countless hours here, kneeling on the tiled floor and praying dutifully to the Almighty and the bishop, for when he was very young, he'd confused the two. Whether clad in the ornate silk chasuble that was his "Yoke of Christ" or his vivid purple and gold cope, the bishop had seemed to Justin to be the very embodiment of God the Father, Lord of Lords, King of Kings, splendid and remote and all-powerful.

Justin put the letters back into his tunic, damning Molly for prodding him into this doomed quest, damning himself for listening to her. Despite all his misgivings, he'd not expected a scene so ugly as the one out in the entrance hall. He understood why his father was so set upon keeping his twenty-year-old sin a secret. Men of God were not saints and they sometimes fell from grace. But a bastard son was a millstone around the neck of a prelate as ambitious as Chester's bishop. Scandal had never been one of the stepping-stones to the See at Canterbury.

He had never seen Aubrey so overwrought, though, so frantic to avoid exposure, and for the first time he wondered if there might be more to the bishop's distress than a fear of public disgrace. What it could be, he did not know, could not even begin to imagine, and an inner voice mocked that he was grasping at straws, unwilling to face the truth: that he was nothing to Aubrey de Quincy but an embarrassment, a source of shame and dread.

Stopping before the high altar, he gazed down at the two tall candlesticks and the elegant silver-gilt crucifix that his father had brought back from Rome. The crucifix triggered an unwelcome memory. After Aubrey had denied his paternity, Justin had challenged him to swear it upon the crucifix. For a moment, his own bitter words seemed to echo in the air. "At least you'll not lie to God."

He stiffened, then, as the door started to open. He heard his father's voice, insisting that there was plenty of time to admire the Tree of Jesse, laughter, and another male voice saying that they could wait nary another moment to see it. Aubrey was backing slowly into the chapel, and behind him, Justin caught a glimpse of the white miter of a bishop. Doubtless one of his father's "highborn guests." Justin raised his head defiantly, fists clenching at his sides, as Aubrey flung a quick glance over his shoulder, then reluctantly stepped aside to admit the others.

Justin was never to be sure why he did it. It may have been the desperate look upon his father's face. It may have been habit, for he had a lifetime's experience in deferring to the bishop's wishes. It may even have been Molly's gentle rebuke, "He tried to do right by you, lover, as much as he was able." But at the last moment, he ducked out of sight behind the high altar.

The quiet chapel was suddenly filled with people, two of them in the sumptuous silk copes worn by princes of the Church. One of them Justin recognized from his years in Lord Fitz Alan's service: William de Vere, Bishop of Hereford. The other bishop was not known to him, a man whose youth was a distant memory, with a girth that bespoke a fondness for good food and fine wine, a florid complexion, engaging smile, and shrewd calculating blue eyes. They were attended by the usual entourage of clerks and archdeacons and priests, who milled about like sheep until Aubrey hastily shepherded them toward a lancet window.

It was soon clear to Justin that his father had been bragging about his new stained-glass panels depicting the genealogy of the Lord Christ. The stained glass was indeed spectacular, but it was impossible for him to appreciate the artistry while crouched down behind the high altar. Already his body was protesting the awkward contortion of his spine, and his legs were beginning to cramp. He wanted them to depart as fervently as his father did, but they lingered, discussing the craftsmanship, praising Aubrey's estimable taste, even making favorable comparisons to the celebrated Stem of Jesse in the west window of Chartres's great cathedral. Because they were all learned churchmen, well versed in Scriptures, someone inevitably had to quote from the prophecy of Isaiah: "But a shoot shall sprout from the stump of Jesse, and from his roots a branch will bear fruit, and the spirit of the Lord shall rest upon him . . ." Someone else was then inspired to lapse into Latin, intoning solemnly, *"O rudix Jesse,"* and Justin grimaced, for his muscles were constricting and he did not know how much longer he could hold his uncomfortable posture.

Eventually, though, Aubrey managed to nudge them into motion, and after a span that seemed interminable to Justin, he was alone in the chapel. Getting slowly to his feet, he sought to stretch himself back into shape, grateful that he'd been spared the mortification of discovery.

What would his father have done? Mayhap accuse him of thievery, the easiest way to explain why he'd been hiding behind the altar.

He was in no friendly frame of mind when Aubrey returned. Closing the door, the bishop leaned back against it, and they regarded each other warily. Aubrey was the one to break the silence, saying in a low voice, "I thank you for not letting yourself be seen."

Justin's shoulders twitched in a half-shrug.

"Why are you here?" Aubrey asked, after another uncomfortable silence.

Justin withdrew the letters from his tunic. "I need you to send these to the queen. I am not sure where she is now, but I thought your messenger could go first to London and learn her whereabouts. There is a second letter for the abbess of Godstow priory." He paused, daring Aubrey to ask questions. "The letter to the queen is urgent. Can your man be ready to ride out today?"

"Yes, of course." Aubrey stepped forward and took the letters from Justin. "I will see to it myself, choosing one of my most reliable men."

Justin nodded, not knowing what else to say. He'd expected Aubrey to leave as soon as he had the letters, but the bishop remained where he was, watching him with an inscrutable expression. "One of my guests," he said abruptly, "was Hugh de Nonant, Bishop of Coventry and Lichfield. I am sure you've heard tales about him, none of them good."

Justin nodded again, for the Bishop of Coventry was rumored to be hand in glove with the queen's treacherous son, John. Aubrey hesitated, subjecting him to another intent scrutiny. "Last December . . . the night you forced your way into my great hall, Hugh de Nonant was here. He was curious about you and the scene you were causing, asked too many questions. He has an unholy ability to sniff out other men's secrets and then use them to his benefit. If he'd seen you again and learned that you serve the queen now, who's to say what he might have made of it?"

Justin did not want to see through Aubrey's eyes. He could not dismiss these fears out of hand, though. Any ally of John's was deserving of suspicion. "You should have told me about de Nonant. Had I known, I would have kept out of his sight."

"Yes . . . I should have," Aubrey agreed, to Justin's surprise. Tucking the letters away, he said briskly, "I will see to this straightaway. I think it best that you remain here a while longer. I will send Martin in to you as soon as it is safe for you to depart."

Justin said nothing, for what was there to say? His father turned, strode over to the door. He paused, then, his hand on the latch. His back was to Justin, his face not visible. "Aline," he said softly. "Your mother's name was Aline."

16

*September 1193
Llanelwy, North Wales*

The River Elwy was a stone's throw away, but the moon had been swallowed up by a passing cloud and Justin could no longer see it. He tilted his head to the side, listening to the soft, rhythmic rushing of the water. So hushed and tranquil was the night that he could easily have been lulled into complacency—were it not for his purpose here in the hamlet of Llanelwy: a secret meeting with a man who was neither friend nor foe, capable of becoming either one.

Turning away from the unseen river, he gazed up at the glimmering lights of St Asaph, the cathedral crowning the crest of the hill. It seemed odd to use so grand a word for so simple a structure, for this humble, wooden church bore little resemblance to the stone and stained glass cathedrals of England. It was perfect, though, for a meeting place. It was only a few miles from Rhuddlan Castle, near enough that Justin could ride out on his own without the need of Sion's escort, and convenient in that he could spend the night in St Asaph's guest house, offer the bishop's gatekeeper a few coins to slip him in and out, and then walk down the hill to await Llewelyn's arrival.

But if it was advantageous for Justin, Llanelwy was a potential death trap for Llewelyn ab Iorwerth, and he wondered why the Welshman had chosen it. It was dangerously close to Davydd's castle at Rhuddlan, deep in the heart of his domains. He supposed Llewelyn might argue that the best hiding place was sometimes in plain sight, but he could not help remembering Molly's tart warning about men who lusted after danger instead of whores. "Unpredictable and reckless," she'd called them. Not the sort of man he ought to be meeting alone at night in a deserted churchyard.

The moon had escaped the cloud's smothering confines, and silvered light illuminated the small cemetery. He'd been told by the guest house hospitaller that Thomas de Caldecott was buried here; his funeral had been held in the cathedral but its hallowed ground was reserved for its own. It was easy to find Thomas's grave; there were only two earthen mounds that indicated recent burials, and one was too small to be anything but the final resting place of a baby. Justin paused before that forlorn little grave, saying a prayer for the soul of its occupant. In England unbaptized infants could not be buried in consecrated ground. He thought the Welsh might be more generous in interpreting God's Word; at least he hoped so.

Moving toward Thomas de Caldecott's grave, he stood staring down at the bare, naked earth, the stark wooden cross. He offered no prayers for Thomas's soul. If the knight were to be forgiven, let it be by the Almighty. Neither the murdered men nor the three missing sailors could offer their forgiveness. And though she still breathed, he counted Angharad, too, amongst de Caldecott's victims.

"Is that the grave of the English slayer?"

Justin was not caught utterly by surprise; he'd taken notice at Aberconwy of Llewelyn's natural sense of drama. But the Welshman's ghostly approach was still impressive; he'd heard not so much as a twig's snap, a pebble's scrape. Turning without haste, as if he'd known of Llewelyn's presence all along, he said, "I ought to introduce you to Molly's phantom."

Llewelyn looked understandably puzzled. "English humor is one of life's great mysteries." Coming forward into the moonlight, he glanced down at the grave, then back at Justin. "A better resting place than he deserves, I daresay. Any idea who might have poisoned him?"

"Is there anyone in North Wales who *does* believe the man was stabbed?" Justin said wryly and caught the glimmer of a quick smile.

"Only those whose wits are addled by drink or grief," Llewelyn said, and Justin wondered if he knew about Angharad. "Sion saw the body and says there was no blood or visible wounds . . . other than *my* dagger thrust, of course."

"Are you claiming credit for another man's deed? Your uncle says Rhys ap Cadell wielded the blade."

"So I heard. Rhys was so pleased that Davydd remembers him." Llewelyn's lip curled. "My uncle is lucky indeed that Rhys was not prowling about Rhuddlan with a knife at the ready. When Rhys wants to take down a tree, he does not waste time lopping off branches, goes right for the roots."

"I suspect that you do, too."

Llewelyn did not deny it. "I suppose I am fortunate that I was not even born when the Archbishop of Canterbury was slain, or else Davydd would be blaming me for that death, too."

Thomas Becket had been murdered in December of God's Year 1170, so Justin had not been born then, either. But he was very familiar with the archbishop's story, as who in Christendom was not? Becket had died in his own cathedral, struck down by four knights who'd claimed that they'd acted on the king's behalf. Henry had passionately denied it, swearing that he'd spoken careless words in anger, no more than that, and eventually he'd convinced the Church. Even those who did not believe him to be guilty, though, did not believe him to be innocent, either. Whether he'd intended it or not, his Angevin rage had unleashed evil, and in perhaps the greatest irony of all, the man who'd been his beloved friend and then his mortal enemy became a holy martyr, canonized as a saint.

Justin had always been intrigued by the enigmatic figure of the archbishop, in part because his father was a great admirer of Thomas Becket. He'd often spoken of his brief meeting with the archbishop, scant weeks before Becket's murder, and Justin had been awed that someone he knew had actually spoken with a saint.

When he entered the queen's service, he'd yearned to ask her about Becket, but he never dared, and only once had she made mention of the tragic feud that brought such grief to both her husband and his archbishop, remarking cryptically that she'd have given a great deal to witness the first meeting between Henry and Becket in the afterlife. Justin had been shocked enough to blurt out, "In Heaven?" for he'd taken it for granted that King Henry would have to endure centuries in Purgatory to repent his earthly sins. Eleanor had looked at him and laughed, reading his thoughts with her usual ease. "Actually," she'd murmured, "I was envisioning them both in Hell," and then laughed again at the stunned expression on his face.

Llewelyn's sarcasm had brought that memory back, and much to his own surprise, Justin found himself telling the Welshman about the queen's sardonic comment. He could not say what prompted him to do so, for he took very seriously his responsibilities as the queen's man, and not the least of them was utter discretion. But

Llewelyn did not seem startled by Eleanor's acerbic opinion of the archbishop. "We have a saying in Welsh," he said with a grin, "*Po agosaf i'r eglwys, pellaf o baradwys.* Nearest to church, furthest from God."

Justin sensed that here was another who did not venerate St Thomas and stifled an urge to defend the martyred archbishop. Instead, he indulged his curiosity and asked Llewelyn if it were true that he'd begun his rebellion against Davydd at the green age of fourteen.

"That is not as remarkable as it sounds. In Wales, a youth reaches his legal majority at fourteen rather than England's twenty-one." Justin caught the glint of laughter in the Welshman's eyes even before Llewelyn added blandly, "We must mature faster than you English do."

"I am sure the Welsh have manifold virtues," Justin said amiably. "It is very *mature*, for certes, to choose a rendezvous that is right under Davydd's nose."

"I was looking out for your best interests." Llewelyn tried and almost succeeded in sounding reproachful. "It is well known that the English get lost with alarming ease, mayhap because they are so often venturing into lands not theirs." He did not wait for Justin's retort, glancing around the silent churchyard as if to acknowledge this was neither the ideal place nor the time for verbal jousting. "Why did you ask to meet me, Iestyn?"

"Whilst I was in Chester, I was able to unearth enough evidence to connect Thomas de Caldecott to the robbery and killings. Regrettably, he got himself murdered ere I could confirm the identity of his ally."

"Very unsporting of him," Llewelyn agreed. "You never did answer my question: who you think killed him. I'd naturally suspect my uncle Davydd, but even he would not have made such a bloody botch of it. What about this ally? Who do you suspect? The Lady Emma?"

Justin could not conceal his surprise. "What . . . you have second sight?"

"So I was right?" Llewelyn sounded surprised, too. "I suppose twenty years of marriage to Davydd could drive any woman to lunacy. But what sort of proof do you have?"

"Enough to fit into a thimble with space to spare," Justin admitted and explained why he harbored suspicions of Emma, concluding with his futile hunt in Chester for Oliver and Molly's "phantom." Llewelyn listened without interruption, his expression intent. Justin was coming to respect the Welshman's intellect, and he was gratified that Llewelyn seemed to take his conjecturing seriously.

"I see what you mean about the thimble," Llewelyn said, after a reflective silence. "But if there is not enough to convict the lady, there is enough to justify further investigation. Why are you telling me all this, though? Mind you, I appreciate your generosity. I am just curious about what prompted it."

"My queen's interest is in recovering the ransom. There'll come a time when she seeks to punish the offenders, but not yet. If I cannot find proof of Davydd's treachery, or if evil befalls me here in Wales, it will be up to you to disprove Davydd's accusations. I want to make sure that you have the weapons you'll need to do it. And remember . . . if I die and you let Davydd win, I'll be haunting you until you take your last breath."

The curve of Llewelyn's mouth hinted at a suppressed smile. "I could become right fond of you, English," he said, "at least until the ransom is found!"

Justin had never seen Rhun look so cheerful. He'd lost that invalid's pallor, the spring was back in his step, and his smile was not far from the surface. He was feeling well enough to earn his keep and was working in the stables now. He'd always had a way with horses, he confided, but he'd never been given the opportunity at Rhuddlan. Justin had come to talk to the boy about returning to Davydd's service. He was beginning to suspect, though, that Rhun had other ideas.

"If you want to come back to Rhuddlan," he said, "we think it can be done. I must stay out of it, for Davydd would deny you just to spite me. I have talked to the Lady Angharad, and she is willing to approach the Lady Emma on your behalf."

Rhun was already shaking his head. "I thank you for your kindness, but I have no wish to serve Lord Davydd again. Master Sion's brother has said he thinks I have the makings of a good groom. And . . ." He paused, lowering his voice conspiratorially although none were within earshot. "I do not think Lord Davydd will rule Gwynedd much longer. God willing, Lord Llewelyn will prevail and the Welsh will rejoice."

Justin agreed with him that Davydd was living on borrowed time and probably knew it, which accounted for his fear-driven rages. His treachery Justin was inclined to attribute to Davydd's deceitful nature, remembering that Davydd had originally obtained power by ambushing his brother Hywel. The Welsh, he decided, could give Cain and Abel lessons in fraternal rivalry. But then, so could King Richard and his jealousy-ridden brother John.

"Master de Quincy . . ." Some of Rhun's newfound confidence was ebbing away. "I have not returned to the ambush site. I did not want to see where the others died. A few days past, one of the grooms asked me where it had happened, and I told him as best I could. He came back later and was sorely vexed with me, saying I'd misspoke, that the ambush had taken place several miles down the road. He talked about the burned hay-wains being near a copse of alder trees, but that is not how I remember it. In my mind's eye, I see a bend in the road and them waiting for us as we made the turn. Now my memory could be faulty, I suppose . . ."

"I suppose it could," Justin agreed. But he did not believe that, and neither did Rhun.

Justin returned to Rhuddlan, planning to set out at first light to search for the hidden wool. He understood now why all previous searches had been in vain. Davydd's men had scoured the area where the burned wagons had been found, as had Llewelyn's men and Justin himself. But the ambush had actually occurred miles down the road, where the wool was likely concealed, and the bodies of the men were then loaded into the empty wagons and driven to the spot where they were burned. He was guessing that Rhun had told him first out of a sense of gratitude. The lad had other loyalties, though. Could he find the wool ere Rhun confided in Sion's brother and word was passed on to Llewelyn ab Iorwerth?

His plans were disrupted, though, almost as soon as he'd ridden into the castle bailey. He was leading his stallion into the stables when Sion slipped in after him with news that changed everything. The Lady Emma was intending to visit the holy well of St Gwenfrewi at Treffynnon, Sion reported, a journey that struck him as suspicious for several reasons. Gwenfrewi, the patron saint of virgins, was much revered by the faithful and the healing power of her holy well was so renowned that King Richard himself had made a pilgrimage there before setting out on his ill-fated crusade. It was close by Basingwerk and Justin had found time on each of his abbey stays to pay his respects to the little Welsh saint who'd died in defense of her chastity so many centuries ago. He saw nothing odd, therefore, in Emma's pilgrimage to such a celebrated shrine, but Sion quickly enlightened him.

Never had Emma visited Gwenfrewi's holy well, he said with some indignation, not once in more than twenty years in Wales. Justin started to point out that Emma would not have been welcome at Basingwerk Abbey, where her sex mattered more than her status as Davydd's consort, but Sion gave him no chance.

"Well, I find it strange that she suddenly shows such interest in a saint she has ignored for all of her married life. I find it strange that a woman who will not go to the privy chamber without an escort is taking only Oliver, one of her handmaidens, and just enough men to see to her safety. The last time she went to Chester, she traveled in a style that the English queen might well have envied. And I also find it strange that she is willing to pass the night in a humble priest's abode instead of demanding that the White Monks admit her to their guest house or returning to Rhuddlan."

By now Sion had won Justin over. "You are right," he conceded. "None of that sounds like the Lady Emma that we know and love not. I will do my best to find out what she is up to, but it will not be easy, Sion. If she has even the slightest suspicion that I am close at hand, she'll never stir from that priest's house."

"That is why you need to announce today that you are going to Chester. If you leave at daybreak tomorrow, you'll get to Basingwerk ere Emma does. If you can keep out of her sight, she ought to feel secure enough to follow through with whatever she is planning. She has said nothing in public yet about her pilgrimage, so she has no reason to suspect that you know. I think she will welcome your absence, not doubt it."

Justin was very glad that he'd shared his suspicions about Emma with Sion. The man was proving to be a useful ally . . . as long as his interests continued to coincide with those of Llewelyn ab Iorwerth. "I think Oliver set up this meeting whilst he was in Chester. I'd wager that Emma never intended to take so active a role herself, not until Thomas de Caldecott got himself so inconveniently murdered."

Sion nodded somberly. "This may be your last chance to find either the truth or the ransom, Iestyn."

"I know." His queen wanted the ransom. Davydd also wanted the ransom. He wondered which one Llewelyn wanted, if it came to a choice. If only he had the answer to that question, he'd know, then, how much he dared trust the Welsh rebel.

17

September 1193
Treffynnon, Wales

A chill drizzle was leaking from clouds the color of lead.
Justin had seen few scenes as desolate as Treffynnon, the
tiny village that had grown up around the holy well of St
Gwenfrewi. Undaunted by the dreary weather, a few
hardy pilgrims had gathered at the spring. Noticing a
young boy dragging a clubfoot, Justin hoped that if the
saint answered any prayers this day, it would be his.

Shifting position, he winced as his back muscles
cramped in protest. He was not surprised that he'd awakened so stiff and sore, for he'd passed the night in a barn.
As uncomfortable as his lodgings had been, at least he'd
been spared a night camping out in the woods. He'd not
dared to stay at the abbey guest house, for it was barely a
mile away at the lower end of the valley, and he was sure
that Oliver would be on the lookout for an Englishman
upon a chestnut stallion. Fortunately, Sion had come to
his rescue, suggesting that he ask for shelter at one of the
abbey granges.

The granges were run by conversi, lay brothers who
took holy vows as the monks did, but who lived under a
less restrictive code of behavior, unlettered men recruited
from the poor and the peasantry to do the manual labor
that the choir monks eschewed. Following Sion's advice,
Justin had packed several wineskins and guaranteed himself a cordial welcome when he'd ridden into the grange

at Mertyn. It was one of the smallest and poorest of the abbey's farms, but the lay brothers had been generous hosts, sharing their plain fare and offering Justin a snug straw bed in the byre that sheltered their cows.

Leaving Copper in the cattle barn, he set out before dawn for Treffynnon. It was not an enjoyable trek, for the rain was cold, the path muddy, and a hole had worn through one of his boots. Thankful that less than three miles lay between grange and holy well, he limped into the hamlet before anyone was stirring. After finding a perch to keep watch, he peeled off a piece of bark to make a temporary plug for the boot sole. His best guess was that the Chester phantom would be arriving sooner rather than later, for he could not imagine the elegant, luxury-loving Emma spending any more time than need be in the priest's small, shabby house. She'd yet to emerge, but Justin had chosen his hiding place with care, one that afforded an unobstructed view of the sacred spring, the adjacent church, and the priest's lodging. He need only watch and wait.

The rain continued to fall, and Justin was shivering and wet and hungry by the time Emma appeared. Justin observed that she did not follow the usual pilgrim's practice of praying at the moss-covered valley stones that represented the penitential stations. Instead she headed directly for the well, where her armed escort made the pilgrims stand aside so she could approach on her own. Oliver produced a blanket, so that she could kneel without muddying her skirts, and Justin watched closely as she blessed herself with the holy water and bowed her head. Her prayer was a brief one, confirming Justin's cynical suspicions about the sincerity of her desire to honor the martyred Welsh saint. Only after she had risen and was escorted into the church did her guards permit the pilgrims to return to the spring and their interrupted prayers.

Although Justin did not yet know it, the rest of his day would go downhill from there. Emma soon exited the church and returned to the priest's lodging. Oliver remained behind and began to approach villagers. Well out of earshot, Justin watched in frustration as the same scenario was enacted time and time again. Oliver would initiate a conversation, only to get shrugs and uncomprehending stares for his trouble. Justin surmised that Oliver was encountering a language barrier; he apparently spoke no Welsh and none of the villagers he accosted spoke French.

Making no progress with the local people, Oliver concentrated upon the pilgrims, but he had no luck until he addressed a tall, hulking youth in the long russet robe and wide-brimmed hat that proclaimed his pilgrim status. Judging by the animated discussion that followed, Justin concluded that Oliver had at last found someone who could answer his questions. But what was Oliver seeking so urgently to find out?

When the canonical hour of Terce drew near, Emma re-emerged and accompanied the priest to the church, where they were soon joined by villagers, pilgrims, and some of the men who'd been staying in the abbey guest house. After the Morrow Mass, the church emptied and people went about their daily chores and activities. Emma was among the last to depart, returning once more to the priest's lodgings. But Justin waited in vain for Oliver.

Once he realized that Oliver must have slipped out the church's side door during the Mass, Justin used some of the Welsh curses he'd picked up from Davydd. He did not think Oliver suspected that he was under surveillance; this was just more proof of the man's innate caution. It was too late to try to pick up the trail. All he could do was to hope that Oliver had not sneaked off to meet Emma's mystery partner. He had logic on his side, for why would Emma have made this uncomfortable journey to Treffynnon if her presence were not needed and Oliver could act on her behalf? Logic notwithstanding, though, Justin felt as if there was a hollow, empty pit where his stomach ought to be.

Oliver was gone for hours, not returning until the afternoon. He moved slowly and his limp was much more pronounced; even from a distance, Justin could see that his boots were heavily caked in mud. He disappeared into the priest's house, and neither he nor Emma was seen again that day. Justin had gotten bread and cheese from the monks at Mertyn, but he'd eaten it at midday, and he found himself bedeviled by hunger as well as fatigue and cold. He'd been sure that Emma had come to Treffynnon to meet someone, so sure. But his faith was waning with each wet, wearisome hour of this vexing, never-ending day.

Darkness came quickly, and the villagers soon retreated to their hearths. The priest withdrew to pass the night at a parishioner's house, and Emma's men-at-arms trudged down the valley toward the abbey guest house. Justin perked up with their departure, surprised that Emma would not have chosen to billet her men in the village. It seemed unlikely in the extreme that she would have put her men's comfort and the convenience of the villagers before her own safety . . . not unless she was expecting a guest and wanted no prying eyes.

The sky was mottled by lowering storm clouds, but Justin's eyes had adjusted to the darkness and he'd found a hiding place closer to the priest's lodgings, so he was reasonably confident that no one could approach the house without his noticing. Off in the distance, a dog barked and was answered with the haunting, lonely howl of a Welsh wolf. Trees rustled and whispered in harmony with the wind. Close at hand, Justin heard the squeak of a small animal that had just met a bloody death. He thought he could even hear the splashing of St Gwenfrewi's holy spring. The muted music of the abbey church bells drifted down the valley, ringing in Compline. Soon afterward, Justin caught a flash of light.

The light vanished as abruptly as it had appeared, and he realized that a lantern's flame had been shielded. The door to the priest's house had creaked open and two mantled, hooded figures now crept stealthily out into the night. Once they'd crossed the churchyard and moved away from the village, the lantern glowed again. Rising soundlessly from his hiding place, Justin began to follow that faint, flickering light.

He assumed that Emma's ally would be close by and was puzzled when they left the pasture behind and entered the woods. Trailing after them at a safe distance, Justin discovered that there was a path winding its way among the trees. It was muddy, strewn with leaves and dead branches, and he had to watch his footing with every step he took. From somewhere up ahead, he heard a sudden cry, and he froze in his tracks.

"My lady, are you hurt?"

"No . . . I just twisted my ankle."

The voices carried back to Justin with startling clarity. None of this made sense to him. Why was Emma's partner not coming to her? Why were they not meeting near Treffynnon?

"Are you sure you can find the way, Oliver?"

"As long as we stay on the path, my lady, we'll not get lost. To make sure, I tied white strips of cloth to trees this afternoon. See . . . there is one now."

"How clever of you," Emma said, with more warmth than Justin had hitherto heard in her voice. "I do see it." Oliver explained that he'd return on the morrow and remove them, and Emma praised his resourcefulness again. "Oliver . . . what in the world are these cloths? They do not look like rags to me."

"I . . . er . . . appropriated one of Father Marcus's shirts. It was the only white cloth I could find."

"Well, we must be sure to leave money in repayment. We are not thieves, after all," Emma said, and then she laughed. This was a new Emma to Justin, one he suspected that few ever saw. She even sounded different; that little-girl breathiness was gone and her enunciation was crisp and confident, utterly devoid of coyness or coquetry.

"This is nothing you ought to be doing, my lady. I wish you'd agreed to let me serve as your messenger."

"So do I, Oliver," Emma said ruefully. "No . . . as unpleasant as this is, it could not be helped. Some news can only be delivered face-to-face."

Justin forgot to breathe, so intently was he waiting to hear her next words. But his hopes of a dramatic revelation came to naught. What he heard instead was an alarmed exclamation from Oliver. Justin halted abruptly, his pulse racing until he realized that they'd not discovered his presence. Oliver had stumbled, fallen to his knees, and Emma nearly lost her own balance when she tried to assist him. After that mishap, they continued on in silence, and Justin dropped back, deciding he could risk following from a safer distance.

The path zigzagged through the woods and, from time to time, Oliver's lantern was no longer in sight. Justin kept his eyes peeled for Oliver's white signals. He thought he had an idea where they were going. The lay brothers had told him about the other abbey granges, perhaps not wanting him to think that they were all as meager as theirs at Mertyn. The most prosperous was the one at Mostyn, ideally located on the River Dee estuary, which enabled the monks to ship their wool to Chester by water. Justin thought he remembered them telling him that Mostyn was about three miles from Basingwerk, and the pathway would be a natural route to and from the abbey. But why Mostyn? Justin still had so many questions. He could only hope that he'd finally find some of the answers this night.

When he eventually emerged from the woods, he saw that his hunch had been right; the Mostyn grange was their destination. He watched as Emma and Oliver disappeared through the gateway, and then cautiously approached the low stone wall that marked the boundary lines of the abbey farm. The night shrouded most of the buildings, but he knew what he'd have seen by light of day: accommodations for the lay brothers, sheepcotes, barns, possibly even a chapel. His nose wrinkled as the wind brought a rank smell his way; it seemed there was also a pigsty. Boosting himself up onto the wall, he hesitated only a moment before dropping down onto the soft earth on the other side.

The sheepcotes were empty, for the flock had not been brought in from their summer pastures yet. Justin darted from one to the other, using them as camouflage. Between the darkness and the distance, Justin could discern only shadowy figures, the silhouettes of buildings. He'd become so accustomed to the night blackness that he was almost blinded by a sudden flare of light as a door opened. Men were coming out, holding blazing torches. The leaping flames lit up a scene as remarkable as it was alarming. These were not monks moving to meet Emma. Nor were they lay brothers. These men were booted and armed, mantles drawn back to give easy access to sheathed swords. As unlikely as it seemed to Justin, it looked as if the abbey grange at Mostyn had been taken over by an army.

Justin had approached as close as he dared, taking cover behind the wooden chapel as he tried to make sense of the situation. The lay brothers were being held in their dorter, doubtless even more bewildered than he was by this unexpected turn of events. No outlaw band would raid an abbey grange, for what could they hope to get? So who were these men? And what was Emma's part in all this?

With the arrival of more men, he had a partial answer, for they were coming from the north, and they were not on horseback. There could only be one explanation: they were from a ship anchored out in the estuary. He was still mulling this over when he found himself in danger of discovery; several of the newcomers were approaching at an angle that would bring them much too close to his hiding place. He made the only move he could and ducked through the partially open door of the chapel.

He almost tripped over a pile of candles scattered all over the floor; it was easy to imagine one of the monks spilling them when confronted by armed intruders. Leaving the door ajar, he continued to keep watch. Emma was ringed by flaming torches, Oliver hovering protectively at her side. A few more lay brothers were being rounded up, herded into the dorter with the other captives. The rain had been falling sporadically since sundown, but now the clouds split, inundating Mostyn in a deluge of icy water. Several of the men were gesturing toward the dorter, but Emma shook her head and, to Justin's horror, pointed at the chapel.

A desperate glance around the chapel interior revealed one possible means of escape: a window in the west wall.

But it was shuttered and he'd never get it open in time. Retreating into the middle of the room, he experienced a moment of utter despair. Then he saw the outlines of another door. Reaching it in three strides, he dived through into blessed darkness.

A small, windowless room, it was blacker than pitch, blacker than sin. He guessed it must be the sacristy. It would be an even more deadly snare than the chapel, but for now, it offered a chance of salvation. He left the door cracked open; if he went down, by God, he'd go down with answers. Torchlights spilled through the chapel doorway, brighter than the sun to moles and bats and Justin, who had to shut his eyes against the glare.

"I will await him here." Emma's voice indicated she was addressing her inferiors; she was very much the lady of the manor again, adding coolly, "I hope it will not be long."

So did Justin. As he'd been able to envision the panic of monks and lay brothers, so, too, could he imagine the fear felt by a cornered mouse with a cat on the prowl. He'd never been uncomfortable in small, confined spaces . . . until now. His back to the wall, he reached under his mantle and let his hand rest on the hilt of his sword.

The sound was a soft one, barely carrying to Justin's ears. But it set his heart to thudding against his ribs, for it had come from a far corner of the sacristy. He stood very still, every sense alert, his eyes probing the chamber until he could peel away several shadows from the obscuring darkness. His mouth went dry with the realization that he was sharing his sanctuary. Almost at once, though, he recognized these new adversaries for what they were: fearful lay brothers who'd taken refuge in the safest place they could find, God's House. He wished he would whisper a reassurance, vow that he was not their enemy. But he dared not risk it, not with Emma pacing impatiently on the other side of that thin, wooden wall.

"Go and seek out their buttery, Oliver. You look like a man desperately in need of a drink." When Oliver said that he did not think the Cistercians allowed wine or ale upon their granges, Emma retorted, "Now why does that not surprise me?" in an acerbic tone that spoke volumes about her feelings for the White Monks.

Justin could not blame her for her animosity, for it had to rankle that the White Monks would bar even their prince's consort from their guest halls. Oddly enough, he was finding this new Emma more sympathetic than the pampered princess he'd seen on display at Rhuddlan. This woman might be in collusion with the Devil for all he knew, but she was showing commendable courage, obvious affection for Oliver, and a steely resolve that put him in mind of his queen.

"The monks must have a lit fire somewhere, if only in the kitchen. Go find it, Oliver, and thaw out." Oliver protested that he did not want to leave her, confirming Justin's suspicions that he was an old family retainer when he spoke proudly of serving her lord father, that prince of blessed memory, Count Geoffrey. But Emma insisted, and Oliver dutifully departed. Almost at once, though, he was back.

"My lady, he has come!"

"About time," Emma muttered, not sounding much in awe of her clandestine partner in crime. She'd begun to pace again, her footsteps echoing as far as the sacristy door and then away. Justin blew on his hands, trying to warm them. In the corner, the lay brothers still huddled, or so he assumed, for they were all but invisible in their dark brown habits. For the first time since taking cover in the sacristy, Justin could feel the excitement throbbing through his veins. Close, so close to learning the truth about this tangled spider's web of conspiracy and intrigue!

Others were entering the chapel. After a murmur of voices, light squeezed through the cracked door of the sacristy, and Justin guessed that a wall sconce had been lit. The temptation to put his eye to that arrow-thin opening was considerable. So far Justin was resisting it.

"I want no witnesses to this meeting," Emma said, and Justin wondered how many of these men knew her identity. Cloaked in a dark, hooded mantle, she thwarted recognition by even her near and dear ones.

"Your wish is my command, my lady." This voice had the distinctive intonation of the highborn, that unmistakable blend of education, expectation, and arrogance. It was also a familiar voice to Justin, one he'd heard all too often at high-risk moments in the past year. He refused to believe what his brain was telling him, though, for that voice belonged to a man who was hundreds of miles away, on the other side of the English Channel.

There was the sound of retreating footsteps, a closing door, and then that silken, sardonic voice again, calling Emma "My dearest aunt," and a stunned Justin could no longer deny that Emma's ally was Queen Eleanor's faithless son, John.

18

"We would be more comfortable in the grange's hall, Aunt Emma."

"No . . . privacy matters more to me than comfort."

Justin was startled by how clearly audible their voices were. This was working out even better than he'd dared hope . . . so far.

"When I heard that you'd left England, I was not sure you'd be back, John."

"Going to Paris is not like going to Hell, Aunt Emma. Men have been known to return from France." John's footsteps neared the sacristy door. "How long has it been since we last met? It has to be a few years . . . I think when Richard made his pilgrimage to St Winifred's Well? But you've not aged a day that I can see. No wonder other women like you not."

"You need not waste gallantry upon kinswomen, John. There is no profit in it."

John laughed. "Just out of curiosity, do you ever let anyone else see the side of you that you show to me? I do not blame you for being vexed with my abrupt departure for the French court. It could not be helped, though, and I did keep my promise. I came back."

"I was not so much vexed as concerned lest all our planning be set at naught. I knew from the moment I learned of Davydd's mad scheme that this was an opportunity that would not come again. Thankfully we had such a reliable emissary, or all would have been lost as soon as you sailed from Southampton."

It was becoming clear to Justin that their plan had been in the works for months, long before the actual robbery. He assumed Thomas de Caldecott was the "reliable emissary," but John disabused him of that notion by saying, "Yes, the Breton was a godsend . . . or devil-sent, depending upon one's point of view." Justin frowned. Who was the Breton?

"It was inspired to suggest him as go-between, Aunt Emma. Neither of us would have been foolhardy enough to commit much to letters. I suppose you met the Breton whilst he was in my father's service?"

"Yes."

"You are not the most forthcoming of allies." John was sounding amused again. "There is much I still do not know about this plot of yours. Such as how you found out about Davydd's plans."

"Does it truly matter? If you must know, Davydd told me. He boasted of it, in fact, said he'd be catching two rabbits in one snare, gaining Richard's gratitude when he recovered the ransom whilst ridding himself of a troublesome rival."

John chuckled. "Is that a Welsh saying. . . . catching two rabbits in one snare? I like it, for that is what I am doing myself with this return to England. I, too, am capturing two rabbits in one snare, and what makes it so sweet is that both rabbits belong to Brother Richard!"

"I do not understand that, nor do I want to. Whatever else you have in mind is between you and the Almighty."

"Such righteousness does not become you, Aunt Emma." John's voice had taken on a discernible edge. "It is not as if your hands are not bloodied, too. It is my understanding that three men died in that robbery. And lest we forget, that Cheshire knight who was found dead in your chapel under such odd circumstances."

"My hands are not bloodied! Those killings were de Caldecott's doing, not mine. I wanted the ransom. He was the one who turned a robbery into murder."

"And I am sure you wept a sea of salt tears for those poor, murdered men."

"You know I did not," she snapped. "But the fact that I did not grieve for them does not mean that I wanted their deaths. That sin is on Thomas de Caldecott, and he has already answered for it."

"Yes, so I heard. Oliver was sparing with the details, though. I do not suppose that you had a hand in it?"

"Of course I did not!"

"I was not accusing, merely asking. I have never been a believer in coincidences, so naturally I marveled that the man should be killed once there was no longer a need for his services."

"I am going to assume that you are making another of your dubious jests," Emma said, with enough ice in her voice to put John at risk for frostbite. "I do not know who killed de Caldecott, only that it was not me."

"A passing stranger, then?" John suggested sarcastically. "Surely you must have some suspicions?"

"Well . . . Davydd was acting so oddly afterward that I did wonder if he'd ordered it done. But it turned out that he was merely trying to put the blame upon his nephew, with his usual dazzling success."

"I hope that my own wife does not speak of me in such loving tones. Surely the man has some redeeming qualities?"

"None worth mentioning," Emma said scathingly. "As I said, I do not know who killed de Caldecott. Nor do I know why you should care."

"Because I do not like surprises, Aunt Emma. No more

than I like riddles. Here is one I particularly dislike: Why is a woman willing to put her own son's birthright at risk? I have no trouble believing that you loathe your husband. Most men would be astounded if they knew what their wives really think of them. But if Davydd loses power, where does that leave your son? Or you, for that matter?"

"My son's 'birthright,' you call it? Davydd seized power over the bodies of his brothers and has clung to it ever since by force, threats, and blind luck. You truly think there will be a peaceful transfer of that power from father to son? When pigs fly! I've always known that my son would never rule North Wales after Davydd. I just did not know the name of the man who would . . . until now."

"And that would be the troublesome nephew?"

"Do you know what I see when I look at Davydd? I see a doomed man, one with a mortal ailment that is slowly killing him. It is only a matter of time. And in that time I mean to do all I can to give my son—and my daughter— a secure future."

"By gaining a friend at court?"

"Why be so modest, John? What we are talking about is king-making. Your chances of seeing yourself crowned at Westminster increase dramatically if Richard does not come home. And then I will have more than a friend at court. I will have the king's favor."

"Yes," John said, "you will. Ingratitude has never been one of my vices." Judging from the sound of footsteps, Justin guessed that John had moved to Emma's side. "So you are taking such a great risk for your children? I hope they appreciate how fortunate they are. My own parents would do anything for the flesh of their flesh, absolutely anything . . . provided it did not involve the actual surrender of an acre of land or the loss of a single vassal."

"I see that you know your father better than I thought you did."

The bitterness in Emma's voice was so palpable that a verse from Scriptures popped into Justin's head, the one that spoke of "wormwood and gall." With John's retort, it was obvious that he, too, had caught the bile behind her words.

"My lord father always had a knack for making enemies. What did he do to incur your wrath, Emma?"

"You need to ask?" Emma sounded startled and then angry. "He forced me to wed a man I despised, separated me from my son, and exiled me to this godforsaken wilderness!"

"Well, yes, he did . . ." John did not sound as if he shared her outrage. "But that is the way it is done, Aunt Emma. Your son was the heir to your first husband's lands, so he could hardly follow you to Wales."

"He was four years old!"

"I was even younger when my parents deposited me at Fontevrault Abbey to start my career in the Church."

"And how did you like that, John? Did you cry for your nurse, for all that was known and familiar to you? My son cried for me."

When John spoke again, the edge was back in his voice, which made Justin think she'd cut too close to the bone. "For the highborn, marriages are made over the bargaining table, not in Heaven. Jesu, Richard even offered our sister Joanna to a Saracen prince! Of course she all but scorched his ears off when she heard, but—"

"I did not have Joanna's right of refusal! Nor am I innocent in the ways of the world. I was married off to Guy de Laval at a very young age, or have you forgotten that? When he died, I learned what most women will not admit, that a widow's lot is better than a wife's more often than not. But then my loving brother Harry decided that pleasing a Welsh ally mattered more than his sister's happiness."

"I doubt that he acted on a whim. Most likely he thought the marriage would help keep the peace in Wales."

"Yes, that is just what he told me when I begged him . . . begged him on my knees! He thought my marriage was a cheap price to pay for peace, and why not? I was the one to pay it, after all!"

"True enough . . . but in my father's defense, I feel obliged to point out that he did not wed you to a crofter or a shepherd, Aunt Emma. He wed you to a prince."

"A Welsh prince!" She all but spat the words. "So it does not surprise me that Richard was willing to marry his sister to an infidel. He was merely following in his father's footsteps, was he not?"

"I am beginning to understand. There is more at play here than a mother's concerns for her son's future. You see that 'price' you paid as a debt, one owed by my father. And since the dead are notoriously unreliable about paying debts, you mean to collect from Richard."

She did not deny it, saying challengingly, "What if I do?"

"In case it has escaped your notice, my father had more than one son. So why does Brother Richard get the lion's share of blood-guilt? Not even my greatest enemies have ever suggested that I am not the spawn of Harry's loins. Do you know something the rest of Christendom does not, Aunt Emma?"

Such a cynical jest shocked Justin; he could not imagine anyone but John daring to joke about so inflammatory a subject as paternity.

"What . . . that you are the result of Eleanor's dalliance with a dark-haired Angevin or Norman lord?" Emma asked, and then laughed. "No, John, I have no doubts about your lineage. Blood breeds true, you see.

You are indeed Harry's son. But you are also the only one who could understand my plight and my desire for vengeance. You already know what it is like to have no power of your own, to be utterly dependent upon the goodwill of those you detest . . . do you not?"

There was a long silence, broken at last by Emma. "You'd best hope that I've satisfied your curiosity, for I'll be offering no more secrets of the heart. This is no confessional, and you are for certes no priest."

"One more question, dear aunt, and only one. Where is the wool?"

"I would," Emma said slowly, "that I knew."

Justin stiffened in disbelief. John sounded no less stunned. "You do not know? What sort of game are you playing now, Emma?"

"I assure you it is no game. Thomas de Caldecott handled the robbery, hiring the men, hiding the ransom, doing whatever must be done. I was not pleased with his killings and let him know it. So he in turn balked at telling me where he'd hidden the wool. He said I had no need to know, not yet. He never quite put the threat into words, but his meaning was clear. As long as he alone knew the hiding place, he was holding the reins and I was riding pillion behind him."

It occurred to Justin that Emma had just given herself an excellent motive for not wanting Thomas dead. He no longer doubted her. Knowing what he now did about Thomas de Caldecott, he knew, too, that the other man had been quite capable of taking such audacious measures to protect himself.

John had apparently come to the same conclusion. "He was a crafty whoreson, I'll give him that. But why did your man not tell this to the Breton in Chester? What . . . it somehow slipped his mind?"

"What would have been the point? The Breton could

not have reached you ere you sailed for England. You'd likely have come in any event, since you've admitted you have other fish to fry here. Moreover, I have not given up. We can still recover the wool. De Caldecott was no Merlin, and it did not disappear in a puff of smoke. It is out there somewhere . . . waiting to be found."

"So is the Holy Grail, but I do not fancy my chances of finding it!"

"Come now, John, do not tell me that you never wager unless the odds are in your favor. I have brought a map of the area for you with the site of the ambush marked. If you put enough men to searching for the wool, they're likely to find it. Hire a Welshman who knows the lay of the land, do whatever you must."

"What if the search fails?"

"Well, you'll still be denying Richard the ransom, and is that not what you wanted? Of course you'd rather have the wool, too. But nothing matters more than keeping Richard captive in Germany, does it?"

The floor was wooden and the boards began to creak; it was easy for Justin to imagine John stalking about the chapel, pondering this setback. When he spoke again, Justin was surprised by the lack of anger in his voice; he'd not expected John to take a disappointment with such good grace.

"You are right, Aunt Emma. I'd burn every one of those woolsacks myself if that would prevent Richard's release. We'll wait a few weeks until all interest in the wool has died down, then I'll send men in to hunt for it. And I will not forget your help once I am king. On that you have my word."

"Many men would not put much faith in your word, John. But I do, for I know you, I know what matters to you and what does not. I think you will be a successful king, a better king than your vainglorious, battle-drunk brother. And now . . . I need an escort to Treffrynnon, for I am not about to walk back through those muddy woods and fields, not if I have to steal a horse."

"No need . . . I'll steal it for you," John offered. "We'll take a few of the grange horses, see you off in fine style."

"And return them to the grange afterward," she prompted, sounding so prim and proper that John laughed.

"God forbid that we steal from the good monks," he agreed cheerfully.

Justin held his breath, not exhaling until he heard the sound of the door opening and closing. Caught up in a surge of relief and triumph that was as intoxicating as any wine he'd ever drunk, he still waited several moments before risking a glimpse out into the chapel. Turning then toward the lay brothers, he said softly in Welsh, "They are gone, but we'd best stay where we are for now."

The darkness hid their faces; they were little more than indistinct shadows. One of them thanked him, though, murmuring "*Diolch yn fawr*" so politely that Justin had to smile, amused that men hiding in a church sacristy should be so meticulous about observing the proprieties. Common sense told him that it would be foolhardy to venture outside yet, but it would be hard to curb his impatience; his brain was racing as he sought to process all that he'd learned this night. The queen must be warned straightaway. He would have to leave Wales as soon as possible, for this information was too combustible to trust to a letter. He knew Eleanor would want no written trail of her son's latest sins. Once he'd reclaimed Copper at the other abbey grange, he would . . .

His musings were rudely interrupted by a sound that sent a chill up his spine: an opening door and raised voices. Men were entering the church. He tensed, his hand dropping again to the hilt of his sword, and then recoiled into the blackness of the sacristy, for John had come back.

The next voice he heard was as familiar to him as John's. "How much longer do you want to wait here, my lord? Are you not ready to return to the ship?"

"Soon, Durand, soon. You'll not be stranded here, I assure you. The rain has eased up but the wind is still high, and I'd rather not be bobbing about on the estuary in a small boat. One future English king drowned when the White Ship sank. I'd as soon not be the second."

Justin was not utterly surprised that Durand should be at Mostyn, too. He was John's veritable shadow, his access to the queen's son making him invaluable as Eleanor's spy. How much had Durand known of John's conspiracy with Emma? Justin did not share the queen's faith in her agent. He suspected that the other man shed his loyalties as easily as a snake shed its skin.

"I still do not see why you had Reynard escort the lady home from the grange and not me. I've a better sense of direction; Reynard has gotten lost on his way to the privy. And I could fend off outlaws in my sleep, whereas he'd bolt if he heard an owl hoot in the night."

"He is fond of you, too, Durand."

"I am not jesting, my lord. I truly wonder if she will be safe with him. Have they far to go?"

"Far enough," John said blandly. "Trust me, you'd have no chance of adding her to your conquests."

"Why not, my lord? Is she yours?"

John laughed. "Even I am not that depraved, Durand."

"What . . . is she a nun?" Durand sounded puzzled, and John laughed again. But his response was lost as more men entered the church. Justin could tell from their deferential tones that these were not knights like Durand; they showed none of his cockiness, the familiarity that danced right up to the border, yet somehow never crossed over into insolence or effrontery. It did not surprise Justin that John quieted them without raising his voice; men learned to obey quickly in John's service or they did not remain in his service.

Now that the storm had broken, John said, he would be returning to the ship. Most would be going with him, but he wanted some of his men to remain behind and guard the grange, keeping the monks in the dorter until Reynard got back. "Since you felt slighted by my earlier choice, Durand, you'll be in command."

"How can I thank you, my lord?" Durand sounded disgruntled; he knew that John was having fun at his expense. "I ask only that you do not forget to send the boat back for us."

"No promises," John said dryly, and the scuffle of feet told Justin that they were moving toward the door.

"We need help here!"

The cry was quickly drowned out by the rising tide of other voices. Daring a peek through the cracked door, Justin saw two men stumbling into the church, one of them bleeding profusely from a gashed forehead. Confusion ensued, for they naturally suspected they were under attack. The alarm soon subsided, though, when it was revealed that the wounded man had split his head open by tripping over a rake.

Transformed in seconds from injured victim to laughingstock, the man was subjected to ridicule rather than sympathy. But because his blood was gushing out like a fountain, someone eventually halted the fun and suggested they get the poor sod a bandage. Justin still did not realize his danger, not until a voice volunteered that there were likely to be cloths stored in the sacristy. He slid back behind the door, his only option to pray that no one would bring a lantern in search of the church vestments and linens. That hope lasted as long as it took for a flaming light to pierce the darkness like a beacon.

"Christ's Blood!" The intruder sprang backward, and the next sound Justin heard was the metallic clink of a sword being drawn from its scabbard. "There are men hiding in here!"

The lay brothers were discovered first, driven at swordpoint out into the chapel. But before Justin could dare to hope that he might escape notice, his hiding place behind the door was exposed and there was a sword pressing against his chest.

The lay brothers were all talking at once, pouring out a torrent of Welsh that meant nothing to their audience. Justin could have translated, paraphrasing their agitated pleas for mercy, their insistence that they were simple men of God, no threat to anyone. He kept his mouth shut, for he well knew that his survival depended upon attracting no attention to himself. But there were too many torches in the chapel for anyone to mistake his dark mantle for the brown habits of the conversi. A grizzled veteran cried, "This one is no monk," and jerked his hood back.

Squinting in the sudden glare, Justin experienced what it was like to be a fox brought to bay by encircling, snapping dogs. Rough hands were stripping away his mantle, laying claim to his sword and eating knife. He stumbled, regained his footing and found himself face-to-face with the queen's son.

"I'll be damned," John said in obvious astonishment. "Oliver mentioned that there was a queen's man prowling around but gave no names. I ought to have guessed, though. I'm beginning to think that I could go to Cathay and meet you coming around a corner, de Quincy."

Justin could think of nothing to say, and his mouth was

too dry for speech in any case. He managed a shrug, and then forced himself to meet Durand's eyes, finding in them exactly what he expected: amazement, hostility, and no help whatsoever. The lay brothers had been herded behind the altar, out of the way, leaving Justin alone in the center of the chapel, surrounded by men who'd kill him without a qualm if John gave the command.

Spurred into action by this unexpected turn of events, John ordered most of the men to head for the beach, taking the injured soldier with them. Others were dispatched to continue guarding their prisoners in the abbey dorter. One by one, he sent them off into the night until at last only Durand stood by his side. "Now . . ." he said, "what are we to do with you, de Quincy?"

"You could give me a ride back to Treffrynnon," Justin ventured, not in the least reassured when John smiled.

"You've long been a thorn in my side, a burr under my saddle, call it what you will. I will admit that there is a certain entertainment value in never knowing when or where you're likely to turn up, and you were even of some use to me at Windsor's siege. And watching you and Durand bristling like a couple of tomcats can be amusing. It is awkward, though, for the lady wants to keep her identity a secret, and we both know you'd be blabbing her name all over the kingdom in the time it took my ship to raise anchor."

Justin knew it was futile, but he made a game try anyway, saying earnestly, "How can I, my lord, when I never saw the lady's face? She could be the Queen of France for all I know."

John's smile surfaced again. "See why I like this lad, Durand?" Pulling up his hood, he strode to the door, saying over his shoulder, "Remember what I said about waiting for Reynard to get back. Once he does, you can let the monks loose and then head for the beach, where we'll have a boat waiting for you."

Durand acknowledged the order and then glanced toward Justin. "My lord . . . what about de Quincy?"

John paused in the doorway, regarding Justin with an enigmatic expression, one not easy to interpret. "A pity," he said, sounding almost regretful, "but he's given me no choice. Kill him."

19

The chapel was absolutely and eerily still, so quiet that Justin imagined the other men must be able to hear the wild pounding of his heart. The Welsh lay brothers were clustered together, uncomprehending but fearful. These hooded, faceless figures garbed in austere monks' habits seemed ghostly and unreal to Justin, not flesh-and-blood men, more like the starkly sculptured effigies on tombs of the dead.

Durand at last broke the foreboding silence, saying very dryly, "Well . . . John was right. This *is* awkward." His eyes moved dismissively over the lay brothers, coming to rest upon Justin's face. "It is no secret that I have no fondness for you, de Quincy. If truth be told, you've been a pain in the arse from our first meeting. But we are on the same side, more or less."

As he spoke, he was unfastening his mantle, letting it drop to the floor at his feet. "If I do not kill you, though, I'll be defying John's express command. Not only will he be sorely vexed with me, he is like to become highly suspicious as well. So I have to ask myself which matters more to the queen, that I continue to serve her by spying on her son or that you continue to breathe."

With a smooth, practiced motion, he drew his sword from its scabbard. "Alas for you, we both know the answer to that question."

At the sight of the weapon, the lay brothers shrank back. Justin forced himself to stand his ground. Durand seemed in no hurry, though. "I'll do this much for you," he said coolly. "I'll not go for a deathblow. If you somehow survive, I can always tell John that I was sure your wound was mortal. So try not to flinch away from the blade or you could spoil my aim. You might want to kneel and close your eyes so you do not see the strike coming."

The mockery misfired, for it kindled a raw, visceral rage. Justin was far from a fool. He well knew that an unarmed man stood little chance against a swordsman as skilled as Durand. In a recessed corner of his soul, he was not even sure if he could have prevailed had he been armed. Durand was Death's henchman, whereas Justin had never killed anyone. But for now his fury was searing along his spine, surging through his veins, cauterizing his fear, and he tensed, awaiting his opportunity.

Durand kept his eyes upon Justin as he jerked his head toward the door and ordered the conversi to get out. Even without a knowledge of French, they seemed to grasp what was happening and burst into agitated Welsh that meant nothing to Durand. "Be gone from here," he snapped, "whilst you still can!"

"They are distraught that you would spill blood in God's House." Justin felt a flicker of pride that his voice sounded so even, so controlled. "They say that you would be committing a mortal sin. They do not know that your soul is already forfeit to the Antichrist!"

Durand spat out an oath, although whether it was aimed at his gibe or the balking monks, Justin could not say. One of the lay brothers then did something quite courageous. His youth was long gone, for he leaned heavily upon a cut-off shepherd's staff, his shoulders hunched under the burden of too many years, too much pain. He did not hesitate, though, shuffled slowly but resolutely toward Durand, and if his voice was reedy, quavering with age and apprehension, his words were boldly spoken—that Durand must not pollute their holy church with bloodshed and violence.

Losing patience, Durand snarled, "The blood shed can always be yours, old man!"

With a thrust of his arm, he sent the elderly monk reeling. There was an outcry from the other conversi, and Justin darted behind the altar, intending to make a grab for the torch sputtering in the wall sconce. What happened next froze him in his tracks. As the old man fell, he somehow entangled the crook of his staff around Durand's ankle, and the knight, already off balance from the shove, went crashing to the floor.

Justin had dared hope that the Almighty might aid him in his time of need. He'd not expected the Lord God to intervene, though, in so spectacular a fashion. But he did not waste time questioning his blessings, and when the sword shot from Durand's grasp, he dived for it. Nothing in his life had ever felt so good as the grip of that hilt in his hand. Knowing that he'd been given a reprieve, not deliverance, he rolled over and came swiftly to his feet, bracing for Durand's counterattack.

It never came. Durand was still sprawled upon the floor, with the aged monk astride him, a knee grinding into his chest, a dagger blade pressing against his throat. "You'd best lie very still, for an old man's hands are none too steady."

There was no need for Justin to translate; the warning had been given in fluent French. Durand took it seriously, not moving so much as a muscle. He felt no anger, not even fear, not yet, just utter astonishment. The monk's hood had fallen back, revealing a head of thick, dark hair that had never known a tonsure, revealing the face of a youthful, triumphant stranger, a man Durand had never laid eyes upon. "Who in Hellfire," he gasped, "are you?"

He sounded so dumbfounded that Justin burst out laughing. "It is my pleasure and my privilege," he said, deliberately drawing the words out, savoring the moment, "to introduce you, Durand, to the next Prince of North Wales, Llewelyn ab Iorwerth."

Llewelyn's companions were already shedding their habits, shaking off, too, the diffidence of submissive, unworldly monks. They wore swords with the ease of men accustomed to making use of them, knives tucked into high boots, and one of them had a coil of hempen rope looped in his belt. He was uncommonly tall, towering over Durand like a sturdy Welsh oak as he dangled the rope before the knight's eyes, looped into a hangman's noose. "Be a good lad and lie still," he said cheerfully, "and I'll fight the urge to see if this fits around your neck."

Durand weighed his chances, decided he did not like the odds, and did not resist as they jerked his arms behind his back. He was soon trussed up like a Michaelmas goose, bound hand and foot and gagged with a strip from his own mantle. He was not cowed, though, glaring up at them and taking comfort from hard-earned wisdom, that as long as a man had a heartbeat, he had hope, too.

For the moment, Justin was being ignored. He was examining Durand's sword, weighing the heft of it appreciatively before sliding it into the empty scabbard at his hip. "I think I got the best of this exchange," he said, and then, "We've no time to celebrate, though. John left men behind—"

Seeing the look of amusement that passed among them, he smiled sheepishly. "I forgot . . . you already know that. What do you want to do about them?"

"They pose no threat. You see, the men in the dorter are not monks. They are mine."

Justin's mouth dropped open, and then he laughed. "I do not know why that surprises me. You've been two jumps ahead of us from the first. Obviously Sion alerted you that Emma was going to the holy well at Treffynnon. So . . . you then put some of your men in the village, posing as pilgrims. My guess is that they overheard Oliver seeking directions to Mostyn. Am I right so far?"

"In fact," Llewelyn said, "we had no need to eavesdrop. Oliver was obliging enough to ask Ednyved." Tossing his head toward the amiable giant, he introduced him as Ednyved ap Cynwrig, and the third man, a dark, slender youth with glittering green eyes, as Ednyved's cousin, Rhys ap Cadell. "Yes, the same Rhys ap Cadell who crept into Rhuddlan Castle to commit unholy murder in Davydd's own chapel."

When Rhys did not take the bait, Llewelyn playfully elbowed him in the ribs before turning back to Justin. "Once we knew Mostyn grange was the site, it was easy enough to get here first and then to convince the lay brothers that we ought to be the ones to welcome the English invaders."

Justin knew that the monks of Basingwerk were not like the monks of Aberconwy; they were English in origin and loyalties, and he could not help wondering how Llewelyn had "convinced" the lay brothers to vacate the grange. His suspicions must have shown on his face, for Llewelyn grinned.

"To answer your unspoken question, Iestyn, the lay brothers are not buried out in the woods. They are burrowing for warmth under the hay up in the barn's loft, and right willingly. You see, the monks at Basingwerk may be dutiful subjects of the English Crown, but their lay brothers are Welsh to the bone."

"Well, however you did it, I am grateful," Justin said. "Of course it might have been easier on my nerves had I known I was not facing down Durand alone. I am not surprised that you fooled him so readily, for I never suspected that you were other than simple lay brothers. A pity you were born to the blood royal, Llewelyn. You'd have made a fine player. The shepherd's staff . . . that was an inspired touch."

"Christ Jesus, do not tell him that!" Ednyved was staring at Justin as if horrified. "He needs no encouragement to strut about the stage. We're just lucky we were shy of time, else he'd have taken it into his head to give us all tonsures to make us more convincing monks!"

They'd been conversing in French as a courtesy to Justin, but now Llewelyn said something in Welsh, too fast for Justin to catch, and the others laughed. Justin was amazed that they seemed so free and easy with Llewelyn, for he could not imagine an Englishman bantering so familiarly with his prince. After conferring with Rhys, Llewelyn sent him out into the rain, but Justin asked no questions, guessing that the young Welshman had gone to alert the rest of their men that the trap had been sprung. He was highly impressed by the efficiency of the entire operation, and now that his initial exhilaration was subsiding, he was remembering what a formidable foe Llewelyn ab Iorwerth could be.

Llewelyn was gazing down at Durand. "So this one spies for the queen against her own son? Is he good at what he does?"

"Yes, God smite him," Justin admitted, "very good." As he looked at Durand, his anger came flooding back, and he strode over, jerked out the knight's gag. "So when were you going to warn the queen that John was stealing the ransom? After he'd gotten it safely away to Paris?"

"I did not learn of his plans until we reached Chester,

you fool! You truly think John shares his every secret
with me?"

"I think that you could teach Judas Iscariot about betrayal! You just proved what I've long suspected, that you
serve only yourself."

"Jesus wept! How will I ever live with your bad opinion of me, de Quincy?"

"Assuming that you do," Llewelyn interjected silkily.
"Live, that is."

Durand's eyes cut toward him, then back to Justin.
"Does the queen share her every plan with you? No more
than John does with me. He is too shrewd to trust all his
chickens to one hen roost. I knew nothing of this scheme
until we sailed, and even then, he only told me bits and
pieces of the plot."

"And what of his other reason for returning to England?" Justin jeered. "Dare you claim to be ignorant of
that, too?"

"So far, yes, but I'll soon find out what I need to know.
I always do, de Quincy. That is why the queen values my
services so highly, and why I could not risk losing John's
trust by sparing you."

Justin shook his head incredulously, and Llewelyn
laughed outright. "How long, Iestyn, ere he is demanding
that you owe him an apology for not letting him kill you?
This one has a tongue nimble enough to lick honey off
thorns."

"No," Justin said, "he has a forked tongue, like any
snake." Leaning over, he knotted the neck of Durand's
tunic in his fist, forcing the other man to meet his eyes.
"So you'd have us believe that you played no part in this
ransom robbery. What about John's dealings with the
Breton? I suppose you are going to insist you know nothing of him, either."

"The Breton?" Durand's eyes widened in surprise, but

Justin could not tell if it was real or feigned. "I've heard of him. Who has not? He is said to be a master spy, one who is as elusive as early morning mist. I've never laid eyes on him, doubt that many have. Even his name is not known for certes. People call him the Breton, but none know if he truly does come from Brittany. What makes you think that he is involved in this?"

Justin could only marvel at the man's gall. "You dare to interrogate me after doing your best to kill me? When did we become a team again, Durand?"

"If you are going to stop John from carrying off the ransom, you'll need my help. Unless you'd rather take vengeance upon me and fail the queen?"

Llewelyn and Ednyved were both laughing, and after a moment, Justin laughed, too, for what else could he do? "I'd sooner take one of Hell's own demons as a partner than you, Durand."

If Durand was afraid, he was hiding it well. "I do not see that you have a choice, de Quincy," he said with a sneer, "not if you want to recover that ransom."

"Actually," Llewelyn said, "he does have a choice." His dark eyes flicked from Durand, over to Justin. "I can see why you'd prefer Hell's dregs to this weasel, Iestyn. But you can do better. What say you that we join forces to find the wool?"

"No offense, Llewelyn, but why would I want to do that?"

"Mayhap because you are a stranger in a land not your own, and you have neither the men nor the familiarity with these woods and hills to make a successful search."

"True . . . but I could get the men I need, hire local guides."

"True . . . but how much time would that take? Need I remind you that time is not on your side? If the ransom payment is delayed, what happens to your King Richard? Nothing good, I'd wager."

He'd not told Justin anything he did not already know. Justin had just been curious to see how well Llewelyn had grasped the weaknesses of his position. Now that he had his answer—all too well—he decided he had nothing to lose by candor, and he said, "I'll not argue that with you. Let's say we do work together, and we find the wool. What then? How do I know you'll not seize it all to pay for your rebellion?"

Llewelyn was quiet for a moment, paying Justin the compliment of taking his question seriously. "In all honesty, I suppose you do not, Iestyn. I can give you my word that I will not, and I am willing to do so. But there is no surety that I'd not change my mind at first sight of all that wool. So . . . yes, you'd be taking a risk. Let me ask you this, though. What are your chances of recovering the ransom on your own?"

Now it was Justin's turn to consider his response. "Probably not very good. So if I am going to wager, I might as well wager that you are a man of honor. You have a deal, Llewelyn."

"Are you out of your bleeding mind?" Durand struggled to sit up, staring at Justin in outraged disbelief. "You trust this Welsh outlaw and Richard will be held in Germany till he rots!"

"Does anyone want to hear his yammering?" Ednyved queried. "I thought not." Reaching down, he stuffed the gag back into Durand's mouth. Rhys had just re-entered the chapel and observed that if they wanted to shut the Englishman up, it would be easier to cut his throat. Justin could not tell if he were joking or not, and neither could Durand, who stopped trying to spit out the gag.

"Are we ready to go?" Llewelyn asked, and Rhys nodded, not volunteering until prodded that John's men were confined and the lay brothers had been summoned down from the hayloft. He was a laconic sort, but there was a glint in those cat-green eyes that explained why Davydd had chosen to name him as de Caldecott's assassin.

"I am guessing that you have horses hidden nearby?" Justin asked Llewelyn. "Can you provide me with one . . . at least until I can get back to the grange to reclaim my stallion?"

"I expect we can find a mount for you," Llewelyn agreed. "Mertyn is only a few miles from here, so we can stop for your horse. That way we can begin our search on the morrow."

"Very good," Justin said, before the significance of his new ally's words hit him. How did Llewelyn know he was staying at Mertyn? "It is flattering that you think it worthwhile to keep such close watch on me."

"Do not let it go to your head," Ednyved said with a smile. "Llewelyn is not content unless he knows what is happening the length and breadth of Wales . . . every fallen tree, every rutted mountain trail, every acorn rooted up by a hungry pig."

"Why not? This is my country, the land of my birth, a land under siege," Llewelyn said, and though he smiled, too, Justin sensed that he was speaking from the heart. It occurred to him that one reason there was such strife between the English Crown and its Welsh vassals was this inbred passion for the woodlands and mountains and rivers of Wales.

Richard was King of the English, but he was also Duke of Aquitaine and Normandy, Count of Anjou, and England was merely one of his domains. Justin was sure that Richard did not think of himself as English. He knew that many of Norman descent did not, even after dwelling there for more than a hundred years. He'd never actually given it much thought himself, for like most people, he was more aware of class than nationality.

But it was different in Llewelyn's homeland. The Welsh seemed to have a strong sense of kinship that their neighbors across the border did not share. While it did not stop them from fighting one another as furiously as they did the English, Justin did not doubt that they saw themselves, first and foremost, as Welsh. For him, bastard-born, raised as an orphan and foundling, never truly belonging anywhere, it was difficult to imagine how it must be to have such deep roots.

"Iestyn? Is it such a hard decision to make as that?"

Justin blinked, returning to reality to find the Welshmen looking at him curiously. "I got lost in thought," he acknowledged. "You asked me . . . ?"

"I wanted to know," Llewelyn said, "what you'd have us do with him?"

Turning, Justin regarded Durand, who met his eyes defiantly. Llewelyn moved to his side, studying the captive knight with the impersonal distaste of a man who'd just turned over a rock and did not like what he'd found. "I doubt that this one would be mourned. His death is more likely to bring joy to any number of men. But he is of some value to your queen. You need to decide if that value outweighs all the very valid reasons for sending him to Hell."

Justin could have dragged out the suspense; God knows, Durand deserved it. But he already knew what he must do. "Leave him," he said contemptuously. "That will give him time to cobble together a story to explain his failure to John." He could not resist pausing, though, in the doorway, for a final look back at the man lying, bound and helpless, on the muddied chapel floor. His last sight of Durand was one he'd long remember, always with fierce satisfaction.

20

Justin took an instinctive step backward, for gazing down into the blackness of the mine shaft was like staring into the abyss. "Well," he said morosely, "so much for that idea." He was too disappointed to hide it, for his hopes had soared when Llewelyn told him of an old, abandoned mine. But one look into those bottomless depths and he knew the missing wool was not hidden here. Picking up a rock, he held it out over the void and let it go. After a long, long time, he thought he heard a faint splash, and he sighed softly.

"I know," Llewelyn agreed, dropping a rock of his own into the shaft. "Even if it were not flooded, how would they ever have gotten the wool back up? Each woolsack weighs more than any two men."

"Look how deep it is," Ednyved marveled, leaning over so recklessly to peer into the pit that both Justin and Llewelyn reached out to pull him back from the brink. "I'm as surefooted as any cat," he protested. "How do you think they dug it so deep? No mines today go down so far."

"They were clever, the Romans." Llewelyn pitched another stone into the shaft. "Think how long it's been since their armies were here—hundreds of years—and yet some of their roads can still be used."

"The old Roman walls still stand in Chester, or so I've

been told," Justin said, almost absentmindedly, for he could not take his eyes from that gaping dark hole. He'd been sure that they were going to find the wool here, so sure. Now what?

Their hunt for the wool took them next to Cefn, where there were a series of deep caves. Llewelyn admitted to Justin that he doubted the thieves would have dared to venture so far with the cumbersome hay-wains, and Cefn lay on the wrong side of the River Clwyd. But it was worth a look, he said, and Justin made no objections, for their search had already ranged over the likely hiding places with no results. They might as well try the unlikely ones, too. The caves at Cefn were steeped in legend; local people whispered that one was Lucifer's own abode. Several soared so high that even a man as tall as Ednyved need not duck his head, and in others there were strange rock formations rising from the floor like stone sentinels. Justin thought that if he'd been seeking to hide a king's ransom, he could have found no safer lair than these eerie, echoing caverns where the sun never shone and the Devil was said to dwell. But the woolsacks were not there.

A brisk wind was undressing the ageless oak that towered above the farrier's shed, stripping away the leaves branch by branch. As they drifted on the current, the morning sun blessed them briefly with gold, and then they fluttered earthward like crippled butterflies, soon to be trodden underfoot. These morbid musings were Justin's. He had nothing to do while the smith replaced Copper's lost shoe, and watching the death spirals of doomed oak leaves was preferable to reliving the failures of the past few days.

Once Copper was shod, he would rejoin Llewelyn and

his men. There was no need to hurry, though, for they were running out of places to look. Thomas de Caldecott had begun to haunt his dreams, a sprightly ghost mocking their futile efforts to find his cache. When Justin reminded him that there would be few occasions for such merriment in Hell, he merely laughed and faded away, only to return the next night, more faithful in death than ever he had been in life, Justin thought sourly.

The scene before him was so tranquil that it was easy to forget so much was at stake. Copper had never looked so sleek, his chestnut-red coat glowing in the mellow morning light. The farrier was going about his task with quiet competence, gentling the stallion with crooning Welsh endearments and calming pats. Each time he spoke, a rangy sheepdog sprawled in the sun would thump his tail in rhythm with his master's voice. Edern, the young Welshman who'd taken Justin to the smithy, was perched on a fence rail, bantering with the smith's son. Edern was a likable lad who'd spent his boyhood in these rolling hills. He'd boasted that he was better than any lymer hound at sniffing out hideaways, and he seemed to be taking their failure to find the woolsacks as a personal affront. Justin was losing hope that anyone was going to outwit Thomas de Caldecott. Only one person had gotten the best of him, his unknown killer.

A sudden flash of movement caught Justin's eye and he turned to see Edern hop off the fence and sprint toward him. He was not alarmed, though, for the youth was grinning from ear to ear. "I think I know where the wool is!" Edern came to a halt, panting. "I was talking with Gwion"—gesturing toward the farrier's son— "and I remembered where there is another abandoned mine."

Justin felt a sharp letdown. "What of it? Why bother searching another flooded shaft?"

"Because this mine must have collapsed long ago, for it

is shallow, more like a cave." Edern's grin got even wider. "I know it is going to be there. My nose is itching, which always happens when I get one of my hunches!"

Edern's itchy nose notwithstanding, Justin did not have high hopes as the men headed back toward Halkyn Mountain. The name was a misnomer, for Halkyn Mountain was actually a hill, dwarfed by the peaks of Eryri, the cloud-crowned mountain range that had sheltered and sustained Llewelyn during the early years of his rebellion. "You English call it Snowdonia," he explained to Justin as they rode along, "but its true name is Eryri, the Haunt of Eagles." Justin merely nodded, for he was only half-listening to this Welsh geography lesson, already brooding about his return to the queen, envisioning the look upon her face when he had to confess he'd failed her.

At least the mercurial Welsh weather was not threatening to sabotage their hunt; the sky was blue and barren of clouds, and a brisk northerly wind brought them the scent of the sea but no hint of coming rain. Led by Edern and Gwion, the smith's son, they soon reached the site of the Roman mine, half-hidden by bracken on Halkyn's wooden slope.

"Who wants to climb down and find out what is lurking at the bottom?" Ednyved squinted into the darkness below, without any obvious enthusiasm for the task at hand. "We could flip a coin, if I had one."

"I'll go," Edern offered quickly.

But Rhys was already unfastening his scabbard, reaching for their rope ladder. Anchoring the metal prongs in the earth, he dropped the ladder down into the mine and then swung his legs over the side. Llewelyn stopped him before he could begin his climb, holding out a second rope. Once he'd knotted it around his waist, Rhys tossed the free end to Ednyved. "Try not to drop it," he told his cousin, and Ednyved acknowledged the command with an amused "Aye, my lord."

"It does not look that deep, but Jesu, it is dark down there. We may need to get a lantern . . ." His voice was muffled now as he descended into the shaft. They could hear the clink of his spurs scraping against the rock as the ladder swayed under his weight. Staring down into the murky blackness, Justin inhaled a lungful of dank, fetid air and felt guiltily grateful that Rhys was the one descending into the pit.

"Christ Jesus!" The ladder swung wildly and then Rhys was scrambling upward, so hastily that his foot slipped from one of the rungs and his lifeline grew taut as he dangled there, fighting to regain his balance. Llewelyn signaled and several of the men grabbed Ednyved's rope, ready to haul Rhys up if he lost his grip. He no longer seemed in danger of falling, but the ladder did not offer a fast enough ascent and he shouted, "Pull me up!"

Alarmed, they did, and as soon as his head and shoulders appeared, hands reached out for him. His face contorted, his skin almost as green as his eyes, Rhys lay prone on the ground for several moments, being pelted with questions as he fought the gorge rising in his throat.

"The stink . . ." he gasped, "so foul . . . I feared I'd choke on it . . ." Rolling over onto his back, he found himself looking up into a circle of concerned faces. "I can still smell it," he said with a grimace, "worse than any pigsty or privy. Rotting flesh—"

"Did you see the body?" Llewelyn interrupted. "Was it an animal? Or . . ." He paused and showed no surprise when Rhys nodded grimly.

"Not an animal—men. More than one."

Justin glanced toward Llewelyn, the same thought in

both their minds. "I think," Llewelyn said, after another pause, "that we've found your missing sailors."

One by one, men were lowered into the mine shaft to attach ropes to the decaying corpses and then pulled out to vomit into the grass. As no one could endure more than a few moments' exposure to that putrid stench, it took several hours before the last of the cadavers was brought to the surface. Even after the bodies had been covered with bed-roll blankets, the men kept their eyes averted. Their Church warned them often of the frailties of human flesh, never letting them forget that their mortal remains would become fodder for worms, dust unto dust. But this had been a view of death that was too close and too personal, reminding each one that this, too, would be his fate and, if he died unshriven as these poor sailors had, he'd burn for aye in Hell.

Justin had forced himself to make a brief examination of the bodies, needing to be sure that their hair color and height matched the descriptions he'd gotten from Rutger. When he was done, his stomach would need days to recover from the ordeal, but there was no doubt in his mind about the identity of the murdered men. Standing with Llewelyn and the others upwind of those forlorn blanket-draped forms, he bowed his head and said a brief prayer for the souls of the greedy Joder, the foolish Geertje, and Rutger's cousin Karl, who left a young widow and baby back in Ypres.

"There is a church less than a league from here," Llewelyn said somberly. "I'll send a man to the priest, tell him to fetch shrouds and a cart. At least we can see that they get a Christian burial. Do you know how to reach their kindred?"

Justin shook his head. "Not unless their ship is still at Chester." He was stunned by the wanton violence of these killings. "How does a man murder with such ease? How could he hold life so cheaply?"

"Killing," Llewelyn said, "can become a habit. From what you've told me, this Thomas de Caldecott had plenty of practice at it."

"Six that we know of, and with a little luck, he'd have added two more to that count," Justin said, thinking of a drunken stroll through deserted streets, a blazing Chester warehouse.

"A man so quick to kill most likely left a trail of bodies behind him. Who knows how many he'd gotten away with. If not for you, Iestyn, none would have known of these murders, either." Llewelyn forced his gaze away from the remains of de Caldecott's last victims, sketching a quick cross on the autumn air. "So now what?"

"I would that I knew," Justin admitted, for the mine shaft had yielded only the bodies of the slain sailors; they'd found no evidence whatsoever of the missing woolsacks.

As disconsolate as if he'd deliberately led them astray, Edern scuffed his boot in the brown, trampled grass. "I do not understand," he muttered. "It has to be here, it just has to!"

The farrier's son had kept at a respectful distance, watching wide-eyed but saying little. Now he cleared his throat hesitantly. "Are you . . ." He swallowed, then mumbled shyly, "Are you not going to search the other shaft?"

The words had no sooner left his mouth than he found himself surrounded by men. Did Edern not remember, he asked timidly. There was a second shaft, sloping in at an angle. "We guessed that it once led to the other shaft. Of course it is all blocked up now, a tunnel leading nowhere . . ." He was talking too much, he knew, but he couldn't seem to rein in his runaway tongue, and he was thankful when Llewelyn cut into his nervous ramblings with a curt command to "Show us!"

The opening was overgrown with brambles and knee-high bracken, and Justin caught his breath at the sight of them, for branches were broken and the ferns flattened down in places, as if something heavy had been dragged through them. "It is here," Gwion said, sounding more confident now, and pulling aside some of the underbrush, he revealed a tunnel entrance.

It was just as the farrier's son had said. What had once been a connecting passage to the main mine shaft was little more than a cave, too low for a tall man to walk upright, the walls shrouded in moss, lichen, and cobwebs, the ground littered with the skeletal remains of prey devoured to the very bone, the air stale and musty. Where Roman slaves had once labored in the earth's bowels, foxes and weasels now made their dens. Justin's boot crunched upon the spine of a small animal, and he was grateful that at least the Flemish sailors had been spared this much; no beasts had been able to feast upon their flesh. Stooping, he moved farther into the tunnel and found his way blocked by an obstacle covered by a large canvas tarp. Llewelyn joined him and together they lifted the tarp, exposing the most beautiful sight that had ever filled Justin's eyes, several padlocked coffers and sack after sack of the fine Cistercian wool meant to ransom a king.

The next discovery puzzled them all: three saddles, half-hidden by the tarp. Saddles were expensive and these seemed intact, in decent condition. Justin was the first to understand their significance. "We are looking at the last stitch in de Caldecott's shroud. These were the sailors' saddles, discarded after he'd let their horses go."

Llewelyn was quick to comprehend. "Of course! What

other reason could there be for casting them aside like that?"

The loose cart horses had been Justin's first indication that he was dealing with more than an ordinary robbery. Once his suspicions settled upon de Caldecott, those pieces of the puzzle had come together. How could one man have handled seven animals? He'd had no choice but to set them free. Until this moment, though, that had been a theory. Now it was fact.

"What did he care about cart horses and hired nags? He had his eye upon a much grander prize." And as he gazed down at the saddles of the murdered sailors, Justin felt a hot surge of outrage that the knight had been spared so much in dying as he had, escaping exposure, disgrace, and the gallows.

Llewelyn's men were still celebrating the successful conclusion of their hunt, eager to shake off the pall cast by the discovery of the dead bodies. When Llewelyn glanced around, though, he no longer saw Justin. After several moments of searching, he found the young Englishman in the tunnel, kneeling down beside a flickering lantern. "Come see this," he said, glancing over his shoulder. "What does this look like to you?"

Llewelyn examined the object in Justin's hand, a rock splattered with a dark stain. "Blood?"

"I think so, too. There is more of it over there, and if you look closely, you can see dried smears on several of the woolsacks. I think this is where the killings began. My guess is that after the woolsacks were moved into the tunnel de Caldecott stabbed one of the men in here, then called out for the others. As the second one entered, he was slain at once. I think the third sailor tried to run and was chased down and caught. The bodies were too rotted to tell me much about wounds, but the back of one man's tunic was soaked with blood."

"May God assoil them," Llewelyn said softly, for he could not help pitying the dead sailors, who'd gotten so much more than they'd bargained for. "Let's talk outside," he said and backed toward the entrance. Justin followed, and they stood in silence for several moments as they stretched their cramped muscles.

"So," Llewelyn said at last, "I suppose this is when you start wondering if it was wise to wager upon my honor."

"I never wagered upon your honor, Llewelyn. I wagered upon your common sense."

The Welshman cocked a quizzical brow. "Would you care to elaborate upon that?"

"Simply put, it is in your best interests to cooperate with the English Crown. I'm not saying you'd not be tempted by those coffers and woolsacks. What man would not, myself included. But you are no outlaw. You are a prince, my lord Llewelyn, a prince in exile at the moment but a prince all the same. And when the day comes that you rule Gwynedd, you will need cordial relations with your liege lord, the English king. At the very least, you do not want to give the English any reason to intervene upon Davydd's behalf. And if they blamed you for the loss of King Richard's ransom, that would be one very persuasive reason." Justin paused, a smile hovering at the corners of his mouth. "Need I continue?"

"Well, you did leave out the most interesting part of the story . . . where you inform the English queen of Davydd's treachery and my invaluable help."

"Jesu forfend that I should forget that," Justin agreed, and Llewelyn began to laugh.

"I know you claim your parents were English born and bred, but you are too clever not to have some Welsh blood," he said lightly, but Justin got the sense that

Llewelyn had been testing him again and that once again he had passed the test.

Justin sent an urgent message to the Earl of Chester with one of Llewelyn's men, with a second message to his father in case the earl had not yet returned to Chester. He then set up camp by the old Roman mine, for he had no intention of letting the woolsacks out of his sight. It was not as uncomfortable as he'd feared, for autumn was still fighting a rear-guard action against winter at the lower elevations. Llewelyn provided men to safeguard the ransom, and stopped by himself on the second day to see how Justin was faring.

White, fleecy clouds were blowing in from the coast, and Justin had been keeping a wary eye upon the increasingly overcast sky. Reaching over to offer a swig from his wineskin, Llewelyn insisted, "There'll be no rain for another day, mayhap two, Iestyn, not with the wind coming from the north."

"You're not the one sleeping at night in a mine shaft," Justin pointed out, "so you do not have as much at stake as I do if the weather turns foul."

Llewelyn started to make a jest about Englishmen melting in the rain like sugar lumps, but instead he tilted his head to the side, listening intently. "Someone is coming," he said. His guards were already on the alert, and within a few moments a horseman had ridden into view. "One of my scouts," Llewelyn informed Justin and summoned the man for his report.

"The Earl of Chester is approaching along the coast road, my lord. He brings a large armed force and several oxcarts. He is nigh on an hour away if he stays with the carts. But if he rides ahead, he'll be here in half that time."

Glancing over at Justin, Llewelyn said, "I'll let you be the one to welcome the earl to Wales."

Edern was already bringing up Llewelyn's stallion. No one appeared to be hurrying, but within moments, the men were all mounted, awaiting Llewelyn's orders. Reining in beside Justin, Llewelyn said, "If you ever need help recovering another king's ransom in Wales, let me know."

"I will," Justin said, "indeed I will."

"Go with God, English."

Llewelyn raised his hand in farewell before swinging his stallion toward the woods. Justin watched and then took several steps forward. "Go with God, my lord prince!" He could not be sure that Llewelyn had heard. He hoped so.

The woolsacks had finally been loaded into the oxcarts; with his usual thoroughness, the earl had thought to bring a pulley and tackle. As he and Justin watched, the carts were covered in canvas tarps. Chester was taking no chances and had brought an escort formidable enough to ward off any outlaw band smaller than an army. Once all had been done to his satisfaction, he called for his own mount, then glanced inquiringly at Justin.

"We are ready to go. You are riding with us, are you not?"

"No, my lord, I am not. I must return to Rhuddlan Castle."

Chester blinked in surprise. "That would not be the wisest move, de Quincy." When Justin agreed wryly that it probably was not, the earl made no further attempts to dissuade him. Beckoning to one of his knights, he conferred briefly with him, and then strode over to Justin.

"This is Sir Adam Fitz Walter. He will escort you to Rhuddlan and—I hope—discourage Davydd ab Owain from expressing his displeasure in a way he might later regret."

"Thank you, my lord."

Once Chester was comfortably in the saddle, he gave the signal to move out. But he'd gone only a few feet when he turned his stallion back toward Justin. "One day, de Quincy," he said, "you must tell me what really happened here."

"I will, my lord," Justin said, ". . . as soon as the Queen's Grace gives me permission to speak of these matters."

Chester regarded him with a faint smile. "I almost forgot. But you never forget, do you?"

"Forget what, my lord?"

"That you are, first and foremost, the queen's man."

"No, my lord earl," Justin said with quiet pride, "I never forget that."

Justin's return to Rhuddlan Castle evoked unpleasant echoes of his first trip into Wales with Thomas de Caldecott. Sir Adam Fitz Walter had known de Caldecott well, and he, too, was a talker, chatting away about the earl, camp-ball, the serving maid at the Bridge Street tavern, his Cheshire boyhood, and—to Justin's dismay—sharing fond memories of his friend, Thomas. Word of his death had brought grief to the city and the earl's household, Adam confided, for Thomas had more friends than a drunkard with money to spend. He doubted that there was a man ever born who'd not liked Thomas, he declared, and insisted upon entertaining Justin with stories of de Caldecott's past exploits, practical jokes, and easy conquests of the fairer sex.

"We could hardly believe it when we learned he'd sickened and died in Wales. At first, gossip had it that he'd been slain, and that stirred up a furor. But when the earl returned and read your letter, he said the Welsh had been mistaken, that Thomas had suffered a seizure after a night of heavy drinking." Adam gave Justin a sidelong, curious glance. "You were there with him, were you not?"

Justin was not surprised that Chester had concealed the truth about de Caldecott's guilt. It was easier that way, and kinder to the dead man's family. It would have been nigh well impossible for most people to reconcile the affable, engaging knight they'd known with the killer of six men. But it still troubled him that Thomas was escaping all earthly punishment for his sins, that so many heartfelt, deluded prayers would be said for the salvation of his soul.

He knew Adam was awaiting his response and said tersely, "I can tell you that he was found in the prince's chapel, not much more than that."

That grudgingly given sentence seemed to provide Adam with solace, though, for after some moments, he said, "At least he died in God's House. Do you know where he was buried? I'd like to visit his grave ere we return to Chester." He seemed embarrassed by his sentimentality and quickly made a joke about giving a promise to one of Thomas's light-o'-loves.

"He is buried in the cemetery of St Asaph's at Llanelwy." The irony of that was not lost upon Justin. He'd solved a crime, but none would be held accountable for it. Neither Davydd nor Emma would face charges. And there would not even be rumors about John's involvement. So why not a cathedral funeral for a killer?

Davydd half-rose from his seat on the dais, looking at Justin in disbelief. "You found the woolsacks? They've all been recovered?"

Adam was detecting strong undercurrents of tension in

the hall. He did not understand it, but his mission was to back Justin up and so he stepped forward, saying loudly, "It is indeed true, my lord prince. By now the woolsacks are back in England and may even be on the way to London already."

Davydd expelled an audible breath, then went limp against the cushions of his chair. "God is good," he murmured in Welsh, and for a moment he was silent, reveling in his unexpected deliverance. Seated beside him upon the dais, Emma had yet to speak or move. Her court mask was back in place; her face could have been carved from ivory or ice, so impassive and enigmatic was her expression. But her hands had clenched upon the arms of her chair, tightly enough that her knuckles were rimmed in white, and this did not escape Justin's notice.

"This is indeed good news, and in truth, I'd despaired of ever hearing it from you, de Quincy." Davydd got to his feet, started down the steps of the dais. "Now that the recovery has been made, what of retribution? What does the queen mean to do about Llewelyn ab Iorwerth?"

"I expect," Justin said, "that she intends to thank him."

Davydd's jaw dropped. "Have you gone mad? '*Thank him*'? For stealing the king's ransom?"

"No, for recovering it." Justin unsheathed a smile that never reached his eyes. "It seems, my lord, that you were wrong in your suspicions. Llewelyn played no part in the theft of the woolsacks. He told me that some weeks ago, and I believed him. Now the Earl of Chester does, too, and so will the Queen's Grace. I'd go so far as to say she'll be grateful to him for his help. You see, nothing matters more to her than retrieving the ransom . . . nothing." His voice had hardened and that last word was thrown out both as challenge and judgment.

Davydd's face flamed. Almost as quickly, though, the

color ebbed, leaving him pale and shaken. Adam had
sauntered over to Justin's side, followed by several of his
men, figuring it couldn't hurt to give the Welsh prince a
subtle reminder that Justin was under the Earl of
Chester's protection. He need not have bothered, though.
Davydd's eyes were blank and unfocused. He pushed
past Justin and Adam without even a glance, as if they
were not there. By the time he'd reached the door, he was
almost running.

The silence in the hall was smothering. Glancing
around, Justin saw that while much would remain unspoken at Davydd's court, it would not remain unknown.
The Welsh prince's scheming was not as secret as he
thought. In the utter stillness, Justin could hear Emma's
voice again, dripping icicles and contempt, telling John
that Davydd was "doomed." He waited until people began to stir, to whisper to one another, and then he walked
over to the dais and paid his respects to the Lady Emma.

She beckoned him closer and he gave her credit for her
gambler's nerves, her willingness to bluff. "You must like
spiced wine," she murmured, "for you seem to have a
taste for bittersweet. With the one hand, you offer my
husband hope, and with the other, you take it away."

He wondered how he'd missed it before, that gleam of
sharp intelligence in those bewitching blue eyes. "The
power to bestow or deny hope is not mine, my lady. I do
the queen's biding."

"I think you do more than that, Master de Quincy."
Leaning forward, she pitched her voice even lower. "We
both know that the recovery of the ransom will not be
enough to restore my husband to royal favor, and we
both know why."

She could not be sure, though, how much he did know,
and he waited, curious to see how she would go about
finding out. By implying that they shared a secret, she

suggested an intimacy between them, even a complicity, all without saying anything explicit, anything he could refute. "It is my hope that Davydd's disgrace will not spill over onto me or my son. This was Davydd's doing, after all, not ours."

He offered a noncommittal response, a bland "I understand your concern, my lady," and caught the fleeting shadow that crossed her face just before she favored him with her most captivating smile.

"I hope the queen realizes how fortunate she is to have a man of your abilities in her service. What you have accomplished is truly remarkable. But how ever did you find the woolsacks?"

"I was in the right place at the right time," Justin said modestly. "I was told that you'd gone on pilgrimage whilst I was away, my lady. Was it as fulfilling as you'd hoped?"

"Yes, it was. But with regard to those missing woolsacks—"

"I visit the holy well whenever I stay at the abbey. It is very peaceful there. I hope you took the opportunity to see the countryside whilst you were in Treffynnon? One place in particular would be worth a visit . . . the abbey grange at Mostyn."

Emma's eyes widened. Her lips parted, but no words emerged. She stared at Justin in stunned silence, and for once in her life, she had absolutely nothing to say.

The sky was splattered with clouds. Hovering low along the horizon, they absorbed the colors of sunset, dulling red into russet and warning the weather-wise of coming rain. As long as daylight still lingered, though, Justin and Angharad continued to stroll the paths of Emma's garden, for this was their first—and likely last—opportunity to speak together without fear of eavesdroppers.

Angharad's hand rested on Justin's arm, a touch that was feather-light and as unsubstantial as cobwebs. It was the grip of a ghost, an illusion furthered by the pallor of her skin and the bruised hollows under those haunted dark eyes. Most women stirred his protective instincts, but none so strongly as this heartsick young Welshwoman. One of the reasons he'd returned to Rhuddlan Castle was to make sure that Davydd and Emma paid a price—if only in anxiety—for their double-dealing. But he'd also needed to find out how Angharad was faring.

"I have gotten permission from the Lady Emma to go home for a while. Mayhap if I could pass time with my family, in surroundings that do not remind me of Thomas every time I turn a corner . . ."

She let the rest of her wish fade away into forlorn silence. Justin bit his lip, acknowledging that he was out of his depth. He did not doubt that Molly would have known how to comfort Angharad. So would Nell. Claudine, too. But the right words somehow kept eluding him. Would it be kinder to let her keep her delusions? Would it be crueler to tell her the truth? If only he knew.

"What I cannot understand, Iestyn, is that no one seems concerned about finding his killer. Nothing is being done, nothing!"

"You do not believe Davydd's claim, then, that it was Llewelyn's doing?"

"No one believes that, not even Davydd. It was a shabby, shameful act, trying to smear Llewelyn with my Thomas's blood. I can barely bring myself to look upon the man's face, Iestyn, I have such contempt for him."

"It might be better, then, if you go to your family and stay there. I would worry less about you, Angharad, if you were well and clear of this rat's nest."

"I've thought about it," she admitted. And when he

sought assurance that her family would not marry her off, as would likely be the case on his side of the border, she smiled, a smile that actually looked genuine. "In Wales, a woman cannot be forced into marriage. If she is a widow, that right is absolute. If she is unwed, her family can object if she marries a man of her choosing, but they cannot make her wed against her will."

"Truly? I might learn to live quite contentedly under Welsh law," Justin said, thinking of the generous provisions for those born out of wedlock in Wales.

"Our women enjoy more rights than yours. That is why I was able to assure Thomas that my family would accept our marriage; he said no English girls of good birth would have dared to make a match on their own."

"For certes, few would. You and Thomas planned to wed?"

"We talked about it often. That is why I was so bewildered when he came back from Chester and was so cold and curt with me. He loved me as much as I loved him, Iestyn, I know he did."

Justin doubted that exceedingly, no more than he believed that Thomas would ever have married Angharad. Which was worse, if she lost her lover to death or to betrayal? Would she be better off knowing he did not deserve even one of her tears? "Men . . . they are not always steadfast, Angharad, and love . . . love can change; it can even die."

"Not Thomas," she insisted, shaking her head so vehemently that her veil slipped and was carried off by a gust of wind. She never even noticed its loss. "The way he was acting . . . that was not the real Thomas. Mayhap he did let himself be tempted by an English harlot, for he always said women in Chester were no better than they ought to be. But even if one did bewitch him, her spell would not have lasted. I made sure of that."

"How?" Justin asked, and even in the fading light, he saw color rise in her cheeks.

"I . . . I fought fire with fire. I gave him a love potion."

"You did what?"

Justin looked so shocked that she regretted confiding in him; men did not understand these things. "I put mandragora in his wine. And it would have worked. There is no love philter more potent than one made with mandrake, which is why it is so costly."

Justin was speechless. He'd heard the stories about mandragora, also known as mandrake or the Devil's apples. Few plants had as many legends swirling around them. It was said to grow only in the shadow of the gallows. People claimed it shrieked when pulled out of the earth and anyone who heard it would die. Its root was shaped like a man, and it was all the more sought after for being so rare, for it did not grow in native soil. A drop or two made a highly effective sleeping draught. Its fame as a love potion was widespread. And it was one of the deadliest of poisons.

"I can see you do not approve, Iestyn. I admit it was a desperate measure, but I was not cheating. I was not ensorcelling Thomas. He loved me without need of charms or spells. The love potion was just to reawaken that love. And if only he'd lived, if only he'd not been stabbed that night, in the morning he would have come back to me. He would have loved me again."

Angharad raised her head when he kept silent, regarding him with a look that was challenging, defensive, and entreating, all at once. "Well? Are you going to scold me, tell me that the Church frowns upon such heathen practices?"

Justin shook his head slowly. "No, lass . . . I am not."

21

October 1193
Chester, England

Sitting up, Molly stretched with feline grace. Her dark hair was loose, appealingly disheveled, her green eyes so wantonly inviting that Justin was seriously tempted to rejoin her in bed. "You look," he said, "like a succubus."

Molly yawned and stretched again. "That had better be good," she warned, with a sleepy smile, for she was not intimidated by his superior education. She liked it that he knew so many things that she did not, confident that she had her own area of expertise, hers the learning that came from life, not books.

"Well . . . a succubus is very good at being bad." Leaning over the bed, he kissed her upturned face. "The Church warns us about these she-demons, who come to men in their sleep and steal their seed."

"And men, being so chaste and pure, naturally resist fiercely. Anyway," she said huskily, "I've already stolen your seed . . . or have you forgotten?"

"Not even on my deathbed, Molly-cat."

"Then why must you be away so soon? I know you and Bennet have some foolish idea that Piers is a seething cauldron of jealousy. It is simply not so. But be that as it may, Piers will be in Shrewsbury till next week."

"Ah, Molly, I wish I could stay," he said, with such heartfelt regret that she stopped trying to lure him back to bed, at least overtly. Watching as he finished dressing,

291

she wrapped her arms around her drawn-up knees, letting the blankets slip just enough to keep testing his resolve.

"So be it," she said with an exaggerated sigh. "London is beckoning, and you must be off with your report. I wonder, though, what you'd say if I were to ask you who it is that you are reporting to." He looked so uncomfortable that she sighed again, this time for real. "Relax, Justin, I am not asking." She paused and then added, ". . . Not yet."

"I will tell you, Molly," he promised, ". . . when the time is right."

She pouted to make it clear she was not impressed. "I thought you were not leaving until this afternoon. So why are you up and dressed already?"

"There is something I need to do this morn. Suppose I meet you and Bennet at the tavern about midday?"

He was expecting her to probe further, but instead she smiled. "Right gladly." Something in his expression alerted her, though, and her smile faded. "You are going to see the bishop, are you not?"

"No, I think it best that I do not."

Picking up his mantle, he kissed her again and then headed for the door. But before it closed behind him, he heard her call out, "Justin . . . go see your father!"

When Molly sauntered into the tavern, she saw Justin sitting alone at a back table and, with a nod to Berta, headed in his direction. "So where is that brother of mine? The sheriff hasn't hauled him off for watering the wine or some such nonsense?"

"No . . . he insisted upon going to the cook shop and getting us what he rather ominously called our 'last meal.' Of course he's been gone so long that he may well have gotten into trouble, which—knowing Bennet—is probably wearing skirts."

Molly pulled up a stool. "Did it go well?" When he looked at her quizzically, she prompted, "Your visit with the bishop."

"I did not see him." In order to fend off her scolding, he had to admit that he had stopped by the bishop's palace, but Aubrey was away, having departed for his manor at Wybunbury on Monday past. He did not volunteer that he'd been greatly relieved to find Aubrey gone, and Molly did not press, satisfied that she'd gotten him as far as his father's door.

"So why do you look so disquieted, then, if you did not quarrel with the bishop?"

Justin was not sure that he liked this eerie ability of hers to read his moods with such ease. "I do have something on my mind," he admitted, but Bennet's arrival interrupted any further revelations.

Bennet had spent money he could ill afford on a variety of foods: freshly baked bread, a crock of pottage, and several hot pies, two made with river eels and pike and one that tasted suspiciously like capon, forbidden on this meatless Friday. Bennet swore it was barnacle goose and therefore permitted, since the barnacle goose was said to hatch in the sea. That had always sounded fishy to Justin, a ploy to evade the strictures of Lent, and although he said nothing of his skepticism, he contented himself with the eel pie.

When they'd eaten their fill, Bennet called Berta over and instructed her to pack some of the food for Justin, then leaned forward, resting his elbows on the table as he studied his boyhood friend.

"Your mission was a great success. Whilst you've been sparing with what you've told us, we know you accomplished what you set out to do; you recovered the missing ransom. It's true you have no evildoers to drag back to London, but when are princes ever arrested, even Welsh princes? I daresay he'll get what he deserves, though, since kings hold grudges even longer than cuckolds. As I see it, the only thing you've failed to do is to solve the death of de Calde . . . whatever his name was. Aside from not being able to thank his killer, what does it matter? So why do you not seem better pleased by it all?"

"Actually," Justin said slowly, "I did solve his killing . . . or at least I thought so when I left Wales."

He had a very attentive audience as he briefly related to them what he'd learned from Angharad in the gardens at Rhuddlan Castle. They listened raptly and were vastly amused when he told them about the love potion, both laughing until they had tears in their eyes.

Molly recovered first. "So much for those Church elders who would have us believe the Almighty has no sense of humor! This was divine justice if ever I heard it. And the Welsh girl, she has no idea what . . . Oh, Jesu, you did not tell her, Justin?"

"Of course I did not! Why would I do anything so cruel? I never thought I'd be grateful to Davydd for his botched attempt to blame Llewelyn, but it was that dagger he had planted in de Caldecott's chest that kept Angharad from guessing the truth. She is a clever lass, and if not for her belief that he was stabbed, she'd eventually have realized that her love potion killed him. I do not think she could have lived with that knowledge . . ."

"Well, she need never know," Bennet pointed out pragmatically. "But what did you mean when you implied you now have doubts?"

"I've been prodding my memory, trying to recall all I could about that evening. I remember seeing Thomas and Angharad in the window seat, drinking, as she said.

But he did not become ill right away. By the time he finally left the hall, more than two hours had passed since he'd drunk her wine, and I've always heard that mandragora acts very swiftly. Rolf said as much, too, and I got the impression that he knows more about poisons than any honest man should. So this morn I visited the apothecary shop near the abbey. I had to find a couple of coins to get his cooperation, but he did confirm it. It was not Angharad's mandragora that killed de Caldecott. If she'd given him too much, as I first thought, he'd have been stricken soon after . . . and he was not."

Justin slumped down in his seat, no longer trying to hide his frustration. "It is not that I *want* Angharad to be responsible. But at least it was an answer and it made sense. Now . . . now it will forever remain a mystery."

Bennet and Molly exchanged knowing glances, theirs the cryptic communication of siblings who need not rely wholly upon words. "You think . . . ?" Bennet asked and Molly nodded.

"We know how you hate puzzles, Justin," she said fondly. "But this is one puzzle we can solve for you. My guess is that whilst the Welsh girl thought she was buying mandragora, she was really getting bryony. It is a common ruse, for bryony is much cheaper and more easily obtained. You remember Toothless Maud?"

Justin did. "People said she was a witch, and we'd run for our lives every time we saw her. Why?"

"Toothless Maud sold love charms and potions, and rumor had it she knew which herbs would help a scared girl get rid of an unwanted babe. She also did a brisk business selling mandragora for the lovelorn . . . only it was bryony. She shaped the root to look like mandragora and her customers went off happily with it, none the wiser. It would not do much good in enticing an unfaithful lover back, but enough of it can easily kill. And unlike mandragora, bryony takes a few hours to act."

Justin considered this for a few moments and then smiled ruefully. "People kept telling me that nothing in Wales is as it first seems. I ought to have guessed that even the mandragora would be false."

Molly and Bennet walked with Justin to the stable where he'd kept his stallion. Copper was now saddled and ready to go. It was Justin who seemed loath to leave. "Remember," he reminded them again, "that if you need to reach me, I rent a cottage on Gracechurch Street. If I am away, Gunter the smith or Nell at the alehouse is likely to know when I'll be back. And they are friends of mine, so they can be trusted."

"Might not the bishop know your whereabouts, too?" Molly teased, and Justin gave her a warning look before silencing her with a very thorough kiss. A quick embrace with Bennet, and he swung up into the saddle, looking down at them both for a wordless moment before urging Copper out into the street.

They waved and Molly called out a cheeky "Godspeed, lover!" When she glanced at her brother, though, she caught his unguarded expression, and she gave his arm a reassuring squeeze.

"He'll be back, Bennet. You wait and see. He'll be back."

Justin was surprised by the austere, subdued surroundings. The cottage would have been perfectly adequate for his needs, but he was accustomed to seeing Claudine in more luxurious settings. "Are you comfortable here?"

It seemed ridiculous to be making polite conversation like this, but there was no denying the awkwardness between them. Was it because they were meeting in a nunnery? That they'd been apart since the summer? Or that there was so much still unspoken between them?

"Comfortable? As well as could be expected."

Had Claudine's response been drenched in sarcasm, he would not have blamed her, for he was acutely aware how foolish he must have sounded. How could she possibly be comfortable under the circumstances, exiled from family and friends, knowing that a baby's birth was too often followed by the mother's death. But there had been no edge to her voice. She was not acting like the Claudine he knew. The high-spirited, carefree flirt had been replaced by a stranger, a wan, forlorn stranger with downcast brown eyes and rounded face, swallowed up within the folds of a voluminous, drab gown that obscured all evidence of her pregnancy.

"How are you faring, Claudine? Have you been getting enough rest, the food you need?"

"Why? Do I look as sickly as that?"

"No, of course—"

"I do," she said mournfully, "I know I do. My face is as swollen as a melon, my hair is as dry as straw, and look at my ankles. . . ." She lifted her skirt for him to see. "You could encircle them with your fingers, and now they are huge! Little wonder I heard from you only once in all these months. . . ."

Justin was astonished. "Claudine, I was in Wales, you know that! I'd gladly have written every week if I could have found a courier to take my letters to Godstow."

When she glanced up, he saw tears glistening on her lashes. "I am sorry. I know how petty I must sound. Your life was at risk in Wales, and here I am bemoaning my swollen ankles and sleepless nights. It is just that I've been so lonely. You are the first visitor I've had, the only one. . . ."

"Only because no one knows that you are here, love."

Joining her on the bench, he took her into his arms. "If the queen had not sent me to recover that stolen ransom, I'd have been camping outside your door, scandalizing the nuns and making you yearn for a royal crisis to get rid of me for a few days. . . ."

As he'd hoped, that earned him a smile. She let him draw her into a closer embrace, cushioning her head against his shoulder. "You always know what I need to hear, Justin," she murmured. "I missed you."

"I missed you, too," he said and tried to ignore the twinge of guilt her words stirred up, for they'd never even discussed fidelity. Theirs had been a day-to-day liaison, with no talk of tomorrows they both knew they'd never have. Their love affair had not survived his discovery that she'd been spying for John, but to his dismay, he'd found that he could still want a woman he could not trust. Her pregnancy had changed everything and changed nothing. The bond between them, flesh unto flesh, had become much more. He was shackled to her by honor more tightly than ever he'd been by desire. But the gulf between them was still there, and marriage was an option she'd not even considered.

"There were times when I was not sure of that," she admitted, with a raw candor he'd never gotten from her before, "times when I wondered if you welcomed the chance to stay away."

Justin was utterly taken aback. "Claudine, that is not so. Your welfare and that of our baby matters greatly to me. How can I convince you of that?"

"I know that we are neither plight-trothed nor wed, nor can we be. I cannot expect you to take a monk's vows. But I need you to make me a promise, Justin. A man is not permitted in the birthing chamber, I know that. Can you be close at hand, though, just in case all does not go . . . well with me and the baby?"

Justin had not fully realized until now how very frightened she was. Thankful that he'd never told her his own mother had died in childbirth, he tilted her chin up, kissed her gently on the mouth. "I will always be there when you and the baby need me, Claudine. That I promise you upon the surety of my soul."

22

October 1193
London, England

Most people lived in tempo with the sun, awakening at dawn and retiring soon after losing the light, for candles and lamp oil were costly and were not to be squandered. The highborn could afford to extend their days by artificial means, and none spent more lavishly than the Queen of England. Eleanor had always followed her own inner rhythms, and her chambers in the Tower were still defying the night long after the rest of London had gone dark and quiet. Knowing her habits, Justin had headed there as soon as he reached the city and, as he expected, the queen was awake, alert, and impatient to hear his report.

She had switched her residence from Westminster to the Tower in order to supervise the collection of Richard's ransom, which was flowing into London from all corners of the kingdom to be stored under guard in St Paul's Cathedral. When Justin was ushered into her presence, she instructed him to await her in the chapel, for nowhere else could she find the privacy their conversation would require.

Justin loved the chapel of St John the Evangelist, a resplendent gem chiseled from Caen limestone. When viewed in a blaze of sunlight, it was dazzling, its walls and pillars gilded in glowing colors, the impression of soaring, celestial space enhanced by the elegant overhead gallery, arched windows, and vaulted nave. Tonight the

air was fragrant with the sweet, earthy aroma of frankin-
cense and myrrh, the shadows were silvered by moonlight, and he felt very close to God. Kneeling before the
altar, he prayed for Claudine and the baby soon to be
born of their sin.

Eleanor entered during his prayer, but she did not interrupt, waiting until he was done. When he rose, he saw
her standing behind him and offered an apology for
keeping her waiting, but she said, "Even queens defer to
the Almighty, Justin," and allowed him to escort her toward a wooden bench.

In her presence he was always surprised by her physical
frailty, for his memories of her were molded in the heat
of her will and that still burned as fiercely as ever. Her
body was not as indomitable as her spirit, though, for
even Eleanor of Aquitaine could defy mortality only so
long. She battled the indignities of age with silk and
emeralds, her face flatteringly framed by the wimple that
hid wrinkles and greying hair, her fingers adorned with
jeweled rings. But the bones of her hand seemed so frag-
ile and brittle that he barely grazed the skin with his lips,
fearing it might be bruised by his breath, and she sank
down upon the bench with a betraying sigh of exhaustion.

The eyes meeting his, though, were the eyes of the
woman who'd taken greater pride in being Duchess of
Aquitaine than Queen of England or France. "Your letters were rather cryptic, and wisely so, but you gave me
enough facts to put together a skeleton. Now I need you
to flesh it out for me."

She already knew what lay at the heart of the conspiracy—that Davydd had staged the robbery to discredit his
nephew, that he'd been outwitted by his wife, and that
her partner in crime was Eleanor's son John. She listened
intently as Justin told her the rest, interrupting only to

ask an occasional incisive question. By the time he got to
the confrontation at the abbey grange, his voice had gotten so hoarse that she noticed and told him to fetch two
wine cups from her bedchamber.

Justin welcomed the respite, for he was coming to the
critical point in his account. In the past he had said nothing of his feuding with Durand, not even disclosing the
knight's treachery at Windsor Castle, sure that Durand
would have found a way to justify his actions, and half-
afraid to find out whose service the queen valued more.
After the episode at Mostyn grange, though, he had re-
solved upon unsparing honesty.

Yet now that he was face-to-face with the queen, he
found that he could not do it. Conspiring to steal a
throne was a favorite pastime for the brothers of kings.
Eleanor was not likely to have been shocked by her youngest son's scheming. Like his brothers Geoffrey and
Richard, John had learned at his father's knee. He'd been
sixteen when Henry had quarreled bitterly with Richard
and, in one of his infamous Angevin rages, encouraged
Geoffrey and John to lay claim to Aquitaine. Striking
back, Richard had set half of Brittany afire. Brotherly
strife was John's birthright.

But ambition was a mortal sin only when it failed,
whereas murder was the one sure road to eternal damnation. Here in the holy chapel of the Evangelist, John's last
words to Justin seemed almost blasphemous. How could
he tell the queen that her son had so casually given that
command to "Kill him." What better proof that the Devil
had already claimed his immortal soul?

Justin had no inflated opinion of his worth to the
queen. He knew his death would have stirred royal regret, not grief. But whatever his transgressions, John was
still the flesh of her flesh, he was still hers, and Justin was
sure that each one of his sins struck her like a stone.

Omitting John's lethal order to Durand, he picked up his narrative after John's departure from the chapel. If he lingered a little too long upon Durand's humiliation at Llewelyn's hands, he thought he could be forgiven for that.

Eleanor sipped her wine before observing, "My lord husband and I used to argue whether it was better for a man to be lucky or to be clever. I am beginning to think that Llewelyn is both."

"Yes, madame, I think so, too." Justin hesitated, but his curiosity was too strong to resist. "May I ask which view you took?"

"Harry was convinced that it was enough to be clever. He was always too clever for his own good, and unwilling to admit that luck alone could determine a man's fate. Harry believed almost until his last breath that a man could shape his own destiny. I'd believed that, too . . . once."

Justin cleared his dry throat, hoping he was not overstepping his bounds. "I would choose luck," he said, thinking of the unlikely chain of events that had led him to the queen. "As for Llewelyn, I think he'd agree that luck matters. But I suspect he'd still choose to be clever, confident that he could then make his own luck."

"It sounds as if you admire the man, Justin."

Justin considered that for a moment. "I respect him, Your Grace. I think he will be a good ruler one day."

"Ah, but good for England or good for Wales? Davydd is neither admirable nor deserving of respect. My husband was right, though, to forge an alliance with him, for he better served English interests than . . ."

She paused and Justin suggested, ". . . A man who is both clever and lucky?"

"Indeed." Justin thought she was smiling, but the chapel was lit only by candles and he could not be sure.

"You need not look so fretful, Justin. The English Crown will not intervene on Davydd's behalf. That would be folly, not to mention futile. Judging from what I am hearing, there seems to be a certain . . . inevitability about young Llewelyn ab Iorwerth's rise to power."

"I hope so, madame," he said, so forthrightly that he surprised himself, for he never forgot their respective ranks. He'd been well aware that he was not neutral in the Welsh conflict. But he had not realized until now how much the outcome mattered to him. "Davydd has done all in his power to get the English Crown to fight his war for him, my lady. Llewelyn asks only that he not be forced to fight uphill with the wind in his face."

"You make a most persuasive advocate, Justin," she said, and this time her smile was unmistakable. "You have done well in Wales. You justified my trust in you."

"Thank you, madame," Justin said, somewhat shyly, for she was sparing with her compliments, which were valued all the more for being doled out so economically.

Eleanor was silent for several moments, gazing down into her wine cup as if it were a portal to the past, and Justin wondered what memories had been inadvertently stirred up. Was she remembering the king who'd had such confidence in his own abilities, the *lord husband* who'd kept her confined for an infinity of sixteen years? Was it her favorite Richard who was staking his claim? Or was she thinking of John, the son who'd grown up during her long captivity, the son she'd seen so rarely from his fifth year until his twenty-first? He supposed his musings might be fanciful—for all he knew, she was deciding what to instruct her steward on the morrow—but how could a woman with her remarkable history not have ghosts in abundance?

"Well," she said at last, "we come now to the second

half of the drama, the half still to be played out. Tell me again John's exact words."

"The Lady Emma had said something about catching two rabbits in one snare and that phrase took Lord John's fancy. He said, 'That is what I am doing myself with this return to England. I, too, am capturing two rabbits in one snare, and what makes it so sweet is that both rabbits belong to Richard.' "

"What further mischief do you have in mind, now, John?" Eleanor said softly, and although she was looking directly at Justin, he knew she no longer saw him.

"Durand claimed he did not know what was planned," Justin said and almost succeeded in keeping the skepticism out of his voice. "He bragged that he would find out, though. I do not suppose you've heard anything from him, my lady?"

"No, I have not. Once he sailed with John for France, it became increasingly difficult for him to send messages."

Justin could not help himself. "I would think that would significantly diminish his worth as a spy, then." Hearing his own words, he winced and said hastily, "Forgive me for being presumptuous, Your Grace. I spoke without thinking."

"You spoke the truth and gave away no secrets. I've long known that you and Durand like each other not. I would prefer that the two of you could work together more amicably, but I cannot say I am surprised by the discord between you. For what it is worth, Justin, most men react to Durand de Curzon the way you do, with suspicion and raised hackles."

Eleanor toyed with the stem of her wine cup and then raised her lashes. It was disconcerting to see John's eyes in her face. "Durand is more than a spy. He has done what I'd hitherto thought impossible: gotten close enough to John to be privy to some of his more outrageous schemes. I have no illusions about the man, Justin. What did you once call him, my 'tame wolf'? The fact remains that John trusts him as much as John trusts anyone, and that trust keeps him at John's side. You might say that his duties are threefold. To discourage John's wilder stratagems if he can. To get word to me if he cannot. And always, always to watch John's back."

So he was bodyguard as well as spy. John's guardian angel, as it were. That thought was so ludicrous to Justin that he almost laughed. Mayhap the queen was right. Mayhap it took one of the Devil's own to protect a man like John. It was not a thought he liked, though, for it seemed to confirm Durand's bravado at Mostyn grange, his boast that he was indispensable to the queen.

"John wants above all else to thwart our efforts to buy Richard's freedom." Eleanor sounded as if she were thinking aloud, but Justin felt confident she expected him to contribute to the conversation. If not, she would have dismissed him by now.

"My Lady . . . when I met Durand in Southampton this summer, he told me that the French king and Lord John intended to offer the Holy Roman Emperor a vast sum to keep King Richard captive, and I passed that information on to you. Have you been able to verify the truth of that report?"

"One hundred fifty thousand silver marks worth of truth," she confirmed. "Say what you will about my offspring, they do not lack for ingenuity."

"Would the French king pay most of that?" he asked, and Eleanor laughed.

"Philippe? That one would sooner drink his own blood than part with a single denier. Moreover, the French coffers were drained dry by the Crusade. He would expect

John to put up his share. They are co-conspirators, Justin, not friends."

"I was wondering how Lord John could get his hands upon so much money. Are his estates that profitable, my lady?"

"In peacetime, mayhap. But his demesnes have been long neglected because of this strife over the crown. And when he fled to France, his lands were declared forfeit." Eleanor was quiet again for a time. "So what do we know? That John would strike a bargain with the Devil himself to keep the ransom from being paid. That he has a great need for money if he is to have any hopes of out-bidding the English Crown for Richard's freedom. That he has a perverse sense of humor, a taste for irony."

Justin did not follow her at first, not seeing how John's humor was a factor in her equation. When it did come to him, he gave an audible gasp. "He said. 'The rabbits belong to Richard.' Would he dare, madame?"

"Oh, yes," she said, "he would dare."

The Bishop of London, Henry Fitz Ailwin, the city's first mayor, and William Fitz Alulf, one of the city sheriffs, were awaiting Sir Nicholas de Mydden at Paul's Cross, the outdoor pulpit in the northeast corner of the cathedral churchyard. The knight was accompanied by a large armed escort, understandable in light of his mission: to transfer a portion of the ransom from St Paul's crypt to the greater security of the Tower.

After amiable greetings were exchanged, Sir Nicholas smiled and produced the queen's writ for their inspection. "I am sure you will want to see this again," he said jovially. "The good Lord forbid that you turn over the king's ransom to any knave wandering in off the street."

They joined in his laughter and made a show of examining the queen's seal, although they had scrutinized it at great length during his initial visit the day before. "In truth, Sir Nicholas," the lord mayor confided, "I will be glad to be relieved of the responsibility. I cannot tell you how many nights I've lain awake, fearing that thieves and brigands are robbing us blind whilst our guards sleep."

"Actually," Sir Nicholas admitted, "I'll breathe easier myself once the coffers are safely stored in the cellar of the White Tower. Imagine the burden borne by those poor souls who'll be escorting the ransom to Germany!"

The knight's men had brought several sturdy wagons, and as they crossed the churchyard, Sir Nicholas explained that the queen thought it would be safer not to keep all of the ransom at one site. He offered no reasons why the queen was suddenly so disquieted about the security at St Paul's, saying only that these were lawless times, a statement they could not dispute. Entering the cathedral, the bishop led the way toward the north choir aisle, cautioning Sir Nicholas to watch his footing as the steps were steep and the lighting poor.

The air in the crypt was cold and clammy, and it was easy to understand why it was popularly known as the Shrouds. A wooden screen ran the length of the vault, dividing the eastern and western halves, and it was toward the former that the sheriff headed. "The coffers are stored on this side, by the Jesus Chapel."

Following after him, Sir Nicholas peered blindly into the dark. "We'll need torches to keep my men from stumbling around like so many drunks. Getting the coffers up the steps will be—"

The rest of his comment was lost as he was shoved suddenly from behind, with enough force to send him sprawling. The air had been knocked out of his lungs by the impact and it was a moment or so before he could find enough breath to protest. "What in Christ . . ." Rolling over onto his back, he found himself surrounded by men with drawn swords. His words caught in his throat as he recognized the Earl of Arundel and Hamelin, Earl of Warenne, the king's uncle, both members of the council named to oversee the collection of the king's ransom.

The sheriff was already claiming his sword, roughly searching his body for a hidden dagger. "You are under arrest, whoreson." Another man was pushing through the circle, and the sheriff gestured toward the newcomer, saying, "Let me introduce you to Sir Nicholas de Mydden, who truly does serve the Queen's Grace."

Glaring down at the imposter, the knight cursed him in language that should never have been uttered in the presence of a prelate of the Church. The bishop did not object, though, understanding his outrage that someone would have dared to sully his family name and honor like this, putting out a restraining hand only when it looked as if the genuine Sir Nicholas's verbal castigation would become physical.

Standing apart from the others, the king's half-brother looked on quietly. Justin felt a prickle of sympathy, for Will Longsword's fondness for John was well known to all. Will alone had defended John, and he looked very unhappy now to have been proved wrong. Becoming aware of Justin's gaze, he mustered up a sad smile. "More fool I for letting myself be duped once again. That writ was the finest forgery I've ever seen. I'd never have guessed that it was not the queen's seal. So what sparked your suspicions, Justin?"

"It was the queen's doing, not mine."

The imposter had been dragged to his feet by Hamelin, a man known to have gotten his fair share of the infamous Angevin temper. "Let's get this hellspawn somewhere where we can put some questions to him."

The man raised his chin, looked defiantly at his captors. "I have nothing to say."

"You will," Hamelin promised grimly, "you will."

Eleanor listened without comment as the Earls of Arundel and Warenne vied with each other to inform her of the events earlier that day in the crypts of St Paul's. The theft had been painstakingly planned, no details overlooked, from the use of a man who bore a passing resemblance to Sir Nicholas de Mydden to the equipping of two sets of carts, the ones carrying the ransom to be driven to the wharves and the others to lumber slowly toward the Tower.

"We are still not sure, madame, if the fake coffers—filled with sand—would have been delivered to the Tower to sow confusion, or if they were meant merely as a red herring in case all did not go as planned at St Paul's. Whatever the intent, the aim was to buy them enough time to reach the docks and load the real coffers onto a waiting ship."

When Hamelin paused for breath, Arundel seized control of the conversation, marveling at the amazing authenticity of the forged seals. "Both your signet and that of the Archbishop of Rouen were well nigh perfect, Your Grace. The mastermind behind this crime seems to have been very familiar with the royal court, knowing, for example, that both your seal and the archbishop's must be provided ere the ransom could be transported."

Standing on the outer ring of the circle, Justin and Will exchanged wry looks. The queen had shared her suspicions about John's involvement with very few, and Arundel had not been one of them. Even those not privy to the truth had been quick to suspect the queen's son, though, and there was some rolling of eyes now as Arundel blundered on with his theories about the theft. John cast a long shadow, all the more obvious for being so studiously ignored.

Eleanor was losing patience with the garrulous earl and interrupted brusquely with a question about the ship. It was Hamelin who answered, saying regretfully that by the time they'd gotten the false de Mydden to talk, it was too late. When they reached Billingsgate, they'd found that the ship had already sailed.

"So they were clever enough to keep St Paul's under watch, and to anchor on the seaward side of the bridge," Eleanor said thoughtfully. "Why does that not surprise me?"

She was not disappointed, either. At least that was Justin's reading of the inscrutable expression on the queen's face. It was a look he'd seen before, whenever one of John's misdeeds came to light. Justin had always had an instinctive sympathy for mothers, in part because he'd idealized his own, the unknown woman who'd died giving him birth. He believed that a mother's love was pure and eternal and unconditional, despite evidence to the contrary all around him. He was sure that Eve must have wept a river of tears over the fratricidal strife between Cain and Abel. As a boy, he'd felt great pity for the mother of Moses as she set him adrift in a basket of bulrushes. And he never doubted that in her heart, Eleanor still saw John as the "son of her womb."

It occurred to him that John was protected by a great conspiracy of silence. Eleanor cared only about foiling his designs on the crown, not about punishing him for them. And the lords of the realm were willfully blind, too. Luke de Marston had spoken for legions during their search of Southampton. "We cannot very well arrest him by ourselves, and I do not fancy arresting him at all, not when the man might well be king one day."

As Justin had expected, Eleanor showed no interest in

speculating upon the identity of the thieves. "What matters," she declared, "is that the thieves failed and not a halfpenny was lost. We have collected enough to convince Emperor Heinrich's envoys of our good faith, and they are making plans to return to Germany with the ransom. It is my intention to do the same as soon as our fleet can be made ready."

She paused and then smiled at the men, a mother's smile as memorable in its own way as the seductive, bewitching smiles of her celebrated youth. "God willing," she said, "I will be spending Christmas with my son, the king. And then . . . then we'll come home."

AUTHOR'S NOTE

A few years ago the Richard III Society asked me to write an article about the role of novelists in shaping history. I have no illusions about the novelist's ability to influence public opinion. How could we ever compete with Hollywood? But I do think the topic raises some interesting questions. What is the responsibility of the historical novelist? How much license can we take in our depiction of people who actually lived and events that truly happened? What do we owe our readers—and the long-dead men and women we write about? (If any of you are interested in my views upon this subject, you can read the article at www.r3.org/penman.)

I have always tried to build a strong factual foundation for my novels, relying upon my Author's Note to tell my readers if I've taken any liberties with historical fact and thus keep my conscience clear. This approach has worked well for my six historicals. But the mystery format is different, and I've been having some difficulty reconciling my two personas. In writing the mysteries, I've given my imagination much more free rein than in my historicals, and while this freedom was fun, it was initially somewhat unsettling.

The essential elements of *Dragon's Lair* are historically accurate. Richard was indeed taken prisoner on his way home from the Holy Land. His mother moved heaven and earth to raise the monumental ransom demanded for his freedom. Brother John did everything in his power to thwart Richard's release, including armed rebellion, an alliance with the French king, and forging the great seal in an attempt to steal Richard's ransom. But all of the other plot twists in the book are mine and cannot be blamed upon anyone else.

In fairness to Davydd ab Owain, I must admit that he did not mastermind a scheme to hijack the ransom. Having said that, I do not think I owe Davydd's ghost any apologies. Those of you who've read my novel *Time and Chance* will understand why I had no qualms about depicting Davydd in such an unflattering light. I don't mean to be cryptic about this; it will all become very clear if you read *Time and Chance*!

Emma of Anjou presented the greatest challenges. We know very little about her. She was King Henry's half-sister, said to be beautiful. She was believed to have wed a French lord, Guy de Laval, bore him a son, and subsequently wed Davydd ab Owain, by whom she had two children, perhaps more. She was dead by 1214, a footnote in Welsh history.

I am not sure why I felt misgivings about my treatment of Emma. Even in my historical novels, I've had to "fill in the blanks" and rely upon conjecture more often than I would like, for medieval chroniclers could be utterly indifferent to the needs of modern novelists. But I still had this vague dissatisfaction, this nagging concern that I'd not done right by Emma.

One of the reasons why I find history so fascinating is that it is not static. It is always in a state of flux, and we never know what unexpected artifacts might be turned up as the tides go in and out. I recently made an eleventh-hour discovery that much of what we think we know about Emma might not be true. While browsing in the

Medieval Genealogy Internet archives, I came upon a spirited discussion about "my" Emma. To my surprise, I found that Emma's marriage to Guy de Laval—accepted by historians for generations—is open to challenge. Citing a thirteenth-century charter to Evron Abbey, the argument was made that Emma de Laval and Emma of Anjou were two different women. Is this claim valid? I honestly don't know, but it is certainly deserving of further study.

Learning that half of Emma's past might be based upon a case of mistaken identity could have been a writer's worst nightmare. Instead, it was liberating. I was reminded that the Emma in *Dragon's Lair* is my creation, and my only obligation is to make her interesting, as "real" as any fictional woman can ever be. And it will not be historians who judge this Emma; it will be my readers. I no longer worried that I was being unfair to the actual Emma, and came to terms with my Emma by promising her a role in my next mystery.

Now on to the more mundane aspects of the Author's Note. I always mention for the benefit of new readers that the bishopric of Chester is a fictional one. Although the title was used in the Middle Ages, it was an unofficial usage, as the diocese was under the control of the Bishop of Coventry, John's crafty ally, Hugh de Nonant. I used Welsh spellings throughout, although Llewelyn is a slightly anglicized version of his name; the pure Welsh is Llywelyn. While daggers were in use in 1193, they had not yet become standard equipment for medieval knights. The area around Halkyn Mountain in North Wales was an important mining center for the Romans, and the horizontal adjoining shaft is called an "adit." The most horrifying fact that I unearthed in my mining research was that Roman slaves were sometimes kept underground until they died, never allowed to go up to see the sun or breathe pure, untainted air. And while chapels were not built on every Cistercian grange in medieval Wales, they were known to have existed on some, so I felt comfortable adding a chapel to the grange at Mostyn.

The theory that the brilliant poet Marie de France, the Abbess of Shaftsbury, was Emma's half-sister is widely believed but not conclusively proven. I hope it is so, for there is something very appealing about the image of this gifted woman penning her worldly verses in the quiet of the cloister. Lastly, Llewelyn ab Iorwerth is not a figment of my imagination. He was indeed challenging Davydd for supremacy in Gwynedd in 1193. He would become the most successful of all the Welsh princes and history has accorded him the deserving accolade of Llewelyn the Great. He would also become King John's son-in-law. For those readers who will want to know more about this remarkable man, he is the central character in my novel *Here Be Dragons*.

S.K.P.
April 2003
www.sharonkaypenman.com

ACKNOWLEDGMENTS

To quote my favorite line from *Casablanca*, "Round up the usual suspects." My family, my friends, my editors at Putnam and Penguin, and my agents on both sides of the Atlantic, Molly Friedrich and Mic Cheetham. I would like to make special mention of the following: Marian Wood, Editor Extraordinaire; Earl Kotila, whose offhand comment about Justin's love life inspired the creation of Molly; John Schilke, M.D., for confirming what I'd learned about decomposing bodies; Lowell LaMont, my computer exorcist; Jill Davies for helping me keep the faith; Marilynn Summers for giving me the benefit of her nursing experience; and above all, Valerie Ptak LaMont, midwife for all my books.

A CONVERSATION WITH
SHARON KAY PENMAN

Q: Like the rest of your fiction, this novel is set in medieval Europe. What drew you to this particular time and place? And what keeps you there?

SKP: Well, I spent twelve years working on my first novel, *The Sunne in Splendour,* and by the time it was done, I was hopelessly hooked on the Middle Ages. It is very familiar terrain to me now, after setting nine books in that era, so each time I begin a new book, it is like coming home. That doesn't mean I'd have wanted to live back then, though; I am much too fond of our century's creature comforts!

Q: Who or what inspired the character of Justin?

SKP: Justin is not based upon any particular person; I never do that for purely fictional characters. He just "came" to me during some long walks in the woods with my dogs.

Q: Justin is such a lonely character. Does much of his loneliness stem from the fact that he is trapped between two worlds—that of the highborn and the lowborn?

SKP: Yes, I wanted a character who would have the

perspective of an "outsider," someone who did not quite belong in either of his worlds.

Q: **What does Justin gain and lose because of his class "mobility"?**

SKP: You might say that Justin is a social chameleon, that he is able to take on the coloration of his surroundings. He can maneuver in the shark-filled waters of the royal court, yet he is also capable of blending in at the corner tavern or alehouse, a very useful attribute for a spy. But he lives in a world in which people are defined by birth, a concept utterly alien to Americans. He is very drawn to Molly; there is a strong connection between them, one that is emotional as well as sexual. Yet it would be difficult, if not impossible, for them to have a future together. The flip side of this coin is that marriage to the Lady Claudine is also beyond his grasp.

Q: **Justin does not let himself think too hard or long about whether or not Richard is worth the money, effort, and lives that his ransom costs. Is the price too high?**

SKP: Knowing what I know about Richard's kingship, I'd say the price was much too high. But I am looking at it from a modern perspective. In Justin's world, few would even raise that question. One of the cornerstones of a class system is that all people are not created equal, and a consecrated, crowned king was at the very pinnacle of the social pyramid.

Q: **Have we heard the last of Molly and Bennet?**

SKP: Not at all! Molly and Bennet appear in the next

mystery, and I expect them to be complicating Justin's life for some time to come.

Q: **Is Justin's understanding of his father going to continue to evolve?**

SKP: Of course. Theirs is an ongoing, evolving relationship, and there will be advances and retreats, backsliding and detours. It is not an easy road, but they are traveling it together, if not always willingly.

Q: **Will we learn more about the identity of Justin's mother?**

SKP: Yes, eventually Justin and the readers will learn more about his mother. I don't mean to sound cryptic or mysterious—well, I guess I do—but his father has good reason for wanting to keep her identity secret. And that is as much as I can say!

Q: **Since Claudine is unwilling to consider marriage to Justin, what is going to happen to their child?**

SKP: You'll have to keep reading the books to find out, won't you? I will tell you that more about the baby will be revealed in the next mystery, *Prince of Darkness*.

Q: **Notable among the many important and thought-provoking themes in this novel (which also appear in your other work) is your focus on the conflicts and differences between medieval English and Welsh culture and society. Would you talk about this tension and what you find so compelling about it?**

SKP: This was a clash of cultures, a war of attrition between a predatory feudal society and a tribal

Celtic one. When I moved to Wales more than twenty years ago and began to research *Here Be Dragons,* I was fascinated from the first by the Welsh medieval laws, by the discovery that women enjoyed a greater status in Wales than elsewhere in Europe. By our standards, Welshwomen were not that emancipated, but in comparison to their French and English sisters, they enjoyed a remarkable degree of freedom. A Welsh girl became her own mistress when she reached the age of puberty and could not be forced into marriage against her will. She was not automatically denied custody of her children if her husband died or the marriage ended, as was the case on the other side of the border. She could even end the marriage herself. And a woman who bore an infant out of wedlock had one great advantage over all of her sisters in Christendom: An illegitimate child acknowledged by the father had full rights of inheritance and was on equal footing with his or her siblings born in wedlock. Medieval Welsh law did not punish the child for the sins of the parents, an enlightened position that can be truly appreciated only when we consider how many centuries it would take to gain widespread acceptance elsewhere.

Q: You make clear the very real limitations women of all backgrounds faced in medieval Europe. How challenging is it to create plausible opportunities and interesting experiences for your female characters?

SKP: It is very challenging, truthfully. Women did not have as many options as men, and I need to reflect that reality in my mysteries. So whether I am writing of a woman of Claudine's class or one of Molly's, I try to stay true to the boundaries and constraints that each would have encountered. A woman of high birth was blessed with certain freedoms that Molly would never enjoy, among them the freedom from hunger or want. But Molly had freedoms that were denied to Claudine, such as the right to chart her own course and make a marriage of her choosing.

Q: **Would you agree that Eleanor and Emma have a great deal in common?**

SKP: Superficially, yes. They were strong-willed women, fortunate from birth, for both were said to be beautiful and both were born into families of privilege and power. Eleanor was the daughter and heiress of the Duke of Aquitaine, married at fifteen to the young King of France. She acquired that high rank through no actions of her own. But when she later became Queen of England, that was very much her own doing. One of the reasons why Eleanor continues to fascinate us so is because she did not always play by the rules of her world, rules that made it virtually impossible for a woman to exert much control over her own destiny. Eleanor dared to break these rules, and although she paid a high price for her willingness to rebel, I like to think that, on her deathbed at the advanced age of eighty-two, she had few regrets. Emma, of course, was never a great heiress like Eleanor; she was the illegitimate daughter of Count Geoffrey of Anjou and thus sister to England's King Henry. Hers was the more traditional fate for women of the nobility, a political pawn wed to a Welsh prince because her brother the king decreed it. We know little of Emma's external life, nothing whatsoever of her interior one. I suspect, though, that she had more regrets than Eleanor.

Q: **Justin leaves Angharad mourning a man who never existed. Was this the kindest or wisest choice Justin could have made?**

SKP: Under these particular circumstances, I think it was both a wise and a kind decision. But if Justin were forced to choose between the two, he would always err on the side of kindness.

Q: **Which would upset John more: learning of Durand's role as Eleanor's spy or as his own protector?**

SKP: Very interesting question. I think John would be most offended by the notion that Eleanor saw him as being in need of Durand's protection. John's jealousy of his brother Richard was a destructive force in his life. Putting it in modern terms, Richard was the Golden Son, the best beloved, and John was the afterthought, John Lackland, forever measuring himself against the Lion-heart and forever coming up short.

Q: **I would like to ask you a question you raise in your author's note: What is the responsibility of the historical novelist?**

SKP: I cannot answer for other historical novelists; I can only offer my own guidelines. In writing my historical novels, I have to rely upon my imagination to a great extent. I think of it as "filling in the blanks." Medieval chroniclers could be callously indifferent to the needs of future novelists. But I think there is a great difference between filling in the blanks and distorting known facts. Whenever I've had to tamper with history for plot purposes, I make sure to mention that in my author's note, and I try to keep such tampering to a bare minimum. I also attempt to keep my characters true to their historical counterparts. This is not always possible, of course. Sometimes all we know of a medieval man or woman are the stark, skeletal outlines of their lives, rather like the chalk drawing of the body at a crime scene. And some historical figures are so controversial—Richard III is a good example—that I feel comfortable drawing my own conclusions. But if I were to deviate dramatically from the traditional portrayal of a person who actually lived, I would feel honor-bound to explain to my readers in my author's note why I chose this particular approach.

Q: **Do you need to work from a detailed outline to ensure historical accuracy?**

SKP: I use a detailed outline for the mysteries, but that is more to avoid any plot holes than to ensure historical accuracy. I use an outline for chapters in both the mysteries and my historical novels, in order to have a road map when I am beginning a book.

Q: **Sharon, you were writing your first novel in your "spare" time while in law school when the only copy of your manuscript was stolen. What happened next?**

SKP: The first manuscript for *The Sunne in Splendour* disappeared from my car when I was moving to an apartment during my years in law school. The car was crammed with the usual college student's possessions, including a small television, but the only thing taken was a notebook containing my novel. At that point I'd been working on it for more than four years, and its loss was very traumatic for me. For the next six months, I would periodically ransack my apartment, deluding myself that I had somehow "missed" it during those other, futile searches, and I was unable to write again for the next five and a half years. I never learned what had happened to the manuscript. The most logical explanation is that one of the children playing in front of the apartment complex had wandered over to the car and snatched the notebook on impulse. It was either that or vengeful Tudor ghosts, and I find it hard to believe any of them were hovering over Lindenwold, New Jersey.

Q: **What is the most notable book you have read recently?**

SKP: I am currently reading a fascinating novel called *Star of the Sea* by Joseph O'Connor; it takes place in 1847, aboard a ship of Irish refugees who are fleeing the Great Hunger and seeking to start life anew in America. I haven't finished it yet, but I can say for a certainty that the first two-thirds of the novel are utterly compelling so far.

Q: **If you could create your own reading group composed of notable historical figures, whom would you include, and what would the group read?**

SKP: My own reading group? I think I would want Eleanor of Aquitaine and Henry II in my group; they'd definitely liven up meetings. And Elizabeth Tudor and Cleopatra and Napoleon and Abraham Lincoln and Mark Twain. I would also invite the Welsh poet-prince Hywel ab Owain, who did a star turn in my novel *Time and Chance,* and the tragic nine-day queen, Jane Grey. Now what would they read? I wouldn't dare suggest my own books to such a high-powered group. I think we'd read one of Shakespeare's plays, possibly *Richard II* or *King Lear* or, if they were in the mood for lighter fare, *Much Ado About Nothing.*

Q: If you could spend a day living the life of one of your characters in *Dragon's Lair,* whose life would you choose?

SKP: I think I would like to follow in Llewelyn's footsteps, for he was blessed with that rare combination of confidence, humor, and optimism tempered by reality, so I'd probably have the most fun living his life—although I'd rather not step into his shoes on a day when he was fighting a battle.

Q: Can you tell us anything about Justin's next adventure?

SKP: Justin's next adventure will be *Prince of Darkness,* which we hope to publish in early 2005. I am working on it now and am giving poor Justin a rough time. Due to circumstances beyond his control, he finds himself on the "pilgrimage to Hell and back," as John wryly describes it, a journey made in the company of the three people

326

he'd least like to be traveling with: his hostile ally, Durand de Curzon; his sometime love, the Lady Claudine; and his unforgiving adversary from *Dragon's Lair,* the Lady Emma. It's a journey that takes him from the streets of Paris to castles in Brittany and then to one of the most celebrated of medieval shrines, the island abbey of Mont-Saint-Michel.

READING GROUP QUESTIONS AND TOPICS FOR DISCUSSION

1. Discuss the pros and cons of being "the Queen's man."

2. In the beginning of the novel, Justin is momentarily taken aback by Eleanor's command that he seek his much-loathed father's assistance, but then he sees the truth. What is that truth?

3. Justin is aptly described as "a natural lone wolf, not happy hunting with the pack." Do you think this wolf will ever form his own pack?

4. Has Justin met the right woman yet? If not, will he ever?

5. If you could plot Justin's future, what would it look like?

6. What do you think would have happened in the chapel if Durand had not been interrupted?

7. Justin recalls being punished as a child for sneaking food to Bennet and Molly. Why was his kindness met with hostility and condemnation from the society around him?

8. Molly helps Justin see his father in a whole new light. Has anyone ever helped you in this way?

9. Justin worries about Piers and his reaction to Molly and Justin's relationship. Do you think his worries are warranted?

10. Justin tells a bereft Angharad that "love can change; it can even die." Discuss the vagaries of love.

11. When is virtue not a virtue?

12. What do you think of Emma's use of her feminine wiles to accrue and wield power?

13. What does Emma mean when she tells John that "a widow's lot is better than a wife's more often than not"?

14. What do you think Davydd would do if he learned of Emma's treachery?

15. John and Emma are kin, but their true bond is their thirst for revenge. Discuss how bitterness has crippled them and imperiled those around them.

16. Two very different kinds of sibling relationships—Richard and John versus Bennet and Molly—are represented in this novel. Do they share any common ground?

17. How do you interpret John's dream of his absent, imprisoned brother?

18. Eleanor's assertion that "all the Welsh are inbred" is a perfect illustration of the prevailing English atti-

tude toward the Welsh. What is the cost of England's cultural and political myopia and imperialism?

19. Other than Justin, which character did you find most compelling? Least compelling?

20. Are you the kind of reader who must solve a mystery in advance or do you prefer to let it unfold before you?

21. What historical figure would make for an interesting addition to your group's discussion of *Dragon's Lair*?

22. How has the group discussion enriched your understanding of *Dragon's Lair*?

23. What book is your group going to read next? Do you plan to read the next installment of Justin de Quincy's adventures?